GATES OF SORROW

AULIREAN GATES II

J E HANNAFORD

*For all the dogs I have loved, and all those I have yet to love.
You are all Moonhounds in your heart.*

Caldera
N
W   E
S
Halfen
Lacton
Clifdon
Eye
Sildet
Pelton
Respite
DAL
Firstal
Redpike
The Edgelands
Redstone
Dark Holt
Port
Scarton
Golden
Anchorage
Blow
Deeper
Hook point
Highwall
Southcrater
Bareplains
Wyrwood
On Holloways; these strange features have become a normal part of travel and transport since the Great Rending.
. Along their length are found a range of accommodations and entertainments for the weary traveller.
Pathway
Holloway

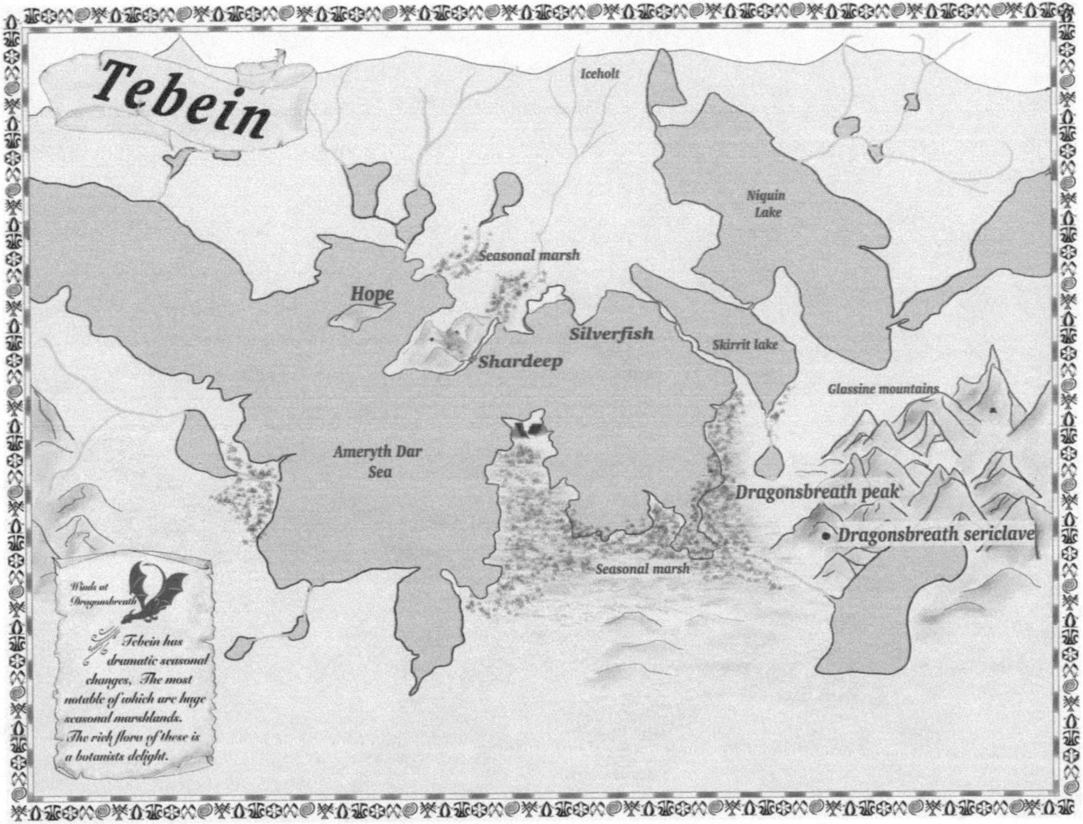

Tebein
Iceholt
Niquin Lake
Seasonal marsh
Hope
Silverfish
Skirrit lake
Shardeep
Glassine mountains
Ameryth Dar Sea
Dragonsbreath peak
Dragonsbreath sericlave
Seasonal marsh
Winds at Dragonsbreath
Tebein has dramatic seasonal changes. The most notable of which are huge seasonal marshlands. The rich flora of these is a botanists delight.

<u>Sorrow's Lament</u>

I hang my head with sadness
I hang my head in pain
I cry out to the sky above
I cry, time and time again.

For I killed too many awldrin
I ended lives in vain
I boiled their souls in fire
Forever, I wear this stain.

My scales have lost their lustre
all company I refrain
I hide now in the darkness
My sorrow forever enchain'd

MOONHOUND

Chapter 1

Suriin

'The binding is not negotiable.'
'What if we ever need our full power?'
'Without the threat of the awldrin, you won't.'
The Negotiations. Watcher's Record-keeper

Her consciousness flew high above Caldera, separated from her physical self, her thoughts floating with her echoglass shard while her body remained trapped in a cell, deep below the peak of the mountain.

⌒ ⋏ ◖ ⚘ ◉

She was soaring, but she wasn't sure how she knew – maybe it was the thinness of the air that rushed past. Occasionally, she bashed against something hard.

Far away, her body vomited.

She could feel which way her physical form was, could reach along the bond toward her body. She tried, but it was too difficult to reach, so she settled back into the crystal.

⌒ ⅍ ◖ ✥ ◉

Rhythmic bumping increased in frequency, and she lost contact with the bottom of the pouch as she dropped swiftly in altitude. Somewhere deep inside, she knew that her body couldn't move any lower. It was the crystal in motion. She was still being carried.

The drop made her body vomit – again.

⌒ ⅍ ◖ ✥ ◉

She was wet. Either it was raining or she was in water. Or both.

A particularly vicious retch brought her broken halves together momentarily, and she saw Gwynn and Fluffy through her own eyes. She knew where she was and what had happened. She reached for them – then, in a flash, they were gone.

⌒ ⅍ ◖ ✥ ◉

Fingers pulled her from the pouch. The leather grazed her sides as she was lifted out into the light.

⌒ ⅍ ◖ ✥ ◉

She accelerated, or maybe the crystal had been thrown? Together, with her crystal, she flew through the air, stopping abruptly as they collided with something. An overwhelming buzz of power echoed through her, and for a moment, she saw.

A tall figure, face twisted in hate, faced her. It threw something to the ground, snapped its arm out and in a single motion, broke the neck of a small creature. The hand reached for her, and metallic hotness covered her senses.

The connection with the magical object severed, as did her view.

Thrown back to her body once more, she shouted, unsure if anyone would hear. 'The Gates. She knows.'

CHAPTER 2

DARIN

*So'Dal have magic because of a twist of fate, a
leakage of power.
Much like the So'Dal, the power of a Howler can
pass to the next generation.
Any Howler's child born, must be kept hidden in
Dal for all our sakes, for children talk too
freely.*
The Hidden Life of the Howlers

She sat with legs drawn up to her chest, shaking in the corner of the cell. Every now and again, the young woman cried out and looked up, her eyes wide yet unseeing. Some semblance of understanding crossed her face, and then she'd withdraw back into herself. She rocked gently, occasionally throwing up into a bag they'd got through the bars to her in a brief moment of lucidity.

'We must be able to help her, somehow,' Gwynn said, for what felt to Darin like the hundredth time.

'Not on our own.' Chase shook his head. He let go of the

lock, which clanged as it swung against the cell door. 'Gwynn, stay with her. Keep Fluffy near her if you can. Darin, we need to talk to the others.'

It was the right thing to do, but Darin felt uneasy about leaving two distraught teenagers alone in the depths of the palace. It brought back strong memories of the time his younger brother had drunk an entire bottle of liquor while their parents were away, then passed out. Darin must have been about Suriin's age, and it had been one of the most stressful evenings he'd had ... Until the fire. They'd kept that secret for years, and he'd let it fade from memory as he grew used to dealing with drunks in the inn.

The sight of Gwynn's face and the smell of vomit brought it back. Seeing Suriin so unwell and leaving Gwynn alone – much younger than he was and with no obvious end to the trauma in sight – sat badly with him.

'One of us could stay with them,' he suggested.

'Darin, we need to go, and soon,' Chase urged. 'Star needs to rest, and this isn't the place.'

Gwynn's brow furrowed, and his hand trembled slightly as he reached out to stroke Fluffy. 'What if they find us before you get back? What will they do to my sister?'

'No one aside from us knows what she did. If we work fast, it can stay that way and no one will ever need to know. She can return to her studies.' Darin felt uneasy saying it. An awldrin was roaming around Caldera. Nothing would be the same. He had no real idea of the severity of the punishment, but theirs was a society willing to poison its youngest, simply to test the potential of new recruits. Secrecy as buried in history and interwoven half truths as that of the So'Dal could allow no leaks.

He needed Gwynn to trust them. 'We'll be back soon, I

promise,' Darin replied. Gwynn stared at him, then gestured at the two hounds.

'Where are your Soul Anchors? Won't their hounds call them?' His pitch rose as panic set in. 'You've already called them, haven't you? I won't let them hurt her.'

Darin glanced at Chase, who shook his head just a fraction.

'No Soul Anchors will come.' Darin gestured back toward Suriin. 'Stay here. If we close the door, it reduces the chance of you being found by anyone who might make the situation worse. For your sister's protection, it's the best plan.'

'Worse? She's unconscious, trapped, and clearly in pain. How could it get much worse?' Gwynn cried. He wiped his eye.

Darin couldn't blame him for the outburst and pretended he hadn't seen the tear.

Gwynn met his eyes and nodded. 'Do it. We'll be waiting.' Then he turned away to reach through the bars and make contact with Suriin.

⌐ ⋏ ◖ ✪ ◉

They left the room, closing the drop-bolts on the door outside. Chase tried his old, single note whistle. Darin watched for it to activate a disappearing magic, but disappointingly, the door didn't vanish. If there was any protection from discovery built into the wood, Darin hoped that they'd activated it. Chase gestured to their left, and they padded quietly down the dark corridor.

'You did well keeping him calm. We'll go through the armoury to reach the howler tunnels. I'm looking forward to showing you this.'

A room full of weapons he wasn't proficient with wasn't something that excited him, but Darin didn't want to spoil Chase's excitement. He changed the topic instead.

'Do you think Bones will mind looking after her?'

Chase chuckled. 'Not at all! He'll be delighted to be part of something for the first time in cycles. If anyone can work out how to free her, it will be him or Fall. Between them, I think they've read almost every book in our hidden library. Even though they could never access the magic, they've been walking spell books.' He patted his pocket where his slider whistle rested. 'Mind you, now we've got new whistles to play the tunes So'Dal can sing, that might change. They can finally start to try them out.'

'Maybe we can get her out ourselves with the right tune?'

Chase shrugged. 'I really don't know. She can't go anywhere in that state – all mumbling and vomiting. She could say anything to anyone, and no doubt would be examined by the Anchor as soon as they took her back. People who break vows and spill secrets have a tendency to vanish here. That lad is right. Someone will come looking for them soon. She looks young enough that she's probably one of the newest batch of Soul Anchors. She'll be missed. We need to work fast to keep her safe.'

Darin paused as they approached the end of the passage. 'I've seen her around. She works with Fresna in the kitchens.' *[Star sleeping]* filled his vision.

[Star walking further, seeing Bones, then sleeping] Darin sent back. Star dragged his paws with exhaustion, the scratching of his nails on the floor somehow still audible in these noise-eating tunnels.

A huge door blocked their passage. Wrought metal hinges extended across it in the shape of sword hilts, and the re-enforcing vertical metal bars were moulded into the shape of spears. A pair of small key-plates crafted into perfect shields guarded either side of the handles. It was a bold advert for a store of weaponry.

'Not very subtle, is it?' Darin laughed.

Chase rummaged in his bag and pulled out two keys, handing one to Darin.

'You carried secret keys around Dal? Do you often need them?'

A frown crossed Chase's face. 'No, I keep a set in that cubby hole we put our travel packs in. I grabbed them in case we needed something from here. One awldrin fleeing the palace was enough of a surprise. I had no plan to meet any more unarmed.'

They slotted the keys into the shields and turned them simultaneously. The taste of oiled metal flooded his senses as they entered. Star raised his head, scenting the air intently. Darin reached into his pocket and pulled out his new whistle. He found the right pitch mark, blew it, and the room illuminated. Blades glinted from their wall mounts, and rank upon rank of spears stood tall against their racks.

'This is the small armoury?' He whistled a breath out.

Chase glanced at him. 'It's impressive, isn't it? What do you notice about the equipment here?'

Darin looked around carefully. All the standard equipment he had seen used by the So'Dal was on display in high numbers. 'Nothing in particular. It's all equipment I've seen before when Hal trained with me. The Collective train with most of this on occasions.'

'Go on ...'

'It's a big storeroom. There are no special xotryl-fighting weapons here. None of the short spears like ours either.' He looked more closely, walking around the room as he studied the wall racks. 'Everything in here is for So'Dal.' Darin couldn't quite put his finger on it, but something was missing from the selection.

'It is, as it should be. Are you ready?'

Darin nodded. Chase strode across the room to the spear racks with Sandy close at his heels. He raised his whistle and blew. Behind the furthest rack, a small, unadorned door appeared.

Chase twisted the last spear-head on the rack. The spear was rusted, unusual in this room of pristine weapons. It had become part of the rack, neglected and blunt – unlikely to be picked up by anyone intentionally.

The door slid open. It moved just like the main entrance in the lift chamber. That was good. If it marked the entrance to the howler rooms, Star didn't have far to go.

Darin and Star followed Chase, turned the main lights back off with a whistle, and used a small push-stone to close themselves in. Darin ran his hand along the wall of the passage. Star was too tired to ask for help; the moonhound needed to save his energy. All the time they'd travelled, Darin had begun to rely on Star's eyes in the dark, but now he had to let that go and use on his own feeble vision.

The wall curved away from his body as the space opened up, and his footsteps rang back at him from a distant wall. Under his hand, the stone was rough-hewn, like many of the older spaces the Howlers inhabited. This didn't feel like a small space.

'Would you like to light it up?' Chase asked.

Darin blew the whistle.

He couldn't help a sharp intake of breath. Arrayed around the edges were suits of delicate armour light enough for a small Soul Anchor to wear. Tall shields engraved and enamelled with various symbols hung around the walls. Staramine ran across the cavern and whined. Above him, a sword pointed upward, inverted, unlike the remaining weapons in the room. Its blade was red as fresh blood and glowed in the light. Darin was drawn to it. He followed Star, and once within arm's reach, he could see tiny symbols engraved in the guard. The pommel stone rippled with light like Mythos' reflection on water. *A staramine blade? What skills must have been used to create such a thing?*

Lost for words, he continued to walk around the room. A pile of leathery armour plates were stacked in a corner. He picked a set up, turning it over in his hands. It was too small for a Skaa-rak. Staramine stood next to him, sniffing at the pile. *[Lots of moonhounds]*

Darin looked more carefully at the plates with Star's new revelation.

'Chase, is this hound armour?'

Chase joined him and picked another piece up, then glanced at Sandy, who was heading to another corner of the cavern.

'It was, yes. Back when the Gates hadn't changed them, they were just large hunting dogs. It's been preserved, like everything, by the Watcher's magic. But I can't imagine that they'd be soft or supple enough to use now.'

Darin lifted a set toward Star, who shrunk away from it. 'What do you think would happen if I removed it from here?'

Chase smiled. 'I don't need to guess – I tried. The leather cracked very quickly. Sandy and I barely got to test it out. It wouldn't help us now.'

Darin's shoulders slumped in disappointment. *A lovely thought while it lasted.*

'Come on, we need to get home. We've other issues to worry about.' Chase strolled across the room, ignoring the treasures surrounding him. Darin searched for Sandy, who had yet to return from the other side of the cavern.

'He's found the meat. We keep moving it, but Sandy always finds it. Give me a moment.' Chase stopped walking and closed his eyes. Whatever argument they were having needed more focus than walking, clearly.

Darin waited until Sandy loped across to join them, drool hanging from his mouth in great strings.

'What do you mean the meat?'

'This place has a preservation spell on it, which we take advantage of to keep much of our perishable foods edible.'

They reached a small door on the far side and continued down the howler passages. Darin urged Star on, sending encouragement to the hound until a musty scent of men and dogs filled the air. He felt a lightness to his shoulders as he inhaled deeply. *A shared problem would be easier to solve.*

They turned into a small, narrow passage and entered the main communal area. Bones sat hunched over a table, intense concentration writ across his face as he studied the stones board. Fall reclined opposite him, his arms crossed as he watched Bones. His chin was slightly raised, and the creases at the corners of his eyes told the impending tale of their game's ending.

The familiar sights comforted Darin momentarily before Chase interrupted the game. He stood on a circle in the middle of the room's floor with Sandy sat at his heel.

'Howler patrol reporting in. Please summon all available members of the pack.'

Darin felt his pulse quickening, the calm of their return lost. They'd intended to return with good news.

Chase remained in position as Bones uncurled. He frowned. 'A formal report? Watcher's breath, things must be worse than I realised. Fall, can you gather the others? Boulder is on the lever, but Aggi should be around.'

⌒ ⅄ ☾ ♣ ◉

Once all Howlers were present, Chase began, 'We have a series of problems, and if I'm honest, I don't know how many we can handle ourselves.' He paused, rubbing his chin, then drew a deep breath audible from Darin's seat.

'There is an awldrin queen roaming freely on Lieus. Two xotryl are terrorising Dal, hunting humans, and there is a semi-conscious girl trapped in a magically locked cell, opposite the seed store, in a room I've never noticed before. She is responsible for freeing the awldrin.'

A collective gasp filled the chamber.

Fall rubbed his forehead. 'Awldrin queen. Start there please?'

Darin opened his mouth to speak, but Bones shook his head and leant closer. 'Chase led this expedition – he reports.'

'The girl was drifting in and out of consciousness, but she was able to communicate that she'd freed an awldrin queen. She hasn't been well enough to say much more, and what she does, is almost unintelligible. Her brother and a mature moonhound are currently keeping watch on her. She's a young lilac – Darin thinks she's a member of the current cohort.

'We saw the awldrin leave the hidden tunnels, mounted on a green xotryl, which has recently arrived in Dal, and we believe is responsible for the spate of violent attacks. If we understood the girl correctly, the awldrin is set on returning home to Tebein and may have already discovered the gates are closed.'

The old Howlers sat in silence. Bones' hand shook slightly, and Fall's knuckles grew white across clenched fists.

'If I could just send the foul creatures back, I would. The Aulirean Gates will never open again. This girl, why's she unwell? Is it guilt?' Bones asked, his voice calmer than his hands.

'We don't know. I hoped you might take a look at her, work out how we release her.'

Aggi growled. 'It doesn't sound like she should be released.'

Darin was inclined to agree, but the regret on Suriin's face had read true to him. 'We should find out why she ended up in this situation in the first place. Before we condemn her, or let the Anchor near her, we need to know what she does,' he offered. 'She'll be missed soon, as will her brother.'

'The boy and hound are bonded?' Fall asked.

Chase shook his head. 'No, he's too young. A year or two away from manifestation, maybe even more.'

Bones sighed. 'I'm too old for this. Darin, Chase, please tell us that at least you managed what you set out to achieve? Give us some good news.'

Darin rummaged in his bag and took out the whistles. He passed one to each Howler in the room. 'They work.'

'Thank the Watcher for small flares of hope in the midst of this furnace of problems!' Aggi said, turning his whistle over in his hand. 'We'll be able to use all that knowledge you and Fall have accumulated in your cycles of reading now.' He waved his whistle at Bones. 'You're far from too old to help. You'll be the key.'

Chase stepped back and sat down. 'Sorry, pack, that it's not all positive.'

Fall shook his head. 'It's not as though any of us could have predicted this. The xotryl attacks were severe enough for us to take steps never considered and create these whistles. I'm sure I speak for the pack when I say I'm glad we chose to break tradition. Thank you both.'

Bones nodded slowly. 'We need to work through this calmly and logically. Darin can take me to the girl. While we're busy with her, the rest of you need to decide exactly how much we report to the Anchor – or if you even think we should. It means exposing ourselves, which may, in turn, lead to exposing the bigger secrets we keep from them, giving them access to power they have not had for hundreds of cycles. Power we promised the Watcher they would never again hold. One awldrin ... Is that truly enough to justify breaking our vow if we can deal with it ourselves? Is our current Anchor stable and strong enough to bear that burden? Also, would someone get the extra chambers ready in case we need them, please?'

Star raised his head from the deep-piled rug Darin rested his sore feet in, the hound's exhaustion leaking into Darin's own awareness.

His vision was filled with *[Sleeping on the bed in their room in the palace]*. Darin felt the question in the image and replied with *[Star asleep on the bed in their howler chamber]* then followed with *[Bones and Darin walking back to the girl, Star sleeping]* To his surprise, Star replied with agreement.

Darin rose and moved close to Chase, leaning down to whisper in his ear, 'Star agreed to stay here. Can you please speak to the others about the dragon bone while I take Bones? I'm exhausted, but I promised Gwynn I'd return. I'd like to keep that promise.'

Star wobbled to his feet and walked slowly to their chamber. Sandy followed closely, curling up alongside Star once they reached it.

Chase reached out and patted Darin on the shoulder. 'Don't worry, Sandy will keep him company while you're busy. As soon as he wakes, we'll have something ready for him, I promise. We're a pack, remember.'

Bones glanced between the two men and the sleeping hounds. 'There's something else going on, isn't there? Something you haven't told us yet?'

Chase nodded. 'There is, but we all made it back. Darin can tell you on the way.'

They returned the way that Darin had arrived. Raised voices followed them down the corridor until they became a murmur of sound. Darin explained the story of the xotryl attack and his fall from the waterfall as they walked. He described Star's self-sacrificing heal and showed Bones the huge scar. Finally, he told of their journey back and the fact that they had managed to create the general heal potion at Tian's home.

'No wonder Star needed sleep.' Bones sighed as they reached the door to the hidden armoury. 'Can you create another heal for him?'

'If I have the ingredients, and once I retrieve the training globe from the cubby near the mountain entrance.'

'I'll send someone to gather what you need once we get back. We should prepare a store, quietly. If we choose to fix this without involving the So'Dal or Collective, we'll need to be prepared. Dragon bone could cure him quickly, but with the dire tidings you brought us, the fragment we have left may be needed far more urgently. Let's try rest and potion heals while we work out a plan. I wonder if I can use the new whistle in some way.' Bones murmured as he pulled one of his old whistles from his pocket. 'Activate your dragon bone, please. Not that anyone should ever be in here. But it's better to be safe under the circumstances.'

As they entered, the pile of hound armour caught Darin's eye again. *Better to be safe.* A flicker of a plan started to form.

'We're going to need help with all this, aren't we?' he asked.

'I fear we will, yes.' Bones blew his whistle and vanished. The push-stone moved in, and the door to the outer armoury opened. 'No one in there. Good. Stay hidden. We can't do the same at the main door. We'll be taking a risk there. If we see anyone, just freeze. Understand?' Darin nodded before he remembered Bones couldn't see him.

'Yes,' he whispered, and they entered the main armoury.

CHAPTER 3

ELISSA

Charvers are strange creatures. Natives of
Mythos and bearing a strong resemblance to
the Mythese themselves, they are a wonder of
ever changing colour and sharp teeth.
Only one has ever been seen in the Edgelands.
Edgelands Anomalies, The Rare and
Wondrous

'You won't be able to teach them.' The quiet voice rang inside her mind as she walked back toward her house, exhausted.

Hope lay curled up near the path, smoke coiling ever upward, and watching Elissa with one half-opened eye.

'Are you talking to me?' Elissa asked, confused.

'Yes.' Hope released more smoke rings, her voice echoing inside her head, loud, although no one else nearby appeared to hear her. 'You won't be able to teach the other humans to use threads of magic. I'm impressed, though. Your control increases quickly as you practise – I could feel it from here.'

'If I can do it, why can't they?' Elissa sat down. She was too tired for riddles. Andra had made her create threads of different emotions for what felt like hours. The woman never seemed to tire, despite her age.

'Because they are not dragons.'

Elissa laughed. 'Nor am I!'

'No. Nor will you ever truly be. You are stuck with aspects of our power, yet none of our strength.' Hope paused. 'I wonder what it will do to your lifespan.'

Elissa threw her hands in the air. 'I'm still here! Can you debate my personal changes when I'm not listening? If it's your power, can you teach me to use it?'

'No.'

Elissa sighed deeply. 'Why not?' Hope had come to save them. That was the feeling everyone, including her, had at the sight of the great, golden dragon. Now, she was slightly less sure. Hope had curled up on the island and not charged off into battle. Elissa wasn't sure she'd done anything to help at all so far, aside from donating a scale to support Elissa's injured foot.

'We do not *use* emotion, we *are* emotion. I cannot explain to you how to access it. Only feel that you are using it. Our powers are greater, less limited. I cannot help.' Hope tilted her head to one side as she studied Elissa.

'I have to work this out alone, then?'

Hope stretched her neck out. 'You will. I am sure of it. Not in your house, though. Trust me on that. It won't like it.' She nudged Elissa, almost knocking her over. 'Did my scale help with walking?'

Elissa smiled. 'Hope, I have a feeling that you know it did.' She watched the scaled snout for a trace of emotion or humour, but nothing changed.

Impassive, Hope stretched out her huge wings.

'I will speak with you again soon,' she said as she crouched.

The huge muscles tensed, then she launched into the air. Downdraft from her wings rustled Elissa's hair, and she stared in awe at the enormous golden dragon spiralling upward on strong wing beats. She'd brought dragons from another moon, through a gate thought forever closed. Only a few tides ago, she had been hiding in darkness. Now she was talking to a dragon – even though she wasn't yet sure how Hope would help. Maybe, with Regret's return, they would have some answers.

⌒ ⚐ ⬙ ⬡ ⊚

'I need rest and food,' she muttered as she walked down the winding path to her cottage. On impulse, she checked the basket by the door. Her hand closed around more wood. Someone must be taking pity on her and refilling it.

She crossed the threshold and scanned the room. The charver eggs were undisturbed, although fresh prints crossed her floor. The parents must have visited while she was out. She wondered what the little ones would eat once they hatched and what they would look like.

The multi-coloured shells shone in the flickering flames of her fire as she tucked into some food Andra had sent her home with. She thought back to the conversations with Hope, and something that had slid past her exhausted mind returned to the forefront of her thoughts. What had Hope meant by the house wouldn't like magic? She reached inside herself for a second, then something on her periphery moved.

A small red creature peeked out at her from behind the chair, chittering loudly. Its pointed snout flared at the end, and gossamer thin wings folded against its side. She leant forward, and it opened them again, chittering louder. Rearing up on tiny, muscular hind limbs, it spread its forelimbs wide. The wings were supported with struts between them and attached to the body near the top of the rear legs. Tiny dark beads stared at her. As the creature turned away, she saw a sail-like fin folding down flat against its back. A ripple of colour flushed across its skin, and its brilliantly glowing red faded to a subtle dark green, the same as the chair it was next to.

She reached inside and grabbed a thread of joy. As she was about to pull it free, the creature shot toward her, jaws agape. Tiny, needle-sharp teeth glinted, and Elissa let go. The creature retreated; this time it flapped up to the nest. Settling down next to the eggs, with its eyes fixed on Elissa.

'You win,' she said. 'No magic near your babies.' Maybe Hope had meant that the charver wouldn't like the magic, rather than the house. It certainly seemed that way.

Elissa finished eating quietly, and as she rose, the small head – almost blending with the pattern of the exposed straw stuffing now – followed her across the room. That was one fiercely protective parent.

Chuckling, Elissa rinsed her plate and retired to her room. She had been released from Andra's presence, but she knew she would be tested all night long by the Chosen. If she wanted to get in touch with Laytha, she needed to work on her dream shielding. She hoped Laytha was still safe.

⌒⋏ 𝆑 ✤ ◦

It felt as though her eyes had barely closed when she heard calls of distress. She sat bolt upright, and listened for them again. Faint now, yet very near. Wordless panic audible in the shrill pitch and quavering call. Elissa leapt out of bed and crept barefoot to the bedroom door. It was coming from the main room. Who was in there? She peered through the cracked open door, but there was no-one in sight. Only the charver, sat atop the nest, repeatedly tapping one of its eggs.

'Hey, little one,' she called out. The noise and assault on her emotions stopped immediately. She tried to push the door open, but her hand went through it. She was dream-walking. *At least I am still in my own house. Is it dream-walking too? Or even genuinely distressed? Am I dreaming it all?*

The charver jumped from the chair and ran at the door, then scratched desperately at it with tiny hooks at the end of its arms. Elissa grabbed at a thread of trust from her store of emotional magic. There was only a tiny ball left to draw from. The one she threw at Andra when they first met must have been huge.

She dropped the thread of trust onto the charver's head, not knowing if it would work in a dream-walk, or if the action was just her imagining she was doing it.

The scratching stopped, and the emotional flood from the charver changed. Hope and optimism flooded her instead. It looked at her with its head tilted to one side, then began to scratch faster at the door.

The scratching intensified until it cut through her sleep. Elissa woke. The noise was still there, although she was now awake. She ran to the door and pushed it open. The charver stared at her chittering; Elissa could feel no emotions from it now she was awake. The charver looked up at her, then hopped and flapped across the room and up onto its nest. It waited until Elissa had reached the nest before gently tapping at one of the eggs.

Cracks were appearing in most of them, and little chirping noises chorused as they struggled their way out. But this single egg was still. It didn't rock like the others, and there was no hole in it. She reached for it and the charver stepped back. It let her pick up the egg, but fierce eyes gripped her with every move.

She lifted it, and closer to her ear, Elissa could hear tiny chirruping sounds. She turned it carefully, looking for a crack to help the hatchling out. There wasn't one.

'I'm going to try to break this shell,' she said, trying to keep a calm, reassuring tone to her voice. *It won't understand me at all, but maybe if I keep talking it will let me help.* She carried the small golden egg to the bench in the kitchen. Elissa twisted a cloth into a makeshift nest, then rummaged in a drawer to find an eating spike. She lifted the egg to her ear again, then carefully placing it with the loudest point upward, she began to tap the egg.

A scarlet charver dropped from the roof next to her and bared its teeth to bite. Elissa ignored it. The other one shrieked from the chair.

'I was allowed to take it,' Elissa muttered. 'I'm only trying to help. As soon as we have your baby out, you'll see.' She braced for the bite, but it didn't come. The argument between the two charver had reached full volume now, and the new arrival flew away from Elissa, flashing yellow and red, toward the one on the nest.

She took advantage of the moment to tap again, trying to angle along the shell rather than into it. A tiny fracture appeared. Elissa tapped again. The chirrups from inside got louder, and she felt movement.

'Okay, little one. This should do it.'

She tapped the edge of the crack, and a large section of the egg fell free. A tiny charver was coiled up inside. She carefully worked the next section of the egg loose to allow it to get its head uncurled. A truce fell between the two adult charver as the chair erupted with a chorus of chirrups and reassuring clicks. The rest of the nest had started to break through.

'I suppose at least that allows me to continue un-bitten,' Elissa said, as she pulled more pieces off. The small charver uncurled its neck and swung the tiny flared snout in her direction. Its skin rippled with blues and purples as it stared at her. The small coiled tail stretched out, and as it started to wobble upright, she saw the small bone strutted fin on its back raise like a sail. Tiny wings clung damply to its body.

Elissa scooped the small creature up and carried it over to the nest. The new hatchlings shimmered blue and purple as they gazed at their parents, but flashed yellow as Elissa leant over them.

She tried to place her charver in the nest, but it also turned yellow and clung on with sharp claws, climbing up her arm and backing away.

The parents tried to coax it down. But it flashed yellow and red at them.

Elissa lifted her hand with the charver still clinging onto it. As she brought it closer to her body, the blues and purples returned.

'Come and get your baby.' She laughed as she tried to untangle the charver from her clothes. The more she tried to put it down, the faster it tried to climb away and more panicked it got. Eventually, Elissa found herself stood in the middle of her house with a baby charver on her shoulder and an adult one trying to coax it over to the back of the chair.

'I have no idea what you eat. You really do need to go to the rest of your family,' she said, finally extricating the creature from her hair. She lowered it into the nest and backed away.

Some degree of instinct must have kicked in, because, although it remained yellow and unhappy, it allowed the parent to regurgitate some food into its mouth.

Surrounded by its calm, blue siblings, the little yellow charver fidgeted and wiggled.

Exhausted, Elissa sat on the other chair and fell back to sleep. Images of tiny flying charver floating through her dreams.

There were no further interruptions to her sleep, and the

gradually brightening sky woke her early the next morning. Through the window, she saw grey clouds gathered overhead, making it hard to judge the time of day. She rolled her shoulders to ease out the aches. A chirruping in her ear startled her. Turning her head carefully, she spotted a small blueish green face peering back at her from her shoulder. The nest was full of the other hatchlings, and the parents were nowhere to be seen.

With her other hand, Elissa gently prodded where she thought its stomach might be. It felt like a small ball.

'I need to go to my lessons in a while. Maybe if I start to leave the house, you will decide to stay with your family.'

She rose and attempted to remove it. The ear-piercing shrieks were enough to change her mind.

'Fine. Come with me then. But you'll probably get hungry and wish you hadn't.' Charver riding on her shoulder, Elissa set off to the tower to meet Andra.

CHAPTER 4

DARIN

They left the armoury without incident, the passageways empty of So'Dal as Darin led Bones to the cell.

After they lowered the heavy drop bolts in place, Bones looked around. He walked to the small alcove, ran his hand along one of the carved shelves, then turned to Darin with a frown.

'How have I never seen this place?'

'Chase said the same,' Darin replied and gestured to the wall ahead. 'Our whistles work on that. Maybe it was Howler built, but we were meant to forget about it?'

'Fascinating. Let's see this girl then. Is she through there?'

Bones pointed at a heavy door with a keyhole glinting by their light globe.

Darin frowned. 'No, we didn't try that door. There wasn't time. Suriin's through here.' He whistled and the wall illusion fell.

The stench of vomit and bile was far stronger than when he'd left, and the drainage hole for the small stream that trickled across the cell appeared to be blocked with vomit; the water had started to overflow its small channel.

Suriin had moved close to the bars, where Fluffy lay as close to the girl as she could get. Gwynn sat near them both and turned his tear-streaked face toward them as they approached.

'She's no better. Can you help her, please?' He sobbed. 'Our Father is dying. Our mother's missing. Suriin is all I have – Suriin and Fluffy.' He reached for the moonhound.

The girl emitted a low groan and rolled over, her eyes squeezed tightly shut and her face screwed up in what appeared to be pain. Gwynn turned in panic, reaching for her.

'Your father?' Bones crouched next to the boy. 'Who's your father?' He studied Suriin as he waited for a reply. 'She looks very pale. Is she hot?'

Suriin looked notably worse than when they'd left. Her skin had paled and her lips were cracked. She moved less, one arm held close to her side, wrapped around her ribs. Until they could get her out, Darin had no idea what other trauma and injuries she was suffering from. No doubt, it was more than she outwardly showed.

Gwynn dragged his gaze away from his sister. 'My father is So'Dal Yorynn. He was attacked on his way here with Suriin.' He gestured at his sister. 'The Anchor sent for us – me and our mother. When I got here, Suriin was missing.' He swallowed hard. 'She got close to the bars just before you got here. Just before she was sick again.' He pointed at a small yellow puddle.

Bones brought his hands together and interlaced the fingers before lowering them with a sigh.

'So'Dal Yorynn.' He nodded. 'I know who he is. The xotryl wound festers still?'

Gwynn shrugged. 'I heard from the Collective who brought me that he'd started to get better, but I haven't seen him. Fluffy let me put her on a Skaa-rak finally, so we got here early. I wanted to surprise my sister.' He gestured at Suriin. 'But she was missing from her room. I thought it would be fun to get Fluffy to track her so I could still surprise her. Then, I found her and ... Watcher's flames!' He collapsed in on himself. 'Well, you know the rest.'

'If your mother has a moonhound, and your father is a So'Dal, you know that you will train as a So'Dal yourself one day, don't you?' Bones asked quietly.

'I guessed I would, yes. What does that have to do with Suriin?'

'It might make a huge difference!' Darin exclaimed, recalling Tralkion's tales about growing up in Redpike. He crouched by Gwynn. 'I need you to be completely honest with me. How good are your plant identifications?'

Gwynn looked uncomfortable. 'I used to borrow my father's books while he was away. I can identify most things – I know I shouldn't have, but I wanted to be ready!' he finished in a rush.

'Your readiness might save her.' Darin squeezed Gwynn's arm, trying to reassure him. The boy frowned and glanced at his sister as she groaned again.

Bones crouched by the bars. 'May I get closer?' Gwynn moved aside as Bones reached over Fluffy to Suriin. I'm going to need you to lift your arm, my dear.'

Suriin didn't respond at first, then she let out a cry of pain.

'Suriin, it's Gwynn. Can you hold my hand?' Gwynn

reached for her and tried to lift her arm. 'Enough?' he whispered.

Bones nodded as he inspected her ribs, prodding gently.

Suriin yelped and curled up again.

Bones retreated from the cell and gestured Darin over. 'Darin, a moment, please.'

They walked further from the cell. 'She's feverish, and I suspect a number of her ribs are bruised, if not broken,' he murmured.

'That's going to be hard to hide,' Darin replied. He looked over at Gwynn, an idea starting to grow. He couldn't go himself, not without people wondering when he'd got back, and where the Master of Hounds was, and then he'd get tied up with lessons. It would leave him and Star unable to help the pack. He could use Gwynn though – remove the pressure of care, and let him feel helpful.

'Bones, I have a plan.' They could use this boy as a go between, a set of eyes and – more importantly – hands in the palace.

Bones stood with his arms folded, watching Darin appraisingly. 'I can see that. One ranging, and you're becoming more Howler by the day. Go ahead, I trust you.'

Darin wished he had Star to reenforce his gut feeling. But Star hadn't been worried about Gwynn.

'Gwynn, the best way you can help your sister is to collect a selection of plants from the crater garden as quickly as you can and bring them back here.'

'Why can't you do it? I don't want to leave her with strangers.'

'That's a long story, and we don't have the time.' He gestured at Suriin. 'I need you to trust me. She needs you to trust me. Can you do that?' Darin tried to look as friendly and supportive as he could.

Gwynn wiped tears from his eyes and shrugged. 'I can't solve anything alone. I don't have much choice, do I?'

'I know, Gwynn, I'm sorry. If it helps, by even coming to see you right now, we're trusting you with huge secrets. If you've been learning on your own, without anyone knowing, you can clearly keep secrets. I promise we will do everything in our power to get your sister out.'

Gwynn shrugged acceptance. 'I don't like it, but if it's the only way, then let's get started. What do I need?' He opened up a bag and pulled out a notebook. 'This is Suriin's. You might want to look at it. There are some really scary drawings in it. I think she's been studying the awldrin for a while. I'm sure she won't mind if I take a page to help her.' He pulled a page from the back of the notebook.

As Darin listed the plants for Gwynn, Bones flicked through the drawings in the book, at one point taking a sharp breath. Darin resisted the urge to ask what Bones had seen; it could wait until later.

'Return to the main palace. I need you to find someone called Conor. He's about my age, with red hair. He's usually carrying a heap of tools, and he's a true man of habit. You'll find him sat on the second table from the counter at mealtimes. If you aren't sure, ask someone to point him out. Tell him you met me in Redstone crater, and that I had said he was the best person to show you the garden.'

'Red hair, tools. Got it.' Gwynn scribbled notes.

'When you have collected these plants, I need you to do two things.' Darin turned. 'Bones, we need a Builder or their tools. The lock is magical, but if there's a way around it, Conor will find it. I trust him.'

Bones shook his head. 'I hate to disagree with your plan, but the head Builder already knows about us. We need him, not an apprentice. Get Conor to deliver a note instead.'

'I can give him a note,' Gwynn interjected. 'Will you stay with Suriin while I go?'

'Yes.' Bones sat next to the cell slowly, lowering himself with aged joints and grimaces. 'Bring the herbs back here. We won't leave her alone.'

Gwynn frowned at them. 'You're hiding something else – you've told me that indirectly. But if you can help Suriin, I'll be as fast as I can.'

He took the note Bones had scribbled and scanned it. 'This doesn't make sense.'

'Not to you. But it will to the person it is meant for,' Bones replied. 'One more thing. Leave the moonhound here.'

Gwynn shrugged as he got to his feet. 'I don't think that will be a problem. She won't move. I think she's worried for Suriin. I can't talk to Fluffy, so I'm not certain, but look at how she's lying. Suriin was always the one who sent her messages, not me.' He pulled a scrap of paper from his pocket. 'I'll try to use this map I found in her bag. I'll see you as soon as I can.'

Bones held his hand out. 'A map?'

Gwynn unfolded it. 'I think we're here. It's covered with her writing. She was looking for something – look at all these crosses on doors.'

Bones rubbed his face. 'It does show part of this room, although not the other door. Keep it safe. When she wakes, we'll have to ask where she got it. Do not show it to anyone.'

'Her secret is safe with me,' Gwynn said and tucked it inside his clothes.

Darin walked with Gwynn to the door. 'If you get stopped, tell them you took a wrong turn. You're new here and you're lost. Ask for the main hall.'

Once Gwynn left, Darin secured the bolts, then turned to find Bones studying the lock. 'I recognise these symbols, though even with the new whistle, I couldn't use them. Let's give your plan a fair try. Otherwise, we're going to need a Soul Anchor to get her out. Once we do that, there will be more questions than we have answers to give.'

'Bones, I know you want to retain the secrecy of the Howlers, and have done so for so long. But we don't have the numbers to deal with this. Pretty soon, sightings of a xotryl with a passenger are going to reach the Anchor. Wouldn't it be better if we just supported her instead of being two men and two hounds trying to fix this?

'She will mount her own offensive in time. But,' Bones inclined his head at Suriin, 'I believe we have a head start. The current Anchor doesn't have anything like the power of the original who must have imprisoned the awldrin queen. She is hobbled, as they all are. Her power is dimmed.'

'What do you mean?' Darin knew they had split the magical training, but surely over time, the So'Dal's actual power hadn't reduced? Or had it? Would the Howlers fade away, too, in the end?

'It's the crystals. It narrows their focus and absorbs their power – effectively diminishes it. They cannot use as much through it at any one time as the So'Dal of ages past once could.'

'Why would any Soul Anchor willingly do such a thing?' If the Soul Anchors, the most powerful members of their society, were reduced – and if it had taken the strongest of those to defeat the awldrin queen previously – they were in even deeper trouble than he'd realised. The So'Dal as a backup plan was possibly weaker than the Howlers would be with their whistles and forgotten magic.

'It's part of the Watcher's pact. The same pact we uphold by keeping those powerful books hidden. The Anchors do it because it's tradition. They know no other way now. They are so scared of using up all their power that they subject themselves to this funnelling without knowing what it really is. Through my position as Master of Hounds, I have heard many Soul Anchors say it's not like being bonded to a hound – part of their mind is anchored in the crystal.' Bones gestured to Suriin. 'Where's her crystal?'

Darin looked carefully. 'I think she said that the awldrin took it, and I can't see it.'

Bones nodded. 'When she opens her eyes, she's staring into space. Look.'

Suriin was turning her head from side to side, eyes unfocused – looking right through them. 'She's also being sick. You say she was assaulted, and there's her damaged ribs. I'm certain that something more than being physically assaulted is going on here, and I'd bet my tail on the fact that it has something to do with the missing crystal.'

'So you think my heal potion won't work?' Darin could see what he meant, but surely her injuries alone needed some help.

Bones laughed. 'Darin, I'm counting on it working! I don't think she'll be able to weft emotions into magic with any strength. But I'm hoping she'll be able to talk, walk, and get to safety.'

Darin sat near Fluffy, stroking the hound. She lifted her head and gave his hand a gentle lick with her rough tongue. 'Gwynn could be gone for hours. What do we do now?'

Bones retrieved his new whistle from his pocket. 'How about you teach me how this works? Then I can start making the links between what I've read over my long life' – he rolled his eyes dramatically – 'and making the magic work.'

'Without my training globe, to get the right pitch, we're a

bit limited. But I can show you how to work it without the wefts?'

Bones nodded. 'That sounds a very sensible place to start.'

⌒ ⋏ ⟡ ✦ ◉

Several hours later, the scraping of door-bolts interrupted them. Fluffy raised her head and whined. The door swung open, and a ruddy-cheeked man strode in. His broad shoulders filled the doorway, then as he strode toward them, two others filed in behind.

'Master of Hounds,' he boomed. 'I heard you needed my help.'

The bolts dropped back into place, and his companions stepped into the light. Gwynn rushed forward to Darin. 'I'm sorry – Conor insisted on coming, So'Dal Darin. The Master of Builders, he also told him to come. I didn't know what to do! I know you said you had to stay hidden, but I couldn't stop him. How is she?'

'Darin, how long have you been back?' Conor stood next to the Master of Builders. Hurt vied with confusion across his face.

'I can explain. Can I?' Darin asked Bones.

Bones wasn't listening to him. He stared at Conor, and a slow smile broke across his face. He turned to the big man. 'So, you've finally chosen?'

'Aye, I have, Lyall, and seeing Darin and Conor together over the last few tides, it's fitting, I think. Timing is everything in building, and the future depends on it.' The Master of Builders reached forward to clasp Bones' hand. 'It worked for us. One day it will work for them. We're getting old, and someone else needs to know how to fix the steam lift.'

Conor reluctantly pulled his gaze from Darin to his own

Master. 'What's all this have to do with the steam lift?' He paused. 'Darin, that's not Star. Where is he?'

'We – I – got in a bit of trouble, and Star helped me. He's resting now. Don't worry.' Darin frowned. 'Did you just call the Master of Hounds Lyall?'

The Master of Builders smiled. 'Aye.' He stared at Suriin. 'I'm used to seeing you in all parts of the palace, Lyall. But not usually with a young Soul Anchor, unless they have a hound in training. What's she doing all the way out here?'

'Suriin is why I sent for you.' Bones replied. 'Can you open this cell?'

By now, Conor was looking ready to explode with frustration. 'Can someone help me understand what's going on? Please.'

The Master of Builders rested his hand on Conor's shoulder. 'Conor, you're being entrusted with one of the oldest secrets of the So'Dal.' He gestured at Bones. 'This man, Lyall, The Master of Hounds, is the leader of a secret society who live under our noses. The Howlers. They have many hidden passageways under the mountain and guard the oldest secrets of the So'Dal. They were entrusted with this task by the Watcher himself.

Conor glanced at Darin and raised an eyebrow. Darin simply shrugged in return. 'You were right. I wasn't telling you everything.'

'Why are you telling me now then, if it's such a secret? Wait, Darin ... you're a Howler too?'

Bones nodded at Conor. 'We are trusting you, and yes, your friend Darin is one of us. One day he may be the only one remaining, unless more are found. Within the Black Palace, the Anchor's knew of us until a few prior to our current Anchor. Otherwise, only the Master of Builders knows.'

And every So'Dal from Dal. Darin shuffled his feet as Conor reached for the bars around the lock.

'When we were young – much as you and Darin did – Lyall and I arrived on the same day for our testing.'

'One of us took each path,' Bones continued. The two old men grinned at each other.

'Now it will be your job, Conor. As I get older, there will be things that need doing. Tasks that require access to the howler tunnels. One of the most key is fixing issues with the steam lift as cogs wear or pistons stick. Only I have had that access for many cycles. Before me, only my Master could fix the lift. Your love of it and all things related to our craft has marked you out from your first day.'

As Conor let go of the bars and looked up at the Master of Builders with colour draining from his face, empathy rose in Darin's core. He knew the feeling of shock all too well. He tried to catch Conor's eye, but his friend stared intently at his master. 'So, is this a roundabout way of telling me that I will become Master of Builders?'

His master nodded, and Bones hid a smile behind his hand before winking at Darin. 'With this knowledge comes responsibility, and you already came close to the Howlers once through Darin.'

Darin blushed as Conor looked at him. 'I promise, Conor, no more secrets. I'm glad I don't have to hide anything from you. You can take this out on me later – again – but right now, we need your master's expertise to get this girl out.'

Gwynn turned from where he'd sat quietly throughout the exchange. 'She's my sister, not a girl.'

'We know. Let's see if we can free her,' Bones replied, placation rippling through his tone. Conor shot Darin a look that promised another beating, then dropped a case of tools alongside the bars.

'The lock is magical and beyond our capabilities. I don't know how she got in there,' Darin said, crouching next to Conor. 'I'm sorry,' he whispered and was rewarded with a thin smile.

'I knew you were hiding something! When did you come back? Why you haven't been to see me?'

'We came straight here and found her. I haven't been back a day yet. Conor, there's really big stuff happening right now. Huge. Watcher's fire, if I hadn't seen the things I have with my own eyes ... Can you get her out? I need to get a healing potion into her. Then we can get some more answers.'

'We'll get her out. Go and make your healing potion. These bars are thick. This will take a while.'

Darin glanced up at Bones and saw the nod. 'Go ahead. I'll stay.'

'Gwynn, do you have everything?'

'It's in the bag.' Gwynn pointed at a Gardener bag he'd dropped by the door. 'Before you ask, yes, it's mine. Please return it.' He sat next to the cell and reached for Suriin. 'I'm back. I'm here. You're safe, Sis. We'll get you out.'

⌒ ⚐ ☾ ✥ ◉

Why would a teenage boy have his own Gardener bag? Darin puzzled as he walked to the howler quarters. That boy and his sister were an odd pair for sure, and with Fluffy, an unusual trio. The world as he knew it became stranger by the day. At least he could share it with Conor now.

He knew he'd struggle to deal with all the changes if he stopped to think too hard about what they meant. As he'd done all his life, Darin focused on the immediate challenge facing him – there was a sick girl, and that was something he could help with. There was no point puzzling over pieces that didn't fit. One problem at a time.

ᴧᴧᴧ

He arrived in the Howler's main chamber to a cacophony of discordant notes bruising his ears. Every Howler was playing a different tune.

'Fall!' he shouted over the din. The Howlers fell silent. 'Fall, I need a spice grinder – do we have one?'

'I'll go find it.' Fall put his whistle on a table and shuffled off to the kitchen.

'Chase,' Darin said, 'can you retrieve the training globe from where we hid it? I'm afraid I don't remember the way.'

'Already done. It's in your room.'

'I need to make a batch of healing potion. The Master of Builders is trying to break Suriin out of the cell, but she's in no fit state to tell us anything.' He looked at the circle of expectant faces around him and felt a small smile grow on his face. 'Shall I show you all how? I know you'll have read it, but doing it is quite different.'

Old faces cracked with delight, and Darin took it as a sign to continue. A moment of happiness amidst the chaos would help him almost as much as the potion would help those who needed it.

Fall returned with the spice grinder, and Darin laid out the plants on a table. He chose the healthiest leaves from the selection; some were quite battered, but most were usable. He ground the leaves, quelling the excitement rising at the anticipation of using magic again. Step by step, he talked the Howlers through the stages in making the heal. The group of old men copied his notes, learning the notch positions for the heal tune. As before, he used the training globe for consistency, then transferred his focus to the potion. The green flash spread through the bowl, and a collective gasp reached him.

He was surrounded by a ring of smiling faces.

'You really did it!'

'Darin, it worked!'

He grinned and gestured at Chase. 'No, *we* did it. Once I get back and we've decided what to do with this girl, we'll have to try some new wefts.'

He poured the concoction into a bottle that Fall offered him and headed for the tunnel. Star struggled to rise and accompany him.

'No, Star.' *[Star resting with Sandy until he came back]* Star accepted the instructions without argument and sank back into the rug.

Chase met his eyes.

'He'll be okay, Darin. I promise.'

'I wanted some of this to be for him, but there's not enough, and we need to get her to safety to get her to talk.' Worry pooled at the pit of his stomach and nausea flooded him. 'I know he'll be okay with you, but I'll be as fast as I can. If he does get worse ...'

'Then I promise I'll do what we talked about.'

Boulder stared at them both. 'Chase, if Star needs something from the stores, I can retrieve it.' He looked around the room. 'I know it takes a full vote, but we've all lost a hound, or come close. We know the hurt, the pain, and, as Star is our future, I believe Bones would add his voice to the agreement if things get dire.' All the men in the circle nodded.

'He would,' Aggi said. 'If that pup *needs* dragon bone, he *will* get it. Darin, go. We need you and Bones back here as soon as possible.'

CHAPTER 5

SURIIN

'Suriin, can you hear me?' The familiar voice cut through her tumbling thoughts. 'Suriin, we're trying to help you.'

It was Gwynn.

She tried to get closer, reaching for him, trying to raise her arm. He was near, and yet he was so far away.

She was utterly disorientated.

She was flying again, she was sure ... or was it her mind? Just her mind, imprisoned in her crystal. Up and up they rose.

'Suriin!' Desperation in Gwynn's voice. She tried to control her distant body, focusing all her effort on reaching out her hand toward where she thought the voice came from.

Her fingers closed on something warm and furry. A soft blanket of calm enveloped her. She was drawn across a distance, down and down, along the thread of consciousness that connected her mind to her body.

No, that wasn't it. Her mind and body should be together. It was the crystal that was apart. As she grew closer to being whole, the rending of her mind hurt more and more, torn between where it belonged – in her body – and the thing that bound it.

She focused on the furry warmth. A familiar blanket that had enfolded her entire childhood ... Fluffy.

Calmness settled on her, and Suriin opened her eyes. She could feel the crystal, its presence a shard of pain in her mind. She still felt nauseous, but she was whole – for now.

Suriin gripped onto Fluffy's fur and tried to sit up. Two men stood at the side of the cell, sawing at the bar with a tiny tool. Her throat was ragged with acid and bile. It hurt to speak.

'The awldrin tried to eat her way out for five hundred cycles. I don't think a tool will cut through these bars.' Their effort was hopeless. She was trapped, and the awldrin was free. What would Natke be doing?

The men turned abruptly. The younger one's face softened as he looked at her.

'We have to try. Does anyone know you were coming here?' he asked.

'No,' Suriin said, her stomach pulsing as it threatened to divulge more of its meagre contents. There couldn't be anything left, surely. 'I had to weave emotions to open this cell in the first place.'

'Can you do it now? Can you get yourself out?' Gwynn was there. He sat the other side of the bars next to Fluffy; his eyes puffy and red. Why was Gwynn there?

'How?' she began.

'Never mind asking me things. Questions can wait,' Gwynn interrupted. 'Keep holding Fluffy. You woke when you touched her. Just try to unlock the gate.'

'I don't know. I have to use my crystal, and I don't have it. The awldrin does.'

'You have to try.' Gwynn looked ready to cry, as though he had been crying for hours. She hadn't seen him like that in cycles. His fists were balled up, ready to punch something.

Suriin kept one hand on Fluffy and pushed herself fully upright. Everything hurt. Her ribs were on fire with pain. She hauled herself up using the bars, then reached for the lock. What were the emotions she'd used? Vigilance, that was one, and serenity. She felt for her stores of magic – the power she'd grown familiar with over the last few tides. Everything inside her was a snarled mess, clouded with an overlaying trace of fear. What was going to happen to her? She breathed deeply to centre herself.

Taking hold of serenity first, she started to push it toward the lock.

The lock was burning. Her head started to pulse, and in a panic, she grasped it in both hands as she rocked in pain. Her mind started to split away. She felt herself losing control again.

'Fluffy! Suriin, Fluffy!'

Suriin gritted her teeth, hearing a rumble of pain growing in her ears from her own mouth. She reached out once more toward Fluffy. Her hand closed on an outstretched paw. Numbing warmth descended again.

'Seems that I can't,' she said before laying alongside the bars. 'I think I need to rest now.'

Chapter 6

Elissa

The awldrin attack our homes, but for now, Cloudsailor has evaded their notice. I hold Hope's compass close as we navigate back through the cloud bank, its golden needle guiding our desperate rush to retrieve the children.
The Captain's Log, Cloudsailor

The charver drew perplexed glances as Elissa entered the hall. While its size was diminutive enough to evade detection, its loud chirruping was not. It had remained, what she now assumed was, a happy shade of purple the whole way to the tower, briefly turning into a living rainbow at the sight of Hope. Once they'd entered, it returned to rippling waves of blue-purple over the tiny body. She couldn't blame the Chosen for staring.

'I'm sure it's not every day that a woman turns up, opens the gate to Mythos, then arrives the next day with a charver on her shoulder,' she murmured. 'I know you can't understand me, but in a place so far from Dragonsbreath, it's nice to have a friend.

As she began to climb the stairs, tiny claws dug in for stability. 'Watcher's breath ... oh.' Elissa fell silent as she remembered the pile of bleached white bones in the Watcher's Gate Hall. It didn't seem right to use that phrase anymore. She was still the only human alive who knew the Watcher had been truly real, and was dead. Even dragons could die.

She'd held to Regret's request and said nothing. After all, any hope for the humans of Tebein in these troubled days was rare, and people put a lot of faith in the Watcher.

Forcing her feet into action to push through her discomfort, now both emotionally and in her foot, Elissa rounded the last spiral to Andra's rooms.

Andra stood with her back to Elissa, talking to the Chosen on message duty. The Chosen gasped in surprise, raising her hand to her mouth when the tiny head peeked over Elissa's shoulder.

'Oh, how adorable! However did you get it to sit on you? Is it part of your shard's powers?'

Andra turned slowly, and a gentle smile grew. 'They hatched! I told you they were something special to look forward to, but shouldn't it be in its nest?'

Elissa sat on the nearest chair. 'You try telling it that!' she huffed. 'These claws are as sharp as shards and the charver shrieks if I try to remove it.'

Andra burst into laughter. 'Did the hatchling see you before its parents?'

'Yes, the shell wasn't cracking. Its parent asked me to help.'

'It's imprinted on you! You are its parent now.' Andra chuckled as she looked at the creature. 'Wait, how did the parent ask for help?'

'It dreamwalked to me.' Elissa shrugged. 'It was scared, so I helped.'

'Another legend brought to life in your presence. Did you know the old name for them was Dreamstealers?' Andra crossed the room to look more closely at the charver.

Elissa shook her head. 'I'd never heard of them until I saw the eggs.'

'They were reputed to inhabit the thin line between wakefulness and sleep.' One side of Andra's mouth raised in a half smile. 'I wonder how many more legends you will bring to life, Elissa Shard-bonded.' She pulled a chair over to face Elissa. 'Let's begin today's lesson – and hope your new classmate lets you focus.'

The Chosen looked warily at the charver. 'I'd forgotten ... Dreamstealers. Andra, will I still be able to receive messages with that in the room? We desperately need an update from Shardeep.'

'Try. If it doesn't work or you aren't comfortable, go down to one of the round cabins and take another with you to act as runner.'

'I think I would prefer to do that,' the woman said, and left the room.

Andra's smile slipped away as the woman left, and sadness filled her eyes. 'Now we're alone, I have a message for you.'

Elissa's stomach clenched in fear. She balled her fists, feeling the tip of her nails digging into her palms. Andra's expression could mean nothing good.

'My nephew got in touch as I slept last night. He'd visited the Dragonsbreath Sericlave on your behalf. Rains has brought them some relief as the river has swollen, and they are able to finally supplement their food. He wanted to talk to you himself, but couldn't reach you.' Andra's face grew more serious, a dark cloud of emotions threatening to break. 'There is no soft or easy way to tell you this news. Your brother Makin has been killed. I'm so sorry.'

Elissa's hands shook. Her lips quivered, and her vision swam with hot, building tears. A sense of emptiness filled her as the knot in her stomach unravelled in despair, and a primal cry escaped her mouth. She lowered her head to her hands and allowed the tears to flow. Elissa's body shook with racking sobs as she struggled for air. Her brother was dead; her last blood family was gone. She was alone.

She could feel Andra's presence, but the old Chosen gave her space. Elissa heard quiet murmuring at the doorway, but didn't listen to it. Through her anguish, she was vaguely aware of the sharp claws on her shoulder as the charver started to work its way across to her hands. Tiny feet scrabbled at her fingers, and a yellow and green snout poked in-between them.

'Not now,' Elissa said through gritted teeth, and tried to put it down. It shrieked in distress and refused to let go, becoming more yellow by the moment.

'Fine, bite me,' she shouted. 'I couldn't hurt more right now, anyway.' She shook her arm, trying to remove it as tears streamed down her face.

A hand rested on her shoulder. 'Elissa, it can't and won't leave you. You are going to hurt, but throwing the charver won't make the pain any less. I am going to try to help.'

'I don't want help!' Elissa sobbed.

A trickle of calm flowed from Andra's hand, tinged with a hint of sadness. Elissa drank it in reluctantly and tried to slow her breathing and tears. She lost awareness of time, unknowing of how long they sat side by side in silence. As she slowly regained control of herself, she clasped the old Chosen's gnarled hand.

'Thank you,' she said, voice still quivering, but no longer coming in gasps. The charver gripped her wrist, slowly darkening to blue and watching her intently. Elissa focused on each breath and watched her charver darken as she grew calmer.

'If you promise not to shriek in my ear, you can get back up.' She lifted the tiny creature back to her shoulder. It curled its tail around her neck and emitted a stream of contented chirrups.

'You can let go now, Andra. I'm not okay, and I won't be for a long time. He was my last family, but I promise I will not break again for the moment. He died protecting me and all the other Untouchables. I owe it to him to get them to safety.'

Tears would have to wait.

⌒ ⋌ ◊ ✵ ◉

A Chosen appeared with a cup of calfa and placed it in front of her before leaving quietly.

'Her brother lived in Silverfish,' Andra said. 'As did mine. The Chosen I was speaking to when you arrived – her parents live in Shardeep, and she has no idea whether they are alive or dead. Almost every Chosen on this island has lost family in the last few days. We are all hurt and broken in a myriad of ways.'

'They must hate me.' Elissa sighed. 'Before I appeared, all was calm.'

'Some do. Yet because of you, they also have hope. You did what we couldn't. You brought the dragons to us and activated the gate. Because of you, our people may finally get off this black moon and go home. As much as your grief hurts, you must use it. We need to find a way to use your ... *unusual* talents.'

'Get me an arrow,' Elissa said. 'I want to wrap it with fear and hatred.'

Andra frowned. 'Whilst I agree with the idea of weaponising your talent, Elissa, I am not sure that increasing your mental instability by encouraging you to draw those emotions to the front today is the right way to do this.'

Elissa sipped the calfa, steaming bitterness filling her senses. 'He used to leave his shoes outside the door to let me know I could leave.' She fell silent, looking out to sea as she took another sip. Somewhere out there, past the fog bank, were the other Untouched, the children of Shardeep, and Laytha. 'I really miss Laytha. I'm sure she would know what to do.'

Andra sat with her, saying nothing while Elissa sorted through her thoughts, some aloud, some she kept from Andra's reach. She scrabbled for a grasp on hopeful thoughts, while others she dismissed almost as soon as they appeared. *What else can my changed magic do? How can I get revenge? How can I help? Did he feel pain? Did they make others watch?* Eventually, with her calfa finished, Elissa put her cup down. She would work on her magic. Hope may not be able to give details of how her abilities worked, but she might get a sense of how best to focus her attention.

'Andra, I would like to go see Hope for a while. Maybe she can tell us of vulnerabilities that we can exploit. Do awldrin feel emotions in the same way, or is it a waste of our limited time?'

Andra gazed out the window as she replied. 'Hope has more to offer us than her mere presence. She has not gone charging off to battle to defend us as I expected. She left us so much, yet does nothing. I am missing something, a piece of this puzzle eludes me. Go, speak to her. I will wait up here for you.'

Elissa stroked the charver and rose to her feet. 'I'll be back soon. Thank you, Andra, for everything.'

She wandered out the door and descended the stairs, still trying to control her tumbling thoughts. Hope had been behind the tower when she came in, so she walked around the edge of the water at its base. The small fish in the narrow pool surrounding the tower were invisible under the wind ripples rolling across the surface.

⌒ ⋏ ʕ ♣ ◉

Hope opened one eye as Elissa approached. The charver fidgeted on her shoulder, and as they drew within a few spans of Hope, it leapt off, wing struts extended, and glided to land in front of Hope, scales flickering with a myriad of colours.

Hope lifted her head and swung it to the side to get a better look at the charver from one eye.

'Hello little one,' she said. 'It's good to see your kind still survive here too.' Then she turned to Elissa. 'These Dreamstealers are from Mythos. Many of them live in the caves around the duskline. Does your foot hurt less?'

'Thank you, yes it does, Hope. I want to talk about the awldrin.'

Hope stretched her wings, and a gust of air passed over Elissa to ripple across the grasses on the hill. 'What do you wish to talk about?'

'Do they feel as humans do? Can our magic create the same emotions in them as in us?'

'They respond to your magic, yes. They are a species with few, mostly primal, emotions. Humans are complicated, and you feel more, different, emotions than both awldrin and Mythese. We see you respond to a range of emotions, but we do not feel all of them ourselves. Take Regret, for example. He reflects sorrow and disgust in equal measure, creating regret. He feels other things, but in very small amounts and insufficient to influence his choices. The awldrin do not appear to be able to meld emotions so easily as you, yet feel more than each of the Mythese individually can.'

She looked skyward, as if scanning the skies for something.

'Why do you ask? Do you wish to speak with them? As much as I would like a peaceful resolution to this conflict, surely that is not wise. The lack of ability to understand each other's motivations is why your species were ever at war.' She sighed, dropping her head back down.

Elissa sat at Hope's feet and stroked her charver. 'I hoped you could help me understand how to defeat them and save our people.'

The huge dragon tilted her head. 'Defeat them? You mean kill them?' her closest eye narrowed. 'Elissa, we are not here to kill the awldrin. This is *their* home. I protected this island to preserve your species for as long as you needed it, but in truth, we expected all humans on Tebein to have died many hundreds of cycles ago.'

'Regret said he regretted what had been done?' Elissa did not like what she was hearing.

'Yes, he does. My brother has ever mourned that the awldrin's lives have been shortened, and his actions changed them as a species. He damaged their home. It was necessary, but he has ever regretted it.'

Elissa's mind reeled. 'So why are you here, then?' Cold shock flowed through her system.

'To protect you, to avoid the annihilation of those who survived against expectation.'

'Then just take us off Tebein and return it to the awldrin!'

Hope shook her head. 'We cannot. Humans would not survive on Mythos. Most plants would kill you – the everdark or everlight sides do not agree with humans. We tried it. Once, we had a few humans who would act as scribes. The last died soon after the gates closed.'

'Then send us back to Lieus!'

'Those gates were also destroyed. Not as yours were, I believe, but they no longer work.'

'So, what has Regret gone to do if not to help us fight the awldrin?' Elissa's charver had climbed back onto her hand and was flickering green and yellow in response to her rising upset. She looked at it and focussed on breathing calmly, on changing it back to purple, as Hope replied.

'He's gone to see the awldrin. To discover what has changed, why they have started a purge of humans now, after all this time. He does not expect a welcome. Though their lives are shorter than those of our kind, there will be those amongst them who remember and recognise him.'

Elissa felt her breath catch, and she exhaled shakily. 'So our families, our friends outside of Hope, are receiving no help? You are merely looking out for us that we do not kill the awldrin?'

Hope blew a small tendril of smoke out. 'I am sorry. I only preserve this island. I will not let them hurt you – or you hurt them – inside my boundaries. To avoid that possibility, I do not intend to let them find you.'

CHAPTER 7

DARIN

*I shall hold the palace steady through the hardest
of times and steer us through the calm times.
That we shall never forget who we are and what
we represent.
The protection of Caldera and its people is my one
goal.
I sacrifice my power for their peace.*
**<u>Extract from the binding of the Anchor
(Traditional wording)</u>**

Darin rushed back to the cell, taking care to ensure he remained unseen. Thankfully, the route remained clear and quiet. They couldn't keep running through the armoury once reports of the awldrin reached the main palace. The Collective would want to act, and no doubt, that would involve accessing far more weapons than were currently in the training ground.

He had been a while, hopefully long enough that Connor and the Master of Builders had cut through the bars. What more could Suriin tell them? Could they really avoid notifying the Anchor? One awldrin against two hounds and a load of forgotten magic weren't the worst of odds.

The carved doors on the other side drew his attention back to where he was. There was something very strange about the wooden door. He stepped back, and when he wasn't directly in line with it, it slid out of view. When he was fully in line with the door and looking for it, he could see it clearly. He was beginning to think Chase was right – there was some sort of magic acting on it. Darin held his glow globe close to the door, searching for white fragments embedded in the swirls and curves of the wood's grain. But on this side, at least, there was nothing. Maybe the books in the howler library held a clue to how it worked.

'I'm back,' he called cheerily as he walked into the room. The false wall was still down, and Conor and the Master of Builders were still trying to gouge bars out from the wall. It didn't look as though it was going well. Burn it, time was against them. There had to be a way to get her out faster.

Fluffy was as close to the bars as she could get. Suriin's arm stretched through them, her hand buried in Fluffy's fur, and she slept. At least she was having some respite, although she remained pale.

'Has she been asleep long? Did she wake? Tell you anything useful?' he asked.

Conor put down his saw. 'Yes and no. Sorry, the other way around. She said the cell's gate was unlocked by magic. That the awldrin stole her crystal and she had already tried to unlock the gate herself.'

Bones interrupted. 'She tried again, in front of us. It clearly hurt, and she almost fainted. Thankfully, this hound protects her – I can only presume because she is the daughter of Fluffy's Soul Anchor. As soon as she let go of Fluffy, she began to lose herself, mumbled and swayed.' He held his hand up, finger and thumb almost touching, and sighed. 'This is how far they've managed to get through just one bar – even with a Staramine-edged blade.'

Darin swirled the potion thoughtfully. 'So it won't be *impossible* to get her out.'

'No, but it could take tides.'

'We don't have tides. She needs to be awake and away from here, and we need to deal with the awldrin.' The words tasted strange. *Like a speech from history. Fighting a long-forgotten creature.* 'Gwynn, please wake her.' If she took the potion, it would help her, and she might be able to get herself out.

⌐ ⋏ ◖ ⊕ ◉

Gwynn leant over Fluffy and shook Suriin gently, talking in a voice too low for Darin to make out.

'Bones,' Darin said quietly, sidling over to him. 'I had another idea. Can I show Conor the other armoury, now he knows about us?'

'I'm not sure that's a good idea – for his own sake. What do you want him to see?'

'The hound armour. Chase said it broke when he took it out because the preservation spells faded.'

'They would break if he were to take them out long enough to copy, but not immediately. Bring a set to the howler quarters and arrange for Conor to meet you at the steam lift so we can bring him in. He'll need to see that route anyway. If he knows what he is being asked to do, he can examine it before it weakens.' He rested a hand on Darin's arm, trying to meet his eyes from beneath his hood. 'It's a good idea, Darin, but is he good enough to make it happen?'

'The Master of Builders can help him,' Darin said.

'What do you want, Gwynn?' Suriin's voice cut through their quiet conversation as she sleepily flailed at her brother. She let go of Fluffy, squealed in shock, and Gwynn made a desperate grab for her arm as she began to roll away.

'I've only just got her. Whatever you're trying to give her, it needs to be soon,' he called.

Darin crouched next to him and held out the bottle. 'She needs to drink this. It will reduce her nausea and pain. I don't know how much. I'm not promising a cure, but it might allow her to talk to us properly or open the gate.'

He stepped back as Gwyn tried to persuade his recalcitrant and semi-conscious sister to drink the bottle of foul-smelling liquid. She eventually sat up and, keeping one hand on the hound, downed it.

Holding it aloft, she called, 'All gone. How fast is it going to work? Eww, It's making me feel sick.'

Darin grimaced. 'Sorry about the taste. It'll take an hour or so, and make you sleepy. If it works as I hope it will, you'll have to keep drinking them. My friend here' – he gestured at Bones – 'tells me that the damage from your lost crystal won't heal itself. We're hoping to help mask the symptoms until you can find a way to unbond from it or replace it.'

Suriin grimaced. 'I'm not sure either of those is an option.' She stifled a yawn. 'Can you make it taste better next time?'

Gwynn grabbed her shoulder through the bars as she began to heave, almost lying on Fluffy to reach her. The huge hound remained in position, unmoving alongside the bars. 'Do *not* throw it up. Hold on to Fluffy.' She reached out and visibly relaxed.

Fluffy was an incredible hound, pushing against the limits of what he'd read they could do. He wondered if Fluffy's bonded Soul Anchor, Suriin's mother, was directing her from wherever she was. He could see through Star's eyes, so why would this Soul Anchor not see through Fluffy's?

'Suriin, you need to sleep, but before you do, I need you to think carefully. If we can't cut this gate open – and it's looking that way – do you have anyone you trust? Someone who won't tell anyone where you are and can let you out?'

'Ronin,' she said, and her eyes began to droop. Darin looked at Bones hopefully.

He shook his head. 'No good for getting her out. He's a Witness – he can't open this gate. Suriin, do you know anyone from Dal?'

'My mother,' she said.

Gwynn stiffened. 'She can't help us.'

Their mother was from Dal; that was interesting. Despite Gwynn's protestation, he suspected she already was helping through Fluffy.

'Skye is from Dal. She's my friend ...'

'Then we need to find this Skye and all be gone before she gets here.' Bones stretched his limbs, raising his gnarly arms and spreading his fingers like coppiced branches. 'Conor, do you know Skye?'

'Conor shook his head. 'Sorry, I don't, but I can find out. The new Soul Anchors swim as two shoals. If she's one of Suriin's friends, I know which group to find her in. What do you want me to do?

'Bring her here. She can get Suriin out by opening the lock. The story is that Suriin lost her crystal somewhere.'

'A lost crystal is easy to claim and hard to prove,' The Master of Builders nodded as he spoke, standing up from where he'd been working at ground level. 'There was a market today. Lots of them went out – something so small could be easily lost or taken. It would imply Suriin was careless and tarnish her reputation somewhat, but it buys you time to retrieve it, and a thief would be plausible.'

'What about me?' Gwynn asked. 'Fluffy needs to stay with her for the moment, at least.'

Bones continued the story. 'You found her on your own – which you did. Then you flagged down someone checking the seed store locks were functioning properly, who happened to be a Builder. Conor then ran for help to the one name that Suriin said aloud. It's a stretch to believe it all, but it's all I've got without asking a full Soul Anchor to open the gate.'

Bones was right. The full Soul Anchors needed to stay out of the loop as much as they could manage it, for now. Although with Fluffy in the room, maybe one already knew.

'How does a crystal-less, disorientated girl get herself locked in a magical cell?' Darin sighed. 'Is this really all we have?' As he looked around, he could see resignation in all their faces. Except Suriin's, who was asleep.

He leant against the wall and shrugged. 'Watcher guide us, we are out of time for anything more elaborate, or feasible. Let's do it. We need to get her back to her room. Gwynn, stick with her. Whatever happens, don't let her talk about the awldrin, and I'm afraid you can't mention us either. Someone will bring you a fresh potion for her later. Keep Fluffy with Suriin. Once she's safe, I suggest you go and visit your father. Do the things that you have come here to do. Behave as normally as you can.'

'As normally as a grieving boy on the verge of losing both parents and whose sister is in a semi-conscious state. As normally as that,' Gwynn shot back. 'You have no idea what you're asking.'

'No, I can't imagine your pain, but do not mourn those not yet dead. They need your hope and love, not your sorrow. You clearly want to become So'Dal – you've been preparing in secret for cycles. You understand that some secrets are too big to share, and you've come across a whole bunch of them in one day.'

'You missed something.' Conor grinned, the earlier tension slightly softened by the hours that had passed. 'When do I get my explanation? I want to hear all you've been up to.'

'Tomorrow? I need to see to Star and sleep. We haven't rested properly for days. You can come visit him, and I'll tell you everything. I need your help with something, so bring a notebook. You'll be met by the steam lift in the morning.' Darin pushed off the wall and crouched to help the Master of Builders and Conor re-load their bag. He glanced over at Conor and whispered, 'It will be a flaming relief to tell you, if I'm honest!'

⌒ ⼊ ◖ ⨻ ◉

Conor left, and the remaining occupants of the room stood quietly for a few minutes.

'Shall we wait in there?' the Master of Builders said, pointing at Darin.

Exhaustion was beginning to grasp a tenuous hold on Darin, and it took him a few moments to realise that they were all staring at the door behind him.

'In here? We can't get in. It's locked.'

'This is one door I can operate. There's no magic here.' The Master of Builders reached into his pocket and drew out a metal key.

Bones laughed. 'Just like old times! I used to love our explorations!'

'It's the only one in use now.' The Master of Builders turned it over in his hand. 'The one the Anchor used to hold has been lost for a long time – ever since an Anchor conveniently mislaid it just before her more power-driven successor claimed the role.' He winked. 'My predecessors decided not to pass the misplaced key on to future Anchors until they felt confident in one again. It's been a while.'

Bones grimaced. 'It says something about those in charge when an Anchor hides the tools of the position from her successor.'

Darin shifted to one side so they could try the lock. It turned with a protesting squeal, then the key vanished back into one of a multitude of pockets around the Master of Builders' outfit. A narrow passage climbed steeply as it vanished around a corner. Bones produced his glow globe from within his sleeve and blew his whistle to light it.

'Gwynn, we're going to check this out. Will you be okay?' Darin hated leaving him again.

Gwynn wouldn't leave his post by Suriin's side.

'I know what to say, I know what I need to do. But if you don't come back, or Conor doesn't, I don't know who to get help from.' Panic tinged his voice.

'We'll be back, I promise.' Darin hoped he sounded more confident than he felt. The boy needed reassurance. He remembered the sick feeling of that night with his brother. A worry only eclipsed by the fear of being across town when he'd heard the family inn was on fire. He'd soon found everyone was safe, but nothing compared to the terror of knowing you might lose your whole family. Gwynn sat in that place now.

Darin swallowed hard. He still looked after his family, his money helping them to rebuild. He still had them, even if they were far away. One day, Darin hoped to see his brother again, introduce his parents to Star. He realised with a pang of worry that Star usually picked up on his emotions, yet he'd felt nothing for a while. His mind was empty and lonely without the strength of their normal bond. Was it his own exhaustion or Star's?

'We're only looking into the area behind a door. Your family will be okay, you'll see,' Darin said.

Bones gestured to the moonhound. 'Darin is right. You keep saying your mother may be gone or lost, but this is not the behaviour of a moonhound in mourning. Take heart from that.'

Gwynn reached out to stroke Fluffy. 'I'll stay here until Suriin is rescued.' He gave them a thin smile and turned his attention back to his sister.

⌐ ⋏ ᕲ ✢ ◉

Where would a door into this hundreds-of-cycles old cell lead to? The three of them peered silently into the dark, dusty space.

'I'll go first.' The words left Darin's mouth before he thought about it. Why did he think he'd be better against unknown dangers than two experienced men, especially as exhausted as he was? They said nothing about his eagerness and moved aside to let him past. With each step, his feet grew heavier, and the climbing, winding tunnel stretched into endless time. Each step up became a mountain, each corner an entire cavern wall. There were no side branches, and they walked further than he thought any passage within the mountain could go. It must be weaving over and through other tunnels, he decided. Time was hard to quantify when every step looked like the last.

'I think we've gone in a semi-circle for this last section,' Bones muttered. It was good to hear doubts from someone less exhausted than himself.

The passageway narrowed, and they had to shuffle sideways for a few spans. Then they reached another door. Darin pressed his ear to it, but couldn't hear anything.

'Let me go first,' The Master of Builders said. 'If it's stiff, you'll need my experience to jiggle this key. I know this palace intimately – one glance will tell me exactly where we are.'

They shuffled back out of the narrow section and changed order, with Darin now at the back. He heard the lock turning. It squealed in louder protest than the first. *If anyone is in that room, they'll certainly know we're coming.*

'Oh!' The whisper was only just audible as a crack of light entered the passage. The lock was immediately closed, and he shuffled out of the narrow section as the others moved back.

The Master of Builders shook his head. 'It leads to the Anchor's rooms. This tunnel was a direct passage between the Anchor and that cell the whole time. Nissa is not the type to ignore a locked door – she'd have asked for me if she knew it existed – so it must be hidden in some way from the other side.'

They walked back down the sloping tunnel for several minutes before Darin spoke.

'There must be records about this awldrin then, surely. What do we do next? How can we find out what Suriin knows if she's back in her rooms?'

'We'll either have to use Gwynn or bring her to us. You and I will need to officially return at some point, rather than have to keep hiding within the mountain, but we should finalise our plans first.' Bones' voice echoed softly down the tunnel ahead.

'When will you tell the Anchor, Lyall?'

'I don't plan to, yet. As kind as her mate is, she takes pleasure from the trials, reinstating the poison section that had been removed ...' He stopped walking. 'I know Hal was your Collective, Darin, but Nissa sets me on edge. If we tell her, she will come looking, will want all our books and all the things we agreed to hide from the So'Dal. She will find out about the awldrin if we fail.

'But, while we have Suriin, I've a feeling we'll have the better system to track it. I suspect Suriin may disappear – with additional consequences for her family if they find out. Nissa already wants to dissect the girl's father. If the rumours are to be believed, she is actively letting him die.' He sighed. 'Five hundred cycles of secrecy, of protecting the So'Dal from themselves – removing the temptation of power – and in one day, we bring three non-Howlers into the secret of our pack. We could try to pretend it means nothing, but sometimes, we need to take the tools offered to us. Right now, they are Conor, Suriin, and Gwynn.'

Darin grinned. 'Four new tools. We also have the whistles.'

Bones turned toward him, and in the faint illumination of Bones' globe, Darin could just make out a smile. 'You did well there. Your next job is to get the hounds protected.'

'Protected in what way?' The Master of Builders asked.

'I'm going to show Conor some ancient legacy armour we have. I'm hoping with your help he can replicate it.' Darin's exhaustion was beginning to override adrenaline once again, and he scuffed his feet a few times, almost tripping into Bones as he caught toes on irregularities in the passage floor.

'We will do our best.'

'You need rest as much as your hound does, Darin.' Bones said. 'I'd like to get you out before Conor comes back. We'll stay hidden to close up this door and the one in the main passage before we follow you.'

Shivers of exhaustion rippled through Darin's legs. As much as he wanted to stay, Bones was right. They cracked the door open. Gwynn still sat by the bars. He looked over at them, tear-streaked eyes swollen with tears.

'She'll be alright, won't she?' he asked.

Bones crouched to meet his gaze. 'She'll be fine,' he said. 'Darin, go. I'll see you later. Don't forget your shard.'

Darin grasped his whistle and let the Master of Builders raise the bars for him – age did not in any way reduce the man's strength. He made it look easy. 'Lock the armoury on your way, though. I'll get Lyall back another way.'

As the door closed and darkness enveloped him, Darin saw a flicker of light from the far end of the passage. He turned toward the armoury and, using his last reserve of energy, set off at a slow jog.

Chapter 8

Suriin

Whilst Moonhounds are only able to bond with
one Soul Anchor,
it has been observed that they are very protective
over children of the family.
Maybe considering them as much their own
puppies as their bonded parent.
Moonhound History and Care

She was being shaken.

'Suriin, wake up. Help has arrived.'

She rolled toward the voice. Was it Gwynn? His eyes were red and puffy. He'd been crying. Skye reached through the bars to try to hug her.

Skye was here? Skye was here! Suriin could finally get out if she could explain how she got in. Oh, no ... she couldn't without telling her friend what she'd done.

'Watcher's breath, Suriin, how did you get in here?' Skye ran her hands over the bars, resting them on the locked gate.

Gwynn spoke quickly before she could respond. 'She said she lost her crystal and then woke up in here.'

That wasn't right. She opened her mouth, but behind Skye, a tall, red-haired man, who looked a little familiar, shook his head violently and raised a finger to his lips. Suriin closed her mouth. She was tired, confused, and sore. She didn't want to confess to freeing Natke – maybe Skye would leave her here if she knew the truth. Instead, Suriin pushed herself more upright, her hand resting in the warm softness of Fluffy's fur.

'I can't open the lock. It's got some symbols on it, but my head hurts, and I can't weft.' She pointed at the lock separating her from freedom.

'Suriin, it stinks of vomit in here. Watcher, how long have you been here? Remind me never to lose my crystal if this is the outcome.' Skye held her hand over her mouth and fought back a retch. 'I don't know if I can unlock it, but I promise I'll try, and if I can't, I'll go get Aslin.'

Suriin buried the panic shoving into her emotional core. If she'd been able to open it, so could Skye. There would be no need for anyone else. Her friend stood by the gate and turned the lock over, exposing the symbols.

'I really don't understand how you ended up in here,' she mumbled. 'Fiery scales, Suriin! This is complicated. How and why did you open it while feeling so sick?'

'It sort of closed behind me, I guess,' Suriin mumbled at her feet.

Her mind and body were back as one person. She felt a lot better physically. Her head hurt less, and maybe she'd be able to stand now. The biggest immediate difference was the loss of nausea. Experimentally, she reached inside for her magic, but that made her stomach clench threateningly, reminding her that she wasn't free of her predicament.

'I've got one!' Skye said. 'One of these is vigilance – I

remember the shield. I will get you out Suriin … just need to remember the others.'

Skye returned her focus to the lock, and Suriin looked at Gwynn.

'I'm letting go,' she mouthed silently. He frowned and reached for her hand. She waved him away. 'I have to know.' She hoped he understood her, that cycles of silent conversation behind their parents' backs would help them now. She lifted her hand from Fluffy and toward the bars. The foul sensation of her mind becoming unmoored was fainter and, with determination, she could keep a tenuous hold on it. With Fluffy out of physical contact, she grew increasingly aware of her crystal. It was moving in the far distance, and behind her. Interesting and terrifying. If her crystal moved, it must mean Natke also moved. She returned her hand to Fluffy.

She could hardly walk around the Black Palace holding onto a moonhound. As well behaved as Fluffy was, there was no chance they could remain in contact in the kitchens. It was a problem for once she was out; for short periods, maybe she'd be able to manage. Suriin glanced at her friend. She'd have to manage.

'I have two of them now,' Skye said. Her eyes were focused on the lock, and her hands gripped it with such force that her knuckles paled. Suriin shuffled forward.

'You can do it, Skye, I know you can.'

The man behind Skye shifted his weight from foot to foot. He appeared impatient, and more than once she caught Gwynn staring toward the big door in the next room.

Suriin had vague, fuzzy images of what had happened since she'd been found. She sorted through them as she waited. There had been more hounds at one point, of that she was certain. Then two men had sawed at the bars, and she hadn't got out – obviously. Fluffy had helped her and still was helping her.

Someone had given her a drink, the healing potion. Those people weren't here now. But Gwynn was, and her friend was. They could get her out, and she could rest before working out what to do next.

How was she going to take part in lessons without her crystal? What would Natke do in the meantime? Guilt rose, laced with bile, and she pinched her lips shut.

'Three ...' Skye sang out. The lock glowed in a range of colours now. Suriin had just locked it with fear, hadn't she? It must have returned to its original setting or drawn something from Natke as it locked.

Suriin leant against the bars again, and took a few slow breaths before opening her mouth to speak, working up the confidence to do so without throwing up.

'Have you tried threading them together with something? Like serenity?' She tried to look down as she said it, worried that her guilt would show in flushed cheeks.

'Oh, good idea.' Skye grew paler, and despite the calmness of her tone, a sheen of sweat beaded her forehead.

'It's moved ... Suriin, it moved!' Skye stared down at the lock. 'Conor, when it pops up, twist this bit,' she said. 'I'm scared that if I move my hands to open it, I'll lose my threads and it will re-lock. Ready?'

The tall man stepped forward and grasped the lock where Skye indicated. He gave her a single nod.

She held her crystal with one hand close to the lock. The glowing symbols illuminated her face. Suriin couldn't hear a single breath or movement. They all waited for Skye.

'Now.'

Conor twisted the lock open, and Skye slid to the floor. Suriin crawled to the gate as Gwynn leapt to his feet and pushed it open. Conor held the lock in steady hands, keeping the two sections far apart. He tucked one in his pocket and the other in his bag.

Suriin left the cell, leaning heavily on Gwynn as Fluffy whined and nosed at her hand. At least 500 cycles. Natke had been in there 500 cycles. She had barely managed a few days.

⌒ ⋏ ◊ ✧ ◦

They left the cell and its adjoining room with Skye leaning heavily on Conor, and Suriin supported by Gwynn and Fluffy.

'We should do something about that door,' Suriin muttered as they walked out.

'I'll come back and sort it once we have you both back in your rooms,' Conor replied. He pulled the door shut behind them and dropped a lock bolt in place. 'Let's go.'

Suriin's legs were wobbly, and she was more light-headed than she could ever recall – even more than the time she and Gwynn had drunk the bottle of berry wine they'd found. Every step was a challenge she accepted for her freedom.

Her crystal had stopped moving. It distracted her slightly less, although its presence remained strong enough that she could chart the direction of their travel by comparing their route to the crystal's pull. Eventually, they reached the more frequently used tunnels. A few people stared as their small party passed.

'No talking, no stopping,' Gwynn whispered. 'I'll talk to you more in your room.'

'I'm going to take Skye to get something to drink,' Conor said.

Skye looked up at him gratefully. 'Thank you. Suriin, I'll be back soon,' she called, as they took the tunnel that led to the main hall and kitchens.

When Suriin and Gwynn made it to her room, they closed the door behind them, and Suriin sank to her bed gratefully.

'I could use a drink too,' she said with a sigh. 'Thank you for finding me ... and staying.' She threw her arms around Gwynn. 'I'm glad you're here.'

'Darin and Chase reached you at the same time,' Gwynn replied. 'Are you awake enough to hear the story they agreed we should share to protect you? They were muttering about people disappearing, and well, I think we need to keep it secret. You could get banished, or ...'

'Or worse.' Suriin nodded. 'I don't know what the punishment might be for losing the crystal. Hopefully, suffering the side effects is considered to be enough.' I can't really think that far ahead right now. I'm exhausted.'

She nodded and rubbed her eyes. It felt good – momentarily relieving the itch of tiredness. Suriin sank back into her pillow and shuffled over to make room for Fluffy, who was determined to stay close to her.

As her brother talked through the alibi they'd decided on, Suriin's mind began to wander. She could soar over the clouds now ... she felt for the thread connecting to her crystal and mentally tugged it. Her mind unmoored, and she slid along the thread, rather than the tug drawing the crystal closer. No surprise there, really. Fluffy nudged her with a quiet growl.

'Do you understand?' Gwynn was finishing up.

'Umm, lost my crystal, can't find it. That made me feel unwell, and I woke up in the cell? Sorry I forgot the bit about why I can't just go and pick it up from wherever I dropped it.' She smiled at her brother, hoping that he'd forgive her tiredness and lapse in focus.

'I don't suggest that you go around telling people that it was taken by an awldrin. Maybe if they tell you to search for it, you can say it must have been picked up by someone passing through because it keeps moving?'

'That sort of makes sense. What about the people who found me with you? Didn't you say it was Darin and someone? Will they be telling the Anchor?'

Gwynn offered her a smile before breaking into laughter. 'Suriin, you found far more than a hidden prisoner. I tried to look like I wasn't listening, but the ones who found you seem to be a secret society within the So'Dal. They have no intention of telling the Anchor. In fact, they seem to be aiming to try to sort the whole situation out without her help at all.'

Suriin felt tension drop from her shoulders. That would make things much easier. If she could work out how to train like this, no one would need to know. 'Gwynn, do you think you could get me some food? That drink helped me feel less sick, but I'm still exhausted.' She held up a trembling hand. 'I could do with eating before we work out our next move. I need to go see our father too. He was getting worse much faster the last time I saw him. He'd started talking about last messages and telling you and Mum he loved you. Which reminds me, once I've eaten, I want to know what really happened to her.'

'I'll go and find some food.' Gwynn squeezed her hand. 'I'll be back soon. Don't go anywhere.'

⌒ ⅄ ◖ ✤ ◉

The door closed. Suriin ran her fingers through Fluffy's fur. Long, soft curls caught on her fingers, and she worked the knots out as they laid on the bed.

'I wish you could tell me what was going on with her,' she said to Fluffy, who licked her cheek in response. *Maybe now I am out of there, I can try to dreamwalk again. Maybe I can ask my father if he is still well enough? A million maybes won't solve the problem I've created, and now I'm left with nothing to rectify the first mistake I was trying to fix. I'll eat, sleep, and then work out what to do. Without my crystal, I can't take part in lessons, for now.*

She was going to have to ask Aslin if anyone had lost a crystal before and how they overcame it. Watcher, that was not a conversation she would enjoy. It could be a research in the library type of question instead. She rested her head against the wall, relaxing in the safety of her room. She should wash, get changed, or something ...

⌒ ⋏ ⟨ ✧⊚

'She's asleep. Maybe we should leave her?'

'She needs to eat. I don't think she's eaten for a day or so.'

'You wake her then!'

Suriin cracked her eyes open to see an exhausted Skye flanked by Merri and Joy.

'Move aside. I'll wake her.' *Oh by the moons of Lieus, already? I thought I might have time to eat at least,* Suriin thought as Aslin bustled into the room, moving her friends aside.

'Suriin, you need to eat. I've sent your brother to see Yorynn. He's worsened again. You will want to see him as soon as you're able to. I've brought you this.' She held a bottle toward Suriin.

A familiar aroma made her stomach churn as she unstoppered it. *I can't let her know I've already had some. It would lead to questions. Surely this can only help me feel better anyway.*

'What is it?' Suriin asked.

'It's a general healing potion. You'll be tired and hungry, as you've been missing for a couple of days, and it will help with the nausea from the crystal separation. Once you drink it, you can have the food your friends have brought to take away the taste.'

Suriin drank the whole bottle as quickly as possible to an approving smile from Aslin and grimaces from her friends, who now stood at the foot of her bed, holding dishes of food.

Joy handed her a plate. She gulped down mouthfuls of pie and fresh fruit; food had never tasted so amazing.

'Thank you,' she managed between mouthfuls. 'Especially you, Skye. Thank you for rescuing me.'

'It was nothing.' Skye sat on the bed and scratched Fluffy behind the ear. 'I'd never have found you without Conor. It's just lucky that Fluffy could follow your trail.' Skye leant forward to hug her. 'You need to get better, then we can all get back to lessons together. If you'd been able to do Aslin's flickering trick, you could have got out yourself!'

Aslin smiled at that, but it was thin and tense. 'No, she couldn't have. Without her crystal, Suriin cannot weave emotion. I am not impressed with your carelessness,' she said, turning to Suriin. 'When you feel better, you will have to track it down. Someone will accompany you in case you get sick. We've all left a crystal in our rooms once or twice, but this is quite different. You should be able to feel the rough direction it is in, which will make it easier to locate'

A knot formed in Suriin's stomach. *Watcher, I have to lie – don't let her see through this.* 'I can feel it, but it moves sometimes, and when it moves, I feel sicker. Someone must have picked it up and is carrying it.'

Aslin frowned. 'That complicates things. But, given your circumstances, I imagine you'd be given a little more leniency than usual. Were any of your friends with you when you realised you'd lost it?'

'No, Suriin didn't get to meet us. We thought she must have been working at first.' Merri looked at Suriin and frowned. 'Could you have lost it in the palace?'

Aslin shook her head. 'If it was in the palace, I'm certain it would have been handed to myself or Nissa by now. Either way, we can't have a Soul Anchor crystal unrecovered for long. You won't be able to use your magic until you regain it. In the short term, suffering discomfort as a punishment for carelessness is enough, and you certainly won't want to lose it again.' She retreated to the door, her hand resting on the handle. 'When she's eaten and rested, could one of you please accompany Suriin to see her father? I don't want her walking around alone in case she feels unwell or disorientated again.'

She looked at Suriin and sighed. 'I'll speak to The Anchor about releasing you from studies until the crystal has been recovered. Suriin, please come see me once you've visited your father. As his appointed guardian, Gwynn is staying with me. Keep the moonhound with you, if she will stay. Gwynn told me that you felt better with Fluffy nearby, and there are already two hounds in my rooms.' She flashed a smile at Suriin. 'We'll get to the bottom of it, I promise, but right now, I am just glad you're safe.' She turned and looked meaningfully at the others before exiting.

Suriin managed a wan smile at her friends. The potion was working again, and she'd fall asleep soon.'Thank you for the food. Aslin is right. I do need sleep. I'll see you all later.'

They filed out the door after Aslin, with Skye at the back of the group.

'I'll come back in a few hours, Suriin. I'll take you to see your father,' she said.

As Suriin's eyes closed, so did the door.

CHAPTER 9

ELISSA

*The longer I remain by his black side, the more I
lose my humanity.
Yet, I would not change this life for any other.*
Journal of Otso Dragon-bonded

Elissa paced along the beach barefoot, feeling the sand between her toes as her footprints filled with water, leaving a trail of little black pools reflecting her despair. *Have I brought our end instead of help? How do I take this news to Andra?*

She scrambled across the rocks, destination-less and running from her own thoughts. The sharp claws on her shoulder finally cut through the fog coating her mind as she lost balance, and the charver gripped tightly to stay in place.

Elissa stopped, looked around, and realised she had wandered far enough from the town that she could no longer make out any buildings. A large rock beckoned invitingly. She accepted its invitation and sat.

A small pile of loose stones had accumulated in a rock pool, and she began to throw them into the sea.

The action gained traction in her thoughts.

This one is for Hut 1. The stone splashed into the water.

This one is for the people, who kept our secrets, being killed by the awldrin. The stone travelled further.

She stood up and yelled as she threw.

'This one is for Makin!' The stone left her hand, flying further than any before, and fire left her mouth.

Elissa stumbled backward in shock, flopping onto the sand behind the rock. The charver landed on her chest, head cocked to one side, and chirruped happily.

Tentatively, Elissa breathed out. Nothing happened. She sat up, nursing a bruised hip, and eased herself upright. She puffed out again. Nothing.

Did I imagine it?

She threw her hand forward, and nothing happened.

Elissa laughed. *I'm so upset that I'm imagining things. As if I can breathe fire. Everyone knows the fire is produced by the firestones that dragons consume. Stand on a tiny bit of dragon glass, and I think I'm different inside.* She shook her head at her folly and pushed herself to her feet.

A huge shadow fell over her, and Elissa looked up at the glistening scales of Hope's belly.

The dragon flew away from her, then turned in a wide, graceful arc to return to the beach. She landed in the shallows with a splash that created rainbows of spray around her, then rumbled as she walked toward Elissa.

'Do it again,' she said.

'Do what?' Elissa asked. No, it couldn't be true. It was ridiculous.

'You know what. Make dragon fire.' Hope stepped closer, waves from her feet washing the beach as she approached.

'I don't know how to.'

'Elissa, I *felt* it. Do it again.'

'I don't know how it happened. I haven't eaten firestone – I couldn't. I was just throwing stones.' The words tumbled out like an avalanche. *I must sound stupid.*

'Why are you talking about stones?' Hope asked. 'Do exactly what you did before.'

'Fine.' Elissa searched around. 'Move to the side, please. I was throwing stones.'

Hope's emotionless face tilted to one side, and Elissa's skin prickled under her scrutiny. 'I will move,' she eventually said, and swung her haunches and tail to the side. 'Throw your stones. I want to see.'

Elissa tried to ignore the huge golden dragon and sink back into her own thoughts. Which was pretty difficult while she was being stared at. She started by throwing a few small pebbles, then built up to bigger rocks. But nothing happened. Frustration filled her, and she started to label each stone again.

For my parents.

This one for Rossi.

'This is one for my friends, abandoned in Dragonsbreath.'

And again she built up, rage and fear mixed as she threw one. 'For Makin.' This time, fire bloomed. It appeared in front of her and travelled with the stone. She realised with relief it was not from her breath, like her threads of magic; it had appeared in front of her chest.

'I did it,' she said. Then sat on the sand, trembling.

'Yes. It appears that you did. This is interesting,' Hope replied. 'It's small, but it is definitely another aspect of our magic.'

'Small?' Elissa laughed. 'It was longer than I am.'

Hope lifted a lip to reveal her teeth and faced her head back toward the gentle waves. She stared out to sea for a moment, then a huge jet of flame shot across the bay. If Elissa's flame was as long as she was tall, Hope's was several times the length of her body.

'Yes, small,' she turned her head back toward Elissa, who was convinced she saw a tiny hint of a smile.

'What do I do now?' As the reality of the situation hit her, Elissa sank to the ground. 'I can hardly go around spitting out plumes of fire! Who ever heard of a human producing fire?' She dropped her head into her hands. 'You wouldn't let me use this to attack the awldrin, would you?'

'No. We wouldn't,' Hope said before falling into silence with her. They sat side by side, staring out over the sea.

Would you allow me to defend myself? Elissa wondered as she gazed down the length of the glistening body beside her.

'I met a human who made fire once before,' Hope said slowly. 'He was the last living one on Mythos. The Watcher was used to having him around and tried to extend his life. They failed. Otso did have control of his flames. They were not as big as yours.'

Elissa's charver practiced gliding from her shoulder to the sand, then strutted back to climb her and soar away again. Its simple, delicate beauty distracted Elissa from her own concerns for a while.

'He comes.' Hope roared out a call that made the water vibrate into a million tiny ripples. 'He is upset. Something did not go well.'

Flashes of green light reflected from his scales as Regret drew ever closer. Hope called out again; this time, Elissa was quick to cover her ears. Regret called back and changed course down to their small cove. He spread his wings wide, using them and his feet to slow his landing. Elissa was drenched by a wave of spray. As her charver clung to her, it flashed red and chittered furiously, shaking water from its wings.

Regret touched snouts with Hope in greeting.

'They are doomed.' He sighed, grey smoke pouring from his nostrils. 'They have no queen. I melted their gate when they had no queen. I have doomed them. They look old, Hope. There are no eggs and no females. The last queen was captured on Lieus just before the Watcher went there, in the battle that rended Caldera.'

'You didn't know there were no eggs,' Hope said. 'None of us knew.'

'Without a queen, even if there had been eggs, they would all have been male.'

'Could there be eggs on Lieus?' Elissa asked.

Both dragons turned to look at her. Piercing green eyes stared at Elissa, then he blinked. 'Hope, she feels like He did.'

'She is like He was,' Hope replied.

'That is complicated, then.' Regret extended his neck and sniffed her. The charver snapped its teeth as his snout got close to Elissa's head, and he withdrew it quickly.

'A charver too? I have only been gone a couple of days.'

'I'm still here!' Elissa huffed.

'Don't get crosser. You'll start to smoke,' Hope snorted. Regret coughed, and both dragons' wings shook slightly as they watched her redden with annoyance.

'Are you ... laughing?' Elissa asked in amazement, as Hope snorted again, smoke rings puffing out from her nostrils.

The parallels with her own behaviour when she and Laytha had first encountered Rossi struck her. These dragons were close.

'No. Everything is too serious to laugh.' Regret collapsed into a wet heap in the surf, wings shaking and smoke rings popping out of his own nostrils.

Elissa and her charver watched the pair for a while until the waters and the dragons had calmed.

'You need lessons in jokes,' she said. 'It really wasn't that funny!'

'You need lessons in dragon!' Hope snorted. 'It was! Elissa, try to stay calm.' Regret popped more smoke rings. 'Return to your normal lessons with Andra. Come and see me in the morning. Regret and I need time to talk, alone.'

Elissa bowed her head to the dragons and walked back toward the town. As she scrambled over the rocks, she wondered idly if she could grow wings with the dragon magic. That would save the pain in her foot.

CHAPTER 10

DARIN

'The pack of hounds attacked, the lead hound
stood taller that the rest,
on his head, a glowing red weapon was mounted.
The awldrin ran immediately for their xotryl,
some ground troops turned to fight, but fell
beneath the sheer size of the pack.'
Battle Strategies of the Awldrin

A major advantage of living under a mountain was that it really didn't matter when day or night was; it was always dark enough to sleep. His bed was so soft, so welcoming, that even after what he thought was a night's rest, he'd be pleased to get back into it soon. Darin was gratefully reflecting on the situation with his hand hovering over the stones board, when a familiar voice caught his attention.

He moved his playing piece quickly and sprung to his feet, almost knocking the table flying.

'Patience, Darin. While you're distracted, I could take advantage and press the attack. Much like a real battle, stones is about keeping a cool head.' Fall moved three stones into new positions – one of which had been facilitated by his ill-considered move.

Darin groaned. 'Watcher's mighty wings, you're going to beat me again.'

Fall chuckled. 'I should hope so too. It would be a wasted skill if I lost to a youngster like yourself. Cycles of practise on the board and in the Edgelands must have a payoff somewhere.'

Conor entered the Howler's home behind Aggi.

'He was brought to me and introduced,' Aggi said. 'Seems a bit young, but then, we're reliant on Darin as our future, so who are we to judge?'

Conor arched an eyebrow from behind Aggi and grinned at Darin.

'No pressure for either of us then – just the future of the continent in our hands,' Darin said. 'Conor, welcome to my other home. I can't show you around it all because, well, some stuff is secret, and I don't know where they've hidden it yet. Also, they keep showing me new bits, so I'm not sure how many secret areas there are.'

'It's hardly a secret if you're telling me it's a secret.' Conor grinned. 'I'm not actually sure whether finding a whole set of hidden rooms or seeing the behind-the-wall workings of the steam lift is the most exciting thing so far today.'

Bones looked across at Darin and winked. 'He's a perfect fit.'

Darin gestured to the galley area so they could talk in private. 'Conor, I'd like your help. I'm hoping you can re-create something to keep Star safe. While we're at it, I can catch you up, with no secrets or omissions, on the last few tides.'

'There're fresh pies in the oven, if you want to test them for me,' Boulder called. 'I'll pick up your side of the stones board and see if I can salvage a draw against Fall.'

Darin removed the pies and set them on a cooling rack as Conor got comfortable. They smelt amazing, but then all the food the Howlers made was as good as his mum's cooking, real comfort food. He picked up the bag and joined Conor on the carved benches. The aroma of cooling pies drifted over and made his mouth water.

'Boulder's pies are amazing. Just wait until they're cool enough to eat. Now, what shall I start with?' *[Star eating pie]* filled his vision, and he held back a laugh. Star must be feeling better too.

Conor's eyes had a sparkle in them today. It was good to see his friend happy and a relief to no longer have to hide anything from him. Despite the trouble he knew awaited them, for a moment, Darin felt at peace.

'The thing you have to show me. Start with that. If it helps Star, then I'm all in. That hound is a treasure on legs – if a drool-filled one. I can guess bits of what you've been up to, and you can fill the other details in over pie.'

Darin hesitated to open it for a moment. Was it more preserved in there? Would it crumble to the touch?

'What I have in here is ancient armour especially designed for moonhounds. It was kept preserved by the magic of the room it was stored in. I'm not sure how long you'll have to study it once we start moving it around – how fast it will fall apart or crumble. You may need to work quickly.'

'You want me to replicate it?'

'Please. Or as close to it as you can get. I know we don't have the same level of technology – or magical technology – as they had before the closing, but I've heard you talk about the things you've designed. If anyone can find a way to copy it, it's you. The Master of Builders has said he will help you too. Star's life and that of Sandy would depend on this armour.'

Conor rummaged around in his pockets. 'Wait a moment. Let me get my tools ready before you give it to me. It sounds as though I may have to work faster than a rockfall.'

Darin put his hand on his friend's shoulder. 'Star nearly died protecting me, healing me. I don't want him to be vulnerable to the xotryl or any other physical attack. Asking you to recreate this armour is the least I can do to protect him.' His own nervous excitement built. It had to be possible.

He lifted that bag onto the table and called Star from the other room *[Star wearing armour]*.

Star trotted in and stood still next to them. *[Armour and a pie]*

Darin sent *[Amour and a bit of pie]*. He'd just have to make sure Boulder didn't see.

'Ready?'

Conor nodded. Darin pulled the large sheets of preserved hide out of the bag, their connecting straps holding well enough to position the armour over Star. Conor sketched and calculated, taking measurements of the thickness of each panel, the position of the attachments. He drew the shapes of every piece from the chest-guard to the tiny overlapping plates on the legs, which allowed Star to move comfortably – and reminded Darin uncomfortably of scales.

The final piece they mounted on Star was clearly too large. Despite its size, the battle helmet was incredibly light. It was the only decorated part of the armour and shone with a red glow. A twisted horn protruded from the forehead, much like a rhinocorn horn.

'I wouldn't like to run into that,' Conor said. 'Darin, I don't recognise what material the armour is made from. I can see how the fastenings between panels could be improved. We can get small links forged to hold them together. But I'd be able to help replicate it a lot more closely if I could take a panel to test.'

'I thought you might need one. Here.' Darin held out a section panel that he'd found loose at the bottom of the box, under the other sets. 'I don't know how long it will stay useful to you, though. It's probably already disintegrating.'

Conor frowned. 'Are we looking at days or hours for it to disintegrate?'

'About a day, from what I understand,' Darin replied. 'It's been in here for a few hours already, waiting for your arrival.'

'Then if you need these to fight an awldrin – which sounds crazy, but after the last day or so, I now fully believe – I'm going to have to test it as soon as I can.' Conor tried to flex the panel and peered at its underside closely. 'Don't worry. I do stuff like this all the time, so no one will notice if I start testing a strange material. Your story will have to wait. I know enough that I won't need to take you sparring to beat it out of you.'

'Thank you,' Darin said. 'Shall I take you back out?'

'You better had. Can I bring a pie? I'll take advantage of lunch and head over while the labs are quiet.'

Darin wrapped a warm pie in a cloth and handed it over.

They left the galley, and he could feel Bones' eyes on them as they left the main area and headed for the waterfall. He escorted Conor out of the howler quarters, then ran back to the others.

'He thinks he can do it! Star and Sandy can be protected.'

Bones' face split in a wide grin. 'Not just these two, Darin. If he creates useful armour, the whole Redpike pack can be protected, though without the headpiece for those who aren't battle trained!'

Chase patted him on the back. 'It was good thinking – if you think he has the skills?'

'If anyone can do this, it's Conor. He's always playing with new ideas and fiddling with small mechanical things. No one will look twice if he starts some other project.'

'Good.' Chase rolled his shoulders and neck. 'Right then, we have freed the fair maiden and armoured the hounds. Now, I suppose we need to find a way to stop the awldrin before she does too much damage.'

'It's too late to say *any* damage by now, I suppose.' Fall sighed. 'You're right, of course. We can't put off building a plan much longer.'

[Star with his feet on the side of the counter, taking his pie] Darin ran to the galley too late, as Star gulped the hot pie in one mouthful.

'Boulder, the pies are delicious, apparently,' Darin called back to the main room before he unstrapped the armour, trying to avoid Star's gravy-covered muzzle. He bagged it up and returned to the others.

'Did you— Oh, Darin. Well, I suppose he must be feeling a bit better if he's become a pie thief.' Boulder roared with laughter at the sight of Star licking his lips as he trailed in after Darin, his tail wagging happily.

Fall stroked Star as he passed to lie on the rug alongside Sandy. 'So what and who can we use? The girl freed the awldrin. The awldrin wants to pass through a set of broken Aulirean Gates to go home. I have no problem with her going back to Tebein – but she can't do it.'

We don't even know for sure whether there are any awldrin left on Tebein. We have no idea whether the gates from Mythos to Tebein still work, even were she to get off Lieus.'

Darin looked intently at Bones. He appeared relaxed, but it was hard to be certain. 'Can the gate be fixed?' he asked.

Bones blinked a few times as he stared into space. 'No, I don't think so. The dragons built them. If they were repairable by the awldrin, I feel sure that they'd have fixed them by now, especially now we know that their queen has been imprisoned here for all this time.'

Fall stood and began to pace. 'I agree. The echoglass pieces that powered it were shattered, creating the crystals that Soul Anchors believe they use as focuses, and the Watcher repurposed to bind and reduce their powers. In order to gather all the pieces, the awldrin would need to take them all, and there's still no guarantee that, even when replaced in the Gates, they would power it. Each crystal is shattered.'

'She took Suriin's crystal,' Darin said. Pieces started to fall into place. 'I'd be trying to rebuild those crystals somehow. She only has to realise that another Soul Anchor carries a crystal before she starts to collect them, one at a time. The awldrin has waited five hundred cycles. If she gets that xotryl to poison everyone who attacks her, she only has to wait a few more. The last thing we want is the Anchor to lead the Soul Anchors out to battle it. Our sliver of dragon bone cannot cure them all. Xotryl alone are a problem, but a xotryl being directed to attack, and a huge warrior with solid skin we can't damage easily.'

'I agree. Directed xotryl could cause devastation. Combined, they could just kill and kill.' Chase said. 'We need to warn the Witness family in Dal. They're the closest to where we think she may be.'

'Have you warned Tian?' Boulder asked quietly.

Chase's shoulders dropped. 'I've tried. I can't reach him. He either hasn't been asleep, or ...'

Boulder twisted his lips into a small grimace behind Chase's back. He leant forward and patted Chase affectionately. 'I'll keep trying for you. I'll get hold of him somehow, I promise.'

'Thank you.' The words were quiet, almost a whisper.

Darin's confident pack mate seemed to shrink before his eyes as the room fell silent.

'We need as much information as we can get. Surely, Suriin wouldn't have let the awldrin out without in some way trusting her, or making some sort of deal. A desperate one – given her father's condition. We need to know all that Suriin does, urgently.' Darin said, trying to break the tension threading around the room.

Chase glanced at him and sighed, shoulders drooping still further with each exhaled breath.

'You're right. Do we bring her here?' he asked. 'Suriin already has enough secrets to keep, and confusion, nausea, and trauma to handle. Can we find somewhere neutral to meet? We don't want to risk Darin and Bones being recognised in any public area until we've decided on our next move.'

Bones stood and started to pace. 'Aggi is right. I'm not sure we could sneak you out twice. We could always use the mountain exit while you remain out of the palace officially. But once you're back, we either expose you – limiting your future training – or include the Anchor in our plans. I'm not sure she'd take being told what to do by a bunch of old men very well.' He grinned and raised an eyebrow as he spoke. 'You're as trapped as I am for a while!'

Darin pushed a stray curl back from his view. 'That's true. I need to do something, though, or I'll go mad. I may know just the place to meet Suriin. The Master was giving me singing lessons in a remote chamber. If I can get to it without being recognised, it could work.'

'You can use one of my robes,' Chase offered. 'I don't use them much. It has the Howler brown trim, so you might want to wear it with that tucked under.'

'Or you could go yourself, Chase?' Fall offered. 'It doesn't have to be Darin.'

Darin started to pace the room. 'No,' he said. 'I can do this.'

Chase met his eyes and rested his hand on Sandy's back as he spoke. 'You can, and yes, you should. It may affect our present, but we're old. It is your future you're fighting for.'

'I'm not old,' Aggi said, laughing. 'I'm just less young than I used to be. I do agree that Darin should talk to her, though. How will we get her to the meeting point?'

'That's easy,' Darin said. 'We'll use Gwynn. Think about Jaer – no one as much as blinks if he's in an odd place. He's just a boy exploring. Gwynn is only a couple of cycles older and new to the Black Palace.'

'I wish we could test that boy,' Bones muttered.

'He's not old enough,' Fall said. 'Would you throw a young lad like him into battle so soon?'

'No, but I have a feeling in my—'

'Bones!' chorused the others. A brief moment of humour in the direst of discussions.

Darin chuckled. They may have been fearsome warriors once but, sat around their stones boards in this cosy room, they reminded him of his grandfather sitting with his friends on the town square back at home. *I feel protective over them,* he realised.

'I'll try to get Gwynn to sing,' he said. 'If he's not a future Howler, we'll know pretty easily. Have you got something I can sketch a map on? Aggi, can you get a map to Gwynn at meal time? I have no idea what time it is. These last few days have been so disorientating.'

He saw looks of concern in aged Howler eyes and sat down.

'I'm fine, honestly,' he said, smiling at them. A warm, happy feeling filled him as Star settled into the rug. Darin crouched to bury his hands in his fur. 'Oh, you smell of sleeping hound!' He inhaled the calming scent. *[Star eating a chunk of meat]* overlaid his vision.

'Do we have anything else for Star?' he asked Fall. 'Something bigger than a pie'

Fall's face lit up with delight. 'Our young pup is definitely feeling better! I'll go and get him something right now.' He wandered off to the galley, whistling.

'I'll take your map to Gwynn,' Aggi said. 'And arrange for him to bring Suriin to meet you tomorrow – that's if she is able to move around freely now.'

CHAPTER 11

SURIIN

There were no So'Dal outside her father's room; they'd abandoned him to die. The suffocating silence of the smooth walls ate at her nerves.

Gwynn sat by his bedside, their father's hand clasped between his own. He raised his eyes, looking at her under furrowed brows.

'Why can't they cure him? Why did this happen to him? He never did anything but good.' Her brother's voice cracked as he spoke.

Skye hung back as Suriin crossed to the far side of the bed and leant forward to kiss her father's cheek. His eyes were tightly closed with crusty ooze dried around his lashes. A tendril of black poison reached up his neck and across his cheek. He was as feverish as before she'd given him the supposed cure. The shallow rise and fall of the covers revealed how small each breath was – mere whispers of hope. She folded the cover down to unbutton his shirt, needing to see for herself how bad it had become.

Blackness engulfed his entire arm, his fingers as withered and dry as kindling. Suriin felt for a pulse in his wrist and found none. The arm was dead. It was only a matter of time before it reached his heart.

Skye rested a hand on her shoulder. 'They should try to stop saving the whole person. Living without one arm would be better than losing the whole fight.'

Suriin gasped. 'Skye!'

Gwynn, however, looked thoughtful.

Skye pushed on with her suggestion. 'It's been done before. Don't look at me like that. You can see that he'll never use that hand again. Have the So'Dal been able to aid in any way?'

'They caused it to retreat slightly,' Suriin admitted.

'So if enough of them worked on him at once …' Gwynn reached to touch the tendril on their father's cheek. Drawing a line back to Yorynn's shoulder as he talked. 'Once it has retreated far enough, they remove his arm? How?'

'I've seen it done,' Skye said. 'One of the men who worked on my parents' farm in Dal had it done after his arm got crushed.'

Suriin stood, her chin raised. 'Gwynn, do you agree it might be his best chance?'

He offered a small, tense smile, but she could see the concealed hope in it. 'Yes.'

Suriin wished her mother was there to ask, but in her absence, it fell to them. If there was a chance to save his life, they had to take it. 'Where do we find someone both skilled enough to do the amputation and willing?'

Gwynn bent forward and kissed their father on the forehead as he re-buttoned the shirt. 'We are going to go now,

Da. Keep fighting it! We'll be back and we *will* save you. We'll go see Aslin. She's Mother's oldest friend – she told me to trust Aslin over all others.'

'You still owe me that story!' Suriin said. 'Skye, will you come with us? I'm not entirely steady on my feet yet.'

'Of course.'

⌒ᚪ☾⚜◉

Gwynn strode ahead. Keeping up with him was exhausting, but Fluffy stuck to Suriin like a shadow while Skye remained at her other elbow. It was a slightly breathless trio who arrived at the large carved door. Gwynn reached forward and pressed the central disk, *like the one in the Anchor's rooms*. The door slid into its groove with a quiet hiss, and a flower-scented breeze tickled at Suriin's nose.

Bright colours swirled across the walls. A door on the far side of the room was open to the crater.

'Is that you, Gwynn?' Aslin called from the balcony. 'How's your sister?'

'She's here,' Gwynn replied. 'We've had an idea, and we need your help.'

Aslin appeared around the door. 'An idea for what?'

Suriin dipped her head in respect. 'I'm sorry for intruding, Soul Anchor Aslin, but we think there's a way to save our father.'

'I doubt you have any ideas they haven't already tried, unless losing that crystal has addled your mind. But go ahead. I'm listening.'

'We think that if the So'Dal can sing the blackness back – as a group – his arm could be removed, which would remove the source of poison.'

Aslin nodded slowly. 'I heard them discuss that. But no

one's carried out that kind of procedure for a long time. Our healing abilities have almost removed the need for it to ever happen. I'm sorry, Suriin, but it can't be done. We don't have the skills anymore.'

'Soul Anchor Aslin, I've seen it done. I know a man who lives with a single arm,' Skye said, her confident poise hiding shaking hands clasped behind her back.

Aslin's face lit up. 'Really? Who and when? Watcher knows I don't want Yorynn to die. Before she went missing, I spoke to your mother and promised I'd help you all to the best of my ability. Up until now, that's been limited to helping you two.' She turned to the desk behind her.

'Let me make a note of this.'

Skye smiled at Suriin while Aslin's back was turned and mouthed, 'We'll save him.' Then aloud, 'I cannot remember the name of the So'Dal who carried out the procedure, only that he had a hound with him. It was at least thirteen cycles ago, and I was very young. But I do remember the farm worker went in with a crushed arm and left the room a few days later, without it. He was always great fun and the happiest worker on the farm. My Da used to say it was because he felt he'd been given a second try at life.' She stopped and blushed pink.' Sorry, that was way more than you asked for.'

'Where are you from, Skye?' Aslin asked, her eyes narrowed.

'Dal. But I've been here since I was young. They thought it was safer for me here.'

'So this was in Dal, and you think he had a hound?'

Skye nodded.

'When I was young, just training, there was a So'Dal with a hound. He can't be much older than me,' Aslin said, walking to look out of the balcony. 'Skye, can you get a message to your home? Find out if anyone remembers his name?'

'I'll contact the Witness family tonight, Soul Anchor Aslin. I'm sure they will know.'

Gwynn nudged Suriin. 'Hounds! Maybe *they* can help,' he whispered.

Them ... she needed to find a way to get in touch with the men who'd found her. The only name she could recall was Conor, but Gwynn must have more details. She needed time alone with him.

Aslin began to pace, her curls bouncing with each step. 'I can get some Gardeners arranged to push the poison back.' She spun and gestured frustratedly at Suriin. 'Who is your father's apprentice? His name eludes me.'

'Ronin.'

'Ronin, yes. We should ask him. I'll find out who else has been working on him. They will be the most familiar with the poison. We should have at least one Gardener, one Witness, and ideally their Soul Anchors to increase its impact. But, in such a small room, we cannot get them in, and I daren't move Yorynn.' She sighed. 'You know the Anchor has given up on him, and this might go wrong. We could still lose him. Do you both understand that?'

The knot in her stomach was already screaming loudly at Suriin about the risk. But her father faced a slow and painful death. He must be in excruciating pain, leading to inevitable and prolonged death from a slow poisoning of his heart. His support withdrawn just so the Anchor could find out the poison's effects. Even if her actions were motivated by the selfish desire to have him alive as long as he could be, it was better than the alternative.

'I think I need to go back to my room,' she said as darkness closed in on her vision, and her legs went from under her.

She awoke in an unfamiliar bed, thick covers pinning her down from the weight of her companions. Fluffy laid across her feet, and Skye's eyes were shut as she lay on the adjacent pillow.

'Still no one there,' she muttered. The bed rocked as she sat up. 'Where ...'

'Hey, you're awake. It's Aslin's bed. She didn't think carrying you back was a great idea. Her and Gwynn have gone for food. I offered to stay with you and try to get an answer about who did the arm in Dal.'

'Thank you,' Suriin said. 'How long ago did they leave?'

'I don't know. I think I fell asleep for a bit too.' Skye blushed. 'Some looker-after-er I am!'

They laughed, and Fluffy joined in the moment by licking both of them enthusiastically. The other hound in the apartment lifted their head and gave them a solemn look before lowering it back onto their paws.

The door hissed open, and Gwynn ran in.

'I'm spending way too much time sat by sick beds,' he said as he plonked himself down next to her. 'But I have the answer. Skye, I know who your mystery So'Dal is and sort of where to find him.' He waved a scrap of paper at them. 'When I went down for dinner, a tall So'Dal handed me this map and told me to go and see The Master in the morning. I'm not talented, yet – I'm not old enough. So I nodded and wondered if it was one of *them*.' He glanced at Skye. 'You know, um, them mistakes that someone had made because I'm new here. Anyhow, it has actual directions for a meeting place. So I'm going to go anyway.'

Suriin laughed inwardly at his attempt to brush off the secret they were hiding. Exposing that would lead to more questions than she was ready for just yet. Even from Skye.

'How does that link to knowing who took the arm off?' Skye said.

'Well, he looked old, so I asked if he had ever heard of a successful arm removal before.' He paused dramatically, looking at them for a sign to continue.

'Gwynn, we don't have time for drama right now!' Suriin nudged him with a foot.

'He said of course he'd heard of one – he'd done one himself.'

'If he's in the palace, why haven't they already asked him to do it?' Suriin shrilled in frustration. The Watcher-flamed Anchor and her wish to study the effects; her almost-wish for their father to die, just so she could cut him up. Gwynn didn't know about that, though, and he didn't need to.

'I'm not sure that they know, Suriin. He wasn't wearing a Gardener robe. I'll meet him tomorrow to find out. Do you want to come?'

Suriin and Skye chorused, 'Yes!' before Skye's face fell.

'I have class with Aslin tomorrow. Suriin, will you tell me all about it later?'

Suriin smiled at her. 'I promise I'll tell you.' *Just not all of it.* 'As long as you share what you learn too.'

⌒ ⌂ ◖ ✣ ◉

Somewhere outside this mountain, birds are singing, and the sun is shining. Going back under the mountain so soon after she'd been released had more impact than she expected, and Suriin felt panic creep up on her as soon as the tunnel walls grew smooth. The map Gwynn carried led them into the tunnel system, but thankfully, only a few turns deeper than the living areas.

They pushed open the door to find a small, round room. Its ceiling was domed, and aside from a couple of stools, it was empty. Suriin walked around the edge, trailing her hand along the wall, willing the So'Dal to appear.

'I hope they found it,' a quiet voice drifted down the corridor.

'I hope it was empty if they did. Can't have more questions about stuff we do in Dal being asked by the wrong people,' a second responded.

'It's him!' Gwynn said excitedly. 'And Darin – one of the So'Dal who found you.'

'I know who Darin is.' Suriin hadn't really recognised that he'd been there, but then she didn't remember much of the last few days anyway, so decided not to berate herself over it. Sharp pain from her ribs had begun to cut through the relief from the potions. She might need another one soon, although she needed to stay awake.

⌒ A ᛰ ✿◦

A hooded So'Dal entered and dropped the hood to reveal his face. It was Darin.

'You look better than last time I saw you. The potion must be doing a good job.'

'Yes and no. I was given another one, too, but my ribs really hurt where she hit me. I haven't told any one about that, mostly because the pain was gone.'

The other So'Dal pulled his hood back. 'Would you like me to have a look at it?' he asked. 'You can call me Silard. Once you've spoken to Darin, I'll come and check you over properly. First, though, we'd like to ask you some questions.'

'What if we don't want to answer them?' Gwynn stood with legs apart and arms crossed. Suriin's heart softened at his protective stance, but he was a child next to both Darin and this older man.

'Gwynn, please,' Suriin said. 'I'll answer them. Don't worry.'

Darin sat on one of the stools and gestured for Suriin to sit on the other.

'Where do you want to start?' she asked. Silard gestured for Gwynn to step away, and they left the room together. She hoped Gwynn would ask about the surgery while she helped to begin fixing her mess.

'How did you know there was an awldrin in that room, and why on Lieus did you let it out?' Darin went straight for the main point. Her aches appreciated his directness.

'I was searching for herbal cures or awldrin relics to heal my father. He was slashed by a xotryl's talon a few tides ago. My research had led me to believe either they weren't affected or had discovered a cure, as they appeared to recover. I read of injured awldrin reappearing in later battles.'

'So you went looking for what?' He leant toward her. 'Go on.'

Suriin focused on the floor as she continued. 'I got hold of an old map a friend found in the men's library. I was trying to find the seed store. I thought that if there were plants from Tebein, they might have been what the awldrin used. At least, that was my hope. I knew I shouldn't be there, so when I saw lights coming in the dark, I took the only opportunity of escape – through the door opposite. While I was waiting for them to go, I looked around, found the false wall accidentally, and couldn't resist trying to get through it. It was a challenge.'

'And found an awldrin on the other side.'

Suriin nodded. 'Yes. Then later, I dreamt of her, but I don't think I woke from my own dream, so she kept visiting me. Natke talked to me and offered hope – a cure for my father.'

Darin sat back. He crossed his legs and tilted his head, much like hounds sometimes did, she thought.

'What was the cure?'

'A white powder in the pommel of her old sword. It's mounted publicly, a relic of power in the Anchor's outer chamber. I got some of the powder out. He drank it, and initially, it made him better. But then the toxin started to come back – faster. She promised me that her shield was out in the world, that she'd hidden it, and we could go and get it. The way she talked about it, I believed that it held a cure.' *Was I really that stupid?* 'It sounds so naïve now I'm saying it aloud. And, well, you know the rest. She stole my crystal, punched and kicked me, then left, locking me in.'

'Did she recognise your crystal?' Darin's tone had a sense of urgency to it now.

'She said she didn't know why I had it and ripped it from me.'

'Watcher's fiery breath. She knows, then.'

'She knows the Gates are broken too. I vividly remember seeing that through the crystal in a brief moment of clarity. She threw it, and while it was out of its pouch, I could see through it. I can still feel it now, but not see through it.'

Darin's eyes widened. 'You can feel it?'

'Yes, we can always feel our crystals. It's – she felt for it, then extended her arm toward the crystal – 'that way. It's moving in that direction.'

'Watcher's breath, Suriin! You can track her. We may be able to solve this much faster than we hoped, and with less bloodshed.'

'It's a stronger pull when I don't have Fluffy nearby, but so strong I lose control. That potion has dimmed it a bit. Maybe with time, I can learn to control my response.' She shrugged. 'I've been told I have to retrieve the crystal myself – as a punishment for losing it. I can help you, if you help me.' The gnawing fear at the pit of her gut re-surfaced. 'I'd like to help, but I'm worried my father will die.'

'Silard will help if he can. We need you focused on the task, and the distraction of Yorynn's health won't help. If we can ease his suffering, you'll help us track the awldrin?'

'I'd help you anyway. It's my mess. I owe you for freeing me.' Suriin glanced up at the man opposite her. His dark curls fell in front of his eyes as he studied her. She'd never really looked at him before, always at his hound.

Darin shook his head. 'It might feel like your mess. But, honestly, we have no idea why it never happened sooner. One day, someone was going to let her out. It just happened to be you. We'll help you make it right if we can – preferably, without alerting the Anchor for as long as possible. You don't want anyone else taking xotryl wounds like your father, do you? Nor do you want to go missing. People do that occasionally in this palace.'

He stared intently at her, and once again leant forward. It didn't feel threatening, but she shuffled back and shook her head, nausea rising as she fell off the stool.

⌐ ⋏ ◊ ⊕ ◉

Her mind slipped along the thread to her crystal. It was out now. Natke's cold hand wrapped around her. She could see blurry shapes, feel air moving past her. Natke shouted, and someone screamed.

Blood.

Iron.

Heat splattered across her surface. She winced, but couldn't move. The blood ran across her view, obstructing everything. She was drowning in someone's blood. Then, she was replaced in the pouch, only now, she was no longer the only crystal; a sharp, shiny surface clinked against her. It was wet where they made contact. Natke had taken another crystal, and this time, she'd done more than punch someone in the ribs.

Suriin grappled with the crystal, trying to extract her mind from it – from the sensation of being clattered around. She reached for the thread, and hand over hand, she mentally pulled herself back to her distant body. Something warm pushed against her hand. Fluffy. She relaxed and let herself flow toward the warmth.

⌐ Ᵽ ◖ ✛ ◉

'Suriin! Not again!' Gwynn muttered. 'You have to stop falling over and being sick in dark caves.' She knew he was trying to be funny. But the spray of blood was seared into her being, and the hot sensation of it running down her vision was so real that she checked her hands and wiped her face.

'She just took another crystal. There was blood – a lot of blood. If she's worked out how to find them or that we all wear one, it's not going to be long before she returns here, is it?' She turned her tear-streaked face toward Darin and Silard.

'I'll help you, whatever happens to my father.' Suriin dropped her head. She needed to know what was happening. She needed to help. Burn it, but she needed to be able to use her magic somehow.

Silard crouched behind her, hooked his arms under her shoulders, and helped her upright.

'We can help you. From what your brother has said, Yorynn is too far gone for healing. He will need to lose part or all of his arm. Can you show me where the injury actually is?'

Groggily, Suriin pointed near the top of her upper arm. 'It's here, below his shoulder. His hand is dead. It's gone. Save the rest of him if you can.'

Darin passed her a small bottle. 'Have some more of the heal, in case you need it. We need to act fast to get you out of here and well enough to track the awldrin. However you are feeling inside, you need to look ready to go.' He turned to Silard. 'Does Gwynn know what he needs to do?'

Silard nodded. 'Two days is all we can give you. This can't wait longer. Can you walk?'

Suriin staggered to her feet and felt her brother's reassuring arm around her.

'Take a sip, Suriin. We'll get back easier?'

She laughed. It was a great idea, but after the last two doses, she knew she'd never reach her room before falling asleep. 'I'll make it.' She buried her hand in Fluffy and leant on her. Clarity breezed through her mind.

Darin helped her to her feet. 'Suriin, get control of yourself so that you're ready to leave the palace. Gwynn, we'll see you as soon as you have what we need. Silard will be ready to assist with the arm as soon as you're ready.'

Gwynn nodded and gestured for Suriin to head out the door. She looked for more from him, but Gwynn wore a very closed expression, and she knew that face. He'd tell her when they were alone, but right now, he was going to do whatever he had just set his mind to.

'Let's get you back to your room so you can rest properly,' he said, and they started the walk back.

Chapter 12

Elissa

All around the coast I could see fire.
The crops we relied on both at Hope and further
afield were burning.
But, far in the distance, small triangles of white
against a purple sea drew us onward.
Sails, survivors.
Captain's Log, Cloudsailor

Elissa closed the door and inhaled the sweet, musty air of her home. Charvers floated past as hatchlings practised gliding. One flew right past her head, and she ducked to avoid disturbing its flight path. Her own charver leapt off her shoulder to join the fun.

'How am I going to sleep tonight with all of you in here now?' She laughed and eased into the empty chair by the fire. Andra had sent her home with a parcel of food. She unwrapped it, and fruity scents drifted up from warm pastries. Before long, a line of small charvers sat in front of her. Her own clicked grumpily at them as it scrabbled down her arm to the food.

'I should name you.' Elissa lifted her arm and turned it around, admiring the colours on her companion. Its flared snout was delicately surrounded by tiny scales. The skin on its body changed colours under her scrutiny, as if showing off. The tiny creature extended its wings and raised its sail. She reached out to stroke it. As she did, ripples of colour bloomed under her hand.

'You look like a field of flowers, or a flash of light from my crystal. But, I think I'm going to call you Dreamer.'

She was midway through her meal when a knocking at her door disturbed them. Dreamer climbed to the usual place on her shoulder as she rose. Elissa reached to put her meal down, but the rush of small creatures toward her hand made her retract it quickly. There would be nothing left if they got their snouts on it. She carried it with her to the door instead.

⌒ ⋏ ◖ ✥ ◉

A Chosen stood outside, soaked to the skin. Her mud-spattered dress clung wetly to her legs, and hair was plastered to her cheeks. 'Elissa Shard-bonded, Regret and Hope have summoned you to the dome.'

'Summoned me? Were they puffing rings of smoke as they said that?' Elissa asked.

The Chosen frowned. 'Yes, they were. How did you guess? Their wings were shaking. It was terrifying. I ran as fast as I could to get you.'

Elisa resisted rolling her eyes and swallowed the rising laughter. 'Without stopping for a cloak, I see. I'm on my way. There's no need to accompany me – I'll just grab my own cloak and head up. Go and get dry, and thank you for bringing me their ... summons.'

She closed the door and chuckled. Who would have

guessed dragons had a sense of humour? Stuffing a few last mouthfuls down, Elissa flung her cloak around her shoulders, Dreamer fluttered back on top of it, claws far less noticeable through the leathery hide. She left the rest of the meal on the green chair for the family; squeaks of joy faded as she closed the door behind her and headed up the hill. The rain was thick and murky, with lights on the hilltop faint through the gloom. She pulled her hood up and bowed her head as she strode into the rainstorm. *I wonder what plan they have come up with.*

⌒ ⋏ ⟨ ⚘ ◉

Hope and Regret sat outside the open wall of the dome. They raised their heads as she approached.

'That was fast. We have made a decision.'

Elissa caught her breath back as they silently stared at her. 'What decision have you made?' Sometimes talking to dragons was infuriating.

'You are going home.'

Her stomach lurched. 'You're sending me back to Dragonsbreath? To the awldrin as a sacrifice?'

'No, we are sending you home.' Hope's eyes span slowly as she turned her head to the side.

Elissa sighed. 'I'm sorry, but I'm confused. Dragonsbreath is my home, but no one is there anymore. They're either imprisoned by awldrin or hiding from them.'

'We mean our home. We are sending you to Mythos. We created this situation hundreds of cycles ago, but we cannot fix it without opening the gates.'

'Then open the gates!'

'We cannot.'

Elissa found herself getting exasperated. She took a deep

breath and sat in front of them. 'So you want me to go to Mythos to open your gates?'

'No, we want you to open the gates in Lieus.'

Elissa's breath caught in her throat. *Lieus.* 'So you can send us all home?'

'Yes, and you must search for awldrin eggs.'

'Regret, Hope, if the awldrin have not been on Lieus for as long as we've been trapped here, how will finding ancient eggs help? That's if there even are any? Also, a small thing, but how do you suggest I open gates on another planet?'

'Sorrow will help you,' said Regret.

'If you can find anything to help the awldrin survive, they will call this attack off,' Hope added.

'Will I come back?'

'Probably.'

Their logic made dragon sense, but Elissa wasn't hopeful that an ancient egg would help. Surely eggs that old would be rotten? Opening the gates, though ... If the dragons believed there was a way, she could get her people home – if they survived long enough. An idea began to grow. She had nothing to lose by asking.

'I will do it – after you do something for me.' Burn it, she'd do it anyway. But they weren't to know. 'Can you carry things as you fly?'

'Hope can. She is biggest.'

Elissa addressed Hope, hiding the tremble in her hands behind her back. 'Please, can you take food to my sericlave? We cannot get them here without drawing attention.'

'I can, but I cannot hold it, as well as hold a cloaking magic. The xotryl can detect all dragons faintly.'

'What about if we made you a harness?' Elissa ducked at the indignant cloud of smoke. 'Okay, no harness.'

'I cloak me, I cloak you. You carry as much food as you can

hold, and I will take you. One trip only, then you go to Mythos.'

Hope had agreed. Elissa held back her rising excitement. She was going to ride a dragon. If a wildbeest was hard, how was she going to stay on a flying creature? She was returning home on a golden dragon. Maybe it would give her friends their own glimmer of hope.

'We will leave as soon as you are ready. You need to go to Mythos before your people are all dead and none remain to take food to. Go and get food.'

These dragons didn't mess around. Elissa rushed to the tower, calling for Andra.

⌒ ⋏ ◖ ⨁ ◉

A short while later, and with packets of dried food strapped all over her, a further bag on her back, and as much as she could hold in one hand, Elissa stood outside the dome, ready to leave.

Hope and Regret took one look at her, and smoke rings started to puff from their snouts.

'You look funny, Elissa. Not like a human now. More like an insect.'

'Are they unhappy?' Andra said behind her hand.

'They're fine. They're laughing at me.'

Andra's mouth twitched. 'You do look a bit bizarre.'

'Don't you start too!'

Regret's wings were shaking. Elissa sighed. 'This food is quite heavy,' she said.

'Come here, Elissa. I will help you onto Hope.'

Elissa walked up to Regret, who crouched lower and let her clamber over him.

'We only do this because you are part of us,' he said very quietly. 'No human would be allowed to sit on a dragon.'

Elissa scrambled aboard and positioned herself between the tall spines at the base of Hope's neck. Dreamer tried to join her, but Regret hissed at it. 'You will spoil the illusion, little one. Stay with me.' To Elissa's astonishment, Dreamer actually stopped.

'Are you ready?' Hope asked. 'Illusion makes my scales chilly. I should test it works before we leave the island.'

A coldness fell through Elissa's body as she finished securing herself to Hope.

Andra gasped. 'Watcher's wings!'

'She's good at this,' rumbled Regret.

Elissa couldn't see anything different, just her and Hope.

'What do you see?' she asked. A Chosen strolled out of the tower, went white, and fainted. 'Whatever you did, looks pretty scary, Hope.'

Andra stepped forward, hands outstretched, trying to feel for Hope, which made little sense to Elissa. Hope was blowing smoke rings again, so she must be pleased with herself. Andra bumped into Hope's wing and felt the scales, her face filled with wonder.

'Elissa, I can feel Hope, but I cannot see her. What I see is an awldrin mounted on a xotryl.'

'It worked,' Hope stated, and dropped the illusion. Warmth returned to Elissa slowly. 'Regret, we will join you at the cove tomorrow.' With that, she sprang into the air, and Elissa's knots were sorely tested. She gripped the spine ahead of her tightly as they ascended.

Hope turned her head back to talk as they flew toward the fog bank. 'We will cross the sea, then fly along the coast. The awldrin are on the other shore, but we must be cautious. You are needed at home.'

Hope reached the fog bank in minutes, and as they passed through it, a now familiar chill descended. 'Are we cloaked?'

'All that is dragon is cloaked,' Hope replied. 'Hold tightly. I am going faster.'

Wind whipped past Elissa's face, and tiny waves far below her looked like a picture from a book. Tiny sails rose in the distance. They sped over the sea without seeing any awldrin, and before long, flew along the coast. They crossed river mouths feeding into the Ameryth Dar sea far below them.

Hope kept up a regular wingbeat for hours, never tiring or resting. Elissa was reminded of how Rossi told her that the dragons could cross space. Sitting astride Hope, Elissa could imagine that she truly had that power. They were so high up that the world below spread like a map. In the far distance, the Glassine mountains studded the horizon. Hope continued around the coast until they were above the marsh, and as the sun dropped below the horizon, they continued on under the cover of darkness. Hope maintained their cloaking even then.

'I shine,' she said simply when Elissa queried it.

Glints of light reflected off the marsh below them as they turned away from the sea toward the big lake above Dragonsbreath. The caves where Laytha and the others stayed weren't too far downriver from the lake, and she pointed the area out to Hope.

'I will land on the lake side of the caves. You take the food, then return to me.'

'Can they not meet you?' Elissa asked, her words stolen by the air.

'A big group of humans walking at night to see a shining dragon would not help them remain hidden.'

'Then may I bring one? The one who is in charge can give the others some hope if she meets you.'

'She cannot take a piece of me.'

Elissa opened her mouth to reply, then saw a smoke ring

briefly as it was whisked away. Hope really did find her own jokes too funny.

⌐ ⋏ ☾ ✧ ⊚

Fires burnt far on the seaward side of Dragonsbreath. That must be where the sericlave had been moved to. Where Makin was killed. The thought speared her heart, and she struggled not to sink into mourning. Hope jolted, and her wings missed a beat. Elissa tried to get a grasp of her emotions; she must be leaking them again. She looked up toward the lake – to Laytha – as she struggled to regain control and not submerge Hope under the weight of her loss.

The sooner she could open the gates, the better. There were only so many deaths the sericlave would stomach to protect the Untouched before someone broke.

Hope banked steeply to the right, and Elissa grabbed at the spines again, her instinct overreaching logic; she was well secured. They flew upstream, toward the top lake, where Hope circled the perimeter, searching for the stream. She swooped down, gliding over its burbling surface. The gentle sound of the water just reached Elissa's ears as they followed it into a wider valley with a flat base – a suitable landing spot. Hope alighted and folded her wings.

'Why were you so sad?'

'My brother was killed. We flew over where it would have been.'

'That would make you sad, I see. Then we must do all we can to get your people from here without the awldrin knowing. We cannot fight them. Regret will not allow it.'

'Thank you, Hope. Will you accompany me part of the way?'

'I will walk with you unless it gets too narrow. Then, you are on your own.'

Elissa untied herself and slid from Hope's back. The food was heavy, and she was unsure how much further they would have to walk.

'Hope, when I leave you, won't the crystal in my foot make me visible to the awldrin?'

Hope tilted her head to one side. 'It will. I will come as far as I can. Can you not do the human magic dream walking thing?'

'Not without actually sleeping.' Elissa sighed.

'That is a shame. But you can make fire. Fire is better.'

Elissa wasn't entirely sure how fire would be better than contacting Laytha, but she kept that thought to herself.

'Will I be able to do other dragon things one day?' she asked as they splashed through the water.

'He could.'

'Cloaking might be useful,' Elissa said, hoping for a hint.

'It would.'

'How do you do it?'

'I do it.'

Elissa sighed. Then she remembered her thought from that morning,

'Will I get wings?'

Hope snorted.

'I'll take that as a no then.' Elissa scrambled over a boulder. Hope hopped over a pile of rocks, a dragon hop leading to quite a thump on the landing.

They carried on in silence, broken only by the sound of their feet and breathing. For such a large creature, Hope was amazingly quiet. The wind picked up as the valley narrowed.

'Elissa, I cannot go much further. You will have to travel alone the rest of the way. Stay in the water.'

'Thank you, Hope. I will be as quick as I can.'

'You will be as long as you will be.'

Elissa stepped away from Hope and watched as the shimmering scales vanished into blurriness.

'Just like the shard.' Safe in the knowledge that Hope was hidden until she returned, she trudged on through the stream alone, increasingly grateful for the scale in her shoe easing her discomfort.

⌒ ⋏ ʎ ⊕ ⊚

Her splashing finally drew the attention she'd hoped for.

'Who's that? Everyone is supposed to be either fishing or in the caves.'

'It's Elissa. I have food for you.'

'Come up here.'

'I can't. You will have to come down to the water for your own safety.'

'It can't be Elissa. She's a long way away – she left here. Who are you?'

Elissa sighed and sat down, keeping her feet in the water. She should have planned ahead.

'Fine.' She untied some of the food and threw a bag in the direction of the voice. 'I'm wearing packages of food all over me. It's not much, I know, but it's all I can bring right now. Check what I just threw at you. Leave one of you watching me if you want while the other gets Laytha. Tell her … tell her everything Rossi told us was true and possible. Tell her I used my key. Please be quick – I need to leave here before sunrise.'

She heard stumbling footsteps in the darkness as they searched for the pack she had thrown.

'I've got it,' one whispered to the other. 'Do we open it?'

'No, don't. It will go everywhere,' Elissa said, trying to

swallow frustration. Eventually, one walked down to the stream, and Elissa removed the rest of her packs. 'Do you have any light at all?' she asked. 'I really can't leave the water, and it's hard to see the knots.'

'No. But when Laytha gets here, we can cut them off you.'

Why was trying to help people so frustrating? Truthfully, Elissa was glad they were being cautious, so she shuffled up the bank a little and laid back on the ground. The parcels made a comfy bed. She realised she still hadn't managed a single night's sleep in her cottage, and if the dragons got their way, she might not for a while longer.

Elissa lay gazing up at the cloudy sky as small patches of stars peeked through the velvety darkness. What would it be like to fly in space?

She must have dozed off, because she woke to an enveloping hug and Laytha's familiar voice.

'Why did you leave her in the water? Help her out of it, quickly.' Arms reached under her.

'I asked them to leave me here. If I'm out of the water, the awldrin will be able to locate me.' She pushed herself back upright. 'Get this food off me and take it to the cave. I need Laytha and one other person to come with me.'

'How did you get here? We thought you were a long way away. You said you couldn't help us.'

'I didn't think I could.' Elissa held her arms out as two others cut more food from her. When they'd finished, she felt light – almost floating.

'That's a relief. I've been wearing that since early evening. It was heavy. Laytha, walk with me. I think your questions can be answered by meeting my companion.'

Laytha chuckled. 'I did hear he was rather dashing and that you were holding hands.'

'He? Oh, no, not the Captain. This is someone you will really want to meet though.'

They walked companionably back up the stream, the lookman hanging back a little to allow them some privacy.

Elissa turned to thank him. 'Please make sure Laytha gets back to the caves. I will not be returning with you.'

In the faint light, she thought that he nodded. 'We need her. I would rather not return than return without her.'

Laytha had hundreds of questions about what Elissa had done since she'd left Dragonsbreath, and as they walked, Elissa endeavoured to answer them all.

'Laytha, I truly thought I'd found us a new home. There's an entire system, like those hidden under Dragonsbreath, across the sea in Shardeep. It would need cleaning and the wild animals evicting, but it could have been ours, until the awldrin spread their attack. They've now attacked and burned just about every human settlement except Hope and here. They need you. It's the only reason our sericlave is still alive.'

'That and the sacrifice of those like Makin.' Laytha stopped walking and embraced Elissa. 'I'm sorry. He was so brave. He believed in you.'

Elissa swallowed hard, fighting tears. 'I won't let him down – or you.'

Laytha nodded. 'I know you won't. If I understand you correctly though, we are trapped, unless every human hides on this one island?'

'Or unless we go home – to Lieus.'

'Lookman Rath did say you mentioned something about being a key.'

Elissa took Laytha's arm and squeezed it gently. 'I've been through the gate.'

'The gate is destroyed.' Laytha peeled Elissa's hand from her arm.

'Not all of it. I have been through. I met someone on the other side, and they came back with me.'

'One of those powerful Souls of Dal?' Laytha gasped. 'No wonder you got here so fast.'

'No, someone else.' She recognised the narrow opening ahead of her. 'Please, stay here,' she called back to the lookman. Hope would be just around the corner.

'Hope, I'm back,' she whispered.

'I can see that,' Hope rumbled. Laytha started at the voice from nowhere and everywhere.

'Please drop your cloak so I can find you.'

'Only you can travel back.'

'I know, Hope.' She whispered to Laytha. 'Get ready.'

Hope's outline became visible by starlight, just visible.

'How much do you trust this Laytha, Elissa?' Hope queried.

'With my life – I owe her everything.'

'Then light me with fire – just once. Mine is too big. We are sheltered, and it is cold. It should be safe.'

Could she do it with someone watching? Elissa tried to produce fire, but nothing happened.

'We don't have long, Elissa,' Hope said. 'Throw your stones.'

Elissa picked up a handful of stones. 'Stay there, Laytha, and look toward the voice.' She ensured she faced away from Laytha, then started throwing stones. This was so inelegant. She hated that she didn't have control. Her irritation flew with the pebble and, whoomph, a small jet of fire spat out, illuminating the great golden form of Hope.

'A dragon? You brought a dragon? Wait ... you rode a dragon?'

'Two dragons,' Hope replied. 'Regret is here too.'

'Here?'

'She means on Tebein. Laytha, they have a job for me. They need me to do something on Mythos. I don't know how long I'll be gone, but when I come back, I hope to take you all to safety. The Captain will remain in touch with you on my behalf. Trust him. If you can get to the sea's edge, he will take you all to Hope. No one can help you while you hide back here.'

'I took some maps. We will see how much food you brought us, and maybe we can brave an attempt.'

'If you can get to a place called Thurra Isle, he told me he can get you to safety. Laytha, in case I don't make it back, thank you – for everything.'

Laytha's choked voice trembled as she replied, hugging Elissa in the darkness. 'Go and save us, my fire-filled girl. I will find your Captain.'

'One last thing. Rossi saved me. He stayed in Shardeep, which is now under attack, and his daughter may lose both her parents. If you make it to Hope, and if I don't come back, I promised to take in his daughter.'

'I'll do it. But you will be back.' Laytha gave her one final squeeze. 'Now go. You don't keep a dragon waiting.'

'But she is,' Hope huffed.

Elissa scrambled aboard with Hope's help and secured herself.

Hope turned around and launched herself skyward. The cold fell on her body as they climbed higher into the night sky and headed back to the island, cloaked in disguise as Elissa's own hunters.

Chapter 13

Darin

Hound in the night, lead me home.
Howl by day, keep beasts away.
Dal children's rhyme

'How did it go?'
'Can he sing?'
'What does she know?'

Darin froze at the barrage of questions and raised a hand. He walked calmly to the centre spot and took the position for reporting back that he'd seen Chase assume previously. Aggi's mouth twitched a small smile, and he nodded his approval. Every Howler fell silent and sat.

'She did get some information before she released the awldrin and seems incredibly embarrassed – almost bewildered – that she would let it out. We have a name for the awldrin, and I'm afraid it's really bad news. The awldrin she has released is called Natke.'

'Not Natke, queen of the awldrin, imprisoned at the end of the war five hundred cycles ago?' Bones spluttered.

'Suriin's father is Yorynn – the Witness the Gardeners have failed to cure. Suriin would have been an easy target once Natke realised she had such a weakness. She was utterly convinced that the awldrin would be trustworthy and help her. Combined with Suriin's pity over Natke's lengthy imprisonment, it was the perfect storm for Natke to exploit.'

'Will Suriin help us?' asked Fall.

Darin nodded and saw his own earlier relief reflected back at him from the circle of faces.

'Aggi has agreed to help save their father – as long as you're all in agreement?' He paused, glancing around the room. No one was giving a sign either way, so, uncertainly, he continued on. 'He will need an amputation. That in itself should not be beyond the So'Dal Witnesses, from what I understand, but we have managed to gather that the most experienced is in Lacton. The Garant doesn't know him, so won't collect him, and we understand the poison is spreading faster since a white powder was administered by Suriin. As for Gwynn, he's as tone deaf as myself. As both parents are talented, there's a good chance he will be both talented and unable to sing.'

'That doesn't automatically make him a Howler,' Chase said quickly. 'Sorry to interrupt – Boulder was mere moments from rushing off to go and find the boy.'

Boulder chuckled. 'You wouldn't be wrong. We need all the help we can get.'

Darin smiled. 'I can't blame you. We don't know for sure yet, but it's better than being certain that he won't be.'

Aggi lifted his hand and raised an eyebrow, so Darin stepped aside.

'The boy has a prodigious knowledge already. He has a fascination with plants and correctly brought us one set of resources. He's our best support in the main palace right now. If we can spare a little dragon bone to help push the poison back – yes, I know – and we rifle through our books for a treatment to numb his father, we can do it. Gwynn can collect the plants we need. One of the siblings can then give it to Yorynn before the So'Dal arrive. I understand he is mostly unconscious, so the Gardeners won't notice a difference.'

'I'll make myself available to Aslin, and we'll amputate. I need a red-trim robe from our stores to help hide myself. I don't think she'll recognise me since she's closer to Chase's age.

'They can use all their song and emotional wefts, but we'll already have delivered the dragon bone mix and something to stop him feeling the cut. Even the most highly skilled Soul Anchor isn't going to keep the pain away with the limits they work under. We need him unaware of the situation, or shock may kill him before anything else. He'll be very weak, and the much-too-small dose of dragon bone I suspect Suriin gave him will not have helped.'

'In return, we gain their loyalty and gratitude.' Boulder nodded slowly, words dropping from his mouth as though they disgusted him. 'I don't like it. I don't have to – I know. But it's worth doing. We need those kids, or we go public. We don't have the resources to fight this battle alone, even with knowledge the rest of the So'Dal don't have.' He gestured to the passage holding the hidden library. 'We need to start working through the new wefts we can use and increase our capability. We all know from battle that practise makes for less hesitation. Confidence, an extra split second between a hit and a miss. Precision in our workings may allow us to defeat the awldrin. We need to attack this music with the same attitude that we took to train as martial fighters.'

Darin felt the palpable tension in the air, unusual for their cosy home. 'Fall, we need to find a way to keep Suriin awake and functional for long enough to track the awldrin. Is there anything to help that in the books? If Gwynn is dropping in later to collect the list of plants he needs to gather, we could add to it.'

Fall shook his head. 'In honesty, I don't know. The crystals are part of the Watcher's deal. They won't have anything written about them – these books predate that binding. If we find a way to unbind Suriin, she might lose the ability to track Natke. But in her current state, she may be unable to function. If we look at older methods of using magic, we might find a way for her to avoid using the crystal as a focus altogether.'

'That would be a start,' Darin said. 'Chase, do you think Star's well enough to do some battle training?'

'If we start with gentle work on positioning and skills, we could.' Chase was dampened, somehow lesser. Darin had hoped he'd get in touch with Tian, but looking at his pack-mate, it appeared not.

'The sooner we get out there, the sooner we can ensure everyone is safe. Would Tian consider coming here just for a little while?'

'To hide in our tunnels, leaving our home and his workshop? No.' Chase pushed himself out of his chair and called Sandy. 'Come on, then.'

⌒ ⋏ ◖ ✥ ◎

Chase led Darin into the armoury. The weapons on display glistened by glow lamp as they cleared a space. He gestured around the room. 'We may need to use some of this stuff, I suppose. If we were ever in need of a little extra magic, it's now.'

'Items that won't rot, so those made of metal.' Darin scanned the room. The hound armour was being replaced. Star would be fine. As good as his screw-tipped spear was, it lacked weight compared to his staff. It would be great to launch at an awldrin on the ground, but would then be lost, and with Natke possibly attacking from the air, it might only give them a single strike.

As he studied the armoury, it occurred to him that most of the weapons would be useless against a flying assailant. He picked at the chain-mail suit, its shimmering hoops drawing his attention, but it was way too small. It might fit Suriin, though – if she were well enough to travel with them. She'd need protection if nausea struck her helpless again. Darin lifted the bottom of the tunic; it was surprisingly light. She could probably wear it under a loose robe too. He moved on, searching the armoury for a weapon that would give him an advantage.

Surely in this great room there must be something he felt a degree of connection to. In old childhood tales, heroes grasped a prized weapon and turned out to be proficient at using it with some natural talent they had hidden throughout their lives. This was his moment.

The red-bladed sword caught his eye again, as it had on their first visit. He'd not used a sword for a long time. It was beautiful, and burn it, but it looked intimidating. Maybe this was his weapon. He lifted it off the wall and swung it experimentally. It was heavy, and his control of the blade was even worse than he remembered. In his hands, it would be as much use as a glow lamp in broad daylight.

'Chase, you could use this,' he said, handing it to his friend before moving along the racks, searching for something more familiar.

He saw the throwing rings next, their shining redness glinting in the light. Darin picked one up. They were perfectly balanced. The outer blades sharpened to a fine edge – he ran a finger along it and winced as it easily sliced his flesh.

'Have you any experience with thrown weapons?' Chase asked.

Darin could only shrug. 'I used them at local fairs, but just as a laugh, never for anything serious. I was good enough to win prizes. They were nothing like these, though. They had dulled edges, and you needed a huge amount of spin to get one embedded in the post. I'd rather find a slingshot. I'm good with one of those.'

'Small pellets won't help us against Natke or the xotryl unless they're magical and going to explode. We can try both. Slingshots are everywhere and easy to find, but perishable. If there's one in here, it won't last outside the enchantment. Are you sure you don't want a bladed weapon?'

'I'm positive. I'm happy with my spear close up – although, I'd rather it was a proper staff. As long as Star is protected, that's the most important thing to me.'

'The rings it is, then.' Chase hung the sword back on the wall. 'It's a stunning weapon, but it's not for me either. It's too flaming heavy. The only person I've seen wield that beast with any efficiency was Aggi, and then only in training. He used your spear most of the time.'

'He could still use it now, I'd guess.'

Chase shrugged. 'He knows it's here if he wants it. We should get started. You can practise with those things a bit later. Show me how you and Star would position yourselves if I was coming directly at you.' Chase mock growled and charged at Darin.

Darin sent *[Star coming in from the side to grab Chase's arm]*.

Star sat.

Chase glanced over and stopped running. 'Hrm, I think Sandy and Star need to have a discussion. Maybe it's better if you attack me first.'

Star had no intention of moving to help Darin attack Chase either. He remained stubbornly sat, sending sad emotion filled with concern toward Darin as he closed on Chase.

'I think you're right. He doesn't want us fighting.' Darin sat next to Star and wrapped his arms around the hound. 'We're still friends. We just need to practise, like you do.' He tried to construct images of moonhounds play fighting, stalking each other with wind-blown twigs before moving on to bigger animals. He sent images of Star playing with his littermates, then followed it up by reminding Star of how they rounded up the Rhinocorn as a team. Then, he sent Star images of the xotryl. Grounded but on its feet, and them trying to kill it.

'It's just like you practised. We need to learn to work as a team, like you and your littermates did.'

[Himself and Conor sparring] filled his vision. Darin felt the question.

[Himself and Star play fighting with Chase and Sandy] he replied.

Star wagged and ran over to Chase, with his gums over his teeth, and softly mouthed his arm.

'I think he's got it, Darin.' Chase laughed and scritched Star on the ear. 'Let's try again.'

⌒ ☌ ◖ ✢ ◉

They wandered back to the main cavern, hungry and slightly bruised from a few accidents. Star had taken to the play-fighting concept a little too enthusiastically. It was a positive thing, Darin decided. They were getting their heads around working as a team.

Their training had exposed another problem. The more Chase taught him, the more Darin realised that the horn on the hound armour could lead to problems for Star or Sandy if they attacked something at the wrong angle. That and the fact that there was a real risk they might impale each other. He'd have to see if Conor could come up with something safer and more effective.

They urgently needed a practise dummy. Darin had no idea how they would get one through the passageways and into the main armoury, let alone anywhere hidden where he could practise with the rings without risking other people. The red throwing rings were the sharpest weapons he'd ever held. He'd found normal ones deeper in the box, and they were still sharp enough to slice his hand open if he threw them poorly.

If he could use them with accuracy against a xotryl, they would cause deep, painful lacerations and potentially shred its wings. With damaged wings, the battle was back in their reach. Grounded xotryl were still fearsome, but the moonhounds were agile. Bones could give them an advantage from old spells.

If they could take one down without an awldrin.

How well the rings would work against an awldrin's outer skeleton – Natke's built-in armour – he had no idea. There would probably be answers in old records. He'd seen it called an exoskeleton in *Battle Strategies of the Awldrin*. They were just like a bug – hard exterior with flesh on the inside. If he could sever the joints, would it stop the creature moving? On humans, joints were a weak spot, but were they the same on awldrin?

Suriin said they ate staramine powder. If their teeth were that hard, could it be incorporated into the exoskeleton too? He shuddered. No, if their teeth were hard as staramine, then chewing through metal bars would have been simple, if slow. If he'd been trapped with teeth capable of breaking down stone, he'd have eaten his way out.

They re-entered the main chamber to find Gwynn sat opposite Bones in a game of stones. To Darin's surprise, he was holding his own. His pieces were even in a slightly attacking position. Was Bones being gentle on the boy?

'Gwynn brought you the herbs, Darin.' Bones nodded at the bulging pouch on the floor.

'Already?'

Fall chuckled. 'You've been in there for hours. It was no big problem to gather the ingredients you'd already asked him to get for the healing potion components once.'

It hadn't felt like hours. No wonder he ached. 'What have you got for us?' Darin moved to pick up the pouch, but Gwynn recovered it quickly and clutched it to his chest. 'Show me how to use the whistle when you make it, please?'

'But you can't access your magic yet.'

Gwynn's shoulders dropped.

He was helping them; it wouldn't hurt. 'I suppose you must have seen Yorynn at work. Did Fall find us anything stronger for the operation?'

Fall shook his head. 'Not in the way I hoped. We'll have to use a tiny bit of powdered dragon bone, enough to reduce the fever and provide temporary relief. Aggi will have to work fast, as it won't last long, and we can't spare much.'

'Anything to help Suriin to unbind or control her nausea more effectively than the healing draft?' Having Suriin almost useful but physically incapable was frustrating.

'Not yet. I'm still working on it. This book looks more promising, but the language is very old, and it takes me a while to decipher it.' Fall waved a red-covered book in the air. It had a strange texture to the leather, the grains far bigger than he'd expect from faat hide. Was it even leather? He resisted the urge to study it more closely. It wasn't important right now.

'Let's get the backup healing draft made and ready for Suriin. I assume you have the dragon bone solution already?'

Gwynn patted his pocket. 'Bones already did it.'

'We didn't want to risk wasting the ingredients on one of us trying the weft for the first time,' Bones said. 'I could probably do it, but we don't have time to waste.'

They walked into the kitchen, where Darin laid the plants out, talking through his selection of each leaf, the grinding, and the singing. He drew his whistle out and retrieved the training globe from its cupboard. As a pack, they'd decided to keep it in everyone's reach for now, so any of them could practise with the whistles.

He played the tune twice, then transferred the focus to the bowl of ground herbs. Gwynn gasped as light glowed through the fluid.

'That's amazing! I always knew I'd struggle because I could never sing like my father, so I thought I'd never be accepted as a So'Dal. I think I'm a disappointment to him in that respect. But there's a way that I could still be one after all.'

'A way that no one outside these secret rooms knows about.' Darin tucked everything away again and gave Gwynn what he hoped was a pointed look.

Gwynn was barely able to sit still. His excitement so strong that Star padded in to see what was happening. 'I know. But I can have hope, right?'

'You can.' Darin bottled up the healing draft and handed it over. 'Silard will see you later. Remember, call him Silard, whatever else you've heard him called.'

Gwynn tucked the small bottle into a pocket. 'Thank you. When do you want me to come back next?'

'Give us a day to really hunt through things and finalise our plan. In the meantime, keep your family safe and close.'

'I will. I'd go finish that game before I leave, but Bones had me pretty beaten anyway.'

They briefly returned to the main room. Gwynn picked up

a glove and slung his gardening pouch around his shoulders. 'I wear it everywhere now, so no one notices anything different.'

'Good lad.' Bones nodded his approval. 'Darin, see him out, won't you? Don't forget your shard – it might let you get out, too, for a short distance.'

As they reached the door, Darin used his whistle to trigger the dragon bone shard and prepared to open the door. He pressed his ear to the wet stone, listening for noise in the huge steam lift chamber. Steam built and built as they waited, the rising whistle of the lift preparing for release, until it hurt his ears.

'Now,' he mouthed at Gwynn, and released the door just after the noise changed. The lift was on its way up. The door opened slowly and immediately began to close. That had never happened before.

'Wait here,' he said, and slipped through the gap.

The hall was packed. Boulder faced the door, watching the tiny crack closing as he reset the lever.

Where were all these people going? Why were so many queueing for the lift? The lift dropped again, and Boulder waved more people on. There must be at least one more platform-full. The Soul Anchors were dressed in very fine clothes, and a number of Gardeners and Witness apprentices looked distinctly less rumpled than usual.

After the last load started to rise, Boulder turned to the door and blew his own whistle. Gwynn peered out and waved at Boulder before scurrying toward the corridors and the main palace.

'What's going on?' Darin whispered in Boulder's ear.

'Bonding ceremony for a Soul Anchor and her chosen. Your timing was awful.'

'Not a lot I could do about it. I'm not sure how we can keep smuggling him in and out this way. Especially without him able to trigger a dragon bone shard.'

Boulder whispered, 'Best you start to think about that. Add it to the pack's challenges. Go. Get back in before someone runs into you. Sorry, Darin, today isn't a good day to sneak around.'

Darin took his advice and returned to the secret door, quietly slipping back to the howler chambers.

CHARVER

CHAPTER 14

SURIIN

They got to Yorynn's room first. Gwynn stood watch at the door with Fluffy, while Suriin lifted their father and helped him to swallow the concoction they'd been given, stroking his neck as she had the first time she'd persuaded him to drink. She talked to him softly, encouraging him as she felt him swallow.

'Well done. This drink will make you sleepy. The Gardeners are coming soon with Aslin and Silard. I'm sorry, Father.' Tears rolled down her cheeks as she spoke. 'I don't know how to say this, but they are going to remove your arm. It's the only chance you have, and it's got to be better than dying.' She sniffled a little, then, as Gwynn's movement by the door caught her eye, she continued, despite knowing he was too unconscious to respond. Suriin needed to tell him what was going to happen. 'They're going to push the poison back, then cut your arm off. Skye said that the person she knows who had this done – he's happy now. We'll help you and do whatever you need us to. It's going to be okay, I promise. I'm so sorry you were caught by the xotryl. I'm sorry I released Natke. I'm—'

'They're coming, Suriin. Silard is talking so loudly, I could hear him across the width of Golden, never mind a hallway.'

Suriin tipped the last of the liquid down her father's throat, continuing to gently stroke his neck to help him swallow. She stoppered the bottle and tucked it into her dress before laying him back down.

'It's all gone,' she whispered.

Gwynn nodded from his position at the door, opened it slightly wider, and came to join her at the side of the bed. He pulled a handkerchief out of his pocket and offered it to her. 'I'd expect you to be upset. Don't worry, Sis – so will they. It's going to be okay. Aslin and Silard will make sure it is.' His warm hand squeezed her own, and she drew strength from his support. No matter what she'd done, he still stood by her.

'In here?' Silard's voice was incredibly loud. He was giving them plenty of warning.

'Yes, I think the children may already be there. I couldn't find them before I left.' Aslin's calm tone carried round the door. Gwynn shot Suriin a last crooked grin. Suriin's hand slipped to her father's good wrist. His pulse still felt as fluttery and slow as it had before they started. Maybe a tiny bit slower.

'There you are.' Aslin was followed into the room by Silard and Ronin. A short, rotund man waddled in after them. His red cheeks sweated, but his eyes twinkled like stars; black curls haloed his face, and he radiated compassion. Suriin took in the green-trimmed robe – another Gardener. They all squeezed in to allow the last person into the room. He was huge. Gold-trimmed robes marked him as one of the Collective.

'Suriin and Gwynn, this is my twin brother – and bonded So'Dal – Orrin.' Now she had introduced him, Orrin's rounded features were a clear match for Aslin. He twinkled at them before he opened Yorynn's shirt and exposed his shoulder. Behind them, Silard mouthed something at them. Suriin tried not to stare as she struggled to interpret his gestures, but Gwynn nodded, so she guessed it had something to do with the potion.

The Collective squeezed around the bed to Suriin's side.

'I'm Nos. I'm afraid I'll need to ask you to move. I must keep your father still while they carry out the operation.' He left her room to move aside. Suriin gave her father a last kiss. 'It's going to be alright.'

Suriin and Gwynn moved to the foot of the bed while the group prepared. Ronin's red-trimmed robe caught her eye. At some point in the last few days, he must have passed that assessment. He hovered by Silard's side, and Aslin squeezed behind them to stand alongside Nos.

Silard laid clean sheets under the now exposed arm and unrolled a set of tools.

'Thank you for stepping in, Silard,' Aslin said. 'I wish one of the other experienced Witnesses could have made it in time to assist you.'

Silard shook his head. 'They couldn't have. This is too far gone.' He drew a line on Yorynn's arm above the centre of the darkness in green ink. 'This is the point I need you to push it beyond. If you can do that, I can cut the bone to leave him a small stump. The muscles around it can then be used to create enough contour for a shoulder. It will be easier for him to manage that way.'

The line was just below the shoulder, two finger widths above the top of the original injury.

Orrin pulled a potion bottle from his robes. 'Are you all ready?' he asked. 'It's the strongest I could make at this notice. Usually they take longer to reach full potency.'

Silard nodded. 'I'm ready. Ronin, we've discussed what I need you to do. Nos, are you ready? Aslin?'

They all nodded, their faces set in a range of determined grimaces. Sweat beaded on Orrin's brow. As he administered the drink, Aslin placed her hands on Yorynn's chest and closed her eyes. A tingle of power floated through the air, but Suriin was unsure which emotions she could sense. Orrin began to sing, wefting an incredibly complex song over her father's body, then Ronin and Nos joined in.

Under the pressure of their song and magic, the black tendrils began to shrink back from his neck. Nothing happened at the other end of his arm. The tissue was dead.

Silard did not join the singing. Instead, he leant over the arm, studying it closely. The intricate harmony picked up in pace and volume. The prickle in the air increased, and Silard selected an incredibly sharp, red knife from his tools.

Suriin tried not to gasp. He had a staramine blade? He stood poised over the arm, ready to move.

'Gwynn, come here,' he said. 'I need you ready to assist me.'

Gwynn nodded solemnly. Suriin's gut twisted that he was being asked to help instead of her. But after her display in the cave yesterday, she couldn't blame Silard for not wanting a second patient in the room. Fluffy remained by the door where they'd left her, and without her reassuring presence, the increasing strength of the wefts and Aslin's powerful magic made her feel queasy.

Suriin sat down, her eyes fixed on her father's arm. She'd brought this on him; she would watch it all.

Finally, the black tendrils passed Silard's line, and almost immediately, the blade cut into his arm. Blood spurted out, flooding the clean sheets, Aslin moved her hands toward Yorynn's shoulder, and the blood flow slowed. Orrin shuffled around the bed, the intensity of the singing slightly lessened. He began to sing a new melody, a calmer one, while Ronin and Nos maintained the initial song.

Silard spoke quietly to Gwynn, who passed tools as Silard worked quickly, deftly slicing as close to the blackness as he could. His fingers reached inside the muscle of her father's arm, and she watched his careful incisions. He was leaving as much as possible intact. Then, he asked for something else.

Gwynn passed him a small, white, serrated blade. No-one else seemed to notice that it was a different colour. Its whiteness stark against the red flowering of peeled-back muscle on her father's arm. Ronin cleared the area around Silard's work, packing the exposed ends into plant lined cloth. His weft changed, so that there were now three melodies in the room. The discordant tunes clashed, but each So'Dal held their role without dropping a note.

Silard glanced up at Orrin. 'Now.'

He began sawing through the bone. The noise grated through her body. She ground her teeth in distress, helplessness and guilt rising to the surface. The continued sawing stretched every fibre of her being into a more traumatised state but she continued to watch.

Gwynn glanced over.

Silard had to ask him twice for something.

Suriin was distracting them. If she was a distraction, then she was putting their father at risk. She could not be the cause of this operation failing. She rose unsteadily to her feet and slipped out of the room.

'I'll be in the courtyard,' she said quietly.

'Take Fluffy,' Gwynn whispered back.

Suriin laid her hands on Fluffy's back and left them to it.

Free of the room and the conflicting wefts, she could think more clearly. She wasn't helping anyone by being in there, and without her, it freed up more space for them to work. Together, Fluffy and Suriin walked out to the courtyard. She wandered aimlessly, following the moonhound. Images of blood and the sound of the saw ran through her head over and over again. Fluffy kept walking until Suriin realised they'd arrived at the hound paddocks.

She sat in the paddock, and a pile of puppies smothered her. Their enthusiasm for all who came to see them a typical response and in direct counterpoint to her emotion.

A small, scrawny female hound snuffled across the paddock toward her. Unusual for any of the moonhounds here, she looked unwell. Her hips and ribs protruded sharply, and her coat was flat, lacking any shine. Suriin held out a hand slowly, and the hound edged closer. Her grey-streaked muzzle twitched.

'Don't move.' A voice floated over the paddocks. 'Please, don't move. She very rarely lets anyone that close.'

Suriin sat as still as she could while the scrawny old hound crept up to her. She ran a hand gently along her side.

'She has lumps under her skin?' she said. Still not moving anything, bar the hand she stroked the hound with. The puppies had wandered away, and Fluffy laid as still as Suriin.

'She does, but hasn't let me check them while The Master of Hounds is away.'

'Does she not have a bonded Soul Anchor?'

The voice was close, and a woman crouched next to her

now, slightly back. Suriin glanced at her quickly and was rewarded with a smile.

'Her Soul Anchor died young. She rejoined the pack cycles ago. It's so sad. She probably doesn't have long left herself now. Those lumps are growing, and they will eventually kill her. She won't let anyone but him handle her – even then it's under protest.'

'What's her name?' Suriin felt a kinship with the broken hound.

'Swift.'

'Hello, Swift.' Suriin kept stroking her side. 'Which lump do you want me to check? What am I looking for?' She couldn't help her father, but in this moment, she could help the old hound.

'She has a soft lump on her side, just behind the shoulder. That's the one I was told to keep an eye on. It should be no longer than your thumb.'

Suriin felt around, locating the lump in question. 'It's still soft. I can move it,' she said.

'Good. I don't know this hound?' The woman stroked Fluffy.

'She's my mother's. Who is ... missing. I'm sure she'll be back soon.'

The woman studied Fluffy. 'So am I. There's no sadness in her eyes. Look at Swift – she drips sadness like a wet rag. Wherever your mother is, she is alive.'

'Thank you. I needed to hear that.' Gwynn's reticence had pushed her to a similar conclusion, but the suggestion from a stranger was more than welcome today.

I should go somewhere they can find me. She rose and stretched. 'It was nice to meet you ...'

'Lea.'

'Come on, Fluffy.' As she rose to leave, she stroked Swift

one more time. 'I'll come back to see you.' On impulse she sent *[herself walking with Swift in the paddock]*.

Swift looked up at her with soulful eyes and wagged.

Lea gasped. 'What did you do?'

'I told her I'd be back for a walk.' Suriin shrugged. 'I've been sending to Fluffy since I was old enough to understand how to. I don't get anything much back. Occasionally, I almost think I can feel a wag – if that makes sense. But I've always done it. Don't you talk to all the hounds?'

'Not unless we are talked to first,' Lea said. 'I ... I didn't think we could.'

'Well, you know now.' Suriin gave Swift a gentle pat and turned to leave the paddock. A low whine followed her. 'I'll be back, girl. I just have to go and check on my father. By the time I get to him, they might be done.'

⌒ ⩙ ◗ ✹ ◦

Resting her hands on the now customary patch between Fluffy's shoulders, they wound back through the tunnels to her father's room. No voices drifted out; no song or wefts pricked at her skin. The air smelt tangy and sharp – remnants of wefts hanging thick in the air.

Nervously, Suriin peered around the door. Gwynn was slumped against the bed while Ronin sat on the other side, facing the door.

'He's made it this far. It's done. Now, we have to hope he pulls through the recovery.' Ronin rubbed his beard.

'Where's his arm?' Suriin asked.

'The Anchor has it – wait – it will help. We need to learn about this toxin. If that xotryl is as aggressive toward others it encounters, we need to find a way to cure it. People dropping dead from necrosis all over Caldera is not the ship she wants to captain. On this occasion, I agree with her need.' He gestured at the sleeping Gwynn. 'He was brilliant. It was a lot to ask of him.' The accusation cut deep. The unstated, 'It should have been you.' But Ronin didn't know about the lost crystal or any of the problems she faced as a result.

'May I see the ...' She wanted to say arm, but there was no arm. Not any longer. It was somewhere in the Anchor's possession, probably being dissected. 'Shoulder,' she settled on, biting back the explanation that she desperately wanted to give. Why she'd run off when her father needed her support the most.

Gwynn raised a tired head. 'Hold up, Sis.' He shuffled down the bed so she could reach. 'Silard was amazing. I want to be like him when I'm older.'

As she pulled the covers back to inspect the shoulder, she half listened to the conversation behind her.

'I'm going to do my next training with the Witness in Lacton. I hear he has these advanced skills too. If times are changing, we cannot keep them to so few specialists.'

'I hope I can train one day. I want to help people.' Gwynn yawned.

'Don't remove the pad, Suriin. It needs to stay clean.' Ronin reached out and rested a hand on her arm. He drew another pad out from his pouch. 'I can let you look if I replace it, but I'd rather not.

'I need to see it, Ronin. Please.'

He sighed and leant over to loosen the dressing.

Suriin wasn't sure what she expected to see. But she was faced with angry, red lines of stitched skin surrounding the swollen stump of her father's remaining upper arm. The skin had been carefully joined over the end and, as carefully as she searched, there appeared to be no trace of the black poison. Though it was hard to be sure through the inflammation, it appeared that they had removed it all. Ronin lowered the pad back.

'Take him' – he gestured to Gwynn – 'away to rest. He's been exposed to a lot of wefts and is in need of sleep to work through it – and all that he witnessed today. Aslin tried to take him, but he insisted on waiting for you.

'Yorynn will not be left alone. I'll be replaced by Orrin in a while, then we'll take turns as he recovers. Can you let Merri know where I am? I was supposed to meet her later. I don't want her thinking I forgot.'

'Of course.' It would be good to see Merri and Joy, and she really needed to catch up with Fresna. 'Thank you, Ronin.'

Ronin bowed his head and returned to his seat as Suriin helped Gwynn to his feet, and they left for Aslin's rooms.

CHAPTER 15

ELISSA

Dreamstealer, nightweaver,
Creeps up in the night
Dreamstealer, nightweaver
Gives your soul a fright.
Children's rhyme, thought to originate
from Shardeep

They landed back on Hope to a rapturous welcome from Dreamer.

'Have it back – it's yours. It will be helpful, so take it with you.' Regret nosed the small charver across to her as soon as her feet touched the ground. The light from the open tower door illuminated a flashing rainbow of happiness. She collected Dreamer, who ran up to her shoulder.

'I take it Dreamer didn't settle quietly while we were gone?'

Regret shook his head. 'It climbed all over me, shouting the entire time. Get ready to leave. We will pass through the gate with sunrise.'

Elissa's tired legs protested the walk down to her house. She grimaced, aware the return would be far worse. Every step was heavy with exhaustion.

Once in her house, she allowed herself a moment to sit. Sleep tried to claim her, and she fought valiantly against it. Through tears, she gathered her small collection of belongings. Everything she had to her name fitted in a small bag: a worn pair of sticky foot wraps from home, a bar of scented wash she'd been given by the innkeeper in Silverfish, a spare change of clothes, the tiny shard of dragon bone Rossi had told her to keep, and a brush. She secreted the small bar of scented cleaner with her things – a reminder of the people she was trying to save. The dragon bone, she wasn't sure about. It felt wrong to carry a piece of one of Hope or Regret's dead relatives around. She tucked it into the back of a drawer.

So that was it. She'd get some food from the tower. Elissa scanned the cottage for anything else that might prove useful on a journey into an unknown world and snorted a laugh. Who was she kidding? She had no idea what she'd need, how long she would be, or even why they were so keen to send her and not fix this themselves. Her gaze landed on the candles. She'd need light.

Maybe Dreamer and her own fire would be enough.

Her own fire.

Her world grew crazier by the day. She shoved the candles into her bag with the other items.

'Right, then,' she said to Dreamer. 'I still think you should stay with your family.' She tried to peel the charver off and place it with the others, but it held on fiercely. 'Maybe when I've had some food, Andra will let me rest in the tower until sunrise, then I can try to explain this to you – like your parent did to me. I'd try here, but I am certain I'd fall asleep, and I really don't fancy being late for Regret.

∘৯ ᚨ ᚦ ⊛ ◉

The tower was silent. No one was running, no panicked Chosen delivered reports. Elissa pushed the door open slowly and peered in. It was almost too quiet.

She didn't know where food came from, she realised – it had just appeared. There must be somewhere they stored or prepared it. She checked behind the stairs, finding a far less imposing door tucked behind the last spiral. The gap around the frame was illuminated, so she took a chance and opened it, revealing a small stairway. The smell of food drifted up. As good a place to try as any.

The kitchen was laid out in a large arc, and in the middle of the immaculately tidy space, Andra sat on a tall stool, cradling a drink.

'I never sleep properly these days,' she said and smiled warmly. 'I thought you might like some supplies, so I prepared you a bag.' She patted a package much like the ones Elissa had taken to Dragonsbreath.

'These are the food parcels we deliver out to the far communities when they have a bad harvest, or to add some variety. There is fruit in them – it's dried. Don't worry, it's not heavy. Some basic grains, dried fish. Everything is dried. I know it doesn't sound appetising, but in a pinch, you could eat it as it is. With time and some water, you can make delicious food. Do you have anything to soak food in?'

'No. I did have, but it got so wet on the way that it's not useable any more.'

Andra pushed a small leather bag at her. 'This bag should work for long soaks, and this for heating.' The strange device she passed to Elissa was made of a shiny metal. Its interlocking rings dropped down to form a bowl as she lifted it up.

'It's so clever and light. Thank you. Do you think I could

have a nap while I wait to leave? I'm really tired, and I'd like to try to persuade Dreamer to stay here.'

'Dreamer? Oh, the charver. There's a recliner in the gate hall. It might be a bit chilly, but at least you'll be in the right place.'

It sounded like a good idea. 'Thank you, Andra.'

She reached out and placed her hand over Elissa's. 'Once you go through, we won't be able to re-open it.' It was a simple statement, but the weight of it lay heavily on Elissa's shoulders.

'I know. I'll be back as soon as I can. While I'm trying to get us all away from here, please promise you'll try to help Dragonsbreath sericlave get to safety.'

Andra's sad smile said what her mouth couldn't. 'We will try. You told them about the Isle?'

'For all the good it does, yes. I don't know how long the new supplies will last. There are about twenty-five Untouched, and I don't know how many more of the rest of the population.'

'Leave their safety with me. We'll try to work out a way. But you know I can't ...' Elissa placed her hand over her pounding heart, trying to calm herself. She knew the reality, but she'd had to ask. 'Andra, I know you have a whole people to get through Hope's fog. I just ask that you also try to save my people too.'

Andra hugged her, a move that threw Elissa a little. 'They are all our people. Come back safe,' she whispered. 'For more than just your own sake.'

'I'll try. I'm going to have a rest while I wait for Regret. Will you be there to help open the gate?'

'I suspect as long as you have a dragon, you'll be fine. Now you have food, I think I'm going to go upstairs to rest.' She let go of Elissa, and a smile flickered across her face. 'I'm no good at goodbyes.'

⌐ ⋏ 𝄐 ✤ ⊚

Elissa was woken by the gentle nudging of a green snout.

'It is time to go.'

'Will you come with me, help me in Mythos?'

'No. I will return here. I need to keep the peace.'

Elissa snorted. 'Peace? They are killing people, Regret.'

'I know. But you are many. They are few.'

She stretched and picked up her bag. 'I don't like the fact you won't help us. But you expect me to help you.'

'I will aid humans to reach safety. I will not attack an awldrin.'

'I know.' Elissa sighed. She could only save the humans on Tebein by saving the awldrin, so the sooner she started, the quicker they could escape. 'Will someone be there to help me?' she asked, tying her foot wraps tight and wrapping her cloak around her shoulders before Dreamer climbed on. She'd tried to emotionally talk to it while she rested, but it was either too young, or she wasn't good enough at communicating yet. It had made a decision, and she knew she'd be glad of its company.

'I hope so. I called our brother before we came through the gate.'

Elissa knew better than to push Regret. He would share what she needed to know, when he was ready to. She trusted his honesty, but she hoped his brother would be more eloquent.

'I'm ready.'

Regret turned to the gate. 'You are needed to open this.'

'How will you get back?'

'We will keep it open for a short time while I explain your task. It will be faster than flying back.'

None of the Chosen had come to see them off. Hope poked her head through the wall.

'Elissa, you can do this. It will be hard. But it is a wrong that needs righting. We cannot do this without you. We are fixed in our moulds, so we put our hope in you. Take our brother's aid. If you help fix this, you will fix more than one set of broken pieces.'

Elissa saw a single tear roll from the dragon's black eye. Her lip quivered in empathy. Burn it, she must be tired; she wasn't normally this emotional. But this clearly meant more to the dragons than their cool exteriors showed.

Regret nodded. 'She is right. Are you ready?'

Elissa pulled her gaze away from Hope to face the small gate. 'I'm ready.' She placed her hand over the crack in the crystal.

'I don't have a tear. I was crying last time.'

'What would make you cry, Elissa?'

'Sadness or pain, sometimes happiness. That doesn't help really, does it?'

'Not really, but you must cry.'

Hope blew a gentle warmth over Elissa. 'If you don't cry, that friend I met won't survive. She will not make it. If you do, if you get through that gate, you can save people.' Very quietly, Hope added, 'And my brother.' Her huge, tear-filled eyes broke Elissa, and the tears flowed. The empathy that poured from Hope was devastating. With a tear added to the gate, Elissa sniffed.

'Regret, I'll need help.' He touched his snout to her hand, and the gate shimmered, growing larger.

They stepped through into darkness. Regret flung a flame to a brazier on the wall. The white bones of the Watcher remained where they'd been the last time. Elissa crept closer. The skeleton was huge, almost twice as big as Hope.

'He was one of the oldest.'

'There were others?'

'There are. You are going to see the oldest. The only dragon alive who might both talk to you and also knows how to make echoglass to fix the gates.'

'Others won't talk to me?'

'Others might, but you may not be strong enough to survive meeting them.'

Elissa shuddered. The dragons she'd met had filled her with curiosity. Regret implied more caution would be needed on Mythos. Not strong enough to survive didn't suggest they would try to eat her, but some other life-threatening challenge. She would deal with that as the problem arose. Anything that didn't involve being hunted gave her a chance.

'We re-make the echoglass, bring it back here, then take it to both sets of gates?' she asked.

'Now I understand why you needed me.' From behind the massive skeleton, a smaller greyish dragon crept out. He was a little longer than Regret, but his posture and hung head made him appear shrunken. His wings drooped as he walked, and his tail dragged on the floor, hissing with each step against the tiled surface. Dull grey eyes studied Elissa intently. Even the smoke tendrils appeared to droop. Elissa's heart ached for him, as she understood what Hope had asked of her.

'Why now?' he asked.

Regret sauntered over to the grey dragon and rested his head gently against the lowered snout.

'Because we should. Because we can. Because the awldrin are dying even more. They have no queen. Because, maybe – just maybe – you and this human can make the glass, get the gate re-opened in Lieus, and we can send humans away from Tebein for good. It's possible there's an egg there. Hope believes. We have to.'

Elissa was stunned by the length of the speech from Regret. She manoeuvred around the skeleton toward Sorrow.

'I will do all I can to help.'

He swung his head toward her.

'Why you? Why a human? What is our plan?'

'She carries echoglass within her. She is 'other' like *He* was. And, she is strong – she opened the gate with a single crystal. She breathes fire.' Regret chuckled. 'It is tiny fire, like a hatchling, but it is a start.'

Elissa folded her arms. 'Still here!'

'I know, I see you.' Regret said, not glancing her way. He was still snout to snout with his brother. 'Take her to Rapture. We can't get in that cavern without an invitation. She can. I am sorry, Sorrow, but I need to return to Hope. We will keep them from killing each other for as long as we can. The rest is in your talons.'

Dreamer fluttered off Elissa's shoulder and alighted on the floor in front of Sorrow. He changed to a yellow colour. Sorrow stared at it absently for a moment, then his eyes seemed to take in what he was seeing. 'Do mine eyes see true? Does he accompany you?'

'He?' Elissa asked.

'He means your charver,' Regret said.

'Dreamer is a he? Thank you for telling me.' Elissa reached out her hand and Dreamer hopped back on, settling against her shoulder, a content shade of blue.

'I'm going to leave now,' Regret called, turning to the gate. 'Close it behind me, then get going.'

Elissa followed him to the gate, with Sorrow trailing after her.

Once his tail passed through, she closed it. She sighed, turning toward the melancholy dragon. His head rested on the floor, and as she studied him carefully, his hooded eyes watched her. Drooping spines and grey scales hinted at a glory long abandoned. Were Elissa to sit as she did on Hope, she would not be secure. The dragon's sadness was all-encompassing, and she struggled to retain her composure.

Dreamer flitted back to him. Sorrow turned his head, following the young charver as it alighted on his back, tucked between the dragon's wings. Chirruping loudly, Dreamer started to scratch at a scale. From under the greyness, streaks of shining silver were exposed. Elissa stared at them and resolutely raised her chin to study Sorrow's grey eyes. They were like clouds reflected on the surface of the sea, swirling, in constant motion. So very unlike Hope's still blackness.

'My name is Elissa. It will be an honour to accompany you to meet Rapture.'

CHAPTER 16

DARIN

I used to love it when the gold-trimmed So'Dal
passed through.
They would often carry small vials, swirling like
a string of gems,
that they would dish out to various occupants of
the village.
I always wanted one of the green ones. They
seemed to sparkle.
A Journey to the Barren Plains

Darin glanced up from his book as Aggi entered the Howler quarters. 'How did it go?'

Aggi looked exhausted. He slumped into a chair and stripped the blood-soaked robe off.

'It's done. He'll probably be okay, as long as the Gardeners keep the wound clean.'

Bones looked up from his book and nodded. 'That's good news. One distraction is removed for her.'

'What will we do once she tracks the awldrin? We can

hardly run along the ground after it. If it's still using the xotryl as a mount, no Skaa-rak will follow it, and none of us have the stamina to chase for long. Even Darin and Star's young legs won't keep them going indefinitely.' Aggi shook his head as he looked across to Darin's room, where Star dozed on his rug, legs twitching as he dreamed.

Darin had spent the last few hours helping Bones, searching old texts for any hint of how they might remove the problems Suriin faced for long enough to use her to good effect. So far, all he'd found were insignificant, small wefts and mentions of combining emotions to do simple jobs, like locking doors and setting alarm wards.

None of it was significant enough, in his opinion, to justify his current book being in the howler collection. There had to be something else that he'd overlooked. Darin looked back at the ward weft; it required only a song weft for the basic version. He scanned the page for the note sequence – that was do-able. The second sequence talked about adding vigilance and a note of emotions you wanted to be warned about. He didn't fully understand the method, but it appeared that they could set a sung ward that would alert you to when someone entered a space with aggressive intent. The added emotion aspect made sense. It would be annoying if your ward went off every time someone dropped by for a friendly chat.

Darin picked up the whistle and took the book into his room. He sat on the bed and tried to play the tune. It wasn't very melodic.

'What's that racket?' Chase shouted.

Being used to Tian's beautiful music must make this sound awful. If it sounded bad to his ears, he could only imagine how it must pain Chase. Darin stood and pushed his magic through the weft, aiming it at the floor of his doorway.

'Can someone come here?' he called. 'I want to test something.'

'If I do, will you stop playing that awful noise?' Chase appeared round the edge of the door. 'What do you need?'

'I need you to walk into the room.'

Chase walked into Darin's room.

'That's odd. I'm sure I did it right.'

'What are you trying to do?' Chase leant over the page and read it. 'It says you'll be alerted through the tug on your vigilance thread and emotion bank. What on Lieus does that mean?'

Darin could only shrug. 'Try again. I'll see if I can feel anything. I guess I just thought it would make a noise or something. But then, it wouldn't be a secret intruder alert. We need Suriin capable, or some other Soul Anchor working alongside us if we're going to use most of this stuff.'

'We can't use another Soul Anchor right now. But if we can work out how to set this up so we can receive the message, then I'll be able to protect Tian – once I know where he is.' Chase's face took on a shade of anguish – an extra wrinkle here, a tense muscle there. They still hadn't made contact, then.

'When Tian is safe, I'm sure he'll get in touch.'

'I don't care how much he hates it. I feel like dragging him back here until this is over.' Chase took a shuddering breath, then bent back over the book again. 'Maybe there's a way the hounds can detect the trap – or help us set it.'

'Sure, tell me how to communicate fear.' Darin looked back at the book. No doubt a Soul Anchor could do it, but the Howlers certainly couldn't. He turned the page and kept reading, certain there must still be something significant in the book. A reason for it to be down here beyond the mix of song wefts and emotion. That in itself was banned, but a few small traps and snares wouldn't do a lot.

Light crossed the floor as they read. Silence in the howler quarters was unusual; no laughter or cheery exclamations of victory at stones. Instead, the quiet was punctuated by an occasional clatter from the galley and the turning of pages. Darin stretched and put the book down, still none the wiser as to how it would help them.

A whine came from the room next door – Sandy. Darin knew that sound. Chase was trying to dream walk. Sandy got very distressed when he did it, much like he had that first time Darin saw it in Kira's house.

The whimpering stopped as Chase moved around. 'I don't like this one bit. I want to head to Dal and see what's going on.'

'Not without weapons and armour for the hounds.' Darin left his room and leant on Chase's door frame.

Chase looked up at him. Wrinkles of frustration grooved his forehead, and his hand shook.

'Not once in all our lives have I been unable to meet him at an arranged time. Not once, ever.' He drew a shuddering breath. 'How long before Conor has the armour, do you think?'

'I'm sorry, Chase. I have no idea. We can ask him to hurry, but I need to practise with those throwing rings so I have better control over them. We still haven't found magic that will help us yet either. All I've found are charms and alarms. Nothing like the huge, powerful streams of magic the old pictures show.'

'No, and you won't be able to use them anyway. We can access the basics, make lost potions, weapons, even. But pure magic – we need a Soul Anchor for that.' Bones lifted his head. 'I think I might have found you some explosives. But we'll need a selection of plants to create them that we haven't got here yet.

With no glass balls, as the gardeners prefer for flash bombs, we may have to find an alternative method of delivery for them.'

Bones put the book down, sympathy etched in his wrinkled features. 'Chase, give us a couple of days, then you can leave. By then, we may have a location for the awldrin, you could have the hounds protected, and I may have found a weapon to help you bring Tian safely back. Someone needs to get hold of Gwynn and either Conor or the Master of Builders. Aggi, could you drop by the main dining hall and get them? You're headed back out to check on your patient, I'm assuming.'

'I wasn't going to,' Aggi muttered. 'But if we need an excuse to get the others in here, then I can. We might need to bring them in another way, though. They are too conspicuous without dragon bone to slip through the main door.'

'Armoury is a bit far and will get busy if news gets out,' Chase said. 'But, unless you have a better idea?'

'Not really. The back door is too far away, although less busy. There's no way they can just pop in and out quickly.'

'What about a pre-arranged meeting in the Master's singing chamber?' Darin suggested. 'It worked before.'

Aggi didn't respond at first. They all waited as he weighed up the other options. 'Agreed. I'll tell them to be there after breakfast tomorrow.'

That worked – Darin could eat, then head over to see his friend. He wondered if Conor knew where to find a training dummy. He really needed to be able to throw more accurately. Two days of practise wouldn't be enough to take down any xotryl they came across, but if he could wound one, it would help. They were big targets – he had a good chance.

He waited in the singing chamber early next morning. Bones had stayed up all night, searching through the texts to find something to help. As a result, Darin carried a small list of plants for Gwynn to collect. He'd added the ones for more healing drafts too. There was no way he was taking Star back into danger without both armour and a pre-ground potion or two of dragon bone – if the rest of the pack would let them. With only two active moonhounds in the pack right now, they were crucial.

Star had saved him; Darin owed his life to his hound. He reached out to Star, sending affection through their bond. Star replied *[chewing bone]*. He held back a laugh. Some things didn't change. He did wonder where Fall got all his supplies from, though. Even hidden kitchens needed real ingredients.

Conor and Gwynn talked quietly as they arrived.

Gwynn entered first. 'Hi, we came.'

'I see that.'

Conor rolled his eyes at Darin and dropped onto a stool. 'What do you need?'

'Gwynn to get these.' He handed over the list of plants. 'It's urgent. Don't let anyone know you're collecting these. And be careful with this one.' He pointed at the one near the bottom of the list. 'Try not to let anyone see you collecting *Scarlet terroris* – not even your sister.'

'With a name like that, I'm not surprised you want it kept secret.' Gwyn tucked the list in his bag.

'Thank you, Gwynn. Conor, do you remember I mentioned Tian when I told you about the trip to Edgelands?'

Conor nodded.

'He's missing, and Chase is going spare. I've not seen him so restless before. We need to go search for him. We can't seem to make contact with Dal, so it combines with what we already needed to do. But after last time and with the added complication of the awldrin ...' He tried not to look at Gwynn or cast any blame or assertions. 'I could really use that armour for Star and Sandy.'

'Darin, it's only been a day or two! I can't make stuff like that so fast.'

Darin swallowed. He knew it had been a slim chance, but he'd had to try. 'How much longer will it take?' He didn't want to push, but he needed to.

'It's tougher than any material I have available, bar metals. I can't make anything as good as that right now. Once I have the material, it needs treating with magic, I suspect. I don't know where to start – or who to ask without arousing suspicion.' Conor shrugged. 'I can make you something temporary, but it would only be boiled faat hide. I have heaps of that. It won't be perfect, but I can hammer some eyelets into it and use light chains to link the pieces so they flex. If I don't get interrupted, I can have two sets ready by tomorrow. They won't be like the ones you showed me and won't stop a sword, but they might deflect a glancing blade. I can keep working on the final set, though. Even when the awldrin is defeated, you will need them as protection against xotryl.'

Darin rubbed his face, covering his eyes for a moment to compose himself. It would have to do. 'Thank you. I'll let the others know about the need for magic. We need to look harder.'

'How soon do you need the herbs?' Gwynn asked.

'As soon as you can get them. Leave them with whoever is on the steam lift lever please.'

'Sure. And you don't want me to mention this to my sister – why?'

'We're trying to find a way to help her, but right now, we need her to focus on regaining some degree of control and getting better, if possible. We need her' – he gestured at Conor – 'we need magic as well as training, and she's no good to man nor hound if she keeps throwing up every time she tries to use her magic. If she can try to track the awldrin, give us an idea of where it is, that would be great.'

'So you can use her?'

Darin shook his head. 'So she helps everyone. She already knows we exist, and all the hidden magic we have access to requires a Soul Anchor, not a Howler.'

Gwynn positively bristled. 'She's not your pet.'

Conor put a restraining arm on Gwynn, keeping him in his seat. 'No, but she did – unintentionally – cause this situation. I'm sure she wants to help put it right.'

Gwynn shrugged Conor's arm off and took a step away from them both. 'It's just a lot to take in, and I need her to be okay.'

'We're working on it.' Darin offered a smile. 'Try to find out where the awldrin is. If she can figure out a way to tell us without having to go walking around the continent searching for it, constantly chasing a flying creature, that would be ideal. Conor, do you think you could arrange for a training dummy to be put in the armoury? I need something for target practise.'

'I'll see what I can do. You're lousy with a spear. You keep talking like an expert warrior now, but I've sparred with you. Almost every Collective is better trained than you and could out-fight you with their eyes closed. What are you planning to use against a mounted enemy?'

'Thanks for the confidence.' Darin sighed. To some extent, Conor was right. But he had Star and equipment the Collective didn't. 'If we could just send them out without exposing their true capabilities, without outing them as warriors instead of travelling healers and wisemen – without throwing ourselves at the mercy of a society that has forgotten we exist outside of Dal, sure, that would be great. But we can't.

'If we upset the balance of what folk outside this castle –

outside our society – believe, it could destabilise Caldera. What if they get caught? If the xotryl start to take down more of them? Who's left to defend the palace if it all goes to flames?' Darin kicked his foot at the ground. 'Sorry, I'm just frustrated. We're trying to do this with the least lives lost to minimise upset for everyone. There simply isn't enough dragon bone to cure every Collective that wants to prove himself.

'Solving problems that shouldn't exist is our job. The Watcher charged the Howlers with protecting the So'Dal from themselves. If they could re-access the power, the spells we have … It might not be pretty. I'm sure you can think of a few people, without even trying hard, who you'd not like to see with that kind of power?'

Darin slumped onto a stool. 'Anyway, you know the blunted fair throwing rings? The ones you slice a pole with to win a prize? There's something like those but sharp enough to cut through something far more substantial.'

Conor grimaced. 'You have access to the kind of magic I've read about in the old stories, and you're throwing rings at the xotryl? You'd have to throw a long way. Are you sure you can do it?'

'We can't use the magic yet. We're working on it, but it will take time – something we don't have enough of. That's why I need a target.' He laughed. 'As you've pointed out, there's no point in trying to use my staff on something flying. If I'm as accurate with these balanced weapons as oddly weighted fair ones, I should be able to do some serious damage. Once we ground the xotryl, it puts us on a more even footing, and every xotryl we ground reduces the awldrin's resources.'

'I'll see what I can do.'

Voices carried along the passageway outside. It was the Master and someone else.

'Go,' Darin whispered. 'I'm sure you can come up with a reason to be here.'

He blew his whistle to activate the dragon bone and pushed himself back against the furthest wall from any light, hoping desperately that he wouldn't have to sit through an entire lesson.

Conor walked toward the door, nudging Gwynn to distract him from Darin's vanishing. 'So, this is one of the training rooms for the Master,' he said loudly. 'I'm sure that he will be in touch soon to begin your singing lessons. I hear lots of people in the palace take advantage of his tuition. Where would you like to see next?'

Gwynn visibly panicked, and Conor nudged at him to speak.

'I think I'd like to meet more of the moonhounds, if that's possible? I think my sister might be out there, and Aslin asked me to take Fluffy some food.'

'We'll go and ask Lea. The Master of Hounds is away at present, and she's in charge. Let's go via the main hall for a bone.'

They walked through the doorway. Darin saw the smooth steps of Conor and the hesitancy in Gwynn's movements as the Master reached the door at the same time.

'Good morning. I don't usually encounter people near my training room.' It was a question as much as a statement.

Conor bowed. 'Greetings, Master. I was just showing young Gwynn around. He needed a walk and some company after yesterday.'

'I understand the operation was a success.'

Darin couldn't see Gwynn anymore or hear the mumbled response. The Master watched them go with a furrowed brow before turning to his companion and entering the room.

'I don't know why they were in here. I apologise, Hal. I

thought we would get some privacy, but it appears that I wasn't the only one.'

Hal sank onto a stool as Darin flattened himself even tighter against the wall.

'Now, what was it you wanted to talk to me about?'

'Something is wrong in Dal. We've always had a very loose liaison with the So'Dal there, but we've heard nothing from them for days, and no one can get through to them.'

The Master sighed. 'Loose is being generous. It's a long way round to them. A journey will take tides and tides and involve crossing the Surface. But they are so close to the Edgelands, it's likely they are facing bigger problems than anywhere else.'

Hal nodded. 'I agree. But if it's got worse there, it's, at least, partly contained. The distance to check on them is the problem. It may be a long journey by Skaa-rak or foot, but it's not far for anything with wings. A big issue there could soon be an issue for us. It's a journey I am reluctant to send anyone else on, but if I could be allowed the garant?'

'Why not ask Nissa? What does she say?'

'She rolls her eyes and says that Dal is of no consequence. That they choose to remain apart from the rest of Caldera, and that if they need help, they will ask for it. She's more concerned with xotryl hunting the faat in the South and food supplies. As much as I love Nissa, none of us are without our faults. She's from the South, and therefore her worries lean that way. But I just can't shift this unease.'

'Give me a few days. I'll see what I can do for you. Anything else?'

'Hmm, maybe. It might be nothing, though.' Hal stood. Darin had seen that expression a hundred times or more. The topic he was about to bring up was his real concern.

'None of the Collective has seen Darin and the Master of

Hounds. They should have reached Darkholt or Firstal – even if they took things very slowly.'

'No one?'

Hal shook his head and spread his arms wide. 'He's a strong young man, but very inexperienced. He can hold his own in a staff fight, but it appears he forgot to reclaim it on his way out. It's still at the town gates. Something isn't right. We've not had reports of any attacks or an increase in crime on the holloways have we?'

'Not that I've heard of.' The Master walked past so close Darin held his breath. If he reached out – if he touched the wall – Darin would be found.

Listening to them discuss him was unsettling. He needed to let the Howlers know. The awldrin may not be news yet, but Hal knew something was up.

'I'm sure they will be okay. The Master of Hounds may be frail, but he knows his way around. You know this, Hal. It's just because Darin was your collection that you've got more attention on him than on other people's apprentice journeys. The Master of Hounds is probably keeping them out of sight. A male bonded to a hound is not common – it would attract attention.'

Hal shrugged. 'I can't shake the feeling that something isn't right.'

The Master walked back toward the door. 'Jaer is fond of him, isn't he?'

Hal laughed. 'Obsessed is more like it. Darin and Star have opened a world of possibilities for Jaer's imagination.'

'Did you want to try to reach a few more waypoints they might have passed? I can watch you while you attempt to make contact?'

Hal lost some tension in his shoulders as he smiled. 'Thank you. The dream paths grow dangerous, and it's not safe to travel unattended at present. Something dark lurks at their edges. Nissa thinks I'm overreacting, and I don't want to worry Jaer. If we could come back here tonight, when I have a chance of making contact, I'd be grateful.'

'I'll meet you here later.'

Hal reached out to shake the Master's hand. 'Thank you. I am sorry for the secrecy. I just don't want to inspire panic if it's nothing. One xotryl attacking So'Dal is an accident. Others going missing, or multiple attacks, would be more. It's something significant that people won't be able to ignore.'

Hal gestured to the door, and the Master led the way out. Darin edged around the walls, waiting for them to be safely out of sight before he ran. There would be no chance of keeping the Collective out of things if Hal started to investigate – or worse, got the garant.

CHAPTER 17

SURIIN

Death is a breaker of bindings, a render of souls.
The ones left behind will shatter before they can
rebuild.
Some will never recover. Lives so entwined
cannot be rewoven with a new set of
threads.
The Bond of Three

Suriin turned her back on Aslin's room and the comfort of her brother's presence with a heavy heart. He needed sleep, and as much as she wanted to curl up in a ball and cry, she needed to look as though everything in her life was normal. Fluffy walked close, almost glued to her leg.

She found herself headed toward the kitchens. It would be good to see Fresna and find out if she could try to do her job or something in the kitchens that was routine. Yes, work was a good idea, a chance to lose herself in other concerns for a short while. At some point, Suriin would have to go through the motions of returning to her normal routine, so why not now? If her hands were busy, maybe it would give her a chance to think about ways to get her crystal back.

She paused at the kitchen door with Fluffy still in reach. Moonhounds wouldn't be allowed in the kitchen, and Fluffy even less so, since they weren't bonded. Their connection was purely through love and family – and possibly whatever her mother was telling Fluffy, if she lived. Lea was certain she did. Suriin had to have hope.

'Oh.'

Suriin stared at her furry companion with fresh eyes. If moonhounds communicated in pictures, was her mother using Fluffy as eyes? She crouched down and let herself sink into the pools of kindness.

'Hi, Mum. I'm okay.'

'Suriin, are you sure about that?' Chef stood with his hands resting on his hips, his head tilted to one side. 'You can't bring that hound in here, even if you try to pretend she's your mother.'

'Suriin!' Fresna ran across the kitchen. 'I've been so worried. Where have you been? What happened to you? You look awful. Doesn't she, Chef? Should you be here?'

'I want to help, and I wanted to see you.' Suriin offered a smile.

'The hound stays outside,' Chef grumbled.

'Yes, Chef.' Suriin sent *[Fluffy sat at the door. Suriin in the kitchen, in Fluffy's sight]*. Fluffy sat.

'It's fruit candies.' Fresna pointed at all the assorted fruits lined up alongside the fragrant vat of boiling, sweet liquid.

'Perfect.' Suriin started to stab the rainbow of fruits onto skewers before dipping them in the candy sauce. Its perfume was sweet and tart at the same time. She lifted them back out and span the skewer as fast as she could, creating a cloud of thin, crunchy fibres around each fruit.

The work was fast and left no room for error. They dipped and span until the entire pile was done, the glistening treats plated onto large glass plates. Suriin appreciated the break from her whirling thoughts. This had been a good idea.

'I have a few things I need to work out because of the last few days, some tasks I need to attend to urgently,' she said loudly enough to carry across the kitchen as she washed her hands. 'I hope I can still do my normal work the rest of the time, Chef?'

He nodded. 'For now. Aslin muttered something cryptic about you needing time to work on a project. Let me know when it will be so we can get someone else in on those days.'

'Yes, Chef. Fresna, will you walk back with me?'

She frowned. 'Don't I usually?' Fresna reached for two candies. 'Come on, then. I want to know all about this secret project.' She winked and crunched into one of the candies as she handed Suriin the other.

The moment they left the kitchen, Fluffy attached herself to Suriin, and she buried her hand deeply in the moonhound's fur. She'd managed the mental burden by being distracted and busy, which was good to know, but when her healing potion's effect wore off, she knew it would be a different matter. They crunched at their treats, and Suriin enjoyed every sweet melting moment and burst of juice that followed as she broke the candy shell.

'So...' Fresna nudged her. 'When are you going to tell me what happened to you? I was worried.'

Suriin looked around, checking they were alone, then whispered. 'I lost my crystal.'

Fresna's eyes widened. 'And you're still standing? I take it you found it again?'

Suriin shook her head. 'I'm just taking a lot of healing drafts

– at Aslin's suggestion. The big project is that I have to recover it.'

'Surely, that's easy. Stop taking the potion, and we'll walk in the direction that makes you feel better until we find it? Can you feel any pull to where you've lost it?'

Suriin shook her head. 'It's in the pouch still. But I think it's moving.'

'Someone has found it and they're returning it?' Fresna's hope-filled words didn't match her demeanour.

'No, that's the thing ... it's getting further away.'

'Watcher's flaming wings. You need to get after it with some Witnesses and reclaim it, all without raising suspicion as to its importance.' She visibly drooped. 'You must be feeling rotten. What awful luck. Where did you lose it?'

'That's just the thing – I don't remember. Maybe it was simply pick pocketed? I just knew I felt awful, then I got lost until Gwynn tracked me.'

Fresna nodded. 'We could ask the guards which direction you came back from?'

'I'm not sure that helps, really.' Suriin tried to swallow her panic. The guards would know she'd never left – what if Aslin had already asked them? She tried not to grip Fluffy's fur in panic. 'I feel as though maybe it's left Redpike already. I'm going to have to find a way to function, then hunt it down.'

Bitter tears stung her eyes as she reached her room. 'I was here so early, from an accident that was my fault, and now ... now I can't carry on my training. Fresna, maybe I'm just not meant to be a Soul Anchor. I'm not a good enough person. I've caused pain to my family ... they're apart and lost, missing limbs and each other. Then, I lose my crystal. The one thing I have wanted more than anything since I was a child, I can't do. All because of a lack of care.'

There was truth enough in her feelings, and Fresna held her

in a hug as she sobbed. Fluffy licked at her hand, and for a moment, the thought cut through her sorrow once again that maybe her mother was using Fluffy's eyes. She was grateful that Fluffy hadn't been able to show why or how she'd got into the cell.

She pushed back from Fresna and wiped her face. 'I think maybe I need some sleep.'

'I think you do too. I'll see if I can think of a way to help you. See you in the morning.' Suriin managed a small smile before she and Fluffy entered her room. She flopped on the bed as the hound sat watching.

Was her mother able to see Fluffy's visions? She knew it wasn't as though she saw directly with Fluffy's eyes – her mother had explained that much. Suriin's gaze landed on her notebook.

She slid from the bed to the floor, reached for *Battle Strategies of the Awldrin*, and opened it up on the image of the painting. Natke sat astride a green xotryl, and the Anchor pushed her back with a stream of magic. Suriin hunted for her map, but it wasn't there. It must have been in her bag, and she had a feeling Gwynn still had that.

A few moments later, Suriin had drawn a sketch of the cell with Natke in it. She hoped that, with what Fluffy had actually seen, she'd be giving the extra information to explain what had happened. A puzzle she trusted her mother to solve.

As she prepared herself, she realised that she'd accepted Lea's explanation after all. She could see no sadness in Fluffy's eyes, only the intelligence and kindness she'd grown up with.

Suriin gathered her visual props and tried to send a picture of herself holding the books, but showing her mother, not Fluffy.

She had no way of knowing whether Fluffy understood her, but she decided to try anyway. Her mother needed warning, wherever she'd gone, that there was an awldrin hunting and killing Soul Anchors.

Suriin held up the book first, pointing at Natke. She sat for a while in front of Fluffy and again tried to send *[Suriin showing her mother the image]*. Then, she held up the first drawing of Natke sat at the back of the cell – much as she'd first found her – followed by a very rough sketch of the awldrin holding a jagged shard with a dead woman at her feet. She'd done all she could think of to warn her mother.

She sat and waited, hoping for some kind of acknowledgement to let her know if Fluffy had understood, but the hound did nothing special.

Suriin sighed. She was being ridiculous. It was one thing sending Fluffy an image, but she had no idea how much of what she tried to send ever got through, or if it was simply her emotions that Fluffy responded to. She dragged herself back onto to her bed and crawled under the covers. Fluffy jumped up and stretched out. There wasn't much room for them both, but Suriin was grateful for the closeness of the moonhound as she settled back onto her pillow.

She should get changed and pick up the laundry too; her favourite dress would be ready by now. Suriin felt the tension drop away as her mind began to wander. Her bed had never felt so soft, so perfectly fitting. Her muscles lost their tension and her thoughts their grip on wakefulness. She fell asleep, secure in Fluffy's blanketing presence.

Panic seized her as she saw the bars and the tiny stream. The impassable gate, once again, locked. She couldn't be back. Couldn't be dream walking. Fluffy was there. Her true dream tormented her – replaying the moments of Natke's release. Moonhounds and unfamiliar faces paraded past, some with limbs missing, their severed stumps poured with blood. Her father's face appeared, contorted into a snarl filled with bitterness and hate. He opened his mouth to speak. As Suriin recoiled, ready for a verbal attack such as she had never received from him, a soft blanket of warmth smothered the images away, cutting her off from the terrors and visions of her traumatised mind. Sleepily, Suriin reached out and wrapped her arms around the hound before settling into a deeper, and this time dreamless, sleep.

⌒ ⚹ ☾ ✣ ◉

She awoke to a banging on her door and half fell out of bed to stumble to open it.

'I'm coming!'

Fresna stood outside with her bag of laundry. 'I thought that this was a small thing I could do to make you feel a bit better.' She thrust it at Suriin. 'I'll wait outside.'

Suriin emptied the contents onto her bed and held up her favourite dress. At least she had something nice to start the day. She slipped into it and glanced up at her scarf for a moment. With no plans to leave the palace, it could stay there. Maybe next time at the market, she could treat herself to a new one.

Suriin caught herself. Next time? She wasn't going anywhere anytime soon. Fluffy stretched her front legs out and raised her tail before leaping from the bed. Suriin glanced at the mirror and was pleased to see that she looked slightly less exhausted than yesterday. Before she joined Fresna, she checked everything was hidden. Her drawings from last night rested on the table, so she tucked them under her mattress, then wrestled her hair into a braid and opened the door.

Fresna looked her up and down. 'That's more like you.' She linked arms with Suriin, and they headed to the kitchen, with Fluffy following close behind.

Suriin's ribs were aching, and as lovely as Fresna was, her

wrist against the bruised or broken bones was increasingly painful. Suriin didn't want to let her know, so she smiled and chatted as they strolled to the kitchens. She had to get through the morning session, then she could see Aslin and Gwynn. She really wanted to catch up with the others too.

'Shouldn't Fluffy go to the hound paddocks while we work?' Fresna looked at the silently padding moonhound. 'Chef isn't going to like it every session, you know, hygiene and everything.'

'Fluffy helps me. You know how you feel when you're too far away from your crystal? She helps that feeling be less. I don't really understand it, but it's a bit like the way they dream shield. She's looked after me my whole life.'

'Aslin's hound has been with her longer than you've been alive, and she's still not allowed her in the dining hall,' Fresna replied. 'Even Sulki isn't allowed in.'

She was right. But Suriin wasn't sure how well she would cope – badly, she suspected. 'Without her nearby, I might vomit,' she confessed.

'How far away is your crystal now?'

Suriin decided not to answer – or to investigate. She'd just try to exist in a magic-free space for an hour or so. Then Gwynn might have to get her another potion, or Aslin ... or ...

She sighed. 'Hopefully, he'll let Fluffy sit outside this morning. After that, I'll see what I can sort out.'

Chef stared at Fluffy as they arrived, but much as she had the previous night, the moonhound stayed outside the door while Suriin worked. They made the flatcakes and stirred the brose; she even thought she might fancy a plate of them. Then, as they neared the end of the morning shift, something changed, and she started to feel clammy. Suriin dropped a plate. Darkness closed on her vision.

Maybe she should sit. The floor looked a good place, less

distance to fall. She slid down the counter, seeing glimpses of worried faces as her view closed in.

She could hear calls for help. The crystal tugged at her again. Were the calls from the kitchen, or from the crystal, far away?

She was moving, picked up and carried. Which part of her?

Even more unmoored, Suriin fell into confusion.

The leather bag surrounded her.

Hands held her.

A hound licked her.

The light hit her from the top of the bag.

The hound licked her.

She could do little but cry. So did the person she could hear. Cries for help – for mercy.

More blood.

Why was she playing at normality when people were dying? Someone opened her mouth. A cool liquid was poured in. Gentle hands sent a flood of serenity into her, a calming wash of hope. Suriin opened her eyes.

'If I'd have known you would try to go back to work, so soon after' – Aslin gestured expansively – 'everything, I would have discouraged you for at least another day.' She tried to support Suriin, reached out, and brushed against her ribs. Suriin gritted her teeth to resist calling out in pain.

'I think I need fresh air,' she muttered.

Fresna wasn't there. Suriin looked around to see her friend back at their workstation, alone but casting worried glances in her direction. Suriin waved. 'I'll be okay. I just need some air.'

Fresna frowned but didn't argue as Aslin helped Suriin to her feet. 'Fluffy will need to go out to the paddocks for a bit. Why don't you take her over? I'll send Gwynn down shortly.'

She'd wanted to see that old hound, Swift, again. They

should spend some time walking, two broken creatures together.

Suriin used Fluffy to push herself up. 'Thank you, Aslin. That sounds like a great idea.' She needed to feel a bit better before she went to see her father. Hopefully, they'd have allowed him to wake by now, and she'd face the reality of his feelings, not the nightmare of last night. She shuddered. Aslin paused in her stride.

'Are you okay? Am I walking too fast?'

'No, I had a bit of a nightmare, that's all. I just remembered it.'

'It's a shame you don't have a bonded hound. Fluffy can only do so much for you,' Aslin said. 'But there's no choosing for a while, and you are nowhere near ready. The Anchor wouldn't let you even try without your crystal.'

Suriin struggled across the courtyard, feeling weak. She'd left the hall without breakfast. Hunger gnawed at her every step.

'I didn't eat,' she mumbled.

'I'll get Gwynn to bring you something. You should really have taken Fluffy to the hound paddocks before breakfast. It's not kind to ask her to wait. I know you aren't yourself, but you need to take better care of her, as she can't tell you things.'

They passed under the arch, and Aslin steered her to a sunny patch of grass. It looked inviting, and Suriin sat on it gratefully, running her fingers through the grass. Fluffy ran off as soon as her paws touched grass to relieve herself, and Suriin felt ashamed that she hadn't considered Fluffy sooner as she ran and played with a group of other hounds.

'I have lessons now.' Aslin pursed her lips. 'I'm sorry, Suriin. If I could work out a way for you to continue your studies, I would. Instead, I suggest you spend this morning's lesson time in trying to pinpoint where you think your crystal might be, so you can prepare to recover it. You look a better colour now, although that might be the healing I gave you.'

She patted Suriin on the head, much like Suriin would pat Fluffy, and left her sat in the grass.

A wet nose nudged at her as she watched the youngsters playing and Fluffy running laps of the field, just like she used to at Golden. Suriin reached out absently to stroke the moonhound sat alongside her. The rough coat and protruding bones told her it was probably Swift without looking. She didn't turn her head, but kept stroking the hound gently. The spine and finger-deep rib gaps were covered by the thinnest layer of flesh. Suriin heard a tail thump as she scratched behind Swift's ear.

Very slowly, she turned her head to face the hound. Dark eyes peered down at her from sunken sockets. She had a knot of fur under her ear flap, and Suriin tried to ease it out. Swift lay alongside her, as close as she could get. Suriin sent a picture of her walking with Swift. After all, she'd sent that as her promise before.

[Suriin sat in the grass with Swift lying next to her, but healthy] overlaid her vision. It was a little like her crystal vision. She felt it as much as she saw it, but the actual image was much clearer.

[Swift eating a big hunk of meat] Lea had said she didn't want to eat. Amidst all the chaos she had caused, she could help this one creature.

[Swift eating the meat]

Suriin looked around her in desperation for Lea, or anyone else. She couldn't leave Swift now, not once she'd agreed to eat. Someone was coming out of a Skaa-rak stall.

'Hi, can you fetch someone? I need Lea, please,' she called.

'Is that Swift?' the man asked as he squinted across at her.

'Yes, please get Lea.' He nodded and walked off at slightly less than a jog.

⌒ ⋏ ◖ ♻ ◉

What felt like ages later, but Suriin realised was probably far less, Lea ran toward them until she was in calling distance. Suriin kept stroking Swift and trying to keep her alongside.

'What's wrong with her? Has the lump burst?' Lea approached slowly as she drew close. Swift didn't flinch.

'No, but she would like to eat some meat. She *sent* it to me.'

'Then meat she will have. Hold on ... She sent it to you?'

Suriin nodded. 'I was surprised too. I thought they only send when they've bonded, and you said she'd already done that.'

Lea frowned. 'Try something for me? Ask her to let me look at her lump.'

[Lea looking at the lump on Swift's side]

Swift thumped her tail and re-sent the image of eating meat.

'If you get her the meat, I think she'll let you look at it.' Suriin laughed. She liked the older hound.

'Suriin, if you can have a conversation with her, you realise what it means?' Lea asked. 'She's reassigned her bond to you.'

Suriin stroked Swift and felt gratitude flood through her. It was stronger than any link she'd had with Fluffy, that was certain. It was amazing.

'Don't you dare hurt her.' Lea leant in close, her intense stare fiercely protective.

Maybe Swift could feel how broken and lost Suriin was too. She'd dreamed of a young pup to train – a small fuzzy youngster. But then, nothing she'd imagined had happened quite as she'd planned, hoped, or dreamed. This hound needed her as much as she needed the support.

'I promise, I won't. I think we were supposed to find each other.' Suriin stroked Swift, and a gentle affection passed through to her, mixed with a lot of hunger. 'I really do think she wants food, though.'

'Stay there. I'll be back soon.'

Lea ran to the main hut and returned a few minutes later with a slab of meat. She placed it in front of Swift. 'I've never seen her eat more than a mouthful.' Swift wagged and bent her head to tear chunks off it. 'You're right. She was ready to eat.'

Lea leant down to check the lump, and Swift paused with a mouthful for a second. They all tensed, a frozen moment of potential, a turning point met. Then Swift turned back to her food, letting Lea stroke the lump.

'Welcome to the pack.' Lea smiled and rose, leaving them alone in the grass.

Her own moonhound.

Chapter 18

Elissa

Captain's log, **Cloudsailor**

Elissa followed Sorrow through the huge doors. The walls appeared so far away that she could barely make them out, yet somehow the doors stood clear, solid, and proud. She walked behind Sorrow as they passed the Watcher's bones, trailing her hand across part of his tail in passing.

The Watcher, on whose command her people were stranded

on Tebein. Emotions warred inside her, and she paused to look at his remains.

'He did it because he cared, so both your species were spared.' Sorrow watched her as she struggled.

'He doomed us.'

Sorrow shook his head slowly. 'Your species is more than those on Tebein. It is the awldrin who truly suffered the pain of his campaign.'

He pushed the door open and gestured for her to follow. She reached out to the bones once more. 'I will try to fix what you broke,' she whispered.

A wall of heat hit her as she reached the door. She'd never experienced anything like it; even in Canicule it rarely reached this sort of level. The air felt heavy, and she was sweating before they reached the outer wall. The cobbled courtyard she stepped into was ringed with huge walls, enclosing enough space to contain her whole sericlave's population and more. And yet, the width of the courtyard was considerably smaller than the size of the hall had led her to expect. Something about the inside made her feel utterly tiny.

Elissa followed Sorrow into the strange light of Mythos. To her right was brightness, and no doubt more heat, stretching as far as she could see. But on her left, a dark line stretched across the entire horizon. Dusk approached.

'Is it about to get dark? Should we stay in the enclosure until morning?'

'The dusk is forever. The sun sets here never.'

'What about beyond the dusk?'

'Beyond the dusk is the Everdark. Plant-light is the only spark.'

Elissa frowned. 'Sorrow, it's just us now. You can't honestly tell me you speak in rhyme all the time? You must struggle to say what you need to sometimes. And it must get pretty tiring when your words don't actually rhyme.'

Sorrow snorted and turned away from her. He gestured toward a dip in the wall with his snout.

'Use your tiny flare. Get us out there.'

'Fine.' Elissa searched the floor for pebbles. There was nothing to throw. She imagined herself holding a pebble and threw it at the dip. Dreamer flew after the imaginary pebble, looking to see what she'd thrown. Elissa stifled a giggle.

'What do you do? Just push it through,' Sorrow muttered.

'I'm throwing my fire. Just give me a moment, and I'll have it.'

'In an urgent situation, this would be quite a frustration.'

'So would your rhyming be! Stop distracting me,' Elissa retorted, and continued to fling her arm outward over and over. Why wouldn't it work? Dreamer gave up hunting for what she threw and returned to her shoulder. She reached up to stroke him. There had to be an easier way; with time and practise, she needed to stop the pebble-flinging.

Eventually, her arm ached from so much repetition of movement. This was stupid. She flung her arm forward again in frustration, and the flame shot out and licked the bowl in the wall. The stonework directly ahead of them sank into the ground, leaving a gap large enough for even Hope to walk through.

Sorrow waddled past her. 'Come along, don't be slow. We have a long way to go.'

Elissa rolled her eyes and followed Sorrow out into Mythos, toward the dusk line. It should be cooler there – some shade would be great. She glanced back to see the wall rising to close the gap. She needed a landmark, something to help her get home should she need to. On a moon filled with dragons and innumerable other unknown beasts, she wanted – no, needed –

to know her way back. A strange tree with broad scales which overlapped along the length of each branch was the closest distinctive plant to the now closed gap.

'Sorrow, can you give me a moment?' He slowed his pace, and Elissa ran back to the tree. She pulled at the thick green scales, snapping the tips and folding them into themselves along the branch closest to the wall. Sorrow rumbled behind her.

'Don't eat the water-leaf, else your stay here will be very brief.'

'You mean it's poisonous?'

Sorrow nodded slowly. 'To you.'

She might not find this tree easily, but at least she'd tried to leave herself a sign. Maybe Dreamer would help in an emergency. Elissa decided to try planting the idea when she next slept.

She turned to follow Sorrow, checking frequently that she could still see the walls as reassurance. She searched the skies, but didn't see anything of a size large enough to be dragons. The plant life on Mythos was lush and green as they walked through the lit area toward what Sorrow had called the Everdark. Leaves fluttered in as many colours as she knew names for. Makin would love it here. So would Laytha.

Elissa stumbled.

Makin.

She'd never see him again, never get to mourn him surrounded by those who'd known him. None of his family could give him a last farewell. Elissa squeezed her eyes shut to stop the tears and put her head down, trudging through the heat after the drooping dragon. She'd make sure his sacrifice wasn't for nothing. He'd believed in her; she would not let him down.

As they neared the dusk-line, the oppressiveness began to lift, a slight breeze ruffled her hair, and some sort of trilling noise filled her ears. Darkness closed in with every step, the transition shorter than she'd thought it would possibly be. Glowing plants swayed as far as she could see, a rippling of light stretching into the darkness. Heavy scents filled the air, heady, rich, and overwhelming in their intensity. In the gently pulsing light of the plants, small creatures flew from flower to flower, illuminated briefly as they landed on each petal, their iridescent bodies glinting like gems.

'It's beautiful,' she breathed.

Sorrow turned his head. 'Sometimes it's easy to forget the beauty in everyday things. We walk through our lives wearing the blinkers of expectation. Only when something is out of the normal do we notice it. Sometimes, someone takes the blinkers off, and we look up and feel. Only then can we become more than mundane ourselves. I flew over the same tree daily for cycles. Only one day when I was deliberately paying attention did I realise that, for all that time, it had been two trees entwined, and see it for what it truly was – instead of just the path-marker it had become to me. Your eyes see what mine have forgotten.'

'Sorrow, you didn't rhyme that.'

He puffed out a small smoke ring. 'Sometimes poetry takes other forms.'

'How long does it normally take to get to Rapture's cave?'

He turned his head and looked along the dusk line. 'A few days in this direction, if I fly. But with you on foot, it may be much longer.'

Elissa looked him over and didn't remark on the lack of poetic statement. He was much smaller than Hope. His demeanour didn't suggest that he had the energy to carry her, but if they were going to get there in time to beat the awldrin, he needed to be able to.

'When did you last eat?' she asked.

'I don't know. I haven't felt hungry for a long time.'

'Days?'

'Cycles.'

Elissa ran her hand over his scales as they walked. They were rough and coated with muck. He flinched, and she withdrew her hand quickly. He'd still not returned to rhyming, and she didn't mention it. She hoped he was growing more comfortable with her.

'Does it rain much here?' she wondered.

'Yes, but not like on Tebein. It just rains some days, not others,' Sorrow said.

The idea of rain always being a possibility was novel, and Elissa searched the horizon for clouds. If she could keep Sorrow out in the rain, he could get clean. Then it would be one less thing weighing him down. If she could get him to eat, he might be willing to carry her. They didn't have tides of time. She had very limited food herself. Elissa sat, pulled her bag into her lap, and started to unpack. Sorrow narrowed his eyes.

'We can't just stop.'

'And you can't keep going,' Elissa retorted. 'Everyone needs to eat, even you.' She found the dried fish that Andra had packed for her. It still smelt very strange. 'Eat this.' Elissa held it out to Sorrow.

He hung his head. 'I can't. You'll die if you eat most things here. You need it.'

'I don't need it right now.' Elissa held it out closer to his snout, noting with satisfaction the small trail of drool it was stimulating in Sorrow.

'You need it later. I cannot eat your food. It would be rude.'

'And we're back to rhyming.' Elissa dumped the entire contents of her bag on the ground.

'Either you eat my food, you go hunt for your own, or I leave it here, and I die. Which means you failed twice to save the awldrin and all the people on Mythos – because you are too stubborn to eat.'

'You wouldn't do that.'

'Watch me.' Elissa stood up and walked straight toward the darkness, hoping the Watcher's dead eyes had her back and that her hunch was right. It was a stupid move, she knew. Makin would never fall for it, nor would anyone else she knew. But she had to hope that Sorrow, the ancient dragon, was so hungry and uncertain that he would. That he'd only needed a little prod. She kept walking, aiming for a distant light in the darkness – and hoping it wasn't moving.

Behind her, a roar filled the air.

'Fine, you stubborn little meat-sack, I'll go eat. But you come right back here and repack your bags.'

Sorrow shot a thin jet of blue flame skyward and shook out his wings. Flakes of dirt dropped from scales, and his dull grey body shimmered in new places as he took off into the darkness.

Elissa watched him with a smile, then returned to her bag. Sorrow's silhouette was clear against the brightness of the lit sky beyond. She relaxed as she re-packed while Dreamer chirruped happily, his own scales flashing blue.

'You approved of that?' She picked up one of the meat pieces and dusted it off, then broke a small section. Dreamer took it delicately from her fingers and flapped a short distance away to perch on a tall bush. As he ate, he watched her. With no idea how long Sorrow's hunt would take, Elissa chewed on the rest of the dried meat. She was used to starvation, and this much food would last her longer than Andra realised. With her growling stomach appeased, she tied her bag up and lay on her back, staring at the sky. Some things looked similar to the view she was used to, except that Lieus was bigger – closer. She could make out shapes on its surface of green and blue. Where on the planet would their Aulirean Gate be? Was she looking at it now?

She searched the sky for the only home she'd known. From here, Tebein was a blackish disk that caught the light. Ominous and foreboding, but home. Elissa closed her eyes, listening to Dreamer chirp over his food.

It shouldn't be *home*. Not from everything the dragons had said. She wasn't supposed to exist; they were a small sliver of hope, a possibility. The humans of Tebein were expected to die, a sacrifice to the cause. But somehow, they'd survived. She lay there for ages, drifting in and out of sleep, while Dreamer's tiny chirps remained a soothing reassurance that they were alone.

⌒ ⋏ ◖ ✥ ⊙

Warm water drenched her awake as a huge, purple dragon shook their head over her prone form.

'What is a human doing here?' The snout prodded her. Elissa barely dared to breathe as the dragon inhaled deeply. 'You smell funny, little human. You smell of dragon.'

Dreamer flapped down to sit on Elissa's chest, chittering ferociously.

The dragon sat back and tilted their head to one side. 'How interesting that you smell so familiar, and a charver likes you. Even more interesting that you are here, when the gates are closed, at a time when Hope and Regret have vanished. This is very exciting.'

Elissa decided that the dragon didn't appear to pose a threat and moved slowly.

The dragon let out a gentle, 'Ooh.'

'Hello. I'm here with Sorrow. We're trying to do a few things, to put some old mishaps right.'

The dragon's jaw hung open. 'You're here with *Sorrow?* Sorrow hasn't left his cave for hundreds of cycles.'

'He's hunting right now. We're in a bit of a rush, and I need to go speak to Rapture.'

By now, the colours of the dragon's eyes were spinning, and Elissa struggled to hold back a laugh. She was so amused by the dragon's antics that she couldn't resist trying her new trick. She threw her arm away from the dragon and glanced back. They were watching. So she did it again and again until *whoosh*. Her best flame yet.

The dragon almost fell over, then started bouncing around as Elissa had never thought a dragon that size could.

'You are amazing!' the dragon shrilled before they settled down to nudge Elissa. 'Do it again.'

Elissa tried again and got so engrossed in entertaining the new dragon that she didn't hear Sorrow arrive.

'What are you doing?' he asked.

Elissa turned to study Sorrow. He looked a bit fatter. He'd clearly eaten something. A few more of his scales looked muck free.

'The human made fire!'

'Yes, she does that. She's like *Him.*'

'I'm still here!' Elissa said, and both dragons turned toward her.

'Greetings, Still-ere. I'm Amazement.'

Now they were side by side, Elisa could see that Amazement was far bigger than Sorrow. A whole dragon-size bigger. It was clear that Amazement would have been of equal size to the Watcher.

'No, I'm Elissa. I was just saying ... oh, never mind. It's lovely to meet you. Sorrow and I need to get going. I may make fire, but my food supplies won't last forever. Sorrow, do you feel strong enough to carry me now? It would speed things up. Hope has carried me before.'

Amazement looked at Sorrow and shook her head.

'He's just eaten, dragony-human Elissa. He needs to fly slowly and digest that food. But if Hope flew you, then I would like to try that too. It will be a very new experience – almost none of us have done that.'

Sorrow hung his head. 'Even in this, I am not good enough.'

'Enough with the pity, Sorrow. You can carry her tomorrow. Please let me help. I never get to do the important things. This sounds like an important thing.'

Sorrow's tail swished a little as he tilted his head and stared at Amazement. 'You really want to help?'

'Oh, yes! I really do. It's a very exciting thing.'

Sorrow's eyes spun slower, and he swung his head close to Elissa. 'Amazement does get easily distracted. Are you sure you wish to do this thing?'

Elissa reached out to touch Sorrow's snout. 'I do. We need to move fast. The humans we left in Hope's care are relying on us, and so are the awldrin, I suppose.'

'Where will you sit?' Amazement's neck was curled as they studied their own back.

Elissa gestured at the spot between Amazement's tall neck spines. 'There. It worked on Hope, and your spines are bigger, so I should be more secure.'

Amazement flattened their neck to the floor, and Elissa was able to scramble up unaided. The difference in the way Amazement was so willing and excited and Hope's kind but formal acceptance was stark.

'To Rapture,' Amazement sung out and crouched low before launching upward with such force that Elissa had to wrap her arms tightly around the spine. Dreamer fluttered alongside her for a while, eventually tiring and dropping back. Elissa risked a glance behind to see Sorrow, trailing behind them, gather Dreamer up gently.

The land of the dusk line glowed with gentle light, and the further from the Gate Hall they flew, the more the vegetation changed. Tall, fleshy blades of green dominated the ground on the lighter side of the zone, while Elissa's eyes struggled to make out more than an overall glow from the leaves and creatures in the dark side.

They travelled fast as Amazement soared with ease toward their destination. No day or night meant that Elissa had no true concept of how long they'd been flying. Eventually, exhaustion overtook her, and she struggled to stay awake. As she swayed, Amazement continued to fly. Elissa shook her head to clear the fog of sleep.

'Amazement, I need to sleep. On the ground, or I'll fall off.'

Amazement didn't appear to acknowledge her at first, but then Elissa felt them change direction slightly, veering toward the lighter side and descending to a small clearing amongst the huge bladed-plants. On the ground, they were far taller than Elissa. She looked at one closely; it was thick and fleshy.

'Are these safe?' she asked.

'I don't know. They are smelly and squishy, and I do not like the taste. But they won't eat you.' Amazement poked at one with a huge foot. It toppled over to lie flat, and a crack at the base oozed liquid back toward its roots. Elissa prodded it carefully further up the leaf. It felt thick and unlikely to break on its own. It gave a little under her weight as she leant on it.

'I'm going to sleep for a little while. Thank you, Amazement. I need a few hours' rest to be able to hold on for the rest of the way.' She struggled to speak, and the last words were a mumbled mess. Amazement sat on their haunches and stared skyward.

'I'll call the others to you. Sorrow should rest too. Then he can finish his food properly. This has been very exciting and very new. Wait until I tell the others I carried a drag-uman on my back.'

Elissa managed a half smile before sleep claimed her.

CHAPTER 19

SURIIN

Gwynn's familiar footsteps advertised his arrival, slowing as he drew near.

'That's not Fluffy?'

'Nice observation. No, it's not.' Suriin laughed. 'You remember when I wished for adventure all those tides ago?'

Gwynn nodded. 'Yup. Waste of a star, I told you that at the time, although you got far more than you hoped and dragged the rest of us along too.' He reached inside his plant pouch and pulled out a soggy paper bag.

'Breakfast?' he asked, offering it to her. It was still warm. Suriin grabbed the flatcakes and stuffed them in her mouth eagerly. *[Flatcake to Swift]* filled her vision, and she laughed before feeding a small bit to the hound. Swift licked at it curiously, taking it with gentle teeth from her palm.

'Are you going to introduce me?' Gwynn grinned and reached out to stroke Swift. She leapt up and slunk around to Suriin's other side.

'Gwynn, this is Swift.' *[Herself and Gwynn, with her family, in their home.]* Would that communicate that he was a safe person? Suriin couldn't imagine anyone in the palace hurting a moonhound, but Swift's actions implied there was at least one. She resolved to find a way to ask once she had Swift's full trust. Something had hurt her moonhound besides mourning.

Her hound.

'Gwynn, umm ... Swift has chosen to bond with me,' she said.

'Of course she has.' Gwynn reached inside his pocket. 'Sis, I think you might need some more of this.' He offered her a small bottle. 'Darin made it for you before the, well, you know. Before yesterday.' Suriin took the potion gratefully. She'd try to get through a little more of the day without it, now she knew that if things got too bad, she had one on hand.

'Swift really has bonded to me,' Suriin said. 'She's talking in pictures and everything, like mother says Fluffy does.'

Gwynn shook his head. 'You're serious? It won't be good for either of you. She's so old, you have only a short period of her life left. Then you may never bond again.'

'Then we shall make what time we have the best I can make it. She deserves love. Aslin wants me to track the crystal, to find out where it is so I can get it back,' she said through the last mouthful of flatcake. She wiped her finger around the last drips of brose in the bag and sighed happily. 'Those were good.' Fresna really had perfected the lightness of the batter.

'I didn't say she didn't deserve love,' Gwynn retorted. 'Just that it will cause you pain. Aren't you dealing with enough?' He tried to reach for Swift again. She flinched, but didn't run away. 'I can feel all her bones!'

'She hasn't wanted to eat, but she does now. I'll fatten her back up.' Suriin stroked Swift, and affection filled her.

Gwynn sighed. 'It makes no difference what I say, does it? She's chosen you. Do you think you can do what Aslin is asking? Will having Swift help?'

'Kind of.' Suriin checked around her. Seeing no one, she carried on in a low voice. 'I can feel where the crystal is, and also that it now has two more forcefully taken companions.'

'Forcefully taken? You mean she's attacking Soul Anchors? Watcher's flames, we need to tell the Anchor. Or someone who has power – someone who can stop this.'

Suriin shook her head. 'She's killing them, and we can't tell the Anchor yet. My gut says that we should trust these people who helped us already.' Telling the Anchor would mean admitting her role, and she'd lose everything. Darin's comment about people disappearing resurfaced in her memory. What happened to those people?

'Remember, *they* say they can fix this. They might not be many, but if the Anchor found out ...' She gestured around her with her free hand at the hound paddocks and the palace. 'On the way here, our father explained why the So'Dal remain hidden, why we pretend to be administrators. The people of Caldera have forgotten magic is real. They are happy and safe. Would they still trust us if they knew? Would they believe we had never manipulated them? All the bonded moonhounds in the world wouldn't save me from the Anchor's fury, from exposing us. Then what would happen? No doubt, I'd be punished. Then the So'Dal will search the whole complex, in case there are more, and they find these men with their hounds? They find the extra magic.' She understood as she thought it through. 'We broke this entire land with our power once before.'

'And the So'Dal use the lost magic to defeat the problem?' Gwynn shrugged. 'What's so bad about that?'

'Everything the So'Dal hide, everything they stand for. All the hundreds of cycles of hiding would be for nothing. And once the magic is exposed, once the forgotten magic is re-learned, that can't be reversed. I'll support them in their endeavours as long as I can before the truth breaks. Please help me – trust me that it's the right thing to do. No one will suspect us of anything. I didn't plan for this, Gwynn. I just wanted to learn how to access my power, maybe fall in love. Like all my classmates – like anyone headed to the Black Palace.'

Gwynn sat in silence, watching the hounds play. Fluffy led a pack of chasing puppies, her tail wagging.

He stood up and offered her his hand. 'I've been helping them already. Mostly to get Silard's assistance with our father. If you're sure that we should carry on and keep everything secret, then I understand, I suppose. Your wasted wish has caused a lot of trouble so far, and We can't sew our father's arm back on now. What we *can* do is go and see him.'

'You'd better call Fluffy then, unless you plan to leave her here?'

'Are you sure Swift can look out for you?' Gwynn looked at the old hound curiously. 'She looks so sick.'

'She's been mourning,' Suriin replied. 'But she's eating now, and I'll take care of her too.' She put her hand in her pocket, and her fingers closed around the small bottle. She could take it now or, see if Swift could help her first. If Suriin found a map big enough to sit on, then maybe she could pinpoint where her crystal was. There had to be a way to locate it without running around Caldera.

She took Gwynn's hand and let him pull her up. Swift

struggled to her feet alongside her, remaining so close to Suriin that she was afraid they'd fall over each other.

Fluffy trotted over when Gwynn called her and touched noses with Swift. Apparently satisfied with the situation, she walked alongside Gwynn.

⌒ ᚠ ᚲ ⚶ ◉

The pink curtains no longer felt as though they reached for Yorynn. He remained a little pale, but sat upright, propped against a stack of pillows.

'Thank you.'

Suriin stopped as he spoke. 'Thank you? We asked them to cut your arm off!'

'And, by making that decision, saved me. I'd almost lost. My arm was lost days ago – the rest of me would surely have followed. So, again, thank you. The Black Palace suits you. You're making difficult decisions. I understand you two also located the person who did the amputation. It's amazing work, so neat and tidy. Look, I can wiggle it!' He proceeded to wiggle his stump around to show them. Suriin couldn't help the smile that crept across her face.

She leant over the bed and gently embraced him. 'I'm so pleased you're awake.'

'I'm better than awake – I'm alive. Ronin and Orin have said I can probably start to get out and about from tomorrow. It will be nice to get out of this overly ornate room and the stench of my illness, and back to normality. I'd like to thank the person who did it. How's your training going?'

Suriin was thrown by his casual swing to daily routine, as though nothing of significance had happened. 'I, umm, I can't train at the moment. I think someone stole my crystal. Aslin has told me to try to work out where they've gone with it. My only work for today is to visit the library and find a big map so I can recover it and get back to training.'

Gwynn frowned at her. 'Go to the crater garden. If you sit at the pavilion, you're pretty much in Redpike. If your crystal has left Redpike, you could try to work out which direction to search. Surely, they can't have gone far, though.' He was trying to play along, to maintain the story. Suriin swallowed hard. She'd shown those sketches to Fluffy. What if she'd relayed them to her mother and their mother had passed them on? She didn't like the idea of lying to her father.

'Have you felt well enough to try to contact mother yet?' Suriin asked.

Yorynn shrugged. 'Truthfully, I feel as though they put more healing potion in my system than I've ever had in my life, plus the strength of the wefts. Dream walking would have been impossible. Hopefully, I can meet up with Eira later.'

He didn't seem at all confused by Gwynn's presence or that of Fluffy. But he did take a long look at Swift.

'I think I've seen this one before. That spot on her nose is quite distinctive. Why's she with you?'

'She chose me.' Suriin decided not to expand on it for now. Her father accepted it and moved on.

'I agree with Gwynn. You should try the crater garden. I'm sure it hasn't left Redpike, though. You'd have to be very unlucky. Pop back in later with a book, won't you, Gwynn? I'd like a chat with you.' Yorynn yawned and blinked away tiredness. 'I'm still not fully over this stuff, you know.'

'That's hardly a surprise.' Suriin sat on the bed, trying not to rock it.

'It itches where the poison was. I keep trying to scratch it – but there's no arm. It just itches, and I...' He stopped. 'I'm sure I'll get used to it soon.' He beamed at them. 'Another day with my family. I think I need more sleep. Go and do what you need to. I'm not moving rooms today. You know exactly where to find me once you've recovered that crystal. I'm safe, so let's get you back to your classes.' He reached out with his remaining arm to stroke Suriin's face.

Reluctantly, Suriin stood up. 'We'll be back soon, when you're less tired.'

Her father blew her a kiss. 'You can still earn your way. Don't let that slide. It will hold you in good standing later on.'

She almost told him that she wouldn't be allowed to work, that she felt too unwell. But he didn't need to hear that, didn't need to hear about any of it. She nodded instead and headed out into the corridor. As they left, she took one last glance back. Yorynn had slid down his cushions. His eyes were tightly closed, and he gripped his stump with his other hand.

⌒ ⋔ ◖ ✲ ◉

'He's hurting more than he wants us to know,' she whispered as they walked away.

'Of course he is. You're hiding your injuries from him too. We're all just playing, pretending everything is normal.' He stroked Fluffy's head. 'It couldn't be any less normal.'

He was right. She gripped the small bottle with one hand and reached for Swift's fur with the other. The hound sent reassurance through their bond.

Suriin tried to reply *[Crater garden, Suriin sat with Swift]*.

Swift wagged. She stuck closely to Suriin's side as they crossed the courtyard and entered the palace passages toward the steam lift. Hissing steam in the chamber greeted them like an irritated Skaa-rak.

The man on the lift lever nodded at Gwynn as they approached, gesturing for them to board.

'That's a lot of interaction for one of the lift men.' Suriin nudged Gwynn and chuckled. 'I remember I joked to Fresna once that they were always so cloaked and mysterious, they could be hidden awldrin.'

He looked at her with a frown. 'I guess that's not a joke you find funny anymore.'

As soon as the words had left her mouth, Suriin had had the same thought. Hidden awldrin the whole time. Fear grasped hold of her once again; she gripped the railing tighter than usual. Gwynn was right. It didn't feel amusing any more.

On reaching the top, they wandered over to the pavilion. Fluffy bounded away, sniffing and following other hounds' tracks through her nose. *[Play with Fluffy]* Suriin sent to Swift.

[Suriin looking upset, Swift by her side.]

Suriin shrugged and kept walking. If that's what Swift wanted, she'd accept it. They strolled as casually as they could through the pathways, stopping to sniff flowers as they went.

Gwynn looked longingly at the plants to either side of the path, and Suriin chuckled. 'Tell me about them,' she said, and Gwynn started to unfurl his knowledge of the plants, much as a flower unfurls from its bud. He expanded on their uses and life habits, on what they looked like in the winter. He plucked one tiny plant and crushed its leaves for her. It wasn't as astringent as Nothelm, and its fragrance was heady and sweet.

'What's that for?' she asked.

Gwynn blushed. 'It's *Femina gracilis*. It helps with, well, *woman* things.'

'Woman things? You mean bleeds and monthly cycle things? Or not having children type of womanly things? Why on Lieus did you look that one up?'

'It can help people who need support with their bodies not doing what they should,' Gwynn said. 'I looked it up because I think it's important to be able to help everyone, and it smells amazing, so I wanted to know what it was used for. Some people pay for Gardeners to make it into fragrances too.'

They had reached the pavilion now. Suriin circled it, trying to work out where to sit. She decided that facing South Crater's tall palms would help her get oriented.

She sat on the floor, with her head resting against the seat. Once she'd done this, she could take the potion and sleep – stop every step hurting and every swallow from feeling like she might vomit those pancakes back up.

'I'm going to close my eyes and try to get a feel for where it might be. Then, I'll point for you to walk in that direction. Do you think it might work?'

Gwynn shrugged. 'We won't know until we try. Do you think Swift is strong enough to anchor you?'

'She was strong enough to live.'

Fluffy pressed her nose against Suriin's hand as she sat on the other side of her. Suriin placed a hand on each hound and let her mind start to drift along the thread connecting her to the crystal. One hound whined and whimpered as though worried, the other made little huffing noises. Suriin was safe.

Her body was safe, her mind floated freely – travelling at speed along the thread. She reached out to make contact with her crystal. It moved with the other two and clinked in the bag. She drew a deep breath and let her mind sink into it. It was high and fast and far. Suriin lifted a hand from a hound and moved it around until it felt right. *That way.* Her body could walk to it, just following the thread with the hounds keeping her safe. She didn't need the body; she could let go.

A wet lick on her face.

A sharp nudge in the ribs where it hurt.

Swift. She needed to be with Swift.

Suriin gripped as hard as she could, forcing her hand to curl, digging her nails in to create pain – a strong sensation, a guide to get back. Swift appeared in her mind, running alongside her, guiding her home. Suriin gripped onto the image of Swift and let herself be carried back.

She opened her eyes.

'You pointed behind you, at the pagoda. Can't really work out more as I'd lose you. You need to try again on the other side.' Gwynn shrugged.

Her breakfast threatened to reappear as Suriin used the bench to haul herself up. She trudged around the pagoda, her body feeling heavy, then sank to the ground once again.

This time, only Swift made contact with her. The connection in their minds was tight, and the hound in her thoughts was steady and calm. As Suriin prepared to reach for her crystal, she was flooded with fear from the hound. Suriin stroked Swift and sent back affection, along with an image of them both asleep in her room.

'Ready,' she said, and tentatively felt for the crystal, trying to keep a tighter grip on her body. For a dizzying moment, she flew, then she realised they'd stopped. Thrumming magic filled her senses, and the pouch was emptied. Hisses and clicks of frustration filled the air as Natke must have tried to do something and failed. If Natke had been human, Suriin would have said it sounded like crying, like pain.

But she wasn't. She was an immortal warrior queen, and surely, something like her would not cry.

Suriin lifted her arm and pointed, but before she even opened her eyes, she knew where she would find Gwynn standing.

Swift dragged her back this time as she started to lose sense of herself. She opened her eyes to see Gwynn walking in the direction of the Edgelands.

Wherever she hunted, she returned to the Gates. Natke had nothing to lose – except her entire hive's lives. She might kill every Soul Anchor in her desperation, and the gates could still never open.

Somehow, Suriin had to help find a way to stop her, stop the futility of the massacre – deaths that were, in effect, her fault and would get Natke no closer to her home.

CHAPTER 20

DARIN

The hounds charged into battle,
snarling and growling as they reached the ranks
*   of gathered awldrin.*
They were a ferocious sight in their glistening
*   armour,*
the lead hound glowed – a beacon of rage.
Battle Strategies of the Awldrin

'Tian needs help.' Chase walked to the reporting spot on the rug. His hand shook slightly, his jaw appeared clenched. Darin put his book down as Fall came in from the galley, and the game of stones was paused.

Chase took a deep breath before beginning. 'Tian rode to Dal Town. The xotryl flights made a number of our small settlements nervous, and he offered to escort those scared enough to leave – thinking that the few of them who wanted to return could do so. Now, they're all trapped. The xotryl with Natke on board is willing to fly into the town, and has now attacked a number of times – one Soul Anchor is dead, and others who tried to help were critically injured. Rumours on the street say that it took something before leaving her to bleed out, so I suspect Natke has killed for another shard. Tian says that the xotryl and awldrin rest on the main road out of the town between flights, blocking their exit, and people are terrified. Darin, we need to go before she kills another and another. How many will she kill before she accepts that broken shards won't open the gate?'

Darin swallowed hard. He didn't feel ready, and Star certainly wasn't there yet, but this was their job. This was what Howlers did. Protect people from the monsters of the Edgelands – and beyond.

'I'd really like to have the hound armour before we leave.' He reached to stroke Star. 'Star and Sandy are too valuable to risk if we can protect them. Conor planned to deliver something temporary by the end of the day. As I told you last night, he's sure we'll need to weft something over the material to gain anything like the strength of the old armour.'

Fall coughed. 'I speak for us all when I say *go*. Rescue Tian and as many others as you can get out of there. Take the awldrin down if you get the chance, otherwise evacuate as many people as possible for now, and give us an idea what we may need to defeat it. While Natke continues to weaponise the xotryl, we may need a Soul Anchor to use the forgotten magic, and one who is unbound. If we'll have to involve someone, it may as well be someone untrained. After all, these methods might be entirely different to what is taught now.'

Darin frowned. 'They might be, or they might need basics she can't access yet.'

Fall smiled at Darin, who felt as though he was being looked at by an affectionate uncle who sees he has missed the point.

'You're going to Dal. You might yet find more people to aid us. Let's use their isolation for good effect. It's their home and their privacy. They won't want Collective crawling all over it and taking their kids.'

Chase nodded. 'We just need to hold on for long enough to get the people out, while you find some useful battle magic and we all hunt for someone to use it.'

'Or we free up one of our tools.' Darin shrugged. 'I asked for a training dummy to be left for us in the armoury. We need to retrieve it so I can throw rings at it and get a feel for weight and rotation before the heat of an encounter.' His stomach knotted at the thought. The big red xotryl had scared Sandy, had indirectly caused his fall. The green one clearly had the taste for blood. A few little throwing rings would do little critical damage, but slowing the xotryl – limiting its range – would be a positive start.

Chase patted him on the shoulder as he walked to his room. 'Then let's go throw some stuff while we wait.'

Bones tried to hide a grin. 'Can we test something, then? I made a thing – well, two things, they have a vibration in them.' He held out a pair of small pebbles. 'They aren't perfect, because, well, it's a first try, isn't it? I set them so they work like a glow globe, I think.'

'They light up?' Darin turned the pebble over in amazement. 'That would be easier than glowsprites.'

Bones chuckled, glee apparent, despite the situation they were in. 'Take yours and run to the end of the galley.'

Darin jogged to the end of the galley, out of sight from Bones. He heard a short tune on Bones' whistle, and the stone in his hand vibrated violently.

'Is it supposed to shake this much?' he called.

'Yes! It's an alert mechanism. We can let you know when we need to talk to you. I just don't know how far away it will work. It was one of a few wefts that didn't need a plant or anything complicated from a Soul Anchor. I couldn't resist trying it.'

'We'll take it with us. Did you have any ideas about the Hal problem?'

'I've asked an old friend to say I've been past.'

Fall chuckled. 'You should have seen the colour of his face as he was trying to talk to her. Even dream walking, he was red.'

'She was a very good friend,' Bones mumbled, blushing.

Darin hid his smile under his hand. Even in moments of darkness, this pack was a joy to be around. He pocketed the pebble.

Chase laughed too, and gestured down the tunnel. 'Let's go throw some stuff,'

⌒ ⋏ 𝟨 ✿ ◉

They found the training dummy in the armoury easily enough and were in the process of trying to get it to the tunnel to their hidden room when the door lock rattled.

Chase nudged Darin, and they activated their dragon bone shards. *This was why they always closed the door.* He could practically hear Chase saying it. One day, he'd be alone and have to think about all these things himself. Thankfully, they'd left the hounds in the larger chamber. Darin sent *[sit in middle of room]* to Star with as much insistence as he could manage. Star replied *[sniffing a pile of tasty things]*. Darin decided he didn't want to know, so he brought his attention back into the room.

Twice in two days was a little more than he wanted to be testing the illusions. He stayed as still as he could as a pair of non-So'Dal entered the room. No robes, but the hand tattoos marked them as Builders. Darin resisted reaching for his cheek. When would he get his or Conor his? Both of them had been told that they were marked to do important things, though neither was yet fully invested into their society.

'There they are,' one mumbled, pointing at a box in the

corner. 'Master of Builders said that we needed to take a suit of old chain mail to his rooms as soon as we could. He's been all secretive and holed up with that Conor all day.'

'What do you think they're making?'

They opened the box, pulling out piles of old mail. About three suits down, they found a set that shone better than the rest.

'This one will take less cleaning,' the older one said. 'No idea what they've been making, but that lad has some crazy ideas. I'm sure it will be special, whatever it is. Probably entirely useless, but special.'

The younger one laughed. 'Isn't that what we all do? We make stuff that does exciting things, then tell everyone it was for some major purpose.'

'Aye. You're not wrong there.'

Darin's hair fell forward. A curl dropped into his eye and tickled the top of his nose. He was desperate to itch it, to reach up and move the treacherous bit of hair away.

They hoisted it over the younger one's back and turned toward the door. Darin decided that now they were looking away, it would be safe to move slightly. He shifted so he could move the hair, and his knee clicked. The closest builder turned slowly.

'Did you hear that?'

'Hear what? With all the chain mail in my ear rattling round, I wouldn't hear a thunderclap in a storm.'

'I heard something.'

'Can you see anything? This mail is heavy. I'd rather not spend all day here chasing ghosts or small creatures.'

'In a locked room?'

He started walking toward Darin.

'Peter, come on. You'd hear a pipe creak as it expanded and be convinced it's a creature. The Watcher would weigh less than this. I've no idea how they used to wear the stupid stuff.'

Peter kept walking. 'I know what I heard. It wasn't a pipe.'

'Yes, yes. But it's in a locked room. We'll get this chain to the Master of Builders, then come back if you really need to investigate. Nothing's getting past this door.'

Peter turned back to his companion reluctantly. 'Deal. Because there *is* something in here, and if something has got in, then it could be damaging the weaponry, and its entrance needs to be blocked.'

Frustration oozed from the chain mail laden builder now. 'Fine, fine.'

They returned to the main doors, Peter still scowling back over his shoulder. Darin barely dared to breathe. They walked out, taking their glow lamp with them, and Darin and Chase were plunged into darkness.

'Wait,' Chase breathed.

The door flung back open as Peter stuck the glow lamp in. Peering around, he laughed.

'Ah, it was worth a try. I still can't see anything. Hoped I'd catch it.'

'Come *on.*'

The door closed, and this time the locks were set. Darin counted to a hundred before he started to move again. They dragged the dummy into the passageway, and Chase quickly closed the door.

'That wasn't ideal,' he muttered.

'No, but they were getting chain mail. I'm sure that will be for the hound armour. Conor was talking about chaining it together. Hopefully, that means they're close. We don't have long for me to try these rings out.'

'Then you'll be throwing them at trees and collecting them as we walk.' Chase shrugged. 'Let's hope you can remember the technique fast, because we don't have time to keep healing your hands if you get it wrong.'

They pushed the training dummy to the furthest side of the armoury, cleared things away from it, and Darin sent *[Star standing behind him, Darin throwing rings]*.

Star moved to where he'd been asked to go.

Darin lifted the first ring. It had small red runes around its edge. He grasped it in his right hand, testing its weight and balance, took a pinch grip and used an overarm throw as his first attempt. It fell a little low, skittering across the floor at the base of the dummy.

'If you're going to use those, you need to mean it.' Chase passed him another.

Darin carefully placed it into his hand, ensuring it was far enough forward that the blade wouldn't catch him, and threw again with considerably more force.

It hit to the side of centre, embedded into the dummy's body.

'It could be worse. Let me try again.'

He tried a side-arm throw, winding up and releasing it with his arm flung toward the dummy. This one went wide and bounced off the wall, rolling across the floor to a stop; clearly, that technique needed practise. He crossed the armoury. The ring that had hit the dummy had sunken in deeply, slashing the body. With a good throw, he could do serious damage.

Darin had yet to try the red rings – they would no doubt resist blunting. The ones with runes in would blunt eventually, but there was no point in dulling their edges unnecessarily. He'd reuse the same set while he got his eye back in.

They spent what felt like hours as Chase suggested different techniques and moved the dummy between objects to make him refine his aim. Darin threw from close and far, from a walk and a run – he missed the moving ones. That would definitely need more work.

Chase pointed up at a So'Dal banner across the wall. It had a long rope hanging from it, presumably used to hang it. *[Star pulling rope around]*

Star bounded across eagerly and gripped the rope in his teeth, growling and fighting it as he did. Sandy barked and grabbed it too, the pair of hounds playing tug of rope with great enjoyment.

It certainly made the fabric move. It wasn't flapping like a xotryl's wings, but if he could accurately put the ring through the centre of the moving So'Dal symbol, then it would give him more confidence when they met one for real.

[Darin throwing hoop into fabric, Star and Sandy not getting hit]

Star's eyes glanced in his direction as he threw the ring, tracking the object in its arc. It sliced through below where he'd hoped for. Passing through the fabric slowed it, and it fell with a clatter beyond the hounds. He tried again. This time, he was too far to the right.

'I don't have time to get this right. I'm nowhere near accurate enough,' Darin growled as he hefted the third one. He threw it with a huge swing, and it sailed through the air, slicing directly above the target.

Chase gestured broadly at the fabric. 'It's not as big as a xotryl, so any hit would have scored a point.'

'We're counting points?' Darin chuckled 'It's a lot harder to aim these than a fair version. The edges are so sharp, I'm probably being too light with my grip – too cautious with the release. But if we were on a points score, I'd still have won the main prize today.'

Chase patted him on the back. 'I agree. But, if the aim was injuring a huge, flying beast, you'd have hit it at least once.'

'One out of three isn't enough.'

'It has to be. We can coat the edges with a flash potion or something that will cause damage when it hits. Then every hit is more dangerous.'

'Hrm.'

Darin gathered up the rings he'd been using and selected five more, including one of the red ones. 'I know it's a lot. But I don't want to damage the ones we'll actually need.'

[Sharp edge of ring. Star carrying carefully]

Star padded over and sniffed the ring. Darin sent the image again and threw the one he'd hit the wall with earlier. The red symbols made him pretty certain that it was magically enhanced in the right hands. In his, he simply hoped the edge would last longer.

He threw one across the floor. Star ran after it *[chase the ring]* and came back suffused with excitement. Darin had to swallow laughter when he saw Star's face as he tried to keep all the edges away from his gums while he carried it.

'There has to be a safer way.' Chase smiled at Star too. The moonhound had retrieved the ring from the floor with his gums pulled so far back, it looked as though he was grinning.

'It's a great idea if you aren't actively throwing. We can work out the details later.' Darin picked up the rings again. 'One more try.'

Chase studied the dummy. 'There's not a lot left for you to aim at now.'

He was right – it was tattered and battered. Its stuffing hung out where he'd pulled rings from it, and slashes at different angles shredded it. Darin would have liked all the damage in one place before they faced a xotryl. It was too spread out for his satisfaction.

Darin took the last ring carefully, letting Star disengage his teeth without moving it. Then, he lined it up in a pinch grip for a last overarm throw. As he released it, the pebble in his pocket vibrated, making him jump, and he missed the dummy entirely.

'What in the Watcher's name was that?'

Darin retrieved the stone. 'If this was buzzing in your pocket, I'm sure you'd have been a little distracted too.' The pebble kept buzzing.

'Doesn't it wear off?' Chase muttered as they trudged back to the main howler accommodations.

'It's still going. At least if our gear has arrived, we can get some sleep and be on the way to Tian tomorrow.' The mention of Tian put extra length in Chase's stride, and Darin had to extend his own to keep up with the shorter man.

As they came into view, Bones lifted the whistle to his lips, and the stone stopped buzzing.

'It worked!' He was clearly delighted.

Darin only hoped that it would turn off when they got far enough away. The realisation that it could have gone off while they were in the main armoury today dried his mouth. Bones needed to work on a way to turn the thing off from both sides.

⌐ ⋏ ◖ ✬ ◉

Conor waved enthusiastically. 'Fall said I could come in, as it was quiet out there. Hello, boy,' he crooned, and Star loped across the room, rolling over on his back for a belly rub. 'I've got something to keep that soft squishy body of yours a little safer.' He turned his attention to Star's ears and found Sandy clamouring for affection, too, both hounds trying to be the closest to Conor.

[Star stood so Darin could put armour on him] Darin tried to break through the puppyish excitement Star showed, but Conor indulged him with every ear rub and stroke. Eventually, Darin resorted to sending the image again with a hand on Star.

Star co-operated almost immediately, and Conor sat back. 'It's good to feel appreciated.' He laughed as he pulled two multi-plated items from his bag. One was smaller than the other. The plates were linked with tiny metal rings, too small to catch a claw in. The hide was tough, and the whole thing slightly lighter than he'd expected. It worried him that it would be too thin, but anything was better than no protection. Under Conor's guidance, he attached the armour around Star's body, securing it in place with small clips. He rested the protective panel over Star's head. A series of articulated panels ran down the back of his neck, and a mix of of chain mail and panels underneath stretched to Star's chest, where it was secured to the main armour.

'I decided that the horn was a dangerous addition.' Conor said. 'It's as flexible and light as I could make it. The rings aren't fully closed – we didn't have time for that – so you'll need to keep an eye on them. The chain under the neck should allow for eating without having to remove the whole thing.'

'I meant to let you know that. We realised it might be dangerous if they impaled themselves.' Darin was relieved Conor had recognised the problem too.

'Do we have the herbs from Gwynn?' Darin asked.

Bones held up a bag. 'Everything I asked for.'

Conor sat back on his heels as Star licked him.

'Gwynn passed me on his way back down from the garden,' Boulder said. 'I took the herbs from him, and he told me that there was another killing, another crystal taken by the awldrin. Suriin had placed him in the direction of the Edgelands.'

'Don't you mean *her*? Natke is a queen?' Darin tried to swallow the words, realising he'd been a bit rude.

Boulder shook his head. 'He definitely said *him*.'

Sandy and Star sniffed at each other's armour, and Chase

chuckled. 'Sandy is sending me mixed-up images of Star and a faat.'

Darin was getting confusion from Star too, but at least they weren't trying to remove it. He rubbed his aching arm and glanced over at the living embodiment of coiled tension that was Chase.

'We can leave first thing if the other Howlers can make what we need,' Darin said. 'I'm getting some sleep after all the throwing. Bones, are you confident to make the healing potion?'

Bones patted the pocket where he kept his whistles. 'Leave it with me.'

'Have you found any way to add fire or other things to weapons?'

'Not yet. I'm not giving up, though. There must be something in this collection worth hiding for reasons other than to simply stop collaboration.'

'Then we'll leave first thing. Thank you, Conor. Hey, at least this time you'll know where I've gone.' Conor helped him to remove Star's armour, then stood a little awkwardly.

'Watcher protect you all,' he said and enfolded Darin in a huge hug. 'Come back safe. I'll keep working on the armour while you're away – Watcher knows I hope you don't need it.'

Boulder pushed himself up. 'I'll take you back out, Conor. Bones, we could use these stones on the lever. If you could make them two-way, it would reduce the risk for our non-wefting visitors.' They waved and headed down the waterfall passage.

Darin and Chase readied their things and headed to their rooms. They would get Tian out. They had to. As he drifted off, Bones' earlier comments returned to mind. There were all sorts of possible magic users in Dal. Maybe there would be a Howler too.

CHAPTER 21

ELISSA

*There appear to be three main types of dragon on
     Mythos.
The Oldest, the most venerated, are truly
     powerful creatures with the most ornate
     horns and features.
They are truly wondrous to meet, even Terror has
     a certain charm when you get to know him.*
Journal of Otso Dragon-bonded

When she'd awoken, Sorrow and Dreamer had dozed alongside her. Amazement had gone, distracted by or interested in something else, Elissa presumed – a sleeping human was far less exciting than a moving, awake one.

Their flight to Rapture's cave had been a struggle, and Sorrow's wing beats grew laboured, his grunts of exertion punctuated by small puffs of smoke.

'There it is. Not far now.' Sorrow pointed his snout toward a mountain. In the dim light, Elissa could just about make out a dark patch near the base. He brought them into a gentle landing, his sides heaving for breath as he sank to the ground. Elissa carefully slithered down his side and crept a little closer.

The cave mouth straddled the mid-line between the everdark and the light. A flock of charver perched on ledges inside the entrance. Their skins rippled, a tide of undulating colours flowing from end to end of the small flock, red to orange and then bright yellow. Elissa's charver stuck its head out of her pack, chittering at them. After a moment, the whole flock returned to match the mottled grey of the rock face.

Sorrow hung back. 'I cannot go with you. You have to take this step alone.'

The cave entrance was huge, and unflattened grasses grew across its width. Clearly, no living thing had passed in or out of the cave for a considerable time.

'Are you sure she's still alive?' Elissa whispered.

'As sure as there are two moons around Lieus. If she'd died, someone would have had the calling. A new Oldest would have been appointed.'

'How deep is the cave?'

'I have never dared Rapture's presence. I am afraid I cannot help you there either. Just remember, show deference, but strength. Power but restraint. And do not look into her eyes, or you will never come back out.'

'Shall I dance whilst remaining still too?' Elissa muttered under her breath. 'I will try to do all you have told me.'

⌒ ⋏ ◐ ✾ ◉

Thick grasses whipped at her as she pushed them aside in the cave entrance; the few that she managed to trample flat cracked in protest. The air grew thicker and warmer as she wove her way between bushes until she was in total darkness. She looked back and could no longer see light. Sorrow had better be waiting, or she'd ... What could she do? Spit a tiny bit of flame at some grass? Shout at a group of charver?

Could she? She stopped walking and scrabbled around her feet, picked up a few pebbles, drew her arm back, then threw one. The noise rattled down the tunnel and echoed back – too loudly. She tried again without the pebble and, after a while, managed to produce a tiny, flickering flame to see by. If she focused on it like an emotion, she could hold it in place for a short time before it fizzled out.

Slowly, and a few flame-lit steps at a time, she made her way through the tunnel into the darkness. After a while, she felt a tug – a pull on her mind, drawing her into the abyssal depths of the cave. Dreamer fluttered his wings, his colours rippling in her small light, clearly as uncertain as she was.

The long passageway was easily big enough to accommodate Sorrow, and Elissa felt awful leaving his dejected form outside the cave. There was nothing in here so far that would have been a problem to him, and his flame would probably have lasted much longer.

She walked for what felt like hours. Rapture had truly cut herself off, so far underground – so very isolated. The tunnel closed in, and the route became crowded with huge boulders. Sorrow could easily move them, and again, she wished his familiar presence was beside her. She squeezed through narrow gaps, scratching her face against the wall as she struggled in the tightest space.

⌒ ⋏ ◖ ✥ ◉

Elissa began to run as the tunnel cleared, her steps gathering pace without urging, drawn onward by a force beyond her ability to resist. Dreamer scratched at her. He was red and agitated, pecking at her to slow down. Eventually, his persistence gave her a window of space, and she reached for him. Elissa stared deep into his tiny, beady eyes, which sparkled by her small flame. He chirruped and settled on her hand, holding her in an intense, unbroken gaze. Elissa dragged in a breath and tucked herself behind a large boulder. The floor was uneven and covered in small rocks. She crouched and ran her hands over their sharp edges.

'If I need pain to slow me down, to keep me aware of my own self, then pain I will allow in.' The pull was starting to build again, so she untied her wraps and removed them, tucking Hope's golden scale into her bag. Barefoot, she stood up. Now, every step cut into her feet. Her toes curled in pain, but it kept her mind clear. With deliberate and careful steps, Elissa continued into the tunnel, battling against the intense pull from somewhere in the darkness ahead. As she walked, the darkness lessened, gentle light marking a change. When her flame spluttered out, she let it remain extinguished while she approached as quietly as she could manage.

The tunnel opened into an enormous chamber. Sunlight streamed through a hole above. Elissa wasn't sure if the hole was tiny or distant, since the dark walls skewed her perspective completely.

Glistening in the pool of light was a crimson and gold dragon. Its back was to her as she entered, but the tail swished as she walked toward the huge beast. The dragon was physically as big as Amazement, but somehow, it felt larger. The presence of this creature filled every part of her, and Elissa realised it was the source of the emotional pull. She wanted to reach forward, to touch the scales ... The tail swished once.

'Do not come closer, little dragon. I feel your presence and admire your fight. I would not let your valiant efforts be in vain. I feel Sorrow outside the cave – even from here, his light is a little brighter. Whatever you have done for that poor creature, I thank you.' Silence filled the cave as the dragon paused. Elissa waited, too, mindful of Sorrow's advice. 'You wear an echo of dragon, but not his; you carry Hope, but it is not her.' The tail swished again. 'Do you have a way to blind your eyes, child? I would see you.' The voice was enticing, like cool water on a hot day or food when you were starved. It filled every part of her being, and Elissa desperately wanted to run toward this creature and give her whatever Rapture desired, for surely, it could be no other dragon.

Dreamer bit her, and she snapped back to the moment.

'I can cover them.' Elissa reached into her bag, then pulled a foot wrap back out. So she'd meet an Older dragon, with a wrap over her face. Flames, Laytha would think this was hilarious. Swallowing the negligible amount of pride she had left, Elissa tied the foot wrap over her eyes.

'My eyes are covered,' she called. Dreamer sat on her arm and, as the wrap didn't cover her vision downward, she could see his tail flash colours she had never seen him show.

⌒ ∧ ◐ ✦ ◉

Hot breath rolled past her. And, despite the mask, Elissa felt a pull on her body toward its source. She stepped forward.

'Stay still.'

Elissa froze, focusing on Dreamer's tail, the pain in her foot, and the claws in her arm – on anything but the draw of this Oldest dragon.

'You are human, yet not.' Elissa felt the air around her being drawn in. 'Now I see why I draw you. You carry Harmony's magic within your body. Your heart beats with her fire, her drive for calm. Her desire to see things in balance, she cannot return until they are.' Elissa heard the head withdraw, a rustle of scales as the dragon repositioned herself. 'You have huge power flowing throughout your tiny body. Child of Harmony, the oldest of us all. You will burn brighter than any human, and faster than any dragon. You have great power available to you, but it will burn you out like a dying star – fast, furious, and fierce. You should use it well.'

'I wish to reopen the Gates. The awldrin are dying on Tebein with no queen. My people die because the awldrin hunt them in what Regret called swarm madness. Regret believes it is worth hunting for an egg on Lieus.'

'Ahh, Regret. And now it all makes sense. What was he doing on Tebein?'

'I brought him there. I opened Hope's gate.'

Rapture laughed, and the cave echoed with her mirth. 'I knew Hope couldn't follow orders and just let you all die.' Elissa heard the scales rattling, settling to a more gentle swish as Rapture's voice calmed. 'On this occasion, her desperation – her need to believe you could survive – has given everyone a slim chance. You wish to open the gates. Do you know how?'

'No. That's why they sent me. Neither Regret nor Hope know how to open the gates with the crystals shattered. They say only you can tell me how to open it now.'

'Only me.' The tone of her voice changed, becoming slower, quieter – almost a whisper. 'I knew I'd felt him leave. Where are my mate's bones? Where do they lie? At his gate where he ever slept? The mistress I could never compete with?'

'The Watcher's bones are in the Hall, yes.'

Elissa felt the sigh. It flowed through her and washed out of the cave, a breaking wave of emotion.

'Then we will use his bones to repair his beloved gates. It seems fitting. He might not approve of us reopening them. I know he felt deeply that it was the right thing to do to close them, even though it was the harder decision.' She paused, her warm air bathing Elissa's skin.

'There must always be a black dragon.' She sighed. 'As much as there will be a crimson and gold one when my time comes. There will be a young Vigilant somewhere – it is the way these things are. We never grow in number. Harmony and balance must return.'

Elissa was a little confused at the purpose of the speech, but decided that waiting patiently might be her best choice. She moved Dreamer back so she could see his colours and gauge how happy he was. His gold tint was a good sign.

'To remake a crystal, we need to combine both the end and the beginning of the journey, along with keys to the destination. We have my mate's end, his bones. Now, you must venture to the Hatchery, in hope that you can find a fragment of the beginning – the shell from a new black dragon. Once you have that, we can talk about the keys. Without the shell, we cannot proceed. Take your mask off. If you must enter the Hatchery, then you will pass more formidable Older dragons than myself. If you cannot look me in the eye and keep hold of yourself, then you will never get past those at the gate. If your luck is good, you will face any of us other than Fury or Terror.'

Elissa reached for the mask, her hands obeying Rapture's words without her consent. It took all her will to resist. This was a test. She pushed her shoulders back and stood tall, trusting in Sorrow's truth.

She leant into the assault, her senses battered by Rapture's joy, her effusive happiness, and the sheer exuberance of being alive. Elissa allowed herself a smile and stored the feeling – saving it for later, when she might need to access it. Below her blindfold, Dreamer swayed with delight, his colours rippling through all shades. He flapped his wings, and one caught her cheek. Just as she thought he'd abandon her to Rapture, the assault stopped.

Elissa stumbled, collapsing to the floor and fighting tears, utterly bereft.

Empty.

Hollow.

She longed to feel like that again. Behind her mask, she let a tear fall. In the absence of joy, there was sorrow. Would he be cancelled out in Rapture's presence? Would he also be filled with happiness?

'Thank you, but I'll manage, I think.' She held her voice steady and was proud of herself for doing so.

'You are this weak after I offer ecstasy. How will you cope with terror such as you cannot imagine? Or anger so pure and total that it warps your mind? You are not born to carry this burden. Show me you can do it. Show me you have the strength, else I cannot help you. The awldrin will die out, and so will your people. Tebein will become a wasteland. And it will be because you are too weak to show you have true dragon blood in you. I'd send Sorrow alone, but he will quail and fade before them. Why else does he haunt the duskline, neither here, nor fully embracing his darkness? He does not have the strength to do this.'

Every word Rapture spoke was filled with passion, with desire. Every syllable dripped with temptation to remove her mask. The assault was fully back on. And Elissa no longer knew whether she should listen to Sorrow. Was Rapture right? Did she need to show her strength? Could she?

Elissa sat. She could think as well on her feet as she could sitting, but it just made it a bit easier when the current assault ended if she wasn't wobbly. With her physical stability settled, Elissa glanced down at Dreamer. If Dreamer could resist, surely she could too? What was going to happen? She was going to throw herself at a huge dragon? Hug and embrace her foot? That was ridiculous. She'd already felt a level of intense joy that she'd not realised was possible to feel. Could she, instead, meet emotion with emotion? Could she weave a small mesh that would protect her? Was protection even an emotion she could use?

What had Rapture called the Watcher? A vigilant?

Rapture continued to croon niceties and threats at her – all coated in the sweetest emotion Elissa could imagine. It was like when she'd been taken in by Laytha and then more. It was like sharing a fish with Makin. If she could have eaten with them both together once. If they could have tried some of the food she'd tried since, with no fear of hunger ...

Makin.

She held the pain, the creeping torture of the knowledge that her accident had doomed him. That her beloved brother had died protecting her and others like her. His protectiveness, her sorrow for him, she held onto those feelings and pulled some threads out, ready to use.

With the image of Makin against her closed eyelids, Elissa removed her mask and looked up into the most wondrously beautiful dragon she could never have imagined. Every scale shimmered with iridescent light, every red-edged golden scale. They rippled across her body as Rapture moved closer, the grace and beauty of her powerful movements at odds with the size of the space they were confined in.

It was a cave, a big cave.

Makin.

Like the one she'd grown up in.

Makin.

She looked up to face Rapture, but her eyes barely saw the dragon. Instead, tears of sorrow, of loss for Makin broke through, the dam of her grief breaking under her intense focus on it. Elissa cried in sweet release.

Rapture sat back, confusion marring her beautiful face.

'Well, that's the first time that's happened. You're supposed to be kissing my claws or swearing undying servitude, worshipping me even! Not leaking from your eyes all over my home.'

Elissa sniffled.

'I'd forgotten the human tendency to leak under pressure – after all, I didn't often interact with anyone but *Him.*' She tilted her head to one side, her eyes spinning as she studied Elissa.

Elissa wiped her sleeve across her eyes. The barrage of emotion had ceased temporarily. It was just there. Not being pushed at her or withheld. Rapture was just simply a joy to be near. Elissa found her mind wandering and brought it back to Makin, setting off a fresh flood of tears.

'Do you need more charvers? Or some air?' Rapture extended her neck toward Elissa, her snout close to Elissa's face. 'Are you doing the leaking on purpose?'

Elissa nodded. 'Sort of. I'm trying to hold your emotion away with a memory, a strong one. My brother died protecting others. I never got to say goodbye. I wasn't there. Oh flames, what would they have done to him?'

Rapture reached out again and touched her snout to Elissa. A barrage of affection washed over her unexpectedly.

'You'd have made a good pet,' Rapture said. 'But you'll make a better bridge between all sides. You will be the path we walk, the route we take to save the awldrin and your people. You will be the last scale on a wing, the piece of the puzzle that makes everything complete. Will you think about being my pet once it is all complete? I was always a little jealous that my mate had Him to write for him, to put his words to permanence.'

No. Elissa paused to look as though she considered the proposal. 'We can discuss that later – if I survive the next step. Where is the Hatchery?'

Chapter 22

Darin

Thunk. The ring sunk to a satisfying depth in the gnarled tree trunk. Their travel had been punctuated with practise, and Darin grew in confidence as he became used to the weight of the rings. Their edges were wickedly sharp, and in battle, he'd have less time to position them well. He might ask Conor to make a flexible glove with a re-enforced section to reduce the chance of slicing his hand.

Chase pointed at a bush further ahead with narrow, twisted branches and fluttering leaves. 'Now that one.'

Darin prepared the ring in a pinch grip, then flicked his arm and wrist outward in a side-arm throw. The ring sliced through a branch and carried on past, skimming into the grass.

'At least it's the right bush.' Darin lengthened his stride to retrieve the rings before Star tried to help. Poor Star still walked awkwardly, his paws lifting a little higher than they needed to, and every jump was over-powered. Sandy wasn't faring much better as they adjusted to the armour.

Darin tried to hold in a laugh as Star hopped like a farbrox over a twig; it was too late.

Star sent sadness his way. He was not enjoying the armour.

There had to be a way to explain to Star why he needed it – without terrifying him. He was still very young to face a real battle. *[Star with spear sliding down armour plates. Star happy. Star with no armour. Spear hits, Star sad.]*

Star replied with *[Star in no armour. Star bites spear.]*

Darin didn't want to start using the xotryl as a reason yet. There was no need to upset the hounds further. *[Star brushes against plants. Plants make blisters. Star with armour. Star unhurt]*

[Star not going near plant that causes blisters. No blisters.] Star loped off ahead, following a scent for a minute, the odd armour forgotten about in the brief pleasure of a scent trail.

'They'll be fine soon,' Chase said as the hounds loped down the trail, side by side. 'Are you ready for the lift?'

'As I'll ever be. I'm just hoping that xotryl is so busy doing the awldrin's bidding, that it's nowhere near the forest.' The memory of the slaughter in the cottage rose unbidden to the front of his mind. He pushed it away, trying to bury it deep. 'Have you heard from Krista?'

'No, but that's not unusual. She can't dream walk, so she usually just catches up as I pass through.'

⌒ ⫩ ☾ ✿ ◎

They reached the top of the crater a few hours later. To Darin's relief, no xotryl marred the sky or horizon, and rain had long since washed away the brown stain on the earth below. His mind supplied the details anyway, recalling the body being dragged into the forest. With a shudder, he tried to coax Star into the basket.

[Star in basket] Darin tried to stay calm as he followed Star in.

He was in control – not the rope, pulleys, or basket. They would descend at Darin's pace.

Chase entered last and closed the door. After ensuring the hounds were both secure and their packs were centralised, he took hold of the rope.

'Untie us. I'll do the work today. I know you can do it, but this isn't the time for a lesson. We need to get down without upsetting you or the hounds.'

Darin leant over the edge of the basket to release the knot. His stomach churned, and as he glanced down to steady his hands, he caught a glimpse of how far they had to descend. His knees began to buckle.

Star. He had to be calm for Star.

Darin took a deep breath. *Slow and steady. In and out. Be calm.* He loosened the rope and checked Chase was ready. Chase gave him a curt nod.

Darin let go.

They dropped at a pace Darin could never have controlled. Chase moved so fast it felt as though they fell. Darin was certain he'd left his breakfast at the top. His stomach had definitely not caught up to the rest of him yet.

'Check below,' Chase said.

Darin peered over the edge. The ground grew close so fast that he braced for impact.

'It's clear,' he replied and rested a hand on Star's back, turning his face away and closing his eyes.

They slowed rapidly before the basket came to a rest on the ground a moment later.

When Darin opened his eyes in amazement, Chase laughed and pointed at a red marking on the rope about two spans above their heads.

'Watch the rope, and you'll be fine every time. Come on, we'll stop by the welcome village in case Krista's back – or anyone else has returned. We could use all the information we can get.'

Darin secretly hoped that no one had returned, that the houses were undisturbed and abandoned. That way, the inhabitants of the other huts were safe. Hopefully, they'd fled to Dal Town like Tian.

Krista had said they'd been invited, but she'd been determined not to leave, certain that their small huts provided more safety than the town. From what Tian had told them, she may have been right.

⌒ ⼂ ◖ ✤ ◉

Birds flitted past, their song alerting others to the Howlers' presence as their tiny wings carried them from branch to branch in search of food. Occasionally, one chased an insect. Fire sprites lit the star-shaped flowers either side of the path, drinking deeply from the nectar before lighting the next star. A small, iridescent-tailed bird glided over their heads to perch in a tree, observing their every move. Darin felt his shoulders loosen. There was no xotryl in the area; the wildlife was far too relaxed.

Grass had grown undisturbed in the clearing between the houses, lush and thick. The broken roof of the cottage where the family had been killed had collapsed even further, one of the walls leaned in, as though the house wished to bury its own horror. It was a scar on the small community. One they would neither be able to hide nor recover from soon.

Chase knocked on the burnt tree stump, and they waited for a while, as they had the first time. It was no surprise when they were met with silence.

'I'm going to make sure Krista took her weapons.' Chase pushed open Krista's door. It swung freely, and Darin followed.

Her home was filled with animal tracks. Strange footprints with a number of spread toes, and distinct claw marks at the front and rear. Chase went into the room at the back and returned with a quiver of arrows and a longbow.

'Can you use a bow? Krista's travelled with her much lighter one. She must have been rushing. Her range won't be enough for something in flight.'

'It's not a weapon I'm particularly good with.' Darin had little reason to need a bow in the inn.

They checked through the hut more thoroughly, and despite numerous footprints, they could see nothing alive in there. There was some wood fungus stacked by the fire grate that was dry to his touch.

'Do you think Krista would mind if I took a slice?' he asked. He wasn't sure how he could use it, but anything that would hold fire like wood fungus could be a useful in a tight situation.

'As long as she has a few disks to warm herself when she returns, I doubt she'd begrudge you any.' Chase winked. 'I'm sure you could repay her if you wanted to.'

Darin felt heat rise in his cheeks. 'Chase, she's older than my mother!'

Chase walked out of the hut, still chuckling. 'Give me a moment,' he called back.

Darin and Star followed him out. *[Krista walking down the path]*. Star started to scent for a trail.

Chase returned from the tree line with a twig. He tucked it under the door, wide side inward, and asked Darin to close the door, holding the thin edge in place as Darin pulled the door shut.

Chase stood up and stretched. 'Try to open it now.'

Darin leaned into it, and with gentle pressure, the wood dug into the floor – too wide to push a door over it. The door remained closed.

'Good. That should stop it smelling even worse when she gets back,' Chase said.

[Krista and other people on the path] Star sent as he started down a trail.

'Let's go. Star has her scent.' *[Darin and Chase following Star]*

Chase picked up his belongings, and with Sandy at his heels, they followed Star. The path wasn't particularly wide, but it was well trodden, and damage to the woods was clear to either side. Broken saplings lay across the path, the jagged shards of their innards exposed, naked and twisted in their death. Shrubs were flattened and, in one area, white shards littered the ground – bones amongst the defecation of the predator.

The xotryl had clearly returned to this spot numerous times.

How could he ask Star if it was fresh? Darin sent *[steaming pile of dung]*. Star hesitated, then walked into the clearing. He sniffed the air and skirted the edge before returning to Darin's side. *[Old dried dung]* he sent back.

'Do you think any of those are human remains?' Darin asked, reluctant to poke around.

Chase's lips twisted in a grimace. 'Probably. I'd like to stop and burn them, to send the dead on their way, but the less evidence of our passage, the better. We will return another time.'

Darin hated the thought of the remains scattered in such a way. Parents, children – the family that had once lived near Krista.

'Watcher guide your wings,' he murmured as he took a moment longer to stare at the bones. Taking in each one he saw, acknowledging their death.

⌒ ☌ ◖ ✥ ◉

They pushed deeper into Dal forest, and the path grew narrower. Star and Sandy settled into their armour more as the day continued, the scents and sounds finally distracting them enough that they started to walk less like newborns and more like the majestic moonhounds they were.

'How far is Dal Town?' Darin asked.

'We'll have to sleep somewhere in the forest tonight, but if we can keep this pace, we should arrive by the end of the day tomorrow.'

As darkness fell, so did the rain. Darin tilted his face up to feel drops landing on his cheeks, grateful for the respite it would bring the town.

'That should keep the xotryl grounded for the night – darkness and rain.'

'Aye, we may as well rest now. We can get underway earlier, then strike out before sunrise.' Chase slipped his pack from his back. 'There aren't any shelters around here.' He pulled out a sheet of lightweight fabric. 'Let's get this up.'

They tied the fabric between some sturdy trunks, then laid out on the mossy ground beneath it. Darin removed a few obstinate twigs from his space and relocated some lumpy rocks, but it was as comfortable as he was going to get.

'Sandy will sit watch to start with. We could use an ear and eye out, given the amount of Edgelands wildlife there is in Dal.'

Darin rolled his aching shoulders and rubbed at his neck. 'Thanks. I'll go second, if Sandy wants to wake me.' He settled back and closed his eyes. A warm breath filled his ear as a tongue slobbered on his face, and Star sent affection through their bond as he snuggled up alongside.

⌒⋏◖✿◉

Well before the sun rose, they were on their way.

'Did you manage to speak to Tian last night?' Darin asked.

Chase shook his head. 'I think he's taking the advice seriously. I've heard nothing since.'

Darin reached out to squeeze Chase's shoulder. 'He'll be fine. Probably playing music to keep people's spirits up or something.'

Chase offered a half smile back. 'Watcher's flames, he'd better not be. I want him safe, hidden in a cellar out of reach!'

'Maybe he is. Maybe that's why he can't contact you?'

'Hrm.'

Darin left the subject alone and instead used the time to ask Chase about the birds and other creatures of the forest. Chase told him about the frilled chorus bird and showed him berries that were good to eat and a few others which weren't. Darin let him talk. It was unusual for Chase to tell him things rather than expect him to work them out for himself. Not once since they left the Black Palace had he said, 'One day, you'll be alone.'

As the day drew on, they started to come across more trails leading into the forest in all directions. *[People on paths?]* he asked Star, who replied with an image of so many people

Darin's mind struggled to build the image he'd been sent. These were main routes and entirely empty of people. Star's image had more people on one path than the others, and it deviated from the route they currently walked.

'Isn't that the main route to Dal Town?' Darin asked as they walked directly past it.

Chase nodded.

'And we are going ... where?'

'To the crater wall behind it. There's an old lift there to Clifdon, and a way in, if we can get past undetected.'

'Why in the Watcher's wings aren't they all just leaving that way, then?'

'Clifdon is almost deserted. No one brings ships past the Edgelands any more. A few people live there, but there's no room to feed an entire town. Although, the holloway to Lacton is still open – maintained as an annual challenge to the youth, a coming-of-age pilgrimage, if you will – the route from Dal to Clifdon is almost gone.'

'They really are self-reliant here, aren't they?' Darin sighed.

⌐ ⋏ ◖ ✛ ◉

The birdsong altered as the trees began to thin, their songs forgotten in a panic of shrieked alerts. Star and Sandy stopped, their muzzles raised, and stared ahead. Birds flashed past them, back into the depths of the forest. Greens and reds, flashes of brightness with tails streaming after them, and fear in their tone as they flew past. Once the exodus from the edge of the trees slowed, Darin stood back up, having ducked to avoid the rush.

'I don't suppose that's a daily migration around here?' He brushed leaves from his trousers.

Chase shook his head. 'We'd better go very carefully.' A

shadow fell over them, and both looked up. Above the trees was the green-scaled belly of a xotryl.

It flew in circles overhead, vanishing from sight for a few minutes at a time as trees blocked their view.

'It would appear the xotryl remains in the area, as Tian suggested.' Darin watched the beast, trying to work out if the awldrin was mounted on it. They crept closer and closer to the edge of the forest. As they approached, crouching in high bushes, he could see the main roadway connecting a walled town and the forest.

Both Krista's reference to being easy pickings and Chase's suggestion that it would be safer to be inside the walls made sense now. While the residents were safe from graaken, rhinocorns, or other wildlife, they were also trapped. Anyone crossing the open ground between the town and the forest would be incredibly exposed.

Behind the town, the rope and pulley system of an old lift swung freely in the breeze, with ropes severed and the cage grounded. Overnight evacuations via the surface were out too then.

'How will we get in?' he asked, hoping for another hidden river or secret system of passages.

'We'll walk.' Chase checked Sandy's harness and tightened his own straps. He untucked the dragon bone charm from his neck and held it in his clenched fist. Darin exhaled slowly. It didn't make them invisible, just made the eyes slide over them; it only really worked, therefore, when they stood still. Moving targets of slipperiness might just be detectable if Natke was looking in that direction.

They crept as close to the forest edge as they could before crouching next to Star. He sent *[blow whistle, Darin and Star vanish]*

[Star staying close to Darin]

Darin tucked his hand into the gap in Star's neck plates, ensuring the tiny shard on Star's neck was in his palm, and put the single dragon bone shard whistle in his mouth. The slider took at least one hand to play, and he needed both. He held his own shard with the other and met Chase's eyes.

'Get to that lift. I'll see you there,' Chase said and took up the same position, also holding the small dragon bone shard they had placed around Sandy's neck.

Chase nodded, and they blew their whistles. The spell took hold.

Darin and Star stepped out of the forest's shelter as the xotryl swung its head in their direction and screeched.

It leapt into the air, the awldrin mounted astride. Scraps of green fabric flapped around it. Natke hissed and clicked as they flew overhead, swooping in a low glide over their positions from a few moments before. They kept moving, steadily and constantly toward the lift.

'My shield does not lie. I know someone used dragon magic over here. Something, someone, or ones. I can wait. You'll be out of the woods again soon enough, then we'll take what I need. And you can be left in peace. I only want my freedom, and I'll give you yours too. Freedom from pain and torture, from imprisonment. Freedom from loss. Forever.' The hissing, clicking speech hurt his ears, and Darin was desperate to run, but the more steadily they moved, the better the chance that they would remain unnoticed.

He was about halfway between the forest and the town when the pebble in his pocket began to vibrate. He risked a glance behind.

The xotryl's head turned.

The awldrin twisted in the saddle to see what it stared at.

In the dim light, as the sun went down, Darin reached out

for reassurance from Star. His hand felt leather. *[Star running to the lift. Darin following]*

Star sent back fear mingled with love, and Darin felt him move away. The pebble was still vibrating, and the xotryl had begun to waddle toward him. Steadily, it closed on his position.

Even if he laid on the floor, the flaming stone would give him away now. Better to survive than have a stone no one could talk to because he was dead. Darin closed his hand around it and threw the pebble as far as he could.

The xotryl changed course. While it looked the other way, Darin began to run, knowing he'd be more visible. He stumbled as Star sent *[Star at lift,]* followed by *[Sandy running with pebble toward lift]*. The pebble had vanished.

No! He'd sent Star ahead to be safe, not to have the xotryl be led to him! The xotryl extended its wings, ready to fly. Darin reached behind him, slowing for a moment. If he could get close enough ... it was a big target, after all.

He untied the throwing ring he'd left on the outside of his bag. It was slightly blunted from all the trees he'd thrown it at, but slightly blunted for a staramine-runed blade was exceptionally sharp for anything else.

He ran after the xotryl. Any minute now, it would take off and be out of his range.

Any minute now, it might catch up to Sandy or Star.

Darin stopped. He took a deep breath and lined up his throw. If he could just catch the wing enough to hurt it.

He'd got his best range and accuracy with over-arm throws, so he drew his arm back and threw with all the force he could muster. As the ring left the protection of his dragon bone shard, it became visible, arcing through the air toward the xotryl. The awldrin saw it too late. The ring sliced across the wing, leaving a gash as it came out on the other side.

The xotryl screamed, all concentration on the pebble lost as it turned to inspect its wing.

Darin ran as fast as he could. Given all the weight he carried, he was certain that the noise of his feet would have given him away if the xotryl weren't so loud.

Silence fell, and it was in pursuit. Cajoled by Natke, it chased after him, and the rain-softened mud soft exposed his trail of footprints.

The other rings were inside his pack, muffled so that jangling metal wouldn't give him away. He gasped for air as the thundering noise of the huge creature bearing down on him intensified.

A second set of footsteps, faster and drawing close. Natke must have dismounted. The futility of trying to fight the pair alone struck him as he tripped on a stone. Darin landed flat on his face. He clutched the dragon bone shard and hoped that they would carry on past, not stop to inspect the ground.

'I will find you, slippery one.' Natke clicked as she stalked closer. 'Your magic attracts my xotryl. It knows you are there somewhere. I heard you fall. Did you trip? Are you nearby?' She started stabbing at the ground as she drew closer and closer. She was huge, so tall, so flame-ragingly scary. Fighting the xotryl with their poisonous talons was bad enough, but having one directed by an intelligent creature was terrifying.

Darin tensed, ready to spring up to run or attack. His heart beat so furiously that it was audible. His breathing quickened. Neither was an ideal option. The throwing ring appeared by his hand, a slippery patch of light that he couldn't look at, giving him a chance. One of the hounds must have fetched it. The ring vanished as he gripped it.

He had one more try – one more throw. The xotryl's great head swung from side to side as it tried to work out where the magic was.

No xotryl meant no way of tracking the magic. No high speed travel for Natke.

Darin took aim at the xotryl's eye. He didn't have long to line it up. As he was about to throw, the awldrin let out a high-pitched series of clicks and lifted their leg, searching for an attacker. Sandy would probably not have pierced the hard casing of the creature, but he had bought Darin a moment's distraction.

He threw the ring. It appeared the second it left his hand, flying directly at the xotryl. He rolled away, crouching and moving as quickly as he could. The ring missed the xotryl's eye, but it did slice off a section of skin above it.

A river of red ran down the xotryl's face, obscuring its vision, Darin hoped. It wasn't a perfect throw, but it would have to do.

While the awldrin searched behind her, stabbing at the ground in frustration, and the xotryl screamed in pain, Darin ran.

That ring was lost to him, but he had more in his pack, and it had given him a chance. He hoped Chase had managed to get to the lift and to Star.

Star must have felt his anxiety as *[Star and Chase behind lift]* flooded his vision, along with *[Star itching at the armour]*.

A wet nose nudged at him from higher than Star's head would be. Sandy and Darin raced to the lift.

He tucked in behind the basket and was greeted by another wet nose and a grunt as he, presumably, stood on Chase's foot.

'How do we get in?'

'We knock, obviously. As soon as we blow these to remove our hiding, she'll know where we went. So, you have to persuade someone who can't see us to let us in.'

'Why me? They know you.' Darin sat down to catch his breath. 'This is one task you can handle better alone. I'll just be here, watching you with Star's nose and waiting. By the way, what happened to that watcher-flamed pebble?'

'It stopped vibrating. Bones must have given up.' Chase pulled it from his pocket and handed it back to Darin. 'We'll check in with them once we get to safety.'

'We need to set a time limit for that flaming thing. Especially now we know that the xotryl can feel it.'

'Agreed.'

[Chase standing and walking to the wall. Chase knocking. Sandy cleaning a cut on his paw.] A hatch in the wall opened, and a face peered out.

Hunger filled their bond, with Star sending *[bone covered in meat]*. Darin reached out to stroke Star. With no idea how long the residents had been trapped, he couldn't promise a bone. He settled for trying to find his ear for a scratch instead.

'Hi, it's the Howlers come to aid you,' Chase said.

'Can't see anyone. How do I know you're not trying to trick me?'

Darin could imagine the frustration on Chase's face even without seeing it and stifled a laugh.

'Did you see the commotion on the ground ahead of the town?' Chase continued, pained patience in his voice.

'Nope, I been down here all the time.' The hatch shut.

Chase sighed loudly and knocked again.

'Told you, I can't let in people who aren't there. Stop hiding, and I'll think about it.'

'Get Krista, Tian, or the Witness,' Chase called as the hatch shut again. 'This is ridiculous. Watcher send me a guard with brains please.'

Darin shuffled to the side to see if the xotryl still pursued them. It had flopped down to the ground, while the awldrin appeared to tend its head wound. It was interesting that the awldrin thought the xotryl worthy of care. There was empathy behind those crystalline eyes, after all. Still, he didn't doubt that were he to unhide, the xotryl would point them out.

He slumped against the wall. At least it wasn't raining.

Chase tried again, but before he could say anything, a commotion came from the other side of the door.

'Invisible Howlers you aren't letting in? Why not, man? Do you want them to get eaten? You've never met one before? Huh.' Krista's voice carried through the open hatch. 'If you don't open that hatch right now, I'm going to—'

The sound of bolts being drawn grated against the stone and the door slid into the wall.

'About time,' Chase muttered.

'It would have been easier if you'd showed your faces,' Krista replied. 'Get in now. I'm assuming you have good reason to spook Cai like that.'

Darin walked to the open door, trusting in Star to ensure he didn't collide with Sandy or Chase.

'We're in,' he said once they were both through.

'Aye, us too,' Chase replied. 'But I want to move away from your entrance before we unhide. That xotryl is pretty sensitive.'

'Follow me, and try not to scare anyone else.' Krista led the way into the town.

Darin tried to stay close behind her to avoid bumping into people. She led them through narrow streets until they reached an old inn much like all the other buildings in Dal. Its sloping walls and erratic wooden beams wore proud mud patching between their gaps. The sign showed a heavily spotted moonhound sat facing the town walls, its ears raised as though paying attention.

'Welcome to The Spotted Dog.' Krista pushed the heavy door open. Its hinges squealed in protest as she led them inside.

The walls were lined with stone, and after recognising the hound on the sign, it should have been no surprise to find that this was a safe place for So'Dal, hiding its protection under a cloak of familiarity.

A single note revealed Chase and Sandy, so Darin released his own magic, and Krista beamed at them. 'It's good to see you both. You took your time.'

Chapter 23

Darin

Only a few patrons sat at the bar. A large chair dominated the centre of the room; in its cushioned embrace sat a woman. An intricately wrapped scarf hid all traces of the wearer's natural hair, but there was something very familiar about the woman's face.

His skin prickled with discomfort as she stared at him. She nodded once and rose smoothly to her feet.

'Thank you for helping to free Suriin, and for all you have done for her and Gwynn so far,' she said as she held out a hand.

Darin glanced at Chase, who stared openly at the woman. She gestured to some empty chairs at the table in front of her.

'Please, join me. I believe I have the Howlers to thank for saving Yorynn as well. As ever, you work in subtle ways.'

'You're Suriin's mother.' Darin shook his head. 'Your family is going mad with worry about you. It was your disappearance that pushed Suriin over the edge. That, in turn, led to *this*.' He gestured to outside and didn't take up the offer of a seat.

'I understand that it would appear that way. Certainly, when Fluffy showed me her presence in the cell – trapped in a problem of her own making, I also felt that way to begin with. Should I have gone to Redpike first?'

'Yes.' Darin clenched his fists. As much as Suriin had made her own stupid decisions, this woman was at least in part to blame for her daughter's emotional state.

'Howler, I can accept that anger.'

Chase did sit. He rested his hand on Sandy's head and leant forward. 'So, Soul Anchor, why on Lieus are you here when you sent all your family to Redpike and told not a soul?'

'You just answered it. Where's the safest place on this continent? Where can I be assured they are all far from xotryl and in the best care possible? Redpike.'

Chase sat back and crossed his arms. 'You're from Dal.'

'The rest of my family is here. Those I cannot send to the Black Palace, those who are old – unable to travel – and cousins who chose to remain here. Yorynn agreed to my travel here. We discussed it in depth. He was going to tell the children, but he grew too unwell. If I could have brought Fluffy, I would have. It turned out she was needed more in Redpike, and having her as my eyes there reassures me that my decision was correct.'

'But they could know?'

'Yorynn does. When the time is right, he will tell the children – any day now, I suspect. I'd have told Suriin myself, but I cannot reach her.' She frowned. 'Something is off there.'

Darin sat then, thumping both hands down on the table.

'You think so? She accidentally releases our oldest enemy, who – for some ridiculous reason – has been kept not only alive, but secretly imprisoned for five hundred cycles, only to be freed by an apprentice in desperation. She's brutally beaten, her crystal is stolen from her, and she can barely reach for her magic without passing out. She goes nowhere without Fluffy by her side, and you think there *might* be something wrong?' Darin clenched his fists and crashed them on the table again, startling even himself.

'Ahh, a lost crystal. That would be a problem.' She nodded, entirely unphased by Darin's anger. 'Before we attempt to engage the awldrin out there, what else can you tell me about it?'

Darin sat back in stunned silence.

Chase rested his hand on his chin, studying the woman. 'You're pretty emotionless for a mother who almost lost her husband and has a very unwell daughter.' Chase said. 'I've seen this before. How much effort is it taking to keep the shield over the town?'

She gave him a thin smile. 'It is costing a lot. We take it in turns, working from in here. We tried to work more freely out on the wall the first day we saw the xotryl. It grabbed the Soul Anchor, plucked her from the walls, and killed her before flying to the East.'

'And each time it leaves, you're evacuating people?' Darin asked remembering the tracks in the wood.

She shook her head. 'No. We let them in.'

'Every kill she makes, Suriin witnesses – through the crystals. Every time she flies to the Edgelands to try to reopen the gates.' Darin reached for Star, to feel some emotion, some anchoring against the apparent lack of care from the woman he faced.

The woman nodded. 'I understand. The second death was

worse. She stood in the town, positioned centrally, for she was not a strong Soul Anchor. The xotryl swooped in, plucking her from the ground. In her panic, she dropped the shield, and the xotryl had access for long enough to bite others – to feast on them before we created sufficient strength of repulsion to force it to flee. There are very few of us left now. The Witness Soul Anchor, myself, and her daughter, who is barely able to hold an emotion.'

Chase sighed. 'Watcher's flames. So we have three of you. Only one with bonded support, but more arrivals daily. Are there others who could be taught?'

'Could be and willing to be are very different things, as I am sure you would know, Chase.' She glanced toward the door. 'Speak of the musician, and he appears.'

Tian ran through the inn door. At the sight of Chase, he sped past Krista and into Chase's arms.

'I'm sorry. I should have let you know, but there wasn't time. And anyway, I knew you'd come here as soon as you could. You had things to figure out first.'

He let go of Chase and studied Sandy. 'Now who's got a nice new set of armour?' he crooned, scritching Sandy. Sandy tilted his head into the scratch, making a low, satisfied rumble, turning his head so far round that Tian had to stop.

'And you too, young fella.' He offered Star a scratch too. Star's tail thudded against the floorboards with the attention. 'You don't want one, too, do you?'

Darin laughed. 'It's good to see you safe, Tian.' The joy that exuded from Tian's every pore had dropped the tension dramatically.

'Get rested,' Suriin's mother said. 'I held xotryl off for the last nineteen cycles at Golden. One more night won't make a difference.'

Tian gestured away from the woman as her eyes glazed over. 'Eira's back in her trance. Come on.' He led them to a table further from earshot. 'I'm going to get you a drink. I can't be dealing with your So'Dal politics right now, so just let me buy them.' Chase nodded, then leant forward when Tian left.

'Keep an eye. I'm going to see what Bones wanted – let him know we're safe.'

Sandy took up his position, and Darin scanned around the room as Chase closed his eyes. Tian glanced back frequently, so Darin smiled at him with reassurance as Chase sat in silence.

After a while, Tian returned and slid in next to Darin, unwilling to move Sandy. 'We received a kind of message when we tried to get in here.' Darin whispered. 'He's just letting them know we made it.'

Tian chuckled. 'I know what he's doing. It's not like I haven't seen it a hundred times before. The getting a message while awake is a new thing, though. That sounds interesting.'

Darin pulled the pebble from his pocket and showed it to Tian. 'Part of the old magic is powering it. We're finding new things to use now because of your whistles. It was the whistles that let Bones make this.'

Tian positively glowed as Darin praised his work. 'Oh, I've just remembered. Do you have the training globe with you?' he asked. 'There's someone here I think you should meet. My instincts say she'd be useful to you, but without a way to check ...'

'Is she unbonded?' Darin leant forward eagerly. 'If she is, we could definitely use her. We need someone who can weft' – he glanced around quickly – 'unaffected by their crystal.'

Tian nodded slowly. 'She's unbonded. But wait until you

meet her before you build up your plans. I'll bring her here in the morning.'

Chase opened his eyes. 'Well, that made a little bit of sense to me. But really, Bones needs to talk to you. Gardener training might make things clearer. He's found a way to add a coating to your weapon.'

That was good, but the slowness of their progress infuriated Darin. They had a library of lost knowledge, of books considered so dangerous they contained the kind of power that existed before the closing – magic able to shatter the land – and yet they struggled to add extra damage to his throwing rings.

Darin smiled. 'Probably something Tralkion could tell me how to do, if I wasn't pretending to be somewhere else! He makes flash bombs and glow lamps. I'm glad Bones has found something. As long as we get the awldrin before she gets hold of anything to augment her own strength – it's just one creature and her very large pet. If we can deal with her, then we can get back to trying to slow the Edgelands incursions and finding ways to reduce their range.'

Chase ran a hand through his hair. 'Bones has almost lived in the deep library for cycles. I assure you, if it was in the normal list of Gardening potions, he'd already have suggested it. I keep hoping he'll find something for wound cauterising or lighting. If we could access fire without a required item, that would make a huge difference.'

'Fire wouldn't have broken the land. There is something much bigger in the hidden library. We're just not seeing it.' Darin pointed at Eira. 'She said there was a Witness here. We should talk to them. If Aggi can perform major surgery, and he was from Dal, I bet they can teach us a few tricks not in the library.'

'We should all have thought that. Age and excitement addles the clearest of thoughts. Not usually Bones and Fall, though.' Chase smiled. 'I'd have got there tomorrow – probably – now I know Tian is safe. But ...'

Tian reached for his hand. 'You're not alone anymore. You didn't need to.'

Darin grinned at the quiet praise. 'No, our pack had it. Let's get some rest in decent beds.'

⌒ ⋏ ʕ ⌘ ◉

When they ate breakfast the next morning, a different woman sat in the centre of the inn. Her eyes were closed, ignoring all who passed by.

Tian excused himself as soon as they'd eaten. 'I need to get Heline. You should meet her.'

An unbonded Soul Anchor would be great, but Darin still wondered why he would need the glow globe to prove anything. She'd either have lilac hair or not.

Purple juice left a stain on Chase's lips as he sipped it. 'Tian will find us. We need to see how close the awldrin is this morning and what she's doing.'

Darin agreed. If they could deal with the awldrin fast, and within the confines of Dal, then they could deal with the other xotryl and whatever might appear in Dal after them. There were a lot of people's lives at risk if more xotryl gained a taste for humans. And that was without considering those creatures they hoped were still contained in the Edgelands. Legends of shadowy creatures in the trees of the surface, of monsters with more spines than a rhinocorn – and worse temperaments.

He drained his own drink. It was tangy and had a lingering, earthy aftertaste. It wasn't unpleasant, but he'd choose a number of drinks before it on any other day.

'Are we not going to talk to her?' Darin gestured at the woman, shorter than Eira, her black scarf shot through with a glimmering thread. It had a subtle glow in the dim light, and he realised it was probably woven from some form of Edgelands plant. He would have to try to get some of that fabric for his mother too. She'd love it.

Chase shook his head. 'let her concentrate.'

They finished their drinks and prepared to leave. Star and Sandy sat at the door to the kitchen, twin puddles of drool growing at their feet. If someone didn't feed them soon, it would become a flood. *[Star walking out next to him]* was firmly replaced by *[Star carrying bone]*. He really needed to eat something more substantial than scavenged bones from kind-hearted people. They could pick something up when they went outside.

'Star won't leave until he's had food.' Darin blushed, embarrassed that he'd failed to call Star to him.

Chase laughed. 'And you think Sandy will leave before then either? These two are pulling their most puppyish faces, and I wish them luck.'

Several minutes later, their powers of persuasion must have worked, as a man appeared at the doorway and gave each hound a fist sized hunk of meat and a bone.

'That's very generous,' Darin called. 'Thank you.'

'Get rid of the creatures, and they can have their pick of a whole faat,' the man replied in a gruff voice before moving back out of sight.

Happiness filled Darin's connection with Star as he gulped down the meat and picked up the bone, tail wagging with delight as he bounded over to join them. Sandy followed close behind.

In the town, things felt almost normal. People carried shopping, and children ran around laughing, chasing each other and playing hunt the farbrox. Darin spotted one child being the farbrox and winked as he ducked behind a barrel. He'd loved the game when he was a kid.

It was a thriving, if over-crowded, town. Chase pointed at some steps, and they climbed them to peer from the wall over the land below. There was nothing there.

'Where are they?' Darin whispered.

'No one has seen them for hours. Could be they moved on finally.' A lanky guard rested his spear against the wall. 'Whole lot of fuss over not a lot if you ask me. I mean, even this.' He gestured over his head.

Darin looked up and around, failing to see what he was pointing at. Chase lifted his hand and ran it through the air over his head. Wrinkles creased his brow. 'She's using fear? It's a brave choice, but with a creature like that on her town's doorstep, I can't say I blame her.'

He took Darin's hand and raised it, moving it in the same way.

Fear overcame him; he could almost feel it filling him up from the fingertips. 'How?'

'That's the crystal's focus being directed into a shield.' Chase sighed. It's not as strong as I'd like.

It was there, but would it enough to repel a xotryl? Darin could understand Chase's concern. 'How much of the town does it cover?'

'All of it. Ain'tcha been around much?' the guard shook his head.

Darin couldn't get used to the casual way in which they accepted the Witnesses protection in Dal. Maybe it would be fine when the rest of the continent learned about their real strength. They were protecting the So'Dal and the people from each other for no good reason.

Darin wanted to believe it – just like he had to believe there would be more Howlers out there to add to the pack. From up here, an area of makeshift tents inside the walls was visible.

'The guard saw him looking and grunted. 'It's getting crowded. Most inn rooms are full, and folk have offered up all their spare space, but it's not enough.' He laughed. 'Who'd ha' thought there were so many of us in this crater?'

Could they get people out of Dal before the situation became critical? Did they even need to? The folk of Dal appeared well protected, as long as the Soul Anchor shield remained up. Food would run out before they were breached, but they could probably hunt in the gaps. He turned back to the clear land stretching between Dal Town and the forest. Where had Natke gone?

The clap of huge wings carried over the wall of the crater as the awldrin and the xotryl she had called her own shield, dived from the surface toward the town.

People screamed.

They ran for cover, panic overriding their belief in the Soul Anchor's shield of fear.

The xotryl drew closer, its huge mouth opened, exposing those vicious teeth as it swooped toward them. Darin waited for the rebound, for the xotryl to hit the layer of fear and pull up. But it merely slowed. The awldrin's will was stronger than the fear produced by a single, crystal-bonded Soul Anchor.

The angle was too steep; there was no way the creature was getting back out. The xotryl passed them, dropping into the central market area, slashing fabric with its talons as traders hid under their tables.

'Avoid the claws!' Chase shouted. His voice didn't carry far above the noise of panic, but it did start a chain of shouts as people took cover from the gigantic beast trying to tear them apart. The Soul Anchor emerged from the inn, raising her hands toward the xotryl and awldrin, her face contorted with effort.

The awldrin leapt off, her heavy feet hitting the ground.

The xotryl bit someone.

Shrieks filled the crisp morning air, cutting through Darin like a blade. 'We need to help,' he urged.

Chase shook his head. 'She's got it. She'll scare it away.'

The awldrin reached forward and plucked the Soul Anchor from the ground, holding her up and shaking her like a dog shakes a toy.

'Is this *it*? The strongest? The best you can pit against me? This trifling fragment of what you once were. You aren't worthy of my time or my respect.' Natke reached out with her other hand and pulled something from the Witness's neck. Dragging the woman with her, she climbed aboard her xotryl. The great beast lumbered into the air, using the houses as a take-off ramp. Up, and up they flew. Then the awldrin laughed – at least Darin thought it was a laugh – and dropped the Witness. People ran to cushion her fall, to stupidly try and catch her, even though they would get crushed. Their own limbs a sacrifice for the good of the town.

They failed. The crack of the Witness's head as it hit the ground was audible from the top of the wall. A flower of blood bloomed from her ended life.

Darin prepared a ring to throw.

'If you have no more strength than that here – in the mightiest of towns – I shall travel and harvest you all until I have what I need.' Natke raised her limb skyward. They cleared the wall, skimming over Darin and Chase.

Light shone through the wings, and Darin aimed his

throwing ring at a main blood vessel, clear and visible in the wing membrane.

The ring sliced through it, and the awldrin shrieked. If Darin had thought her capable of anything but anger, he'd have said it sounded like pain. If there was a link of pain, were they bonded? She'd been able to receive some sort of communication about the magic, and controlled the xotryl in some way.

Blood spurted with each failing wing beat. With each flap of its wings, the scarred green xotryl dropped closer to the ground.

'I did it,' Darin said. 'I actually hit where I was aiming for.'

'Watch the enemy,' Chase said to the guard. Let us know if they get back up. Our hunt will grow faster and more effective if the xotryl is grounded.

He patted Darin on the back and gestured down the stairs. 'We should check on the injured and ensure someone retakes the shield.'

⌒ ⏀ ⟅ ⚶ ◉

They found bodies beyond help, and some folk who were so close to their end that their only respite would be death. All around, townsfolk gathered to treat small wounds and mourn the dead.

Darin found one person who did not appear to be missing limbs but had a few deep puncture wounds. It would be beyond the mending of a normal town healer.

'Here, take this.' He uncorked a healing potion and offered her some. She took it gratefully and returned the partially filled bottle.

Darin looked for others who he could aid on his way to the gate. Another gravely injured person relieved him of the rest of the bottle.

The body of the Soul Anchor lay sprawled across a man of a similar age. Tears streamed down his face, and raw anguish poured from his lips as he wrapped his arms around the corpse.

Darin crouched alongside the man as Chase tended to others with his own bottles of healing draft.

'I'm so sorry.' Words were useless. Words weren't going to mend his body or anything else. 'I need to move her to check your wounds.'

'Watcher take me with her,' the man cried. 'It hurts. It hurts so badly.'

'Look at me.'

The man turned his head, and Darin spotted the Witness tattoo on the man's cheek, his fears made real. They needed this man alive. They needed to learn what they could from him. 'I'm going to move her from you. Please stay still. We'll give her the respect she deserves and is due.'

He crouched down and carefully lifted the Soul Anchor's body from her bonded Witness, laying her alongside him in arm's reach.

The man stared at her. 'She was my everything.' He coughed weakly.

Darin reached for his pocket. Flame it, he'd left the rest of the healing drafts in his room at the inn. Star nudged at him, perhaps feeling Darin's distress. He looked at his hound and the empty bottle, and an idea started to form.

'I can't heal your heart, and I can't bring her back. But I can help you to recover and take revenge. At least, I think I can. I'm Darin – I'm a Howler, and this is Star.'

'Introductions later. You can get more healing draft from our house. My ribs are cracked.' Bubbles of red reached his lips with faint coughs, and his voice grew weaker. They didn't have long enough to retrieve other sources of potion.

[Darin playing the healing draft weft on the whistle, Star touching the man's ribs with his nose. Ribs not broken]

Star replied with confusion.

[Darin's music travelling through Star to heal the ribs] he tried again. He had no idea if it would work, but with Star's innate ability, plus the weft, surely it had to be worth a try. He searched for Chase before he started. 'I need more healing draft,' he shouted. Chase stood, glanced across at the man on the floor and the woman alongside him. His face paled, and he turned and ran.

'Are you ready, boy?' Star wagged his tail. Darin took a deep breath and retrieved the whistle from his pocket. He sat alongside the Witness with Star's nose pushed up against the man's ribs.

'I'd make a joke about your hound licking the blood,' the man said, 'but, flames, that's hurting.' He looked directly at Darin, holding his gaze unflinchingly. His eyes red-rimmed and raw, swelling with tears and anguish.

Darin laid a gentle hand on the man. 'Save your breath. This might not work, but I think it's worth a try. These people need you.'

'So now I'm dinner and an experiment.' The Witness tried to move, but Darin stopped him. A dark-haired woman rushed across the square with Tian in tow as Darin began to play.

'That's not the healing weft.' The Witness tried to hum a tune, but between gurgling foam and the lack of breath, he struggled to hear it.

'No, it's a special Howler one,' Darin replied, hoping he sounded more confident than he felt. The Witness raised an eyebrow, and Darin offered him a smile.

He played the notes over and over again, pushing magic through Star to the man. He hoped that whatever Star's healing abilities were, however they worked, would funnel his weft through the moonhound; to allow his energy to heal the man, not Star's. He played and played, holding the Witness's gaze until the man's eyes closed.

Darin folded slightly as Chase took the whistle from him. A supportive arm reached around his shoulders, stopping him from collapsing. The Witness's face was peaceful.

'I lost him,' Darin said. His shoulders slumped.

Tian gestured at the man's chest, gently rising and falling. 'He lives.'

Chase shook his head. 'Somehow, you've healed him. Just like the power of the potion, it's sent him to sleep to do its work. I've seen him sing a healing weft before, but that was a different tune. There might have been a more effective option, but in the moment, you did the only thing you could think of. You did well, Darin.' Chase smiled. 'I'm proud of you.'

CHAPTER 24

SURIIN

*Moonhounds appear to favour names beginning
with a few specific sounds.
In this article, I will endeavour to prove that they
have a strong preference for names beginning
with voiceless, sibilant, or fricative sounds,for
example, Spot and Flower.*
Moonhound vocal preferences, a study.
T.R. Frome

The old man on the lift lever beckoned her over. Suriin walked slowly while Swift sniffed the air. They were only heading back from the garden; she wasn't doing anything wrong. Watcher knew the lift made her feel rough enough as it was. The lift man didn't speak to her, though. He crouched to fuss over Swift.

'Thank you for taking care of her. She needed it.'

He stood and clasped her hand, a hidden piece of paper in his grip. He left it with her as he withdrew his hand.

'I hope you're making a fresh berry tart or something new

and exciting today,' he said. 'Change may be hard to adjust to, but it's worth it in the end.'

What on Lieus was the silly old man on about? She'd made fruit tarts before. It wasn't anything particularly challenging. Suriin amended that as she felt the paper she'd tucked into her pocket. It wasn't usually hard, but after her last failed attempt to cook, she wasn't sure how to work and earn her way without Swift nearby.

She found herself walking toward the teaching room. Aslin would still be teaching her friends at the moment, but afterward, maybe she could find Suriin something else to do. That way, she would feel part of the palace community still. She stopped walking. They would still be ages, so she'd go to the library to wait. There was no way she could be the first Soul Anchor to lose a crystal. It might not be the main focus or in the library at all, but there would be something in there about healing, something she could use to help herself.

She gripped her hand around the piece of paper in her pocket and changed direction, travelling out to the courtyard and across to the library.

Swift needed a little encouragement to climb the steep stairs to the entrance *[Swift lying on a warm rug under a table]*.

Swift sent back tiredness, but raised her muzzle and climbed slowly. Suriin followed behind, scared that she might lose her footing. The librarian was deep in a book and nodded an acknowledgement as Suriin entered. She walked to the far end of the library and sent *[Swift lying under table]*. Swift complied and sent warm affection back, now tinged with a little hunger. All the help she'd given Suriin today was clearly hungry work. Suriin reached down to stroke her. The soft ears were thin and her hair rough.

Fluffy really liked dried fish. Her mother had always said it was good for her coat. Suriin laughed at her own folly. This far from South Crater and the sea, she didn't think there would be much fish to give Swift, but she was going to try.

She pulled her notebook and a pencil from her pocket, and her hand brushed against the note. She sat at the table and unfolded it.

⌐ ⋏ ☾ ✤ ◉

Dear Suriin,

Your mother is alive and in Dal Town. Your father knows she is there, and her hound watches your family as her eyes. She knows about the missing crystal. The awldrin is outside the gates of Dal Town, but Eira is safe.

Travel to the tower built from the mountain on the north end of the wall after the sun sets tonight. We need to talk. Tell no one.

⌐ ⋏ ☾ ✤ ◉

Suriin read and re-read it, anger and frustration warring with relief. Her mother was alive. She'd deliberately left them in the safest place she could, but she'd risked Suriin's father. What if he hadn't made it? If she'd been here instead, then Suriin wouldn't have felt as though her father was forgotten.

The Anchor would not have dared to let her father reach the threshold of death.

Suriin would never have been searching in the tunnels for a cure.

Her shoulders dropped while she slid to the floor alongside Swift. Tears flowed freely, and she buried her face in the old hound's fur. Swift licked her.

As much as she wanted to wallow in self pity, Swift wouldn't let her, flooding her with waves of love and affection. Suriin ran her fingers through Swift's fur, stroked her ears, and kissed her wrinkled head. She pulled her notebook from the table.

'If there was ever a time that I needed to draw myself calm, this would be it,' she whispered.

She pulled her knees up as an easel and focused on Swift. On the big eyes, on the wrinkled head. Suriin drew Swift as she saw her. Thin with her sparse coat, her angular features which would soften again once she'd eaten more. As she finished shading the hound's spots, Suriin turned the page and drew her again, plumper and with more muscle. She drew a slight sheen across her face, Swift's eyes less sunken. Suriin tuned the paper to show Swift, trying to imagine her as a young moonhound *[Swift with younger features, like the drawing]*.

Swift replied with a wag.

Her wild thoughts tamed, Suriin tucked the note back in her pocket. There was nothing she could do about her mother's choices.

Suriin looked up at the library of knowledge she sat in. What she needed to do was find a way to help her mother. At the least, Suriin needed to learn more about her situation, find any records of previous observations to predict how long the effects would last. Her path had changed slightly with the news of her mother, but before she could return to lessons or find a way to aid her, she had the small issue of a crystal to sort out.

Suriin frowned. She'd not needed it before she bonded, and using her powers had been much easier, more instinctive. What if instead of finding the crystal, she could find a way to unbond?

She'd lose the ability to feel the deaths and know where the awldrin was, but maybe she could re-bond to another crystal. She could still learn from the library until someone realised she was not crystal-bound, or from her mother if she could make contact.

Suriin climbed back onto her seat. There had to be a way around the situation. Were there books on crystal-focused magic in here? The emotion symbols were in small books near the front desk where they usually studied. Seeing Aslin again might be able to wait until tomorrow? Gwynn would pass on anything she really needed to know. She could offer to get Chef all his ingredients, instead of being in the kitchen! It would leave Fresna alone.

Suriin sighed. She was too focused on her own importance. They'd managed the kitchen before she arrived and would do so again without her. Even if she would miss it – and Fresna. Chef probably just needed time to rearrange shifts for a short period. Collecting food might be her best plan.

She wandered to the front of the library to search near the books on symbols. She'd got half-way along the row and not found anything useful when Merri arrived.

'Suriin!'

She turned just in time to be hugged and wrapped in the warmth of friendship from her friends. Skye stood at the back and mouthed, 'Are you okay?'

Suriin nodded. Then, remembering Swift, put a finger on her lips and beckoned for them to follow her.

The librarian had looked up at them, and her frown deepened marginally as Suriin flashed her a grin before leading her friends to the table where Swift waited.

⌒ ⋔ ◊ ✧ ◉

The rest of the day passed in a haze of friendship and ever-increasing nausea. Suriin tried to hide it, to pretend she was okay. But Swift's frequent nudges at her leg and Skye's increasingly concerned face convinced her that she needed to see Aslin for a new potion, or some easing of her symptoms.

She'd found nothing in her reading, but it was hard to talk about what she sought without giving away the truth of her situation. Instead, she'd talked about her crystal feeling fainter, further from her, and hard to pinpoint when Merri had asked.

'I want to get back to lessons if there is any way. I didn't wait this long just to be foiled by some thief,' she muttered when they asked.

'But you have Swift now. You're further down the Soul Anchor route than us,' Joy had replied. She'd looked at Swift with pity. Suriin saw it in her expression, though she could not be sure which of them the pity was meant for.

Swift had eaten well when they went for lunch. The happiness of her moonhound swelled as her stomach did. It anchored and calmed Suriin a little. Once Swift was more sated, she was better able to ease Suriin's symptoms. It still wouldn't be enough to remove them entirely, and before she met with her mysterious letter-givers, she needed a clear head. It was too late for a potion, even if she had one; it would make her sleep, and she'd miss the meeting. Suriin sighed.

'Are you okay?' Merri looked up from her book. They were learning symbol combinations without her, and they were sharing the theory, even though she couldn't practise or focus on what they were trying to explain.

'Aslin was telling us not to add too much serenity to anything today.' Joy looked over Merri's shoulder at the page. 'Looks like she's in agreement with this author. It says here that it can affect your judgement because it can overwhelm other emotions if not used sparingly.'

'I suppose that means that were you to use fear on an enemy, with serenity heavily loaded into it for yourself, then you'd not be afraid, and you'd take less care than you should – be too bold.' Suriin drew on the bitterness of her own experience as she put the pieces together. She'd been so nervous, she must have used too much serenity, way too much. Bile rose in her throat. She was about to vomit. She clasped her hand tightly over her mouth and ran for the steps, with Swift following close behind.

'Thank you, not on the books. Less ale for lunch next time,' the librarian called cheerfully as Suriin rushed past.

Her friends followed close behind, but she didn't dare stop. Instead, she struggled across to the side of the courtyard and fell to her knees, unable to hold her food down any longer.

⌒ ⋏ ◖ ⪥ ◉

She followed the thread of her severed mind, drawn unwillingly toward another death. The inevitability made her retch again.

The awldrin was in Dal.

Her mother was in Dal.

Suriin held back a cry of fear as they flew up and up only to drop steeply, the crystal bouncing around in the bag. Anger surrounded her – it. Anger and hatred, then a sharp twist of fear, but insufficient to make the anger subside.

More fear, not from Natke now. But sharp spikes of fear drawn into the crystal. She was glad that the crystal was in the pouch, that she didn't have to witness the blurry light, the tang and the warmth of the death. No crystal joined her, no wet blood. Suriin dared to hope that this time, the Soul Anchor had got away. That her mother wasn't the target.

She was being licked; her body far away in Redpike was being nudged. Gentle arms lifted her head, held her hair from her face.

Suriin felt for the thread, for Swift. The hound shone brightly in her mind, and Suriin grabbed hold of her presence, dragging herself back. It was far easier than returning previously had been.

She forced her eyes open to take in the sight of Redpike, the scent of the ground and the texture of Swift's fur, the murmuring of quiet voices. Suriin turned her head to see who was helping. Joy supported Suriin's head across her thigh, while Merri held her hair back.

'Thank you,' Suriin croaked. 'It catches me sometimes.' She offered them a weak smile.

'Skye's gone to get Aslin,' Joy said. 'Stay where you are. We'll get you back to your room to recover as soon as we can.'

Swift lay alongside her, and Suriin buried her hands in the hound's fur.

Swift sent *[Suriin being sick, Swift as close as she could be]*.

Suriin replied with affection. She didn't have the energy to construct a difficult sending right now, but she had to. *[Swift and Suriin sleeping, then darkness, and Swift and Suriin walking into the small tower on the end of the wall]*

Suriin searched for the tower the note had mentioned, spotting it on the far wall. It appeared to have no entrance. She had no idea how to get into it.

'I'd like to sit up,' she said. Joy supported her, shuffling forward to sit nearby, a casual arm around her for support. Suriin appreciated the gesture more than she could express.

'Thank you,' she mumbled, then clamped her mouth closed again.

Joy and Merri talked of South Crater and the sea, Merri talked of Ronin, and Suriin hid a smile behind her hands. As much as he irritated her, Ronin had helped her, too, and she wished him his own world of happiness.

Skye must have found Aslin easily, given how fast they arrived, and behind them, Gwynn and Fluffy ran to catch up.

'I get a little sick, and everyone turns out to see me,' Suriin joked. 'I promise it's nothing to worry about.'

Aslin crouched in front of her. 'Maybe, maybe not. I'll get

Orin to make you a fresh healing draft tomorrow. For now, all I can do is offer my own support. May I?'

Suriin nodded. She'd agree to almost anything to stop this nausea.

Aslin placed her hands on Suriin's head and closed her eyes. Suriin felt a trickle of calm, along with acceptance and something else she couldn't quite work out. Their combination made her less conscious of the crystal, less unwell.

'Thank you. What did you combine there to make the feeling go away?' She wanted to say trauma, but, worried Aslin or her friends would read truth into it, she decided on the lesser sensation.

'Serenity, hope, distraction, and acceptance. Accepting our situation leads our body to fight it less. That allows us to heal what is there, not what we worry it could also become. You may feel tired, but not as much as from the potion. Come and see me before the lesson starts tomorrow, and I'll have one ready for you.' She helped Suriin to her feet.

Gwynn put his arm around Suriin's shoulders, and Swift walked on her other side, shoulder to leg with Suriin. She rested her hand in Swift's fur and drew comfort and support from her hound. Aslin's eyebrows shot up as she noticed Swift for the first time.

'What's she doing here?'

'She bonded me.' Suriin shrugged. 'Mum always said I should never say no to a moonhound, so I didn't.'

Aslin chuckled. 'There are times I'm sure you will say no to her. I'm surprised she chose you, but if I'm honest, I thought she'd left us. She was a starving wretch when I last saw her. If she's found a reason to live, we'd better get you fixed up for her.'

'Gwynn, can you escort Suriin back to her room? I need to get to my other class.' She turned to the others. 'Suriin is lucky to have friends like you. We all need someone to hold our hair sometimes.' She turned and strode off, her curls bouncing with every step.

Gwynn rolled his eyes. 'She's been all full of sayings like that today. Half of them don't even make sense.'

'Thank you.' Suriin waved feebly at the others. She let Gwyn lead her away without protest.

'Was it another one?' he asked once they were out of hearing

'I don't know. It was slightly different this time. And no new crystal in my pouch,' she whispered, scared to voice her mind's reality aloud.

Once they reached her room, Suriin closed the door so that they were alone.

'I think *they* want to talk to me. I wonder if they found a way to help me with the crystal. I'm not supposed to say anything, but I need to. I'm to meet them somewhere just after dark. I think I need sleep more than food, but can you wake me as the light begins to fade?'

'With pleasure. I think it's okay to tell me that the Howlers want to talk to you. After all, I've kind of met at least Darin again since we rescued you. Don't tell me what it's about, though. I think they deal in secrets – not from choice, but necessity. I'll wake you in an hour or so, with some food if I can smuggle it out the hall.'

The Howlers. She had a name for the group now, and Gwynn didn't seem worried about them wanting to talk to her. It was a good sign.

CHAPTER 25

ELISSA

*We return to Hope full of children and followed
    by the vessels which fled Shardeep.
Later today, we must tie the first of the Shardeep
    vessels to our stern and guide them through
    the fog.
It may take a number of journeys before we are
    all safely to Hope.
I hope I can recover them in time to meet with the
    Dragonsbreath sericlave.*
Captain's log, Cloudsailor

'We're going to the Hatchery,' Elissa insisted.

Sorrow swung his head from side to side in denial. 'You can't make me.'

'You're a dragon! What's the problem? Just guide me there. I'll walk in and take the bit of egg shell we need to reforge the echoglass, then we return to Rapture.'

'She's addled your brain.' Sorrow hung his head so low that

his snout rested on the floor. 'I knew she would, and so off you go, running to your demise joyfully.'

'How far away is it?' Elissa asked.

'On foot, many days. Many, many days.'

That was helpful. Elissa stroked Dreamer as she considered the next move. She needed a dragon to guide her there, and Hope had tasked her with saving Sorrow from himself. Regret had said that other dragons might not accept her or wish her well, and Rapture implied that there were some of those at the Hatchery. If any dragon should guide her, it made sense for it to be Sorrow, but persuading him to go to there willingly appeared to be an issue.

Fixing Sorrow might have to happen sooner than she'd anticipated. Elissa looked him over. He was so dejected. How had she started to heal, to move forward from her acceptance of how worthless she had perceived herself to be? Elissa thought back to that first bath she'd ever had, the sensation of a fresh start in a new place. Maybe they could start with getting him clean.

'Is there a lake around here somewhere?' she asked. 'I could do with a quick wash.'

'You're changing the conversation.' Sorrow studied her from deeply hooded eyes. Dust crusted the inner corners and rested in the creases of his lids. Yes, a bath would do them both good.

'For now, yes, I am.'

Sorrow leaked sadness like a wide woven fishing net leaked tiny fish. He didn't assault her with emotions like Rapture or lift her spirits in the way Hope did. But she suspected her own sadness had been partly suppressed by the power of his until she'd been further away from him.

'There's a lake over that way.' The half-hearted snout gesture didn't make it entirely clear, so Elissa set off in the rough direction Sorrow indicated. She was a good few dragon-lengths away when Sorrow responded to her unfaltering walk into the unknown.

'You're going the wrong way. Watch out! That plant is toxic to humans. No, don't take that path!'

A small huff from behind her and some slow wing flaps gave him away as he scooped her up in his talons and flew with her dangling beneath him for a short distance before gently replacing her on the ground the other side of some large, thorny bushes. Dreamer chased after them, shrieking in annoyance.

Once her feet were back on the ground, a fragrant scent drifted up with every footstep from the tiny leaves beneath her feet. Sorrow walked alongside, guiding her. Elissa was careful to stay away from the thorny bushes now. There were no real paths here, and although she had been prepared to use them, those that did exist were for creatures far smaller than herself.

She was about to ask what sort of animals made them, when they crested a small rise and below her, extending into the duskline, was a strange, clear-watered lake.

'Is it safe for me to swim?' Elissa called as she ran down to the water's edge. Nothing bar the wind disturbed the surface. The area closest to her was the clearest water she'd ever seen – nothing like the Ameryth Dar's purple, clouded waters. The depth she could see to was a little unnerving. She sat to remove her foot wraps, then stepped forward to dip her toes in. The water was cold, but not unbearably so.

'You will be safe to swim here.' Sorrow dipped his snout into the water and blew some bubbles.

Elissa held back a smile. She waded in, her bare skin soaking up the warmth of the Aulirean sun, and the water caressed her legs. It felt good – as though she could wash away all the dragons' emotional influences for a moment. She ducked under the water, immersing herself completely, washing away everything but herself, her own thoughts and emotions. Only submerged in such a way was it obvious how much Sorrow's emotions had cloaked her.

Elissa was in an incredible place, filled with wonders; she was flying on dragons. She started to struggle for breath and emerged to take another lungful. Sorrow's snout almost dunked her back under.

'You disappeared,' he said mournfully. 'I was afeared.'

Elissa struggled not to roll her eyes. She could take another breath and dunk back under ... or she could do what she'd come here to do.

'Sorrow, that was barely a rhyme.' She forced a laugh. 'Why don't you come in too? I'll scrub your scales, and you will feel a lot better.'

Elissa searched the bank for something to scrub him with and spotted something a little like windweed. She waded toward it and plucked a bunch before sitting in the shallows and weaving the strands through each other roughly, then folding and folding the resulting weave to make a cleaning pad.

Sorrow tentatively waded in, and before he could change his mind, Elissa pounced. She scrubbed his scales, starting with those he could clearly not reach. The water grew murky as cycles – probably hundreds of cycles, Elissa decided as she scrubbed at a particularly well-coated scale – worth of grime washed slowly off.

As she worked, the suffocating weight of emotion she was under flowed more freely, rather than less. Freeing Sorrow from his muddy case also freed his emotional power. Elissa scrubbed and cried, mourning Makin's loss and the potential loss of her other friends. She cried for the sorrow of a species that would die without help. She cried for the lives lost as the awldrin hunted her.

They stayed in the water until Elissa's hands were as raw as her emotions – until she could clean Sorrow no more.

She dragged herself to the shore to dry. Sorrow waded in the opposite direction, immersing himself completely, rinsing all the loose grime that Elissa had freed into the lake. He vanished almost entirely for a moment, submerged bar the tips of his spines, which shook, sending ripples across the lake. Then, he sprung from the water, spiralling skyward with powerful wingbeats. His scales shimmered silver in the light, and he was every bit as beautiful as Hope.

Elissa sniffled as she dressed. The next stage of their task would be a lot tougher than she'd thought.

Sorrow alighted alongside her and shook the last droplets of water out of his scales. Elissa was drenched again.

'Thank you,' he said. 'You were right. I needed that.' He shimmered as he moved, and Elissa winced as light reflected directly into her eyes. 'We need to work out a plan. Walking up to the hatchery, hoping that a new Vigilant has hatched and that the eggshell fragments are still there – plus getting past whoever is posted at the gates – all seems a bit hopeful to be honest. And I'm not her. I need a plan, a back-up plan, and an escape plan.'

The bath really had helped. Food and clean scales, and despite the increased leaking of sadness from him, Sorrow was prepared to try.

'Rapture was adamant that there would be a new Vigilant. She said it was the way things were.'

Sorrow nodded slowly. 'I agree, but two factors are unknown. Is it hatched yet? And, if it did, how long ago?' He tapped a claw on the ground. 'No, there are three factors. By exposing you to Amazement, we have exposed you to every dragon on Mythos. That beast can never keep a secret, nor did I have a chance to tell her to.'

'Why does that matter?'

'It matters because now the others know you are here, they may be more cautious with protecting the Hatchery.'

Again, Elissa shrugged. 'Why on Tebein would my presence make them do that?'

'We have long memories. Humans have used fragments of dragon bone and egg for numerous things, as have the awldrin. If I were on the gate, I'd be eating the remaining egg shell, if it didn't change my very being. Or hiding it. Or ...'

'I get it. What you're saying is that we need to move fast, bring the element of surprise.'

'I don't think finding Surprise is a good idea. Amazement is at least a little more useful and willing.'

Elissa rubbed her eyes, about to reply that she hadn't meant the dragon when she decided better of it. 'We'll sneak in. Get there before they realise I'm away from Rapture.' She stretched the aches of riding from her legs. Could it be called a day if there was no day and night? How did the dragons have any sense of time?

'Let's go, then.'

Sorrow flattened himself, and Elissa took the cue. She scrambled up his leg and sat astride the base of his neck. Dreamer fluttered down to land on her shoulder, having long since abandoned trying to keep up by himself. They took off, flying further into the light. At least they wouldn't meet the Hatchery guardians in the darkness.

The air grew hotter and more oppressive, her sweat beading. She would need to drink a lot in this heat.

⌒ ⚹ ⌀ ⚛ ◎

'You need to be more dragon,' Sorrow called back after she complained for the third time. They'd been flying for hours, and the land below was now sparsely vegetated. There were few tall plants here, mostly just a sort of fine, thin plant that looked a little like windweed. Slender, golden stems rippled beneath in the wake of their passage.

How was she supposed to be more dragon – make wings of thread? It sounded fanciful, even to her, but a few tides ago, she'd had no idea magic existed. No one could help her, aside from the mysterious *Him* the dragons kept talking about. Rapture had mentioned that *He* had created records for the Watcher. If this was Otso the flame-wielder, then he might have documented his own challenges too. Elissa tucked the thought away for later.

As they flew, Elissa delved around inside herself, trying to recognise anything that felt different from how she usually felt. Her knot of emotions remained a tangled mess, with some threads almost glowing to her awareness now she focused on them. She delved deeper, losing track of the world outside as she tried to identify anything new, anything strange. But she couldn't.

She swayed to one side a little too far, and Sorrow shifted under her.

'Falling from the sky is being less dragon,' he muttered.

'I'm not a dragon, though. I'm a human with a bit of dragon stuck in me.'

'Spreading all through you, not stuck in you.'

'So you say. But I can't feel it, can't control it.'

'Find a way.' Sorrow turned a little, and ahead, Elissa spotted a stand of taller vegetation. They dropped lower as they approached, and Sorrow waddled between tall, sharp-edged leaves. The plants appeared to be the same as the ones she'd used as a bed days ago. Jagged tooth-like structures with faint orange stripes protruded from the upper third of the leaves. They didn't provide a lot of shade, but Elissa squeezed herself into the coolest spot she could find.

'We'll rest here. When we next fly, we will arrive near the Hatchery. We should travel slowly and carefully.'

'Can you feel who is guarding it?' Elissa asked.

Sorrow raised his snout to the sky, flicking out his tongue as though he tasted the air. 'I think we are a little too far to tell. Be prepared for any of the older dragons. The biggest, most powerful of us.'

'Perfect.' Elissa stretched out, staring up at the impossibly blue sky. She should sleep. Did humans perish here from the atmosphere and food? Or was it simply that they were so far out of time – out of place – that their bodies gave up trying? She opened her pack and searched for something to tie across her eyes.

It was all too bulky or filthy. She covered her face with her arm and sighed. Dreamer floated down to her from his position atop the leaf-blade and watched her struggle to get comfortable before curling up on her face, his claws tucked in, but his wings across her eyes. Elissa was sure he'd get bored soon, and he was really quite uncomfortable, but she appreciated his effort. She let him stay there. He'd soon move.

⌒ ⋏ ◖ ✢ ◉

Dreamer started to chitter at her a short while later, so she got up and let him lead her a short distance. They were headed toward the hatchery. It was cool enough that she didn't feel sweaty.

'We're going there after I've rested,' she said. Why was it so much cooler? Dreamer hit her with a wall of fear. Oh, they were dreaming.

At least here she could communicate their plan, and he'd gather the gist of what she was about to do.

'There will be dragons guarding it. And I need you to sneak in, to search for a black egg.' She drew an egg in the sandy soil, then cracked it. And tried to find a black object nearby. She had no idea how well Dreamer could understand her, and it might have been better to ask Sorrow to speak with him, but she wanted to see if she could.

Dreamer hopped to the egg, pecking at it with his snout. Elissa cooed at him, praised him, and found an imaginary berry in her pocket to offer Dreamer. It was the first time she'd truly tried to control the essence of her own dream, and she decided she liked it.

'Rest.' Sorrow grumbled from somewhere nearby. 'You're broadcasting your dream and our plans to everything in the area.'

Sorrow had a point. She hadn't set her guards at all. Elissa had felt safe here, away from the risk of xotryl or Chosen wandering into her dreams. In her semi-awake state, Elissa recognised the danger and set her guards properly before drifting back to sleep, her connection to Dreamer cut off.

⌐ ⻔ ◖ ✿ ◉

Dreamer's claws pierced Elissa awake.

'Ow!'

Sorrow stretched out nearby, basking in the sun, his own eyes closed. Her stomach growled; it ached a little too. How long had it been since she last ate? In terms of time, Elissa had no idea, but one less distraction would be essential in the next step of their journey.

Lieus had moved across the sky a little further, and another side of its green and blue-toned wonder showed its face to her.

This landmass stretched around a large section of the planet, with brown scars across the middle and a water mass so huge it almost split the land, but not quite.

She stared up at it in fascination and was still studying it when Sorrow woke.

'On Tebein, there is more land than water. Lieus is the opposite, isn't it?'

Sorrow lifted his head. 'Yes. There's the smaller continent of Caldera, where the Gate is located, and a much larger land the humans call Oubarn and Vatra Estin.'

'So many people,' Elissa murmured.

'Who don't know the others exist. Indeed, a strange world. Are you ready to go?'

Elissa slung her bag across her shoulder and offered her hand for Dreamer to climb onto. He obliged, his skin currently a toned-down grey-ish black. As though he knew they would need to be discreet. Maybe he'd understood her attempt at communication.

⌒ ⋏ ◊ ✢ ◦

They flew for what felt like a full crystal shift in silence. Sorrow's emotional drain on her was more intense when they were in physical contact, and Elissa found herself wrestling with her own sadness as they travelled. She cried until her eyes grew sore.

A more mountainous region rose from the open plain ahead, strange and out of place, the hills speared skyward.

'That's the Hatchery,' Sorrow called back. 'I'll bring us down shortly so it's not obvious we're headed there.'

'If your Oldest dragon sent us, why can't I walk in? I've been invited. Surely, that should be enough permission.'

'Oldest doesn't mean she is in charge. Only Harmony could guarantee a passage, and they are long gone.'

Harmony – the dragon Rapture claimed Elissa smelt of. The second time she had heard their name. She saved the information for later and braced for landing.

⌐ ⋏ ∂ ⚇ ◉

The walk to the base of the Hatchery was uneventful, if exhausting. Sorrow's recent meal had left him with more energy than Elissa, and he allowed her to ride him as her legs grew tired.

Lieus had moved to a higher position, and Elissa decided that it might be longer than the days she was used to, but at least she had found some way to measure the passage of time.

She stared up at the imposing cliff ahead. No paths crossed its steep side, and from here, the spiked plant was obvious. Watcher knew how many other plants might be dangerous to her. She would have to negotiate a route for herself as she climbed.

'There's a ledge at the top of this peak. Below it, there is a slope without plants. It is slippy, and you will be exposed for them to see. You must take great care with each slow, careful step. I still don't know how you will get in unnoticed.'

'Can't you fly in, grab the egg fragment, and fly out?'

Sorrow's features contorted in horror. 'That would be very, very wrong. It is not my egg.'

'Not even to help fix this situation?'

'No. Besides, they would feel me coming, track me easily. You must do it alone.'

'This is crazy. Why can't we just explain it?'

'It's your task. You deal with it as you see fit. I'll sit out here and wait. I hope you come back out and I will be ready to fly us away fast. Remember, whoever is there, you coped with Rapture. You can push through whatever you're hit with.'

'As long as it's just emotions.'

Elissa started to climb. Her flames would do nothing if any resistance grew physical. She scrambled up the slope, trying to avoid contact with every plant. She was certain something stung her through the legs of her clothes. It itched furiously, but she tried to ignore it.

As Elissa grew further from Sorrow, her mind cleared, and she took deep breaths to calm herself. Looking around, taking her time to climb. The heat was her ally, as the plants were more spread out than they'd appeared from the base. Dreamer came to rest on her shoulder as she started the last, steepest section of the climb. At least he wouldn't be visible in the air above the rim.

Elissa stopped just below the crest of the hill, readying herself to face whatever was on the other side.

A silhouette passed overhead, and she glanced up just in time to duck beneath an incoming attack from a small, black dragon.

AWLDRIN

CHAPTER 26

DARIN

A full Howler pack is a rare sight.
With red weapons raised and armour shining,
  these warriors stride fearless into battle.
They keep us safe. And we keep a welcome for
  them all.
Tarnished brass plaque in the cellar of the
  Spotted Dog Inn

They laid the Witness carefully on his bed. Tian sat alongside him.

'She was the last one. We would be defenceless if Eira had not come home. I'll stay with him until his daughters arrive. More than ever, I think you need to go talk to Heline.'

'Who is Heline?' Darin asked.

'The woman who helped us carry him home. She returned to arrange for the Soul Anchor's body to be brought back. She helps look after the hound pack.'

Chase remained with Tian and the Witness as Darin went downstairs. Whimpers wound up the stairwell, a hound in mourning. They should be outside the gates, taking advantage of the xotryl being down, but he had no appetite to fight at that moment.

Star and Sandy laid on a rug, sandwiching a moonhound as broken as the man upstairs. Small cries drifted from her as she trembled. The Howler hounds laid as close as they could, nuzzling her.

Darin looked at the hound. How would he feel if he lost Star? Devastated? Utterly broken? They were a part of each other; it would be horrific to be cut off. That hound must have felt all the terror and pain of the Soul Anchor's last moments. He sent love to Star, who replied with a single wag. His focus was elsewhere.

'She may fade away. She may survive as a shadow of the hound she was. I'll get some of our pack to support her when you leave.'

A dark-haired woman stood in the doorway. 'Her body is in the care of others,' she said, then walked in to the small room and sat across from Darin. Her hair was straight and glossy, her eyes deep pools of sorrow as she joined him. A single ring with a red stone decorated the hand she offered in greeting. 'My name is Heline. Tian was just bringing me to meet you when ...'

Darin rubbed at his eyes. 'Yeah, he seemed to think we should meet you.' He took in the woman in more detail. No head scarf, no lilac hair. 'What can I do for you?' he asked eventually.

She looked a little uncomfortable for a moment, then she shrugged. 'Tian says I have a way with the hounds here. He wanted to test me for magic.'

Darin frowned. 'But your hair.'

'It's black, yes, I know. Did you bring the testing thing?'

Darin shook his head. 'It's back in the Howler

accommodations in Redpike. They need it to try to solve a bit of a situation. Why did he think you had magic?'

She screwed her face up. 'Can you just test me somehow? Please?'

Darin's tired brain wasn't ready for this. He struggled to come up with a solution. The woman was nice enough, she was clearly capable, and she knew the moonhounds well. He didn't want to be the one who dashed her hopes. She talked so openly about a test for magic.

'Can you sing?' he asked.

She laughed. It was a small laugh, thin and tired. 'I've been told my singing would drive the birds into hiding for my entire life.'

'Can you push emotions?' he asked, thinking back to the books he'd read before leaving the Howler accommodations.

She shook her head. 'Not that I'm aware of. I have very vivid dreams of the pups I've helped the Witness family raise. I have nightmares, and I saw that thing' – she gestured toward the south – 'before I even saw it up close.'

Darin leant forward a little as an idea came to him. 'Look, I'm going to show you a thing. It upset the xotryl before, so we have to be to be really fast if the shield isn't rebuilt. Are you ready?'

She nodded.

Darin took the shard-whistle out of his pocket and held the dragon bone, then blew it to vanish.

Heline gasped. 'That's a really good trick.'

Darin blew it again and reappeared.

'I need you to imagine you are putting a cloak on when you blow it.' He handed the whistle and the dragon bone over to her.

She took up the same position, mimicking him exactly, and blew the whistle. She vanished.

'Watcher's fire! Do it again – remove the cloak.' Darin gaped. She reappeared and shyly handed his items back to him.

Chase chuckled from the doorway. 'Heline, I presume.' He strode in and offered a hand to her. 'Tian was just telling me about you, and he was right. Two new Howlers in less than a cycle! Times are changing indeed. Now, the most important thing we need to address is which pup were you dreaming about?'

'The spottiest one. She wags like her tail will fall off when she sees me.'

'Let's go out and see. Darin, come along. We could all use a little happiness right now.' He called Sandy softly. Sandy nuzzled the moonhound on the rug and stretched before accompanying them.

'We'll leave Star with her for company.' Chase led the way out of the Witness house round to a yard behind it, filled with young pups who milled around in confusion. 'She'll need to come back for them soon. They're too small to cope without her.' The pups barked at Sandy, bowing in play at his feet.

Some older youngsters walked out from a shelter nearby. They were of an age with Star and one was the spottiest moonhound he'd ever seen – even more than the one on the Spotted Dog's sign.

Heline reached over to scratch her on the ear. 'She's beautiful. I'm sure she likes me.'

Chase tilted his head, and for a moment, the attitude reminded him so much of Sandy that Darin had to hold back a smile. Sandy walked toward the spotty hound and touched muzzles with her. They stood frozen, staring at each other for a while, then the spotty hound walked up to Heline and sat at her feet.

'Stroke her and relax,' Darin said. If Chase was right, the

next few moments would be a light amidst the darkness of the day.

Heline reached out for the hound and, moments later, stumbled slightly. Darin steadied her as a smile spread across her face.

'I can see a forest and trees. The light falling on the floor through the branches like flecks of gold. Like her. I've dreamed this image before, lots of times,' she murmured.

'She's been trying to tell you her name,' Darin offered. 'Can you name her from the image she gives you?'

'Fleck?' Heline opened her eyes and turned to Darin. 'Is her name Fleck?'

'Ask her, not me.' He was reminded of his own bonding with Star.

She crouched in front of Fleck, and within moments, the hound had exploded into a writhing mass of fur, barks, and wags.

'Welcome to the pack,' Chase said. 'I think she's been waiting a long while for you to realise you'd been chosen.'

Heline beamed with happiness. 'When I was a kid, I saw the Howlers and dreamed of being one. We all did in Dal. Then, I chose a different life to the one I was born with, and the idea of being a So'Dal wasn't even a whisper of an idea in my mind. As I grew older, I thought that door was closed to me. I'd have made the same choice regardless, every time. And now – it shows you really can have it all.' She wrapped her arms around Fleck and buried her head in the spotted fur.

Chase leant down to stroke Fleck. 'You are far from the first female Howler, Heline, and you won't be the last. Bones even told me about records of a lilac-haired Howler once. We know the ability to weft or use the pure emotional magic runs in families, but like many traits, sometimes the magic we inherit isn't quite as clear as it might first appear. As long as the

Watcher's rules are followed, anyone with magic has always found a place amongst the So'Dal.'

'That's two of us who need to learn hound fighting, then.' Darin chuckled. 'Three hounds are better than two.'

They were interrupted by a panting guard. 'I think you'd better see this,' he said as he doubled over, out of breath.

'Do you need a moment?' Chase asked.

The guard shook his head. 'I'll be fine.' He turned and gestured for them to follow.

'I'll stay here,' Heline shouted after them. 'I'll reunite the mother and pups and be here for when Luik wakes.'

Darin called Star, and together with Chase and the hounds, ran after the guard. Darin found himself more exhausted than he expected. The wefting through the whistle must have taken more out of him than he'd realised initially. He paused for a moment as fatigue filled his limbs, and Star nudged him on. *[Darin and Star running through the paddocks]* filled his vision, along with an intense sensation of happiness.

Darin ran after the others, who now leapt up the stairs to the wall, two at a time. Sandy ran ahead of Chase, close on the heels of the guard. As he reached the top of the wall, a shadow he'd initially thought was a bird grew ever larger and redder over the forest of Dal.

'Maybe they'll fight,' he said as he reached Chase.

Chase and the guard stood side by side. Darin peered over the edge to see what the awldrin was up to. Natke paced alongside the downed xotryl, turning to stare at the approaching red one frequently. If the green one was bonded, what was Big Red doing here? Were they territorial opponents? Could they communicate over a distance? Surely, Natke could not command them all? Darin shook himself. It had been a long few days' travel and now he was imagining things.

'Was it the red one you called us to see?' he asked.

The guard shook his head, his skin paling as he tried not to look across to the forest. And Big Red's approach.

'That's appeared while I came to get you. That monster has stopped it now. But I swear, the monster was doing something to the xotryl's talons. Rubbing something shiny against it – a weapon of some sort.'

Darin swallowed. He'd gifted her a weapon. He'd been so busy trying to take them down, the thought of her re-using it didn't occur to him. He could only hope that if he was a bit off target after a cycle or two, she'd be really bad after five hundred cycles.

'We should rush her now,' Chase muttered. 'While she's grounded.'

'We should, but I could barely make it up the stairs.' Darin wasn't entirely sure whether the trembling in his knees as he looked down from the wall was his fear of heights or exhaustion. As Star wasn't also trembling, it was probably tiredness. 'I'll still join you if you think it's our best chance.'

'We have a really small window of time before Big Red gets here. Get your other throwing rings and let's do this.'

Chase ran down the stairs to the town square, where bodies were still being moved and mourned over.

'Join me!' he called out. 'The awldrin is grounded and the xotryl down. We could take her out, could neutralise this threat.'

Some people shuffled forward to listen, a few peered through open doorways.

'We go now!' Chase tried to inspire them into action. But there was little appetite for fighting. A couple of younger men strapped swords to their sides as they strode across to join them.

'Is this it?' Chase asked.

'I imagine it will be. If we antagonise that monster and it

returns to attack us like a poked nest of red-stripes, they don't want to be in its reach. Can't blame them. There's been death every day. I vote we end the creature. Now,' the tallest responded.

Chase clapped the man on the back. 'Come, let's go then. Darin, get your rings and the hound armour.'

'And give her more?' Darin felt the scowl, knew he was looking reluctant, but after arming the awldrin, after hearing that she was trying to wipe it on the claws of the xotryl. He thought that adding any more weapons to her collection would be an awful idea. But he had no others.

They gathered by the main town gates, the wall high enough that they had no idea of how far away the red xotryl was.

'Tactics?' Darin leant across to whisper to Chase.

'No tactics – just attack. We have the numbers. It has to be worth a try.'

They cracked the door open, and the xotryl raised its head slightly. The awldrin turned from her study of the skyline toward them.

'Hit me while I'm down. Cowards and weaklings, every one of you. Unarmed and grounded, you see your chance. I've played this game. I invented it, so trust me, I know the rules. You have no idea who you are trying to kill, or the possible repercussions. Selfish humans – just like you always were,' she hissed, and the xotryl hissed too. Natke's clicks grew more intense with her irritation, and Darin's palms grew sweaty. There were a few of them; surely, they had her outnumbered. He glanced skyward, searching for the red xotryl, but the trees hid much of the sky.

The closest man to Darin ran toward Natke, with the others at their heels.

'For Shona,' one called as he ran.

'Take it alive so we can treat it like it treated us!' a second yelled as they charged.

Natke took a step toward them and lifted two of Darin's rings before throwing one at an advancing guard. Darin's hopes of a bad aim were dashed in an instant as the man's head was partially separated from his neck, and he collapsed to his knees.

'She only has one left.' Darin wasn't sure it would help.

'Try to kill my xotryl, I'll sever your companion's neck.' The other throwing ring flew straight for Sandy.

Sandy leapt sideways and lifted his head, exposing his neck. The ring hit him in the chain section. While the disk did bed in and cut into the chains, it slowed enough that it didn't appear to have cut Sandy. No crimson flowed, and Sandy lowered his head and growled.

Star stood alongside him. Determination flowed through his bond to Darin. He retrieved his ring and threw it. He aimed not at the awldrin, but given the trauma – the upset that the xotryl's pain was causing Natke – he threw it at the xotryl. That xotryl had been hitting humans before the awldrin had claimed, or reclaimed, it. He had no qualms about trying to remove it from the situation.

The ring flew true, but the awldrin leapt to catch it before it made contact with the xotryl.

She advanced now, closing in on them, her long strides showing just how tall she really was. The first of the charging men who had kept running was swept aside like a small insect as his sword glanced off the hard casing around her body. Natke turned to watch him fall. She reached down as he scrambled to his feet and plucked the sword from his grasp. The guard barely reached to half her height. It was like watching Darin's younger brother try to challenge him when they were growing up. The reality of facing this creature was stark. And now she was armed.

A shriek cut through the air as Big Red appeared over the forest line. The awldrin turned away from them, deflecting blows like they were a mere pest. Darin stared at her leg. She had a very slight, uneven gait where two tiny dark spots were near a joint.

'Sandy's bite.' He nudged Chase.

So a direct, clean, powerful hit would pierce the plates; something as powerful as a moonhound bite could get through. His completely red ring might have a chance, but if he missed, she'd have it. And the hounds' current armour could not withstand a true staramine blade.

'How do we fight her?' Darin grimaced. Star was coiled to attack, but he held him back. No doubt watchers would claim them cowards, however, he'd learnt more from the last few moments than he would have dead. The red xotryl flew in to land alongside the awldrin. She reached to touch its nose, then turned back to the green one and hissed at it. With Big Red now alongside her, she slapped the green one with the flat of her blade, pushing it to a floundering take-off. It flapped slowly and unevenly as it just about cleared the trees, blood still dribbling in a thin trail behind it.

'You won't have the satisfaction of picking it to pieces now,' she called.

Darin whistled, and Star vanished. Chase did the same. The red xotryl swung its huge head to face them. The moonhounds went straight for the awldrin, but the rain overnight had left the ground damp. Their trails appeared as they ran, and the awldrin laughed, pointing at a space ahead of the hounds. Big Red flapped lazily and opened its jaws, dropping its head into Star's path.

It bit down.

No hound appeared, and Chase still stood alongside him, staring directly at the awldrin.

'We need to take her before she launches back into the town. At least that beast is too big to get back out if they land in Dal Town.

Darin searched the ground for paw prints, listening for the sounds of their feet. Star sent *[creeping up behind awldrin]*.

Darin readied to throw a ring *[Star about to bite, Sandy next to him]*. Darin swung a huge side arm throw, deliberately over-sized and with all the power he could muster. The awldrin saw it coming and ducked under it. Clicking and hissing came moments later as it was attacked by a pair of moonhounds.

Their teeth pierced the outer shell and made the awldrin buckle at the knees. It clicked in fury, and the huge red xotryl swung its head down as it closed in then gently plucked the awldrin from the ground, flying off with it in its jaws.

'It can't get far, and Natke is an easier target.' Darin started to run into the forest.

Chase caught him up. 'Stop. Where is it going? How will you track it? You can follow the blood trail, but they may not be headed the same way. It might be a trap. We need something bigger – better than hand or thrown weapons. We need magic to take that creature down. We need Bones and his books. As much as it pains to say it, we need an unbonded Soul Anchor.'

Darin agreed. Suriin would have to be unbonded. Or maybe her mother – as she'd abandoned her family to protect her home – it was a choice she might also be willing to make. They turned back to Dal Town, checking the bodies of the fallen and retrieving between them one man who still drew breath.

'While she recovers, we should get some people to safety. As many as we can get out to Redpike? We could always take them over the mountain to the town.'

Chase breathed heavily as they carried the man. They

knocked at the gates to be let back in. Someone poked their head over the top.

'I'm coming.'

The gates opened to let the living enter, while death decorated the road behind them. A road they'd need to travel to retrieve help, and soon.

CHAPTER 27

SURIIN

*Black Pike mountain is as riddled with tunnels
as any insect mount in Pelton.
It simmers with the restrained power of hundreds
of So'Dal, their power weak and faded, much
like the old volcano we reside in. Be wary of
both.*
**Margin note in the Master of Builder's
Recordbook**

Clouds shrouded the moon as Suriin reached the top of the palace wall. With one hand on the wall and the other buried in Swift's fur, she worked her way slowly toward the tower in the dim light. Trusting Swift's nose and four paws was better than trying to find her own way. She reached the tower, then stopped. Much as it had appeared from the courtyard, there was no way in.

Swift paused, sniffing at the wall. The clouds retreated briefly, bathing the palace in gentle green light. Suriin walked to the outer side of the tower, searching for a clue. Swift kept sniffing, eventually letting out a small bark. In the dim green light of Mythos, there was still no visible entrance.

'Well, this isn't very helpful.' The false wall she'd encountered in the cell came to mind. 'Hide secret things in plain sight,' she muttered and reached forward with her eyes closed. She expected to find an archway or edge, like the cell, but her hand touched nothing.

[Tower with no door, open archway, Swift walking through the wall]

A missing wall? Suriin reached out again, keeping her eyes open this time. A tingling sensation rippled across her hand as it vanished into the wall. She pushed through it until everything past her elbow had vanished. Swift had disappeared too.

Suriin checked no one was nearby, then walked forward, closing her eyes as her head went through the illusion. The tingle ran through her body as she walked into the tower. People must fall through that all the time. How strange.

She climbed the staircase to find a small man with dark skin sat near a window, apparently engrossed in a book. She was certain she'd never met him before.

'You found my mother?' Directness was probably best. Given she was still tired, she didn't want to dance with words.

'We did. Before your father was injured, were you the Witness family from Golden?'

'Yes.'

'So your mother can hold a shield almost indefinitely?'

Suriin nodded. 'Even in her sleep, with Fluffy's help. But aside from the one night I saw a xotryl on the crater rim, which was just before I left, we never saw any trouble.'

The man bit his lip and stared out the window for a minute. Suriin waited.

'That one you saw at night is unusual. They don't usually fly at night, but we now know they're attracted to magic and the use of crystals. It had probably chosen to rest there because your mother's shield attracted it.'

'Why is this relevant? Dal is huge, open-sided, and there's not a Soul Anchor on Caldera who could cover it.'

'You're right, of course.' He stood, and his head barely reached her shoulder. Age had stooped him.

'She is defending Dal Town. She's now the last Soul Anchor alive there. A Witness survived the latest attack, although it's unlikely they can work together as well as a bonded pair. Three of my kind are supporting her.'

Her mother was alone, defending a whole town. Suriin drew a shaky breath.

'What can I do?'

'Suriin, we need you to right your wrong. We have attempted to take her down, but the awldrin is too strong to physically fight, especially as she is directing the xotryl to aid her. We need magic strong enough to kill. Magic that only someone not bonded to a crystal can wield. We need you to remove your safety and become raw, pure power. Caldera needs you to unbond your crystal, then we can begin to teach you.'

The call of the power she'd felt when she helped to heal her father was strong. The chance to put things right tugged at her even more.

'If I do this, can I re-bond later, to learn the true work of a Soul Anchor?'

The man laughed. 'What we will teach you *is* the true work. But only you can decide if it's a calling you're willing to pursue.'

'If it stops me seeing visions of deaths, stops the disjointedness of my mind and body – if you are sure we have a chance to fix this before all our secrets are exposed, then I will do it.'

'Don't you want to sleep on it?'

Suriin would be ostracised from her friends, possibly her

family; she would not be welcome in the Black Palace. She walked across to the small window.

The old man sat down again and opened his book, his kind patience unpressuring.

Suriin gazed out over Redpike. The sun's remaining warmth a sliver across the far horizon, the last glimmer of a day before the stars begin to shine. A cloud moved past Mythos, freeing a green sheen to coat the land around them. She looked up, trying to see past the moon, searching the sky for the shadow of Tebein, Natke's home.

The shadow she saw was not that of a cloud. Huge wings crossed the sky.

'I thought you said they didn't fly at night,' she said quietly, and raised her arm to point at the xotryl flying over Redpike. It circled around, swooping low over the palace, then bouncing back as though deflected by something.

'I did. It's not alone.' The man stood alongside her now.

On the walls, guards pointed skyward as they rushed to positions, ready to protect against the xotryl – against those life-stealing talons. How many of them would die once Natke breached the defences of the Black Palace? The xotryl turned, and once again, dived toward the Palace. Suriin reached inside herself.

'Hold on. I may get a little distant,' she murmured. Swift pushed her nose into Suriin's hand; fear filled her, mingled with love *[Swift barking at the xotryl, protecting Suriin].*

[Suriin holding Swift tightly. The xotryl not able to get close] Suriin returned. She hoped that Swift could understand that she needed her support. She sat and hugged Swift close, then let her mind follow the thread to the crystal, staying fully aware of Swift the whole time. It was so close, she could follow its motion.

Her crystal was aboard that xotryl.

If her crystal was, there was a chance that Natke was too.

'I need to try something,' she whispered, hoping that the man heard her. She buried her face in Swift, inhaling the earthy scent of her body, feeling the fur between her fingers, then opened her eyes.

As the xotryl drew closer, she reached inside herself. It was worth a try, a chance to buy some time. The xotryl was so near now that she could almost make out the huge eyes. Behind it, from the darkness, another shadow grew. A second smaller xotryl with very uneven flight.

The man had said they were attracted to magic, or at least the crystals. She reached for her crystal with all the strength she could muster. Her dinner threatened to reappear, but still she reached out, filling herself like a dam about to burst with terror. She drew on the emotions she'd felt when her father was attacked until the knot in her stomach was indistinguishable between the nausea from terror and the sickness of not holding her crystal.

She pushed it as hard as she could toward the incoming xotryl, then doubled over and threw up. The flames of a pain she'd first encountered in the cell engulfed her.

Almost empty, and uncertain whether she had achieved anything, her stomach cramped again, and she tried to recall what Aslin had said about pain.

Serenity and acceptance; she couldn't funnel them anywhere, but maybe she could hold them like a lifeline – them and Swift.

[Suriin wrapped in a dog-shaped blanket and Swift standing between her and the xotryl] filled her mind. Being bonded to Swift was like having a mother desperate to make sure you ate and slept. Suriin bit back a chuckle and pushed herself up to look out the window.

The new xotryl had made a direct line for the initial one,

charging as though they would collide. The bigger one had curled its head around and was pulling away from the palace to avoid the newcomer. Natke and her crystal must be aboard it. The flights of her mind made so much more sense now. The xotryl flew around each other, the big one circling tightly so that it passed back through where it had been, searching for the thing it carried aboard itself.

Shrieks cut through the air, their silent-winged attack foiled by confusion, for now. Natke would be back.

If the shield they'd initially been deterred by wasn't attractive enough, her own intervention must have lit her up like a glow sprite to the xotryl.

Whatever control the awldrin held over her large xotryl deteriorated, and they retreated back over the mountain.

'Did you see her?' she asked.

He shook his head. 'I saw two xotryl, which is concerning enough, but *her*? I presume you mean Natke? No, it was too dark to make out more detail.'

That was good, at least. Those guards below would have struggled to see more, given their angle. It bought a brief respite.

'She was there, I'm certain. I'll do it,' she said. 'How quick can I learn?'

'We don't know yet. The biggest challenge is unbinding you. There are a few books we cannot get into, each with a lock that we suspect requires a Soul Anchor to unlock. If they were left with us, with that kind of protection, then it's for a moment of great need.'

Suriin shook her head. 'You want me unbound, but you don't know how to do it? What kind of offer is this?'

The man looked past her as the shadow vanished into the distance again.

'It's an offer born from desperation – from urgent need.'

He held out his hand. 'Shall we re-start? My name is Boulder. I'm a Howler. One of the Watcher's appointed guardians of Caldera, against the creatures of the Edgelands, and a caretaker of the lost knowledge of the So'Dal. You've caused us a rather large headache, Suriin, at a time when our resources are already stretched to a breaking point. We're yet to work out how, and why, you were the first to access a room, which no one else aside from the Anchor knew about, in five hundred cycles. We need your help, you need our knowledge, and we have very little time.'

'Let's get started, then.' Suriin's nausea started to retreat, but her heart still beat furiously. She would not be returning to her bed that evening.

Boulder opened a previously unnoticeable door and gestured for her to pass through.

'Of course you have more hidden walls. Why don't people blunder through them constantly?'

He smiled. 'Because, sometimes, they are simply walls. Would you try to walk through a wall?' Darkness surrounded them completely, until a whistle from behind lit the glow lamps. A narrow passage stretched ahead, a winding route into darkness with no way to go but down. *A little like my decisions.*

⌐ ⋏ ◖ ✵ ◉

Hissing and whistling intensified as they descended, and Suriin struggled to resist putting her hands over her ears. Boulder placed a restraining hand on her arm to hold her back as it grew louder and louder.

It stopped almost as suddenly as it had begun, and he gestured for her to hurry. They rushed onward.

'Wait here a second,' Boulder whispered, then pulled out what appeared to be a whistle, blew it, and vanished. Suriin reached for Swift and tried not to laugh. Her world grew ever more amazing by the day; it made Aslin's flickering trick appear small. It would be really useful to be able to vanish. How close could she get to animals to draw them?

[Boulder opening a doorway and walking through] filled her sight. Suriin stopped and waited for the man's return. If Swift could see him, then the vanishing wasn't a case of vanishing after all? It could be all about her perception.

'Follow Swift,' Boulder whispered, and Suriin sent *[Swift walking through the door and Suriin holding onto her]*.

Swift nudged her, and together they walked into the main steam lift chamber under the crater garden. Had they followed that tunnel so far?

The man on the lift lever pointed at a section of wall behind him.

[Boulder?] Suriin sent, and Swift replied with an image of him stood by a section of wall. They hurried across. The hall was empty, and by this point, Suriin was entirely unsurprised to see a door slide into a wall channel, exposing another passageway.

It closed behind them, and Boulder reappeared.

'Let's go. Bones will be waiting for us. He'll be delighted to see Swift.'

Suriin frowned. 'How do you know her name is Swift?'

He laughed at her. 'Moonhounds don't change their names. We all know Swift. You have to admit she's rather distinctive, for all the wrong reasons.'

Swift padded alongside Suriin, constantly in reach. Her head lifted, she scented the air, and her tail began to wag. Slowly at first, then building up to an undulation that worked its way down the length of her skinny body. As they entered a warm, airy space with deep rugs on the floor, she burst forward with an energy Suriin hadn't known she possessed, wagging and licking at an old man. He was almost knocked off his stool by her arrival and appeared as surprised and delighted as Swift was.

'What are you doing here? Who's a wonderful girl? You look happy, Swift! You're wagging.' He got off his stool and looked up at Suriin, a small tear trickling down his cheek as he fussed over Swift, who now lay on a rug with her legs in the air as he tickled her tummy.

'Is she with you?' the man asked.

Suriin sat next to them and nodded. 'She bonded me.'

'I'm Bones.' He smiled at her. 'I'm also the Master of Hounds. Are my other hounds happy? I miss them.'

'Lea is caring for them wonderfully. Swift was the only one she was having trouble with ... you know, her lumps.'

Bones slid his hand around Swift's side and checked the area. 'They're no bigger. With proper food, exercise, and love, given as well as received, they might remain that size.'

[Meat] filled Suriin's field of view.

'She's been eating a lot, I think she's hungry again.'

'What moonhound isn't?' A third man strolled in from another room, carrying a bone with meat fragments hanging from it.

'Why do you have that in here? Don't you eat in the main hall with everyone else?' Suriin asked.

'No, we mostly prefer our own company. We buy our own supplies from Redpike and forage in the crater garden, the same as others do. We aren't many. And we have certain areas back here where preservation of supplies is possible.'

Suriin stifled a yawn. 'I'm sorry, that was rude. It's just, I tried to push the awldrin away just now. I'm exhausted and don't feel well. It's only Swift who's kept me going. Trying any magic without my crystal is horrific and makes me feel utterly awful. But the crystal is becoming more distant, so I'm confident that, for the moment, we've pushed her away.'

'What did you just say?'

Boulder reached for Suriin, squeezing her shoulder. 'I'll tell them. You did brilliantly. I promised you a healing draft, and I think a rest before we try to open any book would be a good idea.'

Suriin looked up at the small chambers around the main area, each with their curtain pulled back.

'In there?' she asked.

Bones shook his head. 'Despite our reputation, which I now realise you don't know, there have been occasions of female Howlers in our pack, and even a bonded one once. Follow me. We have some more private spaces through on the other side of our small library. I've cleared one of them out.'

'We don't have time for me to rest. We need to make me into a weapon.' Suriin tried to get to her feet, but her legs wobbled and she ended up back in the rugs.

'Maybe just a short rest?' Bones encouraged, taking her arm and supporting her as she stood again.

'Maybe,' she agreed. 'I'll need to be back in the main palace for the morning. Aslin will expect me.'

'Leave that with us. We'll try to buy ourselves a full day with you. If what you saw tonight was noticed by others, they will be too busy sending out dreams to blanket the town's awareness to notice your absence.'

'I ... I don't think I understand?' Bones helped her walk, and Swift picked up her bone to trot alongside them.

'Rest is all you need to understand right now.'

Suriin couldn't help thinking that he was awfully calm for a man who'd just been told that an awldrin was over the Black Palace. They walked through a long, thin library – a single wall entirely covered in books with ancient, leathery spines. Some of them glimmered with shiny lettering. The symbols from Aslin's table adorned the covers of many, and at the end, a small room opened out. A comfortable chair was pulled up to a table with a glow lamp on it. Several books rested on the right-hand side, each held closed by a lock. She reached for the top one, but Bones steered her away.

'When you've rested,' he said and pressed a push-stone. The door slid open to reveal a room much like hers in the main palace.

She tried to sing the glow lamp to life, and it responded, filling the room with gentle, golden light as she swallowed the resulting nausea. Bones offered her a small bottle.

'It's the same healing draft. Don't take the whole bottle. You need a short sleep, and we need you awake after.' He pointed at a block of staramine next to the door channel. 'That's the closure. You'll see when it shuts that there's a white block inside the door. You don't know us, and I appreciate that you're deep under a mountain with a group of strangers. The white block serves as a lock. I'm sure you can work out how to set it, given what you did in the awldrin's cell. I'll knock to wake you in a few hours.'

He turned and walked away, leaving Suriin in the room, staring out at the desk of books. She took a step forward to get one, but Swift blocked her way *[Suriin asleep]*.

'Fine, Swift. I'll do what you say.' Suriin pushed the red button inside the room, and exactly as Bones said, the door closed. She pressed it again, and it reopened.

'I'm not trapped, then,' she muttered, realising that checking that first would have been the best plan. Or at least leaving Swift outside to re-open it.

She closed it one more time and searched for the small white block. 'I don't know if I can do this, Swift, and if I can, there's no guarantee I'll feel well enough to open it later.'

Suriin left the lock. They'd told her about it, and that was enough; they'd expect her to have locked it. She shuffled back and flopped onto the bed, unstopped the healing draft and poured a small amount onto her tongue. There was plenty left in it, so she put the bottle on the table and rested her head on what smelt like freshly washed sheets.

They smelt of flowers. With her mind filled with images and memories of home, Suriin allowed herself to give in and sleep.

CHAPTER 28

ELISSA

As events on Tebein and Lieus peak, so the
*   dragon's power peaks.*
We often know of war or famine, celebration and
*   mourning,*
long before a messenger will reach us on Mythos.
Journal of Otso Dragon-bonded

'This place is not for you,' the dragon shrilled as it scraped at her shoulders with outstretched talons.

'Oww!' It flew upward, only to return for a second dive at her face.

'I will guard this place, protect it. Go away, fleshy creature. This is a dragon place, not a soft-thing place.'

The dragon was only about twice her size, but more than big enough to almost knock Elissa over. She dug her feet in and gripped a tall rock. There were stinging bushes just below her, and she had no desire to land in them. Elissa raised her other arm to protect her face as the small dragon circled back at her.

'I want you to go away.' This time, it caught her arm.

Dreamer's skin flashed red and black as he took off from her other shoulder to snap at the dragon's tail, leaving Elissa precariously balanced and trying to avoid both creatures as they shouted at each other just above her head.

'This is ridiculous,' she muttered, and pulled herself back to the top of the ridge. She crouched as the black dragon came in for another attack and checked her foot wraps were tight. Then, as Dreamer bit the dragon's wing, Elissa ran down the scree slope, aiming for the gravel pit at the centre of the ring of hills.

She slipped and slid, struggling to remain upright as the increasing flow of pebbles around her feet grew, carrying her downward unsteadily. There was no solid ground ahead that she could see. The only way was down. The noise of her approach, and the shrieking pair at the top of the hill, lost her any pretence of stealth.

Elissa tried to look up, to search for the shaded passage between the hills Sorrow had mentioned. It was clear she wasn't getting back up this slope. She thought there was a darker area to her left, but her precarious balance took all focus away from escape and back to survival.

As Elissa reached a less steep incline, she tried to slow her progress. The scree did not, and her legs were swept from beneath her. She slid the last section of the slope, finally slowing as it flattened.

Elissa arrived in a crumpled and bruised heap at the outer edge of a steaming pit. Larger pebbles surrounded other pits in the ground across the centre of the hatchery. The air smelt faintly, the unfamiliar stench almost sharp, hurting her throat and lungs as she backed away from the heat. They fitted the description of the nests. One of these must have the egg shells in; all Elissa had to do was find it and get out of there.

She hobbled to the closest, aching from the fall. Rapture hadn't really helped with how much she'd need. But the Gates in the Hall of the Watcher were huge – she'd take what she could carry.

At the edge of a nearby nest, Elissa spotted a small fragment of what looked like shell. She reached for it. It crumbled to dust at her touch.

'Watcher's flames, no one is getting home if I can't get a bit of this flaming egg,' she muttered.

The black dragon alighted opposite her, its teeth on full display. 'Go away!'

'You know, your predecessor would help with this. They are the most famous dragon in human history. And the one we all respect.' She stood square to the dragon, her hands resting on her hips. Her bag contained no weapons, as the dragons had deemed food more important to her survival. Without Sorrow, she was defenceless. Her protection was, right that moment, cowering outside the hatchery. He might still carry the weight of his actions, but if only he'd been willing to atone for them and risk helping her.

Elissa studied the black dragon intently. What would happen to him if his sorrow was appeased? Would he fade away and a new silver dragon be born to replace him? If this youngster was anything to go by, within each incarnation was room for interpretation.

'I never knew him, and I don't care. I am the Vigilant, and I will ensure this place is guarded and protected. I stand guard over the hatchery.'

'Just you?' Elissa asked. She didn't want to start a fight, but if it was just Vigilant, then maybe a little fire would be enough, or a few shreds of hope, dropped across his snout.

'No.' Vigilant smiled.

A much larger shadow fell across the hatchery from a dragon that would rival Amazement or Rapture for size. As it passed over her, Elissa's knees buckled. She cowered on the floor as her body trembled uncontrollably. Panic rose inside her as she was overcome by the desire to vomit, or run, scream or all of them. She needed to hide, to bury herself in the gravel, so she wouldn't be seen; her hands began to dig, almost of their own accord. Flaming dragons and their emotions.

'It's not real.' Elissa gritted her teeth, trying to stop at least one part of her body from shaking. 'It's not real.' She reached into her pocket and took a few shuddering breaths before donning the mask Sorrow had helped her make.

A moment was all she needed. A chance to fill herself with another emotion, but the mask didn't help this time. The shadow enveloped her entirely.

The smoothest voice she'd ever heard – cold, calm, and utterly terrifying – swept through every part of her body and soul.

'What do we have here? You should not exist in this place. I can fix that easily.'

'The walking meat won't go away,' Vigilant huffed.

'No, it wouldn't. Whatever it wants, it has overcome impossibilities to get here. I can make it go away forever.'

Tears trickled down Elissa's cheeks, and she swallowed deeply as she tried to regain control of herself. She reached for a strand of hope, and grasped a thick thread of joy, of rapture. Elissa drew on the overwhelming strength of the emotional reserve she'd soaked up from her recent encounter. Then she lifted her head and removed the mask.

'Why thank you.' She paused, surprised at the colour of the dragon she faced. 'I thought you'd be a different colour.'

The great pink dragon bared his teeth at her. 'Are you not afraid?'

'Oh, yes. Very. Can you not see my body shaking?' Her legs really were quivering, and she held out a trembling hand, even as she held her head high.

Terror, for that was who it must surely be, studied her. His great emerald eyes span slowly, and he puffed a large cloud of unruly smoke toward her. It embraced her in his strength, and it took every bit of her consciousness to hold on to the thread of rapture, the lifeline she had been given.

'Your body shakes, your voice does not. Why is this?' He drew himself upward, spreading his wings wide and opening his jaws even wider as he descended on her.

She was going to get eaten, and no one would ever know. No one would ever be safe. Her family was dead, her friends would be too. Elissa was alone. Everyone would die in the battles on Tebein ... Round and round her thoughts went. She cried out in fear – in anguish.

Dreamer flew below Terror and gripped his talons into her head as he fluttered in to land.

Terror snapped his jaws shut a finger's width above Dreamer's wings.

'Interesting. An impossible human in an impossible place with a cousin-companion. Maybe eating you should come after the questioning of you.'

Elissa drew a shuddering breath.

Vigilant flapped around near Terror's head. 'We should find out what she knows, be prepared – be ready for more of them. Then we can defend our home.'

'Even for a Vigilant, you are very intense, youngling.' Terror laughed, and the walls shook; scree slid toward them on multiple sides. Elissa scrambled to her feet, ready to run.

Running would work. It was probably something she could easily persuade herself to do. Terror and fear were emotions she had not felt with any depth since she'd used her stores up at the Shardeep caves. It turned out that she didn't miss them.

Elissa looked up at the huge dragon and tried to draw the flooding of his emotion into a single cluster, condensing it down into a solidified mass of terror. She tried to keep it away from her other tangle. Easier to access in a time of need. For the briefest of moments, she considered throwing it at the Vigilant to buy some more time and distance.

Instead, she tied it as close as she could, then stood tall, funnelling the flood of terror into one impossibly dense ball. Should she face another xotryl, she could use it, or maybe she could add it to the weapons Andra considered possible.

Elissa took a slow, deep breath and looked directly at the dragon, trying to ignore her trembling body.

'I am an impossible human, with dragon magic running through me.' Her voice wavered, but she pushed on. 'I am here at the behest of Hope, Regret, Sorrow, and Rapture to find a way to reopen the Lieus Aulirean gate.'

'The gates must remain shut,' Vigilant trumpeted. 'We must remain on guard at all times.'

Elissa ignored him and focused on Terror. 'Was the Watcher like this too?'

Terror smiled. 'He cared a lot for you small creatures. That's why he took over the gate – to ensure your safety as well as that of our own.' He reached his snout down, inhaling her scent so strongly that her hair stood on end.

Elissa tried not to quake, but her body had other plans. 'You have the feel of the oldest of us all. Maybe there is something in what you say.' He regarded her closely. The danger in every syllable that slid past her ears was excruciating. Her muscles were taut, her breaths fast and shallow.

The heat of the air and her body's response to him led to rivers of sweat forming on her palms and under her arms. She doubted she would smell anything but her fear if she were him.

There was the exit! Light fell through a gap in the hills, a passage to freedom, away from the dragons. Elissa started to edge toward it. Sorrow would have to retrieve the egg fragments himself. She was too small, too tasty. If she didn't escape, then the gate would not open anyway. If she lived for another day, there was still hope.

She found herself edging toward the exit, her steps small and inconspicuous. As she turned to run, Dreamer nipped her ear and screeched at her. He flashed blue to yellow and fluttered around her face, making it hard to see where she was going. His distraction broke the moment, and Elissa stopped running.

She kept her back to Terror, looking at the exit. 'I need the fragments of Vigilant's egg shell. From the end to a new beginning, from the Watcher to a watcher reborn. Rapture said it was the only way. If I take it to her, she will aid me to make a small number of echoglass sections. Then we can attempt to right the wrong done to both awldrin and humankind by the Mythese.'

'I wasn't involved in that. Although, I suspect I would have enjoyed it.' Terror chuckled. It was venomous and threatening.

Vigilant landed in front of her, blocking her exit.

'The black dragon is the most loved and feared. The most treasured of all your kind.' Elissa gestured toward Vigilant. 'If humans were to meet you in the future, they would fall to their knees in your presence.'

'They like me?'

'They like your predecessor. You have the opportunity to follow in his footsteps, to become a symbol of what is good about the Mythese. Their strength and fairness. Their power.'

'Why do you need to open our land to your kind?'

'We don't plan to. We wish only to pass through the gate, to search and hope to find an awldrin egg, a chance to birth a queen in Caldera. We wish for the humans of Tebein to return to Caldera, to let both species have their homes and natural lives back.'

'Why would you believe there is an egg after all this time?' Terror rumbled.

'Regret seems certain it's worth the hunt. He believes something triggered the awldrin to action, and not just my existence.'

'Face me, Child of Harmony.'

Elissa turned slowly, holding tightly to a thread of joy that she plucked from her knotted mass of emotions. She thought of Laytha and the nest of charvers. She looked for Dreamer; far on the other side of the hatchery, he flitted from nest to nest. He'd remembered, or understood her. She added a small thread of hope, then quietly, she blew both at Terror.

He paused, and Elissa grasped a thread of trust, turning quickly to send it at Vigilant. She waited.

Both dragons remained silent, staring at her. Vigilant was first to speak. 'I think you have a good plan. We should let you take the egg. With Dragon in your own being, you wouldn't be planning anything that harms us.'

Terror's eyes slowed, and a tiny tear trickled down his face.

'Thank you,' he said. 'I know there is a lot of terror and fear out there, because I have grown stronger recently and more out of balance with the others. You remind me that we Mythese need to work toward harmony. She may be long gone, but we should still strive for the balance that would bring her re-birth. I believe many of us have forgotten that should be our aim. I am needed, but so are hope and joy. Take the shell, Child of Harmony. Use it wisely.'

He raised a talon, pointing it across the hatchery. 'To reopen the gate, you will need more than the full circle Rapture has sent you for. You will also need anchors.'

'What's an anchor?'

'A thing entirely of Lieus. You'll need a thing of Mythos

too.' Terror moved aside as Vigilant flapped slowly toward Dreamer.

'My nest was back here. Let me take you,' he called back.

Elissa pursued Vigilant over uneven ground. As they neared a small boulder-ringed circle in the centre of the hatchery, heat assaulted her. This nest was notably hotter than the others she'd passed. Her foot wraps were no match for the warmth of the ground, and she shifted from side to side, trying to reduce her contact. A pile of sharp, black-veined shell rested on the edge of the steam vent.

'Take what you need,' Vigilant said. 'I'll hide the rest to keep it safe. Come and find me if you need more.'

Elissa crouched to select several pieces. They'd only needed one crystal to open Hope's gate, but she had no idea how many would be needed to open a full gate. She tucked them in her bag and replaced it on her back. Out of Terror's shadow, she was calmer, could think more clearly. The way to the exit was clear as Terror had flown up to rest on the rim of the hatchery.

'I know you hear me, Sorrow,' he bellowed. 'I feel your presence. Come, ease your injured hatchling to safety. It has been through enough. It reminds me we should work together. Though I doubt you wish for my aid, I will give what I can. There is only one way to get to the gate, Sorrow. Are you truly strong enough?'

A silver streak shot skyward, spiralling in an ornate dance, met by Terror mid-flight. Sorrow dived, and Terror flew alongside him. They soared higher and higher, Terror chasing Sorrow so high that she could barely see them. They were two shimmering specks in the distance. As fast as the dragons had flown away, they returned, Terror leading now, while Sorrow chased behind, his smaller wings unable to keep up with the large pink dragon. Terror swooped down, catching Elissa in his claws and lifting her higher and higher until he flew above Sorrow.

'Catch,' he called, and let her fall.

Elissa screamed. Her arms flailing at the air, she dropped toward the green land below.

Sorrow caught her.

They descended slowly, Sorrow lowering her to the ground as they landed. Dreamer's shrill calls followed as he chased them down.

'I have the shell.' Elissa gasped for air and collapsed. 'What on Tebein was that all about?'

'I was proving I am strong enough for the task.'

'And that had to involve me almost dying?' she shouted. 'Couldn't you just say "yes?"'

Sorrow's eyes span slowly. 'It would mean nothing without proof. I am sorry you were involved. I didn't expect him to test me that way.' He leaked so much emotion that Elissa believed him.

As Dreamer caught up to them, Sorrow lowered his shoulder and offered her a chance to climb aboard. 'We should get away from here.'

CHAPTER 29

___

SURIIN

*Mythese is guttural and musical at the same
time. It both hurts to hear it and inspires
wonder.
Like all the Mythese do, every phrase is full of
contradiction.*
Journal of Otso Dragon-bonded

Gentle, insistent nudges drew her from the depths of
sleep. Wet licks and a knocking on the door brought her
to wakefulness. Swift whimpered a little and paced around the
room. Once again, her hound's needs had not been at the front
of her mind; Suriin had to do better. She shuffled over to the
door and pressed the button.

Bones looked up at her asShe rubbed sleep from her eyes.

'Glad you're back with us. That potion really knocked you
out. I'll get you something herbal to wake you a little.'

'Thank you. Swift needs to relieve herself,' Suriin replied.

'No problem. Tell her to follow me, and I'll take her
somewhere she can do that.' Bones stroked Swift. 'Then, we'll

get you some more food, shall we, girl? We'll feed you while you're willing.'

Suriin tried to send an image to Swift *[Swift following Bones, then Swift weeing]*. Swift wagged and looked expectantly at him.

'If you want to take a look at those books, I'll be back with Swift and a drink shortly.'

'Thank you.' Suriin sat on her bed for a moment as she tried to wake up properly. The awldrin had been at the Black Palace. Somewhere on that table might be a way for her to make up for what she'd done. She could sing more strength into her father without the crystal too. If she was going to rebel, she may as well make the best use of it.

Suriin yawned. The healing draft had done its usual work of making her tired, but she felt a lot better. Whether she could access her magic was another question, but she only had to access it for long enough to free herself, and then the well of her emotions would be returned to her with the filter of the crystal removed. She could pretend she'd found it in town and wear a fake one around her neck.

She smoothed her rumpled skirts and left the small room, closing the door behind her. It was time for all her library research to be put to use.

There were two seats in the room, one behind the table, which Suriin had seen before her rest, and another with sunken grooves and a sagging seat tucked in the corner. A few cushions were propped against its back, with their own dents curved around an absent body.

She took the seat at the table and laid the six locked books out in front of her. The chair was comfortable, although she suspected she'd catch her elbows on the carved arm rests more than once in her tired state.

The books were gilded with mostly familiar symbols,

though Suriin was certain that they wouldn't be the same ones needed to unlock the books. What use was a lock if you wrote the combination next to it?

There were many symbols on Aslin's table, and she was well on the way to knowing what they all were. In all the books on the long wall, there must be a guide to the rest. The gilded spines were adorned with them here. Who knows what secrets they hid so far from the women's library filled with gentle spells and hidden histories?

She ran her fingers across the symbol on the biggest book. It could be a double bluff, anticipating someone to beleive they weren't the key, and therefore try anything but those symbols on the cover or, the symbols could have been added after the book was locked. That's assuming they were locked with the same combination as they were supposed to be.

Suriin was way too tired. She rubbed at her temples and studied the least ornate book. Would she have hidden the biggest secrets in the most overtly ornate book in the library? She decided that if it was her, they'd be in something unobtrusive.

The lock on this book was subtle. She'd have overlooked it altogether if it wasn't on the pile.

People must have lost crystals before; the secret to binding and unbinding must be in this library somewhere. She sighed, glancing down the long room in search of Bones and the promised drink. If people had lost them before, then surely, they'd be out in the main library, where Aslin would have known all about them.

One unlikely event – which should, by all reasonableness, have happened numerous times before – of her finding the awldrin wouldn't mean that all the secrets of the So'Dal would just land at her fingertips.

She retrieved her notebook from her pocket, the corners a

little crumpled from sleep, and started to take notes. First, Suriin numbered each book. Then she searched their covers, noting down each and every visible marking related to the symbols she'd studied.

She was on her second book, having failed to recognise a few symbols on the first, when Bones returned with a steaming drink and a wagging hound. Swift loped in with a chunk of meat in her jaws.

Suriin smiled at Swift's wagging tail. 'You'll have to show me how that preservation area works.'

'I think I found that somewhere. I imagine they still teach it if you studied long enough. It doesn't seem like the kind of thing that would be offensive or problematic.' Bones sat in the armchair. She suspected that he fitted its grooves perfectly. 'How are you getting on? Have you tried to open any yet?'

Suriin tapped the page of her notebook. 'I may only have one attempt before I have to rest. We need to be sure it's the one we want to try.'

More awake and refreshed, she realised that she had seen him before. 'I recognise you now. You saw me in that cell – I know you did, you saw how painful it was for me to try to use magic. I'm honestly not sure I can draw enough power to open any of these.'

'Boulder said you managed fine up on the tower.'

Bitterness wove through her voice, despite her best effort to temper it. 'Because the water-flamed awldrin was so close that I could use my crystal. Because all I did was channel to my crystal. Just enough to confuse them, to give the watchers time to re-enforce the shield. It's far away again now.'

'We know you can feel it. Thought we'd keep you as a tracker to start with, but there's little point. What we need is someone willing to break their vows, to unfasten from their crystal, and to break the Watcher's trust. Someone willing to risk it all.'

Suriin winced as each word hit her, a rain of tiny barbs to her soul. 'I only wanted to save my father.'

Bones offered a smile, the sharpness hidden. 'And now you can save many more people. We need to find a way to unbind you, and fast.' He settled back in his seat. 'Before we start, I should explain something to you. Your crystals are not a focus. They are not a way of filtering or saving your magic. Everything you have been told about that aspect of their use is false.'

He stopped and shuffled his weight into the grooves a little deeper.

Suriin wasn't surprised entirely by what he was saying. 'Why?'

'Because of the war. Because the Watcher allowed us peace and shattered the crystals from the Gate on condition that they were used to reduce the power of the So'Dal. That every woman born to power was bound to the crystals.'

'Why not the men?'

'We could never do much damage. Our strength has dimmed little – it's yours which must be truly limited.'

Suriin sat back for a moment, her fingers caressing the forms on the book. 'If we unbind me, I will have access to more power? Be able to achieve bigger things?'

'At a bigger cost, yes.'

Suriin nodded. Aslin had been clear with her on that, and presumably the crystal's filter made it hard for someone to drain all their emotions. It reminded her of her mother. Sometimes fearless, often flat or lacking empathy. Suriin wondered for the first time how much effort it must have taken to maintain Golden's shield for all those cycles, alone with no break and through the crystal's limits.

'So these books contain all the abilities we used to have?

Powers and skills the Watcher wanted us to forget, to lose the strength for?'

He nodded. 'You've got it, gal.'

'How long have I got?'

Bones shrugged. 'How long does rain fall? How long can we store cheese? You have as long as we have – until time is up, until the cloud is empty, or the cheese spoils. We think it's a matter of days, but it could be hours, it could be tides. You won't work alone, though. We'll help.'

Flames, if it took her tides to find the answers, they were in serious trouble. Natke would want to act fast. Yet, compared to five hundred cycles, a few tides would be fast if she had patience, and that second xotryl had not flown well. Natke had lost the element of surprise, so maybe Suriin's small act would buy them a few days.

Suriin glanced down at the books. 'I need a book on the symbols and their meanings to figure out the last ones. Do you have one here? I know there's one in the women's library.'

Bones nodded. 'Let me see what I can find. There's not likely to be a teaching manual, but across a selection of books, I suspect I've come across most of them and can give you a good idea of their meaning. Between us, we can work the symbols out. How many are there to find?'

Suriin tried to picture Aslin's table in her mind; two rings of eight and one jagged alternating row with about twice as many. 'Thirty-two,' she replied.

Bones pushed himself out of the chair and smiled, like her dad used to after she did something daft. 'I'm old and not clear, I suspect. I meant how many symbols you didn't recognise? I'll pop back and get Boulder. Three heads are better than two, and he knows these books as well as I do.'

As he left Suriin and Swift, she realised that, surrounded by friendly faces, she still felt alone. How long would she be able to maintain the fallacy that she had lost her crystal and re-found it? Would Aslin know when she attended training? Suriin needed to get back to class, to learn other things – things that she needed to help her work safely. She bit back a laugh. She had knowledge at her fingertips that no-one had been able to use since the gates shattered and a mistake to rectify.

Her family were spread around Caldera because of the xotryl, because of her. Her mother desperately needed Fluffy if she was now working alone. Suriin needed to step up and stop dreaming of a life that was, for now at least, out of her reach.

She took a sip of the herbal drink and turned back to the symbols. There was no point in planning a future filled with powerful magic if she couldn't use what she had now. If Suriin failed, the Howlers were better getting someone else to do the work, someone as yet unbonded.

She searched the covers for a symbol that she'd used in the past, something familiar that she could access. There was a vigilance symbol on one. She slid it closer, carefully moving the small book and its list of symbols to the side. Her instinct still led her to believe it was important, and she didn't want to damage its lock.

Suriin placed her hand on the new book and tried to reach for her power. She couldn't feel much at first, then her guard shattered, her strength became unstable. Her mind started to drift.

Swift nudged her as she slumped forward, and Suriin felt a surge of protectiveness flow into her. She grabbed at it and pushed it through the symbol.

It glowed, and Suriin sat up in surprise. Swift's tail thumped on the floor as she wagged with her head resting on the table.

Low voices carried toward her just before Bones and Boulder reappeared.

'Master of Hounds,' she began.

Bones raised a questioning eyebrow. 'Yes?'

'Moonhounds can send us emotions, can't they?'

He nodded.

'I can't feel mine as well as I should be able to, and if I attempt to use them, I fail. I just tried, and was about to faint when Swift funnelled her protective vigilance to me.'

He nodded for her to continue.

'I could redirect it though and it worked as my own would have.'

Boulder shrugged at Bones. 'Makes sense to me. Otherwise, how would the Howler magic work? We can't use the emotional magic, but the hounds produce it, and we use it. Think about healing.'

He turned to Suriin. 'Healing with a moonhound requires a desire to see you no longer hurt because your hound cares for you.'

Bones rushed down the bookshelf and returned with a simply bound grey book.

He flicked through the pages and opened them, pointing in triumph at a page illustrating what Boulder had just been saying. The symbols for Love and Vigilance were clearly inscribed in flowing strokes across the page. The surrounding paragraphs were filled with strange comments and suggestions in a variety of scripts.

'What are these?' Suriin pointed at one that appeared to be discussing feeding moonhounds their favourite food early in the bonding process and not letting others feed them.

'Ways to encourage a hound to send you a particular emotion,' Bones said. 'Maybe *you* can't open these books, but if we can work out which one we need, and how to get Swift to send you the right emotion, she might be able to.'

Suriin nodded slowly. 'Okay. All I have to do is find the

right words to unbind. Allow my mind to be dragged toward the crystal, and then, taking Swift's emotions with me as support, use my binding emotions – plus presumably Draconic words – to free my mind.' She stroked Swift's ears. 'This feels dangerous for her.'

'She has a lifetime of emotion to draw on. You couldn't ask for more.' Bones looked down at Swift with fondness.

'How old is she?'

'Swift is pushing toward thirty-five cycles. Although, given how deeply she mourned, I didn't think she would make it past twenty-seven.'

Suriin cradled her drink. 'I don't mean to be difficult. But if I wanted to reduce the powers of a people who were too strong by making them quote Draconic words to bind them, I don't think I'd leave them a way to break that binding. And certainly not in a form that spells out *this is how to break my agreement with you.*

She sipped again as the two old men stared at her. It was a kind stare, not one that worried her, but she felt certain that they already realised this. They were just waiting for her to solve the puzzle herself. Like some sort of test.

'You speak Draconic, too, don't you?' she muttered.

Bones laughed. 'Now you're being ridiculous. I've not had time to learn Draconic while being Master of Hounds.'

She chuckled despite herself, enjoying their relaxed company. Even under the pressure of time, they still smiled.

'But I do.' Boulder winked at her.

Suriin laughed louder then, from exhaustion or the madness of the situation, she couldn't say, but Boulder's smile, his almost black eyes that twinkled with joy, held no threat or promise of enormous power. She felt sure that in earlier life, these men had been a formidable combination, and their easy friendship relaxed her.

Would she and Fresna be old together like this? Or would it be Skye? Would any of them make it to old age if the population found out about the So'Dal?

If these Howlers couldn't bring the awldrin under control before she attacked Soul Anchors further afield than Dal, and the Anchor or So'Dal had to work together to raise enough power to bring her down, the truth would be exposed.

Boulder had mentioned dreams and a way to suppress the memory. How far would things have to go before that was no longer an option?

So many questions, so many possibilities. Suriin needed to act, not ponder. 'The binding for the crystal is in a language I've never heard before. If you're saying that it was created by the Watcher, that's why I thought it might be Draconic. I can't remember it exactly, though. If you heard the words that bound us, could you work out the words to unbind us?' She doubted she could recall them well enough to be of any use, but she knew someone who could. If she could find a way to make Aslin say it.

Boulder shrugged. 'I've read most of the things we have in Draconic. It's all the really old stuff, some almost illegible with time. We could try reading it to you? I can choose phrases that might have a relevance and work backward from there. We used to use words to bind the hounds and other creatures, as well as bond each other. If we can identify any similarities, we might be able to find the opposite effect.'

Bones opened his palm to show a small pebble. 'We used some Draconic to bind two pebbles to each other recently. We could start there?'

It sounded like as good an idea as any. Suriin nodded. Boulder started reading from a book he'd brought, and Suriin settled back into her seat, listening to the strange words he spoke. It could be a long night.

After a while, all the words blended into one, and Suriin couldn't tell where one ended and another began. She thought that they'd identified several sounds that felt familiar, but her optimism in the plan was fading along with her concentration. She rubbed at her eyes and stifled a yawn, grateful for the appearance of a tall So'Dal she realised was Silard.

'We just switched shifts. People are headed to breakfast.' He studied their faces. 'Have any of you slept?'

They all shook their heads.

'I need to go,' Suriin said. 'I need to visit people before they think I've got trapped or collapsed somewhere again.'

Silard offered his hand to help her up as she swayed a little.

'I think you need to sleep first. I'll take you back to your room, but it will have to be the long way. It's way too busy for you to appear in the lift chamber.'

Boulder pulled a necklace over his head. 'Borrow my shard instead. Keep your hand on Swift as you leave the rooms. You don't have time or energy for the long way. Eat and be seen, visit your father. We'll keep reading, and one of us will make contact later today.'

CHAPTER 30

DARIN

Summer 504 Town games; Archery
One Hundred Span distance results
First place, Alicia Wanstall Score 590
Runner-up, Krista Liftins Score 585
Dal Town records

'We need to get them out.'

A group of people were trying to wash the blood from the cobbles, but the stain stubbornly refused to shift. Darin couldn't shake the image of the falling Soul Anchor from his mind, and these people had lost loved ones. As sad and disturbing as it might feel to him, it would be many times worse for them, and with only Eira left to protect them, it was only a matter of time before more died.

'We might not have long, but they flew off injured. If we're going to evacuate the town, it's as good a chance as we'll have.'

Chase sighed. 'I don't think it's as simple as telling them that. People from this crater value their privacy – their autonomy. None of them wants to spend their lives faking an ignorance of magic to the So'Dal of the Black Palace, or those from further away. There is a saying here, Darin. Born of Dal, always of Dal.'

'Is that why Suriin's mother is here? Her ties to this place are stronger than her marriage?'

'I doubt they're stronger, but she would have been in touch with someone here, known there were few Soul Anchors with the raw strength to shield the town. She knew her children were safe.'

'While she remains – while any of the So'Dal remain here – they are to the xotryl like nectar to fire sprites. Natke will keep coming back, over and over again.'

'I agree.' Chase stroked Sandy's ear as he glanced skyward.

[Meat] filled Darin's view.

'No matter what we decide, or who we try to evacuate, these hounds deserve some food. They were amazing today.'

Chase laughed. 'You just got that request too? I think we'd all benefit from food and a chance to work out our next step.'

Darin filled Star's bond with love and pride before taking a last look around the square and heading for the Witness' home.

Three Howlers. He considered it as they walked. The Surface was dangerous at the best of times, but getting all these people to safety, with just three of them would be a serious challenge.

They nudged the door open and found Heline and Fleck sat on the floor staring into each other's eyes. Darin well remembered the early moments of wonder and resisted the urge to stroke the very spotty moonhound as they passed. They sat quietly at the table and waited for her to join them.

'How's he doing?' He gestured toward the stairs with his head as Heline stood up.

'He's still well and truly out of it. What next?'

Was she referring to her and Fleck? Or the whole situation?

Darin wasn't sure, but as he was trying to decide on an answer, Chase leant forward, resting his elbows on his knees.

'Heline, do you think we could persuade either those without magical abilities to leave for their own safety, or those who have it to leave to preserve the others?'

'No waiting for the rain to fall there!' Heline's face screwed up in thought as she considered the situation. 'What do you think Tian would do?' she eventually asked.

'He'd refuse to go to the Black Palace, that's what he'd do. You know it. I know it. Flames, we all know it. I suppose it would be the same for all the others who have chosen to avoid it.'

'And others like me,' Heline said. 'People who don't always fit the expected rules, those who don't yet know they are capable of magic, or even use it unintentionally.'

'Does Luik know who has abilities?' Chase asked.

Heline shrugged. 'He may have some idea, but not a full list. We still send lilac-haired women to the Black Palace, but anyone else? No. All we have are their family links to work from.'

'So, we'll move the people away from Dal until the threat is neutralised.' Darin shook his head. 'It sounds as though it would be easier to move a mountain.'

Heline gestured upward. 'The fastest way out of the crater would be over the Surface to Clifdon, but the path will be overgrown, lost in places. It's been many cycles since the lift ran for the trade route. It would be a dangerous walk and take a few days.'

Clifdon again. They needed to repair the lift and get everyone who would travel out. These walls were no defence against the smaller xotryl. Once it healed, they were back on the menu, with or without the awldrin. Dal Town was certainly defensible, but with only one Soul Anchor, alone and exhausted, there was a limit to how long they could hold out. If Suriin's mother was taken, would the awldrin leave them alone? Go in search of crystals elsewhere? Darin really wished he could speak to Conor. He'd know how to fix the lift.

'Are there any Builders here?' he asked.

Heline frowned. 'I'm not sure what you mean. But it's a town – we have folk of most trades here. What do we need?'

'I think we need to get that lift working as quickly as we can.'

Helene patted Fleck once more, then walked across the kitchen to open a drawer. She searched through oddments of things shuffled away from sight. Darin's dad had a drawer like that back in the inn – before it burnt down. He'd probably started to build a new one by now.

'Found it,' Heline said, raising paper and a pencil in triumph. She sketched a diagram of the lift, the pulleys, and the cage.

Chase glanced over at them. 'I'll leave fixing the lift with you. I need to make contact with Bones, and then persuade Tian to get on board with the evacuation plan.'

He didn't wait for a reply, and Sandy followed him out of the room.

Darin and Heline studied the diagram she'd drawn carefully.

'We're going to need a lot of rope,' Darin said. 'Is the cage still safe to carry weight? It looked green and rotting when I hid behind it. I don't think I'd trust it with my own weight, let alone a group of people.'

She tapped the pencil thoughtfully. 'It's been grounded for cycles. You may have a point.' Next to the diagram, she wrote: two hundred spans of rope, basket repair.

'If it's been grounded for cycles, do we even know if the pulley-wheel works?'

'Do you want the honest answer or the hopeful one?'

Darin sighed. 'Honesty, if people's lives are at stake. We aren't planning to get them stuck halfway up the wall as a fly-past snack station.'

'That's a horrible vision – thanks for that,' Heline replied, pushing long hair back from her face. 'First, I think we should get the basket.'

'I agree. Without that, the rest is a waste of our time. Time we'd be better using to cross the crater to the working lift.'

⌒ ⋏ ◖ ✤ ◉

As they tipped the basket over to move it, the base remained beneath the pulleys. Plants growing through the woven floor ripped the panel from the frame.

It needed a new floor.

Fleck and Star pushed the basket by the supporting struts. Star's adventures had started to fill him out, and his muscles, though a long way from the size of Sandy's, were defined under his rough coat. Fleck was of an age, but softer. Life had left her less strong. Their uneven pushing made the task a little harder, but Darin was reluctant to ask Fleck to stand back. Pack worked together, and they would find a way.

They pulled and pushed, shoved and rolled, until they got the broken basket through the gate.

'This'll do,' Darin puffed as he nodded to the man on the gate. He slid the bolts across to seal them back in.

Fleck wagged in time with Star as they loped ahead of Darin and Heline, with Fleck pausing to look back frequently. The rutted streets in this part of town meant that they walked one to each side, while Heline and Darin used the skaa-rak track down the centre.

As small as Dal Town was, Heline hadn't understated the

range of skilled people. In a town that didn't pretend magic never existed, there was a hum of creativity in the air. If they were connected to the rest of Caldera, they would have so much to offer.

They reached a large building, and Heline knocked on a small door under a swinging sign that simply said 'office'.

A woman opened the door and squinted through glasses at Darin. 'I don't know you,' she said. 'Should I?'

'This is Darin,' Heline said as Fleck moved alongside her.

The woman looked at Fleck, at Star, then back at Darin. 'Oh, you must be the new Howler. Pleased to meet you.' She extended a filthy hand, and Darin shook it.

'I'm a Howler, yes, but Heline is the newest.'

'Is that really true?' She raised her eyes to look up at Heline, a broad grin breaking across her face. 'I knew you were special – I told you so when we were kids!' She enveloped Heline in a hug, squealing with joy.

Heline gently uncurled her. 'Thank you, Lillith, but we're not here to see you for that. We need the lift basket repaired.'

Lillith scratched her head. 'It's doable. Who's it for? Who's restarting trade at a time like this?'

'We need to evacuate Dal,' Darin replied.

Lillith laughed. 'In that thing? To where? How long do you think we have before the monster is back? If you take everyone in one group, we'll be stood on the clifftop as an offering to the creatures of the Surface. I'd rather walk alone through the Edgelands.'

Heline shrugged. 'It won't be easy, I agree. We won't force anyone to leave. But either those who draw the xotryl here need to leave, or those who don't, leaving the others to protect themselves.'

Darin was more than willing to force people to leave if it kept them safe, but he kept his mouth shut.

'Can you do it?' he pushed. 'As soon as possible?'

'Sure. Let me grab a few folk, and we'll collect the basket. I'll have it back with you before long.'

'Thank you.' Heline hugged her once, and Fleck licked Lillith's hand.

'Next up, rope.' Darin gestured down the path. 'Lead on!'

He was confident that they'd arrived at the rope-maker's house as they rounded a corner. The entire building at the end of the road was entwined and woven from plants and threads. The walls coiled around the floor, growing upward in a spiral while the roof was made from rows and rows of ever-decreasing thicknesses of twine.

'Where does he grow the plants to make all this?'

'There are crop clearings throughout the forest and around the northern edge of the crater. Once, when the port was living and busy, we sent rope to Clifdon. A lot of rope. These days we only grow enough to meet our needs and little more.'

'But you never repaired the lift?' Darin ran his hand along the rope work. It was solid and heavy. He imagined an inn made from it, how travellers might pause to take in the unusual nature of the structure. But no. He couldn't get enough out of Dal, let alone across Caldera. He wondered if he could persuade his parents to relocate closer once the xotryl problem was dealt with. If they lived in Dal, he'd not have to keep secrets from them. The idea planted a small seed in his mind. One he could nourish later.

'Like my house, do you?' Curly dark hair, much like his own, framed the bearded face of the man staring at him in bemusement.

'It's amazing. I've never seen anything like it.'

The man's chest puffed a little as he stood taller. 'Why thank you. You haven't come to stroke my walls, so what are you after, Heline? What does the Witness need now?'

Helen slumped. 'Davii, have you been working?'

'I've been working on some fine stuff, yes.'

'We were attacked again. All our trained So'Dal have been killed aside from the visiting Soul Anchor and Luik. The Witness is badly injured and is resting at home. But we must keep fighting on, so the Soul Anchors didn't die in vain. We need rope.'

'You want to fight with rope?'

'Lillith is repairing the basket. We need enough rope to work the pulley and re-build the lift.'

'Come with me.' Davii gestured them through the door; inside was warm and cosy. Davii opened a door on the far wall. 'I've always been ready for today,' he said. 'Just waited for someone to need it. Expected it to be for trade, not an evacuation, though. How do you plan to get it through the top pulley?'

'I'm going to ask Krista,' Darin replied. There was a huge length of rope in the room beyond, certainly hundreds of spans long, if it was a single length.

'That's as good a plan as any. You'll be needing some of my finest strong thread, too, then.' He stepped over the coil of rope that dominated the room and returned with a large ball of thread.

'It's spider silk far stronger than the rope. It's taken me a long time to perfect the technique, and a whole lot of singing to the spiders to persuade them to spin. I usually sell it to the dressmakers – it adds a sparkle to their weaving.'

'You sing the spiders to spin?' Darin rubbed at his eyes.

'Yes, they seem to like it.'

'Can you arrange for the rope to be brought to the base of

the lift?' Darin took the ball of thread, and despite knowing its source, he was surprised at its lightness. 'We need to find Krista.'

It turned out that Krista was looking for them too. She rushed up to them outside the Spotted Dog. 'I heard you're planning to get people out of here? I'll want to go home when all this settles. Someone has to be there for the lift. In the meantime, I'd be more than happy to get out of here and help you get others out too. We can't all leave because there's the skaa-rak flocks, and the faat, and the crops. You'll have to leave some people here, or we'll starve when it's safe to return.' She took a deep breath to continue, and Darin raised his hand. 'I'm glad you're willing to help. Because we need you and your bow.'

Krista relaxed slightly, the panic and urgency of her delivery turned to purpose. 'I can do that. What do you need me to shoot?'

'Go get the big one we brought and some arrows you trust to fly true, then meet us on the town wall, and I'll show you.'

'I'll be right there.' Krista ran off, her silver-threaded curls bouncing with each step.

'I'd like to check on Luik and the hounds if you don't mind,' Heline said. 'We've been gone a while. I'd hate him to be alone when he wakes.' Her sadness was reflected in Fleck's drooped tail.

'I think you might need to be a little more careful with how you broadcast your feelings in the future.' Darin pointed at the hound. 'Fleck is going to feel what you feel. Nerves, tension, sadness. It's not easy to lid everything, but I'm sure you'll manage.'

'Fleck keeps sending pictures of food, and it's making me hungry too,' Heline admitted.

'Then feed yourselves and go put your mind at ease. A worried hound won't build confidence as we try to persuade people to leave their homes.'

The newest Howler and her hound strode off, Helene clearly still anxious about something by Fleck's behaviour. They would have to work on that communication themselves.

[Star and Darin on top of the wall] he sent, and Star loped ahead, his tail wagging as he ran.

⌒ ⋏ ☾ ⊕ ◉

Krista looked up at the pulley. 'You want me to shoot an arrow through that gap?'

'No, we need you to. The thread is carefully laid out so it won't tangle as the arrow flies.'

'Then you'll pull the rope through with it?' Krista nocked the arrow. She stood still, her breathing slow and steady as she stared upward. Then she aimed her bow and drew the string. Darin held his breath as she loosed it.

'Watcher's flaming wings, it's short. Okay, okay, I can do this. Let's try again.' Krista stared up at the pulley. It was an easy hundred spans from where they stood. Darin pulled the thread back up, laying it carefully along the town wall to let it fly tangle free. There was a bush below them, and he tugged the arrow through carefully. If it snagged, he'd have quite a walk to retrieve the end of the thread.

The second shot hit the pulley, the noise of the arrow glancing off it raised his hopes a little higher. 'So close. You can definitely do it.' They'd drawn a small crowd now, and a few of them shouted encouragement.

'If anyone can do it, it's you.'

'Krista, you've shot further in the Dal target shot last year. It's in your range.'

A small child started to chant, 'Krista, Krista ...' Soon, others joined him until they were hushed into silence.

Because of its deflection, the arrow was easier to retrieve this time, and Darin stepped back as Krista lined up for the third time. 'Three times is the charm.'

She stood so still she appeared to have stopped breathing, totally focussed on the pulley at the top of the cliff. The third arrow clipped the support structure above it. An audible sigh came from the crowd.

Krista frowned. 'It's the wind. It's just a little high and a little exposed as it reaches the top. I'll get it eventually, but we could be here a while.'

'Would you like a little help, Krista?' The crowd parted to allow Eira and Chase through.

'I won't say no, that much is sure.'

'Pass me your arrow.' Eira reached out her hand.

Darin carefully passed the arrow down. It looked a little battered at the flights, so he smoothed the feathers straight.

Eira took the arrow in her hands and closed her eyes. Her lips moved silently.

Darin took the arrow back when she offered it and passed it to Krista. She held it and smiled.

'Thank you for whatever you did to it.' She drew her bow one more time, and the arrow slipped through the gap above the pulley to drop on the other side. A cheer rose from the spectators, and this time, the chant was allowed to continue.

Now all they needed was the rope, the finished basket, and time.

CHAPTER 31

ELISSA

*The last boat is through the fog bank, and our
    fleet now sets sail for Hope Isle.
I will finally meet the great dragons in the flesh!
We were through just in time, as I have recently
    heard news of
xotryl beginning to risk short flights over the
    water.*
Captain's log. Cloudsailor

Elissa thought a lot about Terror's advice as they flew away from the hatchery. Anchors, ways to secure each end of the journey, made a sort of sense. There must many things on Mythos that she could use if Rapture deemed them suitable. The bigger issue was an anchor to Lieus. If the echoglass would be fitted at the gate, was there a way in which she could join an anchor once there? What she needed was some kind of artefact that had been brought here.

As they landed to rest, she laid on the ground, staring up at Lieus.

'Did anything from Lieus ever arrive and stay here?' she asked. 'Charvers are on Tebein, and they came from here, and there are even small furry creatures all the way from Lieus on Hope Island too. Terror said I needed an anchor from Lieus to forge working crystals.'

Sorrow stretched out next to her, his wings extending over her before he settled them back against his body. 'I won't pretend to understand all the things involved in creating new echoglass,' he said. 'But Terror is primal – much like Rapture – and always has been. Whilst one day, he may fade, there are always small acts of terror fuelling his existence, much as personal sadness fuels my own. He would have been around the last time echoglass was made, even if he won't admit to it.' Sorrow blew a smoke ring, and Elissa watched it float away, widening until it fragmented.

'That would also imply he once had a responsibility to contribute to Harmony.' Sorrow turned his huge head so one of his eyes was close to her. 'Many of us find the concept of being a lot less self-centred rather difficult, even if we have a responsibility to try.'

'Were you around then?'

Sorrow shook his head. 'No, I was hatched later. I am not the first of my line. You saw the state of me when you arrived. I wasn't eating, I was filthy and self-pitying. You have helped me embrace the understanding that sorrow is necessary, but I do not need to let it consume me. There have probably been more of my incarnation than most others on Mythos, aside from Grief. We drown in our own sadness.'

They rested companionably for a while. Elissa took the opportunity to make some food; Sorrow heated her special dish with gentle streams of smoke. Once rested and with a belly-full of warm food, Elissa felt ready to continue the journey.

Sorrow lifted his snout toward Lieus while Elissa packed her bowl away. 'I suspect that the anchor will need to be both created on, and of, the fabric of Caldera, not just a creature with that origin. You are a creature of Tebein – though you may rile against the thought. Your bones are born of Tebein's minerals, your meat is formed of the plants and grains you grew in that thin soil. Your tempered spirit has been cooled and sharpened on the blades of your life in the shadow of the awldrin. You are of Tebein.'

'Do we need bones made of the minerals from Lieus? What about books or things *He* brought here?'

Sorrow encircled Elissa, his warm body doing little to aid her in her search for a breeze or respite from the heat.

'You're cooking me,' she muttered. Sorrow said nothing as he extended a wing over her head moments before the skies opened and water poured down as though it were Rains.

'Oh, I needed this.' She laughed and stepped out from the shelter he offered, turning her face up to the new layer of clouds that began crowding the sky.

'That is one thing I know for certain, yes,' Sorrow said, as she let the rain drench her. '*He* was from Lieus.'

'You dragons are always talking about a Him or He,' Elissa said as she ducked back under the canopy of silver wing. 'Rapture said she wanted to keep me as a pet, like the Watcher had *Him*. But isn't Otso long dead? The reason you know that I won't survive long-term here?'

'Yes, He is dead, and I know where his bones are buried.' Sorrow shook his head, spraying droplets of water all over her. They hung off his silver spines like gems, his scales creating a little extra magic where they reflected through them.

'Are you suggesting that we dig up a dead human from Lieus to meld his bones with those of the Watcher and the Vigilant egg?'

'Yes, apparently, I am.'

'We know the Watcher would agree, and Vigilant gave his permission. Are you sure that Otso would willingly allow this?'

Sorrow tilted his wing to angle the rain away from Elissa as it ran off in streams between the stiff wing-struts. He said nothing for a while, and they sat together while the rain continued its barrage. Elissa leant against Sorrow.

'I cannot say. Maybe he has left his thoughts on paper somewhere,' Sorrow replied.

⌒ ⚲ ◖ ✠ ◉

As the rain dried up and the clouds retreated, they stretched and readied to leave.

'Which way?' Sorrow asked.

'The Hall of the Watcher. I want to find these records, see if there's anything of use in them. I'd rather dig up a body that would have been happy to be used in this way than disturb Otso's bones to use them against his beliefs. Obviously, I will do whatever it takes, but I'd feel easier if I knew he'd not be opposed to it.'

Sorrow offered a dipped shoulder to allow her to mount.

'Dead is dead, little dragon. But I do understand your thoughts. There could be something else of Lieus there that we could use instead.'

They flew until the darkness grew close, and Lieus kissed the horizon. The huge walls of the Hall rose from the green of Mythos's lush vegetation. Elissa braced herself for a bumpy landing, but Sorrow soared over the walls to land inside their perimeter.

'These walls weren't meant to keep things out, were they?' Elissa asked.

'They were to keep you and the awldrin confined.'

The huge size of the blocks now made sense, as did the

hidden exit. Elissa slid down Sorrow's flank. There was nothing in the courtyard aside from the entrance to the Hall; no extra buildings or doors. 'Are there any hidden doors? Where did Otso live?'

'With the Watcher – always with the Watcher.'

They pushed the huge doors open and walked in.

'Can we leave them open for light?' Elissa felt lost in the vast, impossible space. The Aulirean Gates shimmered in the light from outside, their crystals embraced by tendrils of golden metal. She approached it with trepidation. The echoglass gems on one side were filled with movement. Through fractured crystals, she could see a whole world.

Scenes of humans and large furred creatures, big enough to make the farbrox look small. There were so many faces and landscapes. She reached out to touch one fragment of a large crystal, a room filled with people. Lilac-haired women moved amongst them. A flurry of movement caught her eye from another crystal; a streak of red dripped across it. Elissa stared at it. As the blood cleared, she caught a glimpse of a face. One with sharp, pointed teeth and green-hued skin.

'Did you see that?' She pointed at it frantically. 'Tell me you saw that?'

Sorrow shook his head. 'I see a lot of crystals, a lot of lives. I can see how easy it would be to become lost in watching these lives. You can see the one you came through. There's a single human sat in front of it. Do you think they are waiting for you?'

'Yes, they wait and hope.' Elissa dismissed the thought. 'Sorrow, I am sure with every part of my being that I just saw an awldrin on this one.'

'That's Lieus.'

Elissa sighed with exasperation. 'I know that, but it's there.

Now, it's gone dark. But I really am sure. I'd stake two days' food on it.'

Sorrow glanced across at the Watcher's skeleton. 'Are you willing to stake the bones of one long dead? Are you willing to risk it?'

Elissa didn't reply. She searched every other crystal, all the fractured views, all the faces and places. The views that simply held other crystals. In none of them did she see any sign – any trace or possibility – of an awldrin.

'I need to tell Regret. We need to open the gate to let them know, but it took all of us to re-open it. I need you to hold it for me, just for long enough to pass on the information – for me to tell them. Then we'll find the bones and return to Rapture.'

Sorrow tilted his head to the side. 'If you are so certain, I can do that. Be fast, little dragon. I cannot hold it indefinitely.'

Elissa dropped her bag and ran to the Tebein gate, placing her hand on the only echoglass she could see with a person inside. It wasn't Andra. That would have been too easy.

'Let's do this,' she said. Sorrow put his snout to the gate and pushed. A small section opened, and Elissa took a deep breath before she plunged through into the darkness, then out onto the tiled floor of Hope.

'I need to speak to Andra and Regret, or Hope.' Elissa called as she sat to regain her bearings and settle her stomach.

The woman's eyes widened as she looked at Elissa. 'Yes, Shard-bonded,' she replied, and ran out through the hole in the wall.

Elissa straightened her clothes and moved to sit on the recliner where she knew Sorrow would be able to see her.

A few minutes later, Andra bust into the room, followed by a number of other Chosen, and Hope arrived at the open wall.

'Regret is away at the moment.' She paused and studied Elissa closely. 'I like it.'

'Like what?' Elissa asked. She didn't have time for Hope's games today.

Andra reached for Elissa's face, turning her chin toward her. 'Your eyes, my child. Your eyes are changing, and your skin is starting to shimmer.'

'I probably have Sorrow's scale powder or something on my face.' She shook her head. 'Anyway, I'm not important. It appears that, with help, I can open the gate to Lieus. I just need a few things, one being something that entirely originates from Lieus. Is there any artefact or object you know of?'

Andra shrugged. 'I am not certain. How crucial is its origin?'

'Our lives depend on it.' Elissa leant forward in hope.

'Then I am not certain enough, but that's not all you came for, is it?'

'No.' Elissa turned to Hope. 'I found one. I don't know if it's who the awldrin seek, but I found one on Lieus. I saw it through the gates. It looked like the awldrin in the pictures, not those who are here now.'

Hope snorted rings of smoke. 'That is possibly the best news I've had in hundreds of cycles. You must open the gates and bring it here.'

'If the awldrin are there too, will we not be running from one battle to another?' Andra asked. The other Chosen muttered between themselves, torn between staring at Elissa and listening to her words.

'I only saw one. In the many, many other lives it was possible to observe, there is no sign of them.'

Hope shook her scales, stretching her wings as ripples of gold flowed toward her tail. 'We must do this thing. Do whatever it takes, Elissa. It will not be easy, and I cannot promise you will survive, but you must try.'

Elissa grimaced. 'Thank you for that, Hope. Sorrow keeps the gate open for me. I must rush back.'

'Is he?'

'He shines again,' Elissa replied, and Hope puffed smoke rings. 'There is a new Vigilant too.'

'Go, little dragon,' Hope said. 'We will prepare at this side for your next return. I have no doubt that it will be to tell us the migrations can begin.'

'Before I return, Andra, is there any news from Dragonsbreath?'

'The Captain sails that way on his next voyage. He is due here with the survivors of Shardeep any day.'

'He promised to stay in touch with them.' Elissa slumped slightly, worry for her friends, for Laytha, overwhelming her now she was back and facing the reality of the situation on Tebein.

Andra leant heavily on the closest Chosen for a moment. 'Meet him somewhere in your dream. Nothing should stop you crossing that divide, even being on another moon.' The work or magic they were exerting was clearly taking a toll.

'Tell him to meet me in my cottage by the green chair,' Elissa said. 'You can let him in so he can get his bearings. Only, I have no concept of day or night on Mythos. The sun never sets. It is one thing to see it and quite another to live it.'

'Then use the gates to tell when it is dark,' Hope offered. Elissa glanced through the wall; the light looked as though it was afternoon. She might still be in the area in a few hours, so she nodded and turned back to the gate. 'I should get back. Sorrow is waiting.'

'You said that.' Hope reached her head in to the chamber and nudged Elissa toward the gate. 'We are all counting on you. In so many more ways than I first realised. Your biggest challenge is yet to come, and I hope that the changes you have started to show will happen fast enough for your survival.'

Elissa slipped back through the open gate, into the darkness, and it swallowed her up until she felt the cool breeze of the Watcher's Hall and saw the glint of Sorrow's scales.

He moved back and allowed the gate to seal behind her.

'Just us again,' Elissa said, as the pain of leaving everyone she knew hit her. She allowed herself a moment to sit and let the tears to flow. It was entirely possible that being away from Sorrow had simply made his influence more obvious. So Elissa soaked it up, bundled the emotions, and then reached for her bag.

'I should have asked them for a spade,' she muttered. 'Let's go and dig these bones up. Then I need to have a quick chat with someone before we return to Rapture.'

⌐ℛ ⌂ ✦ ◉

They stood over a large stone at the back of the Hall. It was plain, rough, and sat at a slight angle where it had been placed on uneven ground, then partially sunk over the intervening cycles.

'Not out in the sun? Or at least the courtyard?' Elissa crouched alongside it, resting her hand on the large stone. 'Did Otso change too? Regret told me he could use fire.'

'A little. He had a blacker shimmer than you. You are starting to turn white. He is buried in here because the Watcher wanted to keep him close. He didn't want him eaten or dug up.'

Elissa nudged at the slab. There was a chance that the bones had totally decayed by now. There was a chance that they didn't hold the power they needed. 'If he changed, does that not make him of Mythos as much as of Lieus?' She tried to get her fingers under the edge, to lever it up.

Sorrow blew a gentle cloud of smoke her way. 'I can help, if you want.'

Elissa shrugged and moved back. 'I'm not too proud to say yes. The faster we get them, the better.'

Sorrow pushed at the slab until he could get his claws under it. In his talons, the slab looked small. It was still a struggle, though, and he shuffled it slowly to one side as Elissa stood by, watching helplessly.

In the hollow space below it lay a skeleton, curled in a sleeping position. The tiniest bones were pretty much gone, but fragments of the longer bones were present in the shadow of the body's remains. There wasn't much left to collect. Elissa hung over the edge, almost scared to breathe in case they crumbled. Amongst the bones was a long, red object. She peered closely at it, holding her breath.

'What's that?' she asked. Sorrow peered down into the pit.

'It's what he used to write with. I'm not surprised he was buried with it. He never went anywhere without it.'

Elissa reached down to take the red object, and the nearest bone crumbled at her touch. She had been right to be cautious. 'It's almost glowing, like lumina.'

'It's made of staramine, the hardest rock in the Aulirean system. The one the awldrin need to stay alive – the thing they mined on Caldera for.'

Elissa sat on her heels, trying to remember the story that Rossi had told her back in Dragonsbreath. 'They used all the Tebein supply before they arrived on Lieus. Staramine was only found on Lieus.' She looked toward Sorrow, who glinted in the light of the fireball he juggled. 'We don't need his bones. We have our anchor.'

As they pushed the lid back over the resting place of the last human to live on Mythos, Elissa wondered where he had come from, how had he become so beloved and trusted by the

Watcher. Light glinted from something else in the grave, and before she thought properly, she reached in and picked it up, finding that she held a small black scale, far tinier than any she'd seen on a dragon – even on Vigilant. She tucked it in her pocket and helped Sorrow replace the lid.

⌒ᚨ☾☧◉

With a section of bone from the Watcher's wing tip and the staramine writing tool safely stored in her bag, Elissa and Sorrow left the Hall. The skies were still light in the Tebein crystal, and they didn't have time to wait. She'd just have to try repeatedly over the duration of their journey. Surely, she would reach The Captain eventually.

They launched into the sky directly from the courtyard as Elissa hung on by sheer determination. Dreamer perched on her shoulder, his talons piercing her clothes. It was time to make echoglass.

CHAPTER 32

SURIIN

The rending buried the mines and towns alike
We tried to recover the bodies.
Those buried in the rubble of fallen beauty were
easier to find,
But those taken by the awldrin to search for
staramine,
Those souls were lost to us forever.
History of the Crater-lands, Post Rending

Silard hustled Suriin away from the lift chamber, and as soon as the corridor was clear, he took the necklace back from her. Someone appeared at the far end of the passage, and he turned back the way they came without another word. These Howlers were strange.

The scent of breakfast drew her onward. Whilst the herbal concoction had kept her awake, she was utterly starving. If she'd have had four legs and a tail, no doubt she'd be just fine. Swift still carried her bone, and contentment flowed through their bond.

Suriin could really do with eating a meal that she didn't throw back up. Food, then rest. She'd be skinnier than Swift soon, otherwise.

She needed to see Aslin today, though – if she could work out a sensible reason why she might need to hear the words of binding.

'Hey, Aslin, can you speak dragon?' Or maybe, 'I was reading about how our crystals are so connected, so maybe if I spoke my binding again, I could get more information about its location.' Suriin laughed at herself. Neither of those would do. But she could hardly open with, 'I need the words of binding, so I can tell them to a secret group, then I can unbind me and can use really powerful, banned magic to kill an awldrin that I accidentally freed.'

But before that, before Suriin tried anything, she needed food and to see her father. The hall was packed, and she'd walked straight across to the serving counter before she realised that Swift had stayed at the entrance. At least one of them knew what they should do. She sent *[Swift in the paddocks, Suriin eating]*.

Swift replied with friendship, affection and, unusually, no hunger. The Howler's meal must have helped more than the things she had been giving Swift. That, or she'd finally eaten enough to feel full.

⌒ ⋏ ◖ ✧ ◉

Suriin collected a plate of food and slipped into a nearby seat, too tired to seek out company. Sleep should be her priority, but before she fell asleep again, or in case something went wrong with her binding, she needed to see her father. The fact that he knew far more than he had let on was eating at her. Did her mother know she was responsible for the awldrin? Did he know?

Suriin barely tasted the flatcakes as she drowned them in fruit and brose, eating as fast as she could. She returned her plate to the clear-up zone and then wandered across the courtyard to the Star Tower.

One of the laundry workers left the chamber, carrying a bundle of sheets. 'Excuse me, has So'Dal Yorynn moved?' Suriin asked.

The man nodded. 'He's back in the main accommodations for visiting Witnesses.'

'The guest hall?'

The man shook his head. 'The garden-side ones, third floor. There's a room for each crater.'

'I'm sorry, how do I get to the third floor?'

He frowned at her. 'You need to spend more time out of that kitchen. You do make good fruit baskets, though, so I'll tell you.' He leant in as though it was a great secret. 'Crater edge, near the Halfen flower beds, is a staircase. That's the main route up.'

'Thanks.'

He whistled as he hefted the bundle of bed sheets to carry them away.

There would be more privacy in private quarters, something she could really get behind, given the conversation they needed to have. Sleep would have to wait. A little food had refreshed her, and if it was full quarters, like Aslin's, she could sleep there anyway.

⌒ ⋏ ◖ ⚵ ◉

[Lift to crater garden,] she sent to Swift.

Swift sent a wag through their bond, and as Suriin crossed

the courtyard, the hound ran back from the paddocks to rejoin her. They strolled as casually as she could manage back to the steam lift. Swift left her side for a scratch from the Howler on the lift.

'Sorry,' she said as she reclaimed her.

'Aren't you supposed to be asleep?' Fall whispered.

'I'm just going to visit my father. He's moved rooms,' she replied, and with an energy she didn't feel, she boarded the steam lift with a hop.

The lift shot upward, and Suriin walked off the top with considerably less energy. [*Yorynn walking down the path*] filled her view as Swift started to scent the path ahead. Suriin rested her hand on Swift's back and let her lead them to a staircase. She hoped it was the right one. The garden map normally made sense, but she was too tired to be certain.

Every step of the staircase was a challenge. She caught her toes on the next step more times than she could count, and only Swift's gentle pushes from behind – and the desire to find out what her father really knew – kept her moving upwards.

They rounded another landing, and Swift nudged her away from the stairs. Suriin wove along the curving passageway, looking at the signs on the doors. Eventually, she found one that said Golden, and knocked.

Gwynn opened it and grabbed Suriin as she crumpled with exhaustion. 'Dad, do you think you can help? It's Suriin!' he called.

'I can do it.' Suriin dragged herself over the threshold. There was a comfy chair. She could sit in that and ask her questions.

'I know where our mother is,' she said as she sat down, her father and brother both standing over her.

'Good. That will make our next conversation a lot easier.' Her father smiled. 'Now sleep.'

He started to sing a gentle song. His voice was hoarse from lack of use, but Suriin remembered the tune from her childhood. She relaxed a little, unwilling to give up her fight with wakefulness, but with Swift's comforting head on her lap, she soon lost the battle.

⌒ ⪢ ⟨ ✥ ◉

'Now you're going to be less tired and, hopefully, far more logical,' her father began several hours later. 'It would appear we all need to share a little honesty.'

'Wouldn't it have been less traumatic for me to know where she was from the start?' Suriin replied.

Gwynn laughed. 'Yeah, you were right – she needed sleep. Even after a rest, she's as grumpy as a farbrox who just lost its dinner.'

'I am not,' Suriin retorted, wincing as she did. 'It's just a lot. We had a whole load of other things going on. It would have been good to know our mother was safe and hadn't been eaten alive. She could have answered Aslin?'

Her father nodded. 'If I'd been well enough, I'd have told you. But we wanted you to focus on your studies, to live your dream. You were already feeling guilty.'

Gwynn raised an eyebrow. 'And me? I was under the impression she was trying to collect a cure, that it was highly borderline that the Black Palace would allow it, and so I was sworn to secrecy. That's pretty different from the fact that she went to fight monsters!'

Yorynn rubbed his stump as he sat down. 'We did what we thought was right. The rest of her family is there – family you've never met. You were both safe, and they needed her.'

'If we'd known it would lead to this,' he gesticulated widely around, 'then we might have made another decision. I'm sorry.

We made a mistake too.'

'What do you mean by "this?"' Suriin leant forward. How much did he really know?

'Suriin, I know you would not lose your crystal. You would have reclaimed it immediately and chased the thief down. Your mother has seen the awldrin take crystals. She has seen the creature kill for them. She also knows you have seen it. You tried to warn her, she says, through Fluffy, and one of the So'Dal has told her all about it.'

Suriin sat back, her pulse racing as her father stared at her.

'I don't know how you found it, or where it was, but as sure as night meets day – as sure as the Watcher is black – you had something to do with the awldrin being released.'

Suriin let the tears flow. There was no hiding now, and her father didn't look angry. His voice was calm. She sobbed as Swift nudged her and Fluffy watched, and probably her mother, too, through those gentle eyes.

'I was trying to cure you.' Suriin sobbed. 'I didn't mean to do it. I thought she'd help me. She gave me a substance that she said would cure you and told me that she had more. I believed her. I know I'm stupid. It was reckless. I thought Mum had been eaten – I couldn't lose you too.'

'And as a family, we need to put this right.'

Suriin stopped, her eyes raised in disbelief to her father. 'I can't even cast a simple emotional magic. I can't do anything. I'm crippled without my crystal.'

Her father sighed. 'Your mother always says she is crippled *with* it. She said those words were burned into her memory, and she'd wished from the day she'd bonded it that she could have removed it. When things were hard – when too many creatures approached – she'd curse the thing.'

'She knows the words still?' Suriin stood up. 'I need them! If I have them ...'

Suriin's mind raced. Which was the fastest way to get hold of her mother? To get the words to the Howlers?

'If she could unbind from it, do you think she would?' she asked slowly.

Her father laughed. 'If there was a way, I suspect that, yes, she'd do it. Facing an awldrin in battle with your hands tied behind your back is not a fight I'd want to take on. She says she has help. That there is a group of special So'Dal there who are aiding her.'

Gwynn interrupted. 'Darin? Is one of them called Darin?'

Their father frowned. 'I don't know.' Suriin and Gwynn looked at each other. Gwynn rubbed at his face. It wasn't their secret to break, but it sounded like the same Howlers who had helped her were now with her mother, otherwise how would they know?

'I need a moment,' she murmured, and walked toward the source of the breeze coming through the room. A wide balcony opened up, and she could see other people on their ledges, oblivious to the trouble in Dal. She looked down at the garden – the map spread far below her – and over at Dal, to her left.

'What else do you know?' Her father placed a gentle hand on her shoulder. 'Come back inside, sweetheart. I'll close the doors, and we can talk.'

Suriin sighed and nodded. He was as good as his word and closed the main doors to the crater.

'There may be a way to unbind me, so I no longer feel so sick and can access my power.'

'If you can be unbound ...' Gwynn's eyes widened.

'Then so can our mother.'

Their father paced the room. 'Wishing for a thing and actually having it are two different things. Watcher knows she needs the strength. So far, the awldrin has shown no magic, only the ability to communicate with the xotryl.'

'And she can dream walk,' Suriin added. 'She's strong. I made this mess, but if I can get to Mother and learn from her instead – if I am unbound – I can fight. The awldrin was here last night. I saw her, I felt her, and I chased her away.'

'How?'

'She still has my crystal and was close enough that I could use it.'

Gwynn arched a brow. 'That sounds pretty unlikely. Sure you haven't unbound already by accident?'

'Trust me on this – I'm sure. There's a way, using Swift, that I can access my magic. But our bond is new. It's not going to be easy, and I still need the right words. To find those, I need the original words of binding.'

'Let me ask her opinion. If we attempt this, we'll be removed from the So'Dal if they ever find out.'

'If we don't, the So'Dal will have no choice but to reveal themselves. The normal folk may turn on us. You explained all this to me before. I don't care about finishing my training here. I have Swift, and you're alive. We'll move to Dal!'

'There's my daughter.' Yorynn smiled. 'If your mother agrees, you will have to join me in a dream walk to collect the words yourself.'

'Okay.' Suriin scritched Swift's head. 'How long do we need to wait?' The sun was dropping, and she suddenly realised that the Howlers might not wish to risk collecting her if they knew she wasn't alone.

'As soon as night falls.'

⌒ ⋀ ⟨ ⚘◉

Her father opened his eyes. 'You need to join us in the market,' he said. Gwynn sat on the floor, playing with the hounds as

Suriin rested her head on the pillow. She wasn't tired enough really, but somehow, this had to work.

She felt the bony head of Swift push under her arm, the warmth of her body alongside her, and relaxed.

Suriin closed her eyes, trying to picture the market and build the image of Redpike in her mind, but instead, she was pushed far from the market, deep under the mountain, back to the cell.

Natke stood over her. Suriin's instinct to curl up and protect herself kicked in.

'I see you. I know what you did to my xotryl. I will get home, and none of you can stop me. I'll kill every last one of you, if that's what it takes to rebuild the gate. I hope you rest badly, because I'll be there to see you again soon. And this time, I'm reclaiming everything.' Natke towered over her. She didn't wear the red and black armour this time, nor the green dress Suriin had last seen her in, but an ill-fitting piecemeal set of armour. If she'd found it, then she'd returned to a place of the awldrin, somewhere on Caldera.

Suriin tried to gather herself. 'My father lives, despite you. You will not break me so easily.' She hoped she sounded braver – stronger – than she felt.

'My people rise. They know I live, and they will come for me. We will take back what we need.'

'Your people are worlds away. They cannot help you.' Suriin reached for Swift, feeling for their thread of connection. She needed to get to her mother fast.

'I'd kill you, but I want you to suffer, to see what your foolish love did to your home – how you broke it with your weak blindness.' Natke said, her hand raised as though to strike.

Suriin grabbed the thread and *pulled* herself back.

She sat up, sweating, and vomited over the side of the bed. She didn't think Natke could live out her threat, didn't believe it was possible, but what if it was? What if there would soon be more of them?

She shook her father. 'I can't get to you. The awldrin rules my mind every time I try to sleep walk. She finds me.'

'Just now?' he asked.

Suriin nodded. 'She said her people know, that they will try to return. They know she lives. I can't get to you. Tell Mother ...' She glanced at Gwynn. 'I have to – there's no other way.'

'We promised.'

Suriin closed her eyes tight. 'Tell Mum to pass the words to a Howler. They need to reach Boulder.'

'That makes no sense.'

Gwynn stroked Fluffy. 'Then we broke no promises. Just repeat that to her.'

Chapter 33

Darin

*Clifdon is a small harbour, only accessible by
land from Lacton.
Once, great ships would dock there, bringing
wares from faraway lands.
Since the great rending, no ships visit.
We are forgotten, and it has fallen to ruin.*
A Traveller's Guide to Caldera

With the basket attached to the rope, all that was left to do was get it to the top. Lillith had found another pulley in some bushes, and raised it in triumph above her head.

'This changes the game!' she'd yelled, and ran with it back to her workshop. Now, with a new copy of it in her hands, she was getting ready to test the basket.

Darin stared up at the cliff and shuddered.

Chase laughed. 'There are some tasks best left to experts. Thankfully for you, this is one of them. Once they're up and getting the rope rigged through the pulleys, we should start rounding up the passengers. I left Tian and Eira with Luik to decide who comes. It's their town and their decision. We'll guide those who wish to evacuate to safety.'

The basket started to rise as Lillith and one of her workers hauled themselves up. It would be slow and difficult on a single pulley. But as he watched, a group of others, led by Davii, picked up the descending rope, and the basket rose faster.

'They've got this in hand, Darin. When it was a trade route, they used to lift heavy goods without passengers regularly. All we had to do was set them on the right path. Come on. We need to get ready. On this side of the crater, there will be far more wildlife to deal with. No matter how they split the town, we're going to attract a lot of attention, either from xotryl or other opportunists. Our pack won't be sleeping much for a few days.'

Darin would worry about the Surface when he got there. He watched the speed the basket rose at with the sinking realisation that he would have to ride in it soon, then turned to follow Chase.

⌒ ⋔ ꟼ ✲ ◉

Unfamiliar scents filled the room as they entered the Witness's home. Luik appeared slightly agitated, his tone clipped and short, although they couldn't make out the exact words passing between him and Heline. She sank to a chair with her head in her hands. Fleck stood behind her, tail between her legs.

Star nudged him *[Heline sad. Darin helping]*.

Darin took his cue from Star. Luik looked as exhausted as Heline was distressed. Suriin's mother appeared very distracted, and Tian beamed a smile at Chase before gesturing him over for a quiet conversation.

They needed Heline to help herd the people. Whatever the problem, she was a new pack member. Darin headed toward her.

'Are you okay?' he asked quietly. 'Can I help?'

Luik glanced over at him. 'Unless you can sing, which Howlers famously can't, no. I'm still blocked by the healing draft. You need to leave as soon as possible, and Heline should go with you, but she needs a potion, and I can't make it.'

'I agree we need her, but if she needs this potion, then we'll find a way.'

Heline stroked Fleck, whose head now rested on her lap. Her long, dark hair hid her face.

'Darin, with your whistles, can you play any tune?'

'If I know it, yes. They allow me to access the same wefts a So'Dal can.'

Heline uncurled a little. 'Really?'

'What do you need? Luik, can you sing the tune?'

Luik nodded, then started to sing. The tune began slow and deep, then it changed and grew high-pitched; complicated sequences of notes ran into each other. It wasn't long, but Watcher, it was complex. Darin swallowed hard as Heline stared up at him, her gaze fixed on his fingers. She was a Howler now, and apparently she needed help. He stumbled over the first notes and clenched his fist in frustration.

'Hold a moment. I can do this, but I need help. Tian, can you pick up this tune, please? Luik can't weft it, and I can't learn it without hearing it repeated.'

Tian rushed across the room and hugged Darin. 'You wonderful boy. You have no idea what a help this will be! Of course I can. Luik, start again. I'm listening.'

Tian nodded along as Luik sang it for a second time, then began to join in. Before long, Tian was note perfect. He took the whistle and replicated the tune. 'I've got it now, Darin.'

'It doesn't do a full glow on landing,' Luik said. 'When the weft settles, a delicate red sparkle will flicker for a moment.'

Darin studied the herbal mixture. 'There's quite a lot there.'

'I have to take it every day to keep feeling like myself.' Heline said quietly. 'I prepared it, not thinking about Luik being unable to weft. I don't know how long we'll be away for, so I didn't want to run out.'

'What's the contents? If we can gather them on the way, you'll be able to make your own once you're better with your whistle.' The mildly astringent smell was pleasant, and Darin breathed it in deeply.

'Mostly *Femina gracilis*. It's not rare around here,' Luik replied. 'It's more commonly used to help with other feminine issues, but it's essential for Heline to keep being her wonderful self.'

'Oh ... oh.' Darin looked at Heline. She shrugged. 'I think I understand now. The black hair, the dreams of being a Howler. This matters far more than you're suggesting. Tian, let's get this tune learnt.'

They worked on the weft over and over until Tian and Luik were happy that he was note-perfect. Darin focused his weft through the music to the bowl. As the red sparkles settled on the liquid, he lifted his eyes to find everyone beaming at him. Even Eira clapped a little.

Heline sighed, and Fleck wagged. 'We should focus on everyone else now, please,' she said. 'We have a town to evacuate.'

⌒ ⌀ ◖ ✥ ◉

With the lift running smoothly and the ground team pulling people up at a much faster rate, the queue for the lift soon began to grow. It was mainly made up of families. Young children fidgeted with impatience, wide eyed as their friends stepped into the basket and were lifted to the crater rim. Tian and Krista had gone up first, followed by a basket of tools and food. They were followed in turn by a team who would clear vegetation from the old path.

Eira appeared alongside him, watching quietly as the next basket was raised.

'Take care of them. They are needed back here when this is over.' He glanced at her. She remained oddly distant, disconnected almost. 'I need one of you to send a message to someone called Boulder,' she said.

'Chase is better at that than me.'

She nodded. 'You should know, Suriin plans to attempt to unbond herself with Howler help. If she is successful, I will do the same. I know it has risks – I am burned out already – and I accept that. But if I am able to finally protect people as I should have always been able to, I will not be returning to the Black Palace. I would like my family to be brought here. Sending Suriin there was a mistake. I thought it for the best, but I regret it now. I trust the Howlers will get them here safely.'

She turned away without waiting for a reply and tapped Chase on the arm. He followed her a moment later.

Darin checked Star's armour was properly in place, lifted his pack, and joined Heline near the front of the queue.

'We should get up. It's going to be getting crowded soon.' He sent *[Star in the lift with Darin]*.

Star replied with *[Star and Darin, as well as Heline and Fleck in the lift]*. He'd got quite attached to the other youngster.

'When can we get armour like that?' Heline stroked an exposed ear, and Star wagged with delight at the extra attention.

'When we go back to the Black Palace. I have a friend there who's making enough for the whole pack.' The cage landed, and they climbed in.

Darin swallowed the fear; he would not let Star worry. This was lower than the other lift. There were more people lifting them. He would be fine.

He grasped the rail as the basket started its ascent, his resolution of calm barely holding intact.

'It's exciting, isn't it?' Heline stared over the edge, looking down.

'It's certainly something,' he muttered as they shot up to the rim of the crater.

Tian stood near the top as they were ushered out. 'Chase warned me you might struggle. Come and sit over here for a moment while we bring the rest up.'

Darin collapsed where Tian indicated and tried to count the people already up. Children investigated their new surroundings, while parents tried to keep them in the group. More Dal folk were rebuilding a cart that had been sent up in pieces, and he had no doubt that others would follow. They all moved so much, he had to give up counting.

'This is going to be a long walk.'

⌒ ⋔ ☾ ✠ ◉

Later that evening, Chase appeared over the rim, and the lift was lowered for the last time. Several carts were now in various stages of being built. They wouldn't carry much weight, but if he had to bundle all the small kids into one to speed their progress, he was willing to do it. Food and water filled a couple, and a last was empty to carry the tools. Each cart had bars and straps for people to pull them with. Aside from the carts, each family carried only what they needed.

Chase said that Boulder predicted a two-day walk to the cliffs overlooking Clifdon. Apparently, there were a few routes down to the beach from there, but his memory was hazy on the details.

As they stood together, Chase rubbed at his chin. 'We'll have to split up. I don't like it, but the group is too large to protect otherwise. Keep your hounds on alert for anything that isn't human.' Chase frowned at the milling people. 'We also need to spread leaders they trust as part of the escort team. Heline, you travel in the middle. Darin, take the front with Krista.'

Lillith strolled over with a bag tucked under her arm. 'I'll travel with Heline,' she said. 'Can we hand these out through the line?' She withdrew a hinged wooden object from inside the bag, took one part in each hand, and clapped it together quickly. The sound carried far enough that those gathering at the front of the line turned to see what it was.

'It's effective. I'll give you that!' Darin was impressed.

'The noise will carry as far as the whistles, and far less skill is needed to use them.' Tian reached for one. 'I should have thought to bring some myself.'

'We use them out in the fields to warn each other of incoming trouble. Everyone in Dal knows what they mean.'

Darin took a set from the bag. 'Let's distribute them and get moving. Travelling overnight is going to be bad enough as it is.'

'That was an eventuality I did prepare for.' Tian chuckled. 'Every family has been given a jar. As night falls, they can fill it with fire sprites. It will only give a dim light, but should attract a lot less attention than glow lamps. Not that there were enough of those in Dal, anyway.'

'And that's why I love you.' Chase leant over and planted a kiss on Tian's cheek. 'You always think of the bits I miss.'

'Let's go, then.' Darin stretched as he got to his feet, sending *[Star and Darin leading the line, Star sniffing ahead]*.

Star replied with *[meat]*.

[Star killing a farbrox, Star eating it] 'If you can kill it, boy, you can eat it.'

'Good luck.' Chase clapped Darin on the shoulder. 'Keep

the throwing rings handy, Star on alert, and trust Krista. Her instincts are usually right.'

⌒ ⋏ ⟨ ✾ ◉

Star loped ahead, sniffing the air and occasionally pursuing some small creature into the undergrowth. The vegetation on the Surface wasn't as different as Darin had expected. There were a lot of plants he knew well from his work with Tralkion, and a fair number from Dal. It made sense, though. Why would seeds not be carried up here? Some plants would be bound to cope with both environments.

Unlike the mountain route from the Black Mountain to Dal, there were a lot more trees. In places, they had to stop to clear fallen trunks from the path.

The track wasn't quite deep enough to be a holloway. They walked on rock, and even with regular passage, it would probably not get much deeper. The sides were still steep and distinct, which stopped them from getting lost or children leaving the track accidentally. As dusk fell, fire sprites lit the walls ahead, and they became a procession of silhouettes carrying bobbing lights. Darin usually enjoyed the silence of night, but as the children realised they weren't stopping to sleep, cries and whines filled the air.

Darin wanted to quiet them, to ask the parents to stop the noise; they would attract too much attention, but he bit his lip, and they pushed on. When they got too tired, he'd encourage them into the cart. For now, they would keep moving.

It was fully dark when they heard the first roar.

A second answered from further back in the line. Star sent confusion to him. The scent was clearly unfamiliar *[Four vague shapes, to their right]*.

'Star thinks there are four.'

Krista's face was illuminated by her glow lamp as she turned to face them. 'Four what?'

Darin tried to recall any of the creatures from the bestiary of Lieus animals, their twisted shapes, their varied sizes. Whatever was out there was bigger than a graaken, that much was certain. 'I don't know yet.'

He unscrewed the top of his staff and prepared it for a fight. *[Star bite shadow]* filled his vision. It was good to know their training was working.

'Put the smallest children in the nearest cart,' Krista called back. 'Be prepared for anything. Do not get between us and the creatures. If you see it, let us know.'

The path was only as deep as his waist, his head at a level he really didn't like. Star yelped as he stood on something, and Darin bent down to check on him.

Star was okay, but surprised. He licked a thank you, then turned to face the roars. Darin picked up the sharp object under Star's paw and held it close to Krista's light. It was a tooth. A very distinctive tooth, with serrated edges and two points, one longer and wider than the other.

'It's roilken.'

'That's a tale from childhood stories.' Krista laughed. 'Here, let me look.'

'They are as real as So'Dal and skaa-rak. And I suspect there's at least four of them hunting us.' Darin handed her the tooth.

'Let's say I believe you. How do we fight a creature that slips in and out of the darkness?' Krista peered into the dark.

'You keep everything light. No shadows, lots of movement – be unpredictable, but stay inside the path. I need you to keep the people safe and, unless you see them, leave the actual fighting to the Howlers.'

As they talked, a small cry came from behind them. Darin

turned to see a woman scream and run into the trees. For a moment, he thought they were already undone, but she returned, cradling a child. Krista took charge, calling orders and getting the group huddled along the centre of the path, the fire sprite lanterns to the outside of the long line of people. Once he was confident that Krista had everyone under control, and the wooden clapper had been sounded to alert those behind them, Darin returned his attention to Star.

'How shall we do this then, boy? A few over-sized farbrox can't be as scary as a xotryl, right?' He sent *[Darin with Star's eyes, seeing the shadow and throwing the throwing ring]*.

Star sent reassurance back, then Darin saw everything double, his senses tied in to Star *[Two shadows behind the trees ahead]*.

He climbed to the Surface and crouched slightly, aligning his vision with Star, and prepared a throwing ring. The closest shadow shook as another growl filled the air, and Darin took his chance. He threw the ring overhand with as much power as he could muster when the creature passed between trees.

[The blur of the throwing ring, a spray of heat as it hit the shadow]

A high pitched yelp from the direction of his throw.

[The shadow turning toward them, charging, another holding back, moving to his right]

'Krista, there's one coming toward you,' he called as he stared through Star's eyes at the incoming creature. Teeth glinted in the light; those serrated teeth that the roilken grew and lost continuously, rows of sharp danger ready to take a chunk out of him.

He threw another ring directly at its head and reached for his spear – any second now, he'd be face to face, the light from the fire sprites just bright enough to use his own vision.

Anger, hatred, and pain filled the next roar. The ground

shook as the roilken charged. Blood poured from the fresh wound where his ring protruded. Star crouched alongside him. He sent *[Star between the creature and the people. Star attack under throat]*.

[Star biting the roilken] filled his vision. He sent agreement, and they moved into position.

Star barked from his side, the roilken glanced in Star's direction, and Darin struck the exposed side of its neck, stabbing and withdrawing the spear. It dragged as he tried to pull it back out, and the blunt, tooth-filled snout turned toward him. Star leapt at its throat as Darin stuck the spear into its eye.

He was covered in blood as Star shook the creature, and it collapsed to its knees before falling still.

Darin wiped the end of his spear on the grass, retrieved the ring, and wiped that clean too.

[The second roilken approaching Krista] Star sent.

Another screamed from further back, and Darin hesitated. Should he take this one on too? Were the others okay? *[Sandy and Chase standing over a roilken corpse]* filled his view. *[Fleck barking at another, Lillith throwing something]*

As the roilken stalked the fringes of the group near the wagon, so Darin stalked it through the trees, using Star's vision to help. It circled around Krista, poised to pounce.

Star snapped at its rear legs, and it spun to face them. Darin threw the ring toward it, but it bounced off a tree, deflecting away from the roilken. It charged at Star, who replied in kind, his armour protecting him from a glancing bite. Darin wielded the spear, stabbing at the roilken's face. He missed.

Star snapped at it from the other side, darting in to attack and withdraw as Darin readied for another spear strike. The roilken snarled.

They were close to the light now. Too close to the children.

Krista called out, but Darin couldn't make out her words.

He tried to get between the children and the roilken to give Krista a clear shot.

A loud noise intruded on his thoughts – flapping.

A shout from above.

Light bloomed. Darin was blinded by a flash. The scent of burning flesh filled the air. The roilken was aflame. Darin looked up as his vision settled to see a garant extending its wings and glide in to land.

CHAPTER 34

ELISSA

They arrived that day, exhausted and broken
Not for them the hope of our island,
they had seen their families burn.
These children needed more than Hope to heal
the scars they carried.
The Black Planet

'We need to land.' Elissa struggled with the weight of the bag as they flew toward the dusk line. There had to be a better way to secure it before they took back off. Her shoulders ached and her back and neck were agony; the extra weight of the items they carried was just a little too much. After hours of flight, she was in desperate need of a rest. Sorrow tucked his wings in tightly and dived. Elissa held back a panicked scream as the ground rushed toward them. Sorrow spread his wings wide and glided in to land, leaving her a slightly quivering wreck.

'You sounded worried,' he said as she slithered to the ground, her knees still shaking.

Elissa shrugged the bag from her shoulders. 'Terror must have got to me more than I realised. I'm not worried as much as hurting. You need to take the weight of this.'

Sorrow picked it up in his claw. 'It's not heavy.'

'Good. We'll tie it behind me. Can you keep a watch while I try to dream?'

Sorrow curled around her. 'Do what you need to do.'

⌐ ⋏ ◖ ✦ ◎

It took way too long for her liking, but eventually, her house and the little green chair with its straw nest of charvers came into view. The whole family of them were besieging the Captain.

'You might have warned me.' He gently swatted one away. 'It's a nice house. Comfy bed.' He winked at her.

'You're in my bed?'

'Well, I thought you might be a while. Andra said that you couldn't tell the time, and I need to get back out to sea as soon as I can.'

Elissa tried to sit in the other chair but realised too late that she still didn't really have enough control to do so, catching herself as she crumpled. 'How many survived?'

'*Cloudsailor* was full to the waterline, and we had three further small boats with us from Shardeep. There are more of Shardeep's people hiding in the old sericlave tunnels. We believe they will reach the coastal side soon, if they survived the journey. Many more are staying beneath the mountain in the older tunnels, hidden for now but ready to salvage what they can.

'The awldrin and the resistance at Shardeep fought for days. Rains gave them a short respite, but all their crops are burnt. There will be little food to go around this Winds, either for survivors or the inhabitants of Hope. If we survive the fight, we may still starve.'

The pressure of the task she faced grew with every word. A dire situation faced not only by those in Dragonsbreath, but the Chosen and the families who'd made it safely to Hope.

'Rossi? His daughter?'

The Captain looked down. Even in the dream state, his emotions were clear for her to read. 'I cannot tell of any specific adults. There was no sign of any of the Chosen on my last visit to Shardeep. I believe all the children made it to Hope, along with a small number we rescued from Silverfish. Andra was assigning them to families in Gallimaufry when I headed up here. They are safe, for now.'

For now. She needed to ask about Laytha, but she also needed a moment to regather herself.

'Take my hand,' she said.

The Captain clasped her hand. 'Where are you taking me?'

'Somewhere we will not be overheard. Somewhere no living creature on Tebein has seen.' She gripped him tightly and stepped into Mythos.

The Captain stared around in wonder. They stood where she actually slept, with the dusk zone in front and the everlight to their backs.

'Oh, hello,' Sorrow said, as Dreamer joined them too.

'Sorrow! You're supposed to be watching we're safe!'

Sorrow closed his eye. 'As you say, little dragon.'

The Captain chuckled. 'It looks like you have a better dream guardian than my collection of rogues. This is Mythos?'

Elissa gestured toward the distance. 'Far in that direction is the Hall of the Watcher, where the gate will bring you. We travel onward, deep into Mythos to the cave of Rapture, where I hope to make some new echoglass with her help.'

'How?'

Elissa shook her head and ran the fingers of her free hand through her hair. 'I don't know yet. I'm trusting that as I need to know things, they will be revealed.'

'How will you get them to Lieus?'

Elissa winced. 'I'm trying not to think about that. No one will tell me. But the dragons were able to build all the gates before there were gates. There must be a way.'

'They are dragons, Elissa – you are human. Your limits are not theirs.'

Elissa reached into her pocket and withdrew the tiny black scale. 'I think the more time I spend with them, the more their magic impacts me. They keep saying I smell of Harmony.'

The Captain nodded. 'You appear in this dream as you were the last time I saw you, but my aunt said that your hair has lightened, your eyes grow pale, and your skin now shines like Hope's scales. I wish I could see it.'

Had she changed so much? Elissa glanced at Sorrow's scales; none were smooth enough to allow her to see herself.

'Maybe this change is good.' She sighed. 'I didn't bring you here to talk of me. How are those at Dragonsbreath? Be truthful with me.'

He squeezed her hand. 'I'm sure you are still beautiful, no matter how dragony you become. I spoke to Laytha two nights ago. They are travelling to the closest headland opposite Shardeep – it lies in the shadow of the coastal mountain. Rains has been good to us, and the marsh is a-flood. Less xotryl patrol the skies on that coastline, as they took the bravest to Shardeep. Some of your sericlave have chosen to stay. With the burning of Shardeep's fields, the crops from Dragonsbreath may yet be needed if you ...'

'If I fail.'

'You won't. I believe in you. We all do.'

Dreamer fluttered his wings in an agitated fashion. Elissa

glanced up to see a silhouette far above them. 'I can't guarantee your safety, even with me. There are those here who fly across both wakefulness and sleep.'

'I will be collecting the refugees from Dragonsbreath at Thurra Isle as soon as I can. I will eat, sleep, and head back to sea on the next tide.'

'Thank you,' Elissa said. 'You can sleep in my bed if you want. You may as well now you're already there.'

He reached for her with his other hand. 'I'll see you soon. I'll get all who live to Hope, I promise. You have to get them the rest of the way – to safety.' He let go of her hand and stepped away. Alone again, her hand left empty.

'He was nice,' Sorrow said. 'You should rest properly now. Then we'll fit the bag to me.'

⌒ ⚲ ☾ ✧ ◉

They flew and rested again, then prepared for the last stretch to Rapture's cave. The lone peak appeared ahead of them, the dark scar of the cave at its base visible from their height.

Sorrow landed softly and with their post-flight routine now as smooth as a wildebeest's hide, Elissa dismounted.

'You're coming with me this time, aren't you?' she asked as Sorrow hung back from the cave entrance. Clusters of charvers greeted his arrival with excitement, fluttering out to swarm around him eagerly. Sorrow puffed some smoke rings, and the charvers dived through them, weaving in and out, playing with them.

'You don't need me,' he said.

Elissa paused before walking back to him. 'No, I don't. But if you can manage it, I'd really like your support. Sadness helped me balance my emotions against Rapture last time. If you balance each other out a little, it might be easier to do whatever I have to without fighting so hard against her.'

Sorrow blew another smoke ring. More charvers arrived from the bushes around the cave. She thought he was choosing to ignore her at first, but his flanks heaved a huge sigh, reflecting sparkles of light around him. Charvers pursued them as though they were fire sprites.

'If you're certain it will aid, I will be by your side.'

Together, they entered the tunnel to Rapture's cave.

⌒ ⋏ ⟆ ✧ ◦

'I can feel you coming,' she sang out as they drew close. Sorrow stopped mid-step.

'I can't do it.'

Elissa rested her hand on his cheek. 'You can. You need me to do impossible things, remember? I need your help now, because I need to know I can rely on you then.'

The clouds in Sorrow's eyes spun slowly; his scales rattled as he approached the central chamber. They entered the cavern together with Dreamer perched on Elissa's shoulder, his claws digging in tightly. Elissa supported Sorrow with a gentle touch, loaded with trust.

Rapture uncoiled as she saw them. 'No eyes covered today?' She didn't approach. Instead, she let them come in, her gaze fixed on Sorrow. Her eyes span faster and faster as he fully entered the room. 'You look good. I had worried that you would be not long with us.' She spoke in a soothing, calm voice, with none of the hard-edged passion that Elissa encountered on her previous visit. 'I am glad to see you flourish. The human might be better as *your* pet. She is doing you good.' Her joy washed over Elissa then – a wave of emotion that threatened to drown her. Sorrow reared back, as though he had been attacked, with panic in his eyes.

'It's okay.' Elissa drew as much of the emotion in as she could. It grew easier every time.

His muscles remained tense, and his tail swished, but he returned his feet to the floor. Rapture edged closer. Now she'd encountered Terror, Elissa could see that Rapture was no bigger. Her snout drew close, and she swung her head to study Elissa.

'You are both like Him and entirely unique. I felt what you just did. Have you been doing that with the others too?'

'Storing their emotions for later? I was advised once that I should embrace all experiences to replenish my own stores.'

Rapture laughed. 'That may be the case with human experiences. That is not what you are doing here. You are embracing our emotions, yes, but our power – the very magic we weave – is made from emotion. You are storing reserves of magic. Your body is not big enough, not dragon enough, to hold it all, so some of it is leaching out and changing you. Otso only ever took in ambient magic from the Watcher. Over his lifetime, that was enough for his skin to scale with tiny black scales, his fur to grow black, and his fire to be stronger.'

She nudged Elissa around, turning her in a circle. Elissa didn't resist. She was in a cave with two huge beasts. No matter how friendly they were, she still didn't know if she could trust one, or rely entirely on the other.

'Your hair is turning white. Your skin grows rough and also shimmers white. Tell me, little one, whose emotions have you been stealing?'

'A little of Amazement, Sorrow, Terror, Vigilant, and your own. But it's not stealing, you're throwing it at me, all of you.'

Rapture looked at Sorrow. 'You haven't stopped her?'

'It is what she needs – what we all need. If she is to survive the voyage, she will need more. More change and more power. You know this as well as I do.'

Elissa didn't like the sound of the journey, although she suspected she knew, deep down, what everyone was asking of her. The Captain and Andra could not know what it truly involved. She couldn't accept that they would ask her to risk everything to fly to Lieus.

One step at a time. Elissa strode forward, and as she did, she realised that her foot had stopped hurting, though she didn't really remember when. She sat, ignoring curious gazes of her companions, and removed her foot wrap and Hope's scale. Elissa squeezed her foot, and no matter where she pressed it, the pain was gone.

'The shard in my foot doesn't hurt any more.' She shook her head and retied the foot wrap.

'Given how much you've changed on the outside, that isn't really a surprise. It is in you – Harmony spreads throughout your body. Now, we have work to do. We can all admire your new scales once we've made the echoglass. You will have to finish their fitting once you reach the Lieus gate. For now, we will simply create the main lump of crystal. I assume you have the shell and the bone?'

Elissa tipped the contents of her bag out on the floor, recovering the bone, the egg shell, and the red shard of staramine rock.

'Terror said I would need anchors too – not just a completed journey, but a start and end anchor. I thought this might work.'

Rapture sniffed the staramine. 'It's probably not the easiest thing to work with, but he's right. I should have thought of it. I was too excited to see you – too caught up in dreams of our future.'

Elissa ignored the hint and picked up a rock from near the

entrance. 'This should work as the end point. How do we do this?'

Rapture picked each object up between sharp talons, studying them. She snapped a little of the egg shell off and put it to one side; she broke the Watcher's bone into smaller pieces and smashed the remaining shell fragments into a pile before combining them in a single heap. The staramine, she stuck in the middle, alongside the fragment of cavern wall.

'Now, you melt it with dragon-fire,' she said.

Elissa stared in horror. Melting all that would take her a whole season. There was no chance she could do it.

'Can you not melt it?' she asked. 'It would be quicker that way.'

'Then I would have to be the one to fly to Lieus to fit it. And, as much as the idea of revisiting that beautiful land fills my heart with ecstasy, until I have passed on all my knowledge, I cannot risk the flight. Besides, although I may appear powerful, my wings have long since lost their strength. I wouldn't make it.'

Sorrow closed his eyes slowly as Rapture explained, and Elissa tried to quell the panic that threatened to overcome her. She bathed instead in the positivity of Rapture, choosing to soak up her energy.

'You're doing it again,' Rapture murmured.

'Sorry, is it rude to do that?' Elissa opened her eyes and laid a hand on Sorrow for balance.

'It's unusual. Now, make me some fire.'

Elissa took a deep breath and readied herself to create her small flame. Before she had even pulled her arm fully back, fire exploded in front of her. A shimmering mass of flames licked the edge of the pile of bones. Maybe this wouldn't be so bad after all.

CHAPTER 35

SURIIN

Freedom is never underrated.
Graffiti on a bench in Dal Town

The Howlers came for her at dinner.

'Bones wants you, now.' Silard did not look happy.

'May I finish my food?'

'Does the world matter less than a plate of crostun?'

Suriin looked at the crunchy, meat-filled parcels on her plate, picked up one more, and shoved it in her mouth.

'Lets go,' she mumbled. Silard started toward the main passage immediately, and she shook her head. 'I need Swift first.'
[Swift meeting her at the hall doorway]

[Swift running] It wasn't long before the hound was at her side.

Suriin had to jog to keep up with Silard as they returned to the lift chamber. Before they reached it, he passed her a necklace like the one she'd used on the way out. He blew his whistle, and they faded away. Although fear dogged her steps, she felt a tiny thrill that they were moving almost unseen through the Black

Palace. She kept her hand on Swift as they sneaked toward the hidden door.

When the chamber cleared, he whispered, 'In the door.' Suriin and Swift sidled into the passage behind the lift. Silard closed the door and immediately held out his hand for the necklace.

'It's not yours and never will be,' he said.

They entered the chamber to a semi-circle of Howlers, all with somber expressions. Silard walked past her to a seat.

'We received a message from Chase. He told us a Soul Anchor in Dal wanted to speak directly to me. Why does a Soul Anchor in Dal know to pass me a message?' Boulder's face gave no emotion away.

Suriin raised her chin in defiance. 'It's my mother. You know full well that she's out there, and you Howlers already told her about what I did.'

Boulder laughed. 'You were right. They are Draconic, you clever girl. She said that it was urgent, and that you'd have extra news we'd need. She also said that she was willing to break her bonds to help her people. I don't agree with the offer, but the situation there is dire. Unless you had a garant, you could not get there in time to aid them.' He looked around the room. 'I'm sorry. I couldn't keep it up.'

Bones rose from his seat, his arms spread wide. 'You did well.'

Suriin relaxed. 'I thought you were all mad at me. We broke our promise.'

'Technically, you didn't, although you weren't to know that, in Dal, we are simply accepted as part of life.'

'So we have the words? Do we know what to do? Can we unbind me?'

Boulder nodded. 'Yes. I was able to work out the opposite binding from the words we have and the format used. We haven't yet sent them back to your mother. I thought you might like to attempt your own unbinding and let you pass it on yourself, as long as it works.'

'If it works, I've got a whole list of defensive things I need you to put in place.' Bones held up a piece of paper, covered in writing. 'Are you ready?'

⌐ ⚶ ◖ ✿ ◉

They sat in a circle with Swift's head in her lap. Suriin's hands shook, and the acrid stench of fear emanated from her favourite dress. It might yet go wrong. She could get trapped in the crystal, or lose her way back – she might fail. Suriin buried her hands in Swift's fur. She couldn't. Swift needed her. A small hook in her soul with a big need.

The hound sent affection and reassurance through their bond. Image after image hit her. Swift's previous bonded Anchor must have done things that scared her often enough that she was tuned in to fear, despite the freshness of their bond.

[Swift and Suriin in the market, eating something Swift really liked. Swift and Suriin on a very soft bed. Swift, Suriin, and her friends in the library] The last one hit Suriin the hardest. While she'd been trying to find answers, Swift had been connecting with her life. Suriin could do this, *would* do this.

'I'm ready,' she whispered.

Bones sat alongside her. 'We've got you safe,' he said. 'Know that whatever you face, your body is not in a cell. You are in the safest place in the Black Palace.'

They'd agreed to try to keep her mind on positive emotions until she needed to unbind. Suriin had told the Howlers about her suspicions. That the strongest emotion she could access would be needed for this. As she prepared for the trial ahead, she held regret close, certain that she'd either need to access it or the opposing emotion. After much discussion between them over food and a warm drink, Bones and Boulder had decided that the opposite of regret was probably love.

Bones was certain that he would regret a bad meal, but feel only joy and comfort from a really good one, and the other Howlers all found similar examples. It fitted with her recollection of the opposing side of Andra's table too. So as she laid in the soft fur rug, Suriin prepared herself to use both.

Swift settled next to her. She tucked her hands into Swift's fur and closed her eyes. The healing potion had worn off very slowly, as is the way of things you wait for.

With it out of her system, even the action of lying down made her nauseous. That nausea – the pain of her connection – would lead back to the crystal. Suriin embraced it. She felt for the tiny thread and pointed in the direction she thought it was. One last gift she could leave the Howlers, in case things went wrong – Natke's current location.

Then she tried to draw on her magic.

The pain hit as soon as she tried to summon love.

⌒ ↟ ◊ ⬡ ◉

She flew through the darkness. Her body, far from her mind, felt safe and warm. Suriin reached back for her connection to it – to Swift – reassured that both felt secure. She flew on, holding love. She could feel the pain of her body, knew that she would vomit on the soft rug any moment. Her crystal drew her close. She flew toward it, her mind calming as they joined. Serenity settled over her, the bond between herself and the echoglass now reforged.

Suriin could feel the pouch they were in, the soft leather of the outside and the hard edge of the other crystal inside. She sat quietly, not wishing to attract attention from the xotryl, should any be near. Now she was present, she withdrew her hold on love.

She accepted the situation, hoped for an opportunity, and rested. Suriin reached for the thread back. It was faint, but still felt secure.

The last few times, she'd been dragged here against her will. The fear of separation had overtaken every other emotion. The terror of being lost and unmoored. This time, Suriin felt safe. She briefly considered how easy it had been.

Her body was still vomiting. It was messy and distant, but nothing she had to worry about. It was safe.

They were moving. Wherever they went, they moved slowly, steadily. At a walking pace, not that of the xotryl.

That might mean they were away from the xotryl, which gave her a potential window of time to attempt to unbind.

Suriin readied the words. She had practised them over and over as they waited for the healing draft to wear off. Boulder had made her repeat them, tweaking every inflection until he was happy.

She had no mouth – how would she say them?

Did it matter when her very being was entwined with the crystal? It surrounded her, shielded her. A shield she needed to break through.

Suriin gathered as much love as she could pull together and pushed it at the shield around her mind. She said the words as carefully as she could; once, twice. She pushed as she said them until the shield around her mind began to pulse a gentle green. Watcher, but this was hard. Suriin poured everything into it, yet her stores reduced with little impact. The shield glowed with a gentle pink pulse. If the crystal glowed, too, she was given away.

Light flooded her. Suriin stilled her thoughts, trying to think of nothing.

The light faded, the pouch closed, and Suriin reached for regret. She pulled on the memory of her father and the black spider of poison ravaging his body. The xotryl flying in for the attack. She focused on the moment that the awldrin turned on her. She built and built it, releasing everything against the shield around her mind as she screamed the unbinding. She felt the words leave her mouth and fill her mind. The shiver of magic flowed through every part of her via the thread of her consciousness. With all she could gather, she struck the shield with her pain.

It shattered, and Suriin floated free. Her body was far away – separate. The world felt brighter, her mind no longer confined. With the connection to the crystal broken, she was drawn back toward her body along the thread of self, with Swift calling her.

Her body breathed calmly. She could feel no nausea. Suriin caught onto Swift's bond, utterly exhausted, and let Swift pull her back to wakefulness as her mind returned to a body lying entirely still on the rug.

She lay there for a moment, revelling in the normality of the feeling. In how she owned herself once again. She opened her eyes briefly to be sure the bond was gone. Suriin closed them again while she reached for love and trust. To her delight, she was able to direct their flow to Swift. Hearing a tail wag, she opened her eyes.

'I think it worked. I should let my mother know. She needs it more urgently than me.' Suriin closed her eyes and pictured the Redpike market. The awldrin was on the move, so it was as good an opportunity as she would get. She appeared in the market to find it empty; neither parent was there. It had been a faint chance anyway. She'd have to let her father pass the news on.

Suriin opened her eyes and tried to sit up. Every part of her hurt, and despite Bones' support, she felt as though she had been beaten again.

'That was some impressive vomiting.' Bones wore streaks of her last meal down his clothes.

Fall looked sadly at the rug. 'Well done, girl. I'm glad it was out of the spare room, but that's no use to hound nor Howler now.'

Boulder picked up the list eagerly. 'Let's test it out. Darin found some alert traps in a book he was reading. We could test that first, then try to set them off.'

Bones shook his head, and Suriin withdrew her hand from the offered paper. 'Give her a brief rest and some water and food, or she'll collapse before we're even part way through the list.'

'Natke is on the move,' Suriin said. 'I should rest, but we certainly can test the traps out. If she returns as she has threatened to do – either to here, or to Dal – we need to be prepared. Traps and early alerts are useful, but I need to know how to fight, so I can take her down, for good. My mother needs to know too.'

Fall sighed. 'For our entire history, we have prevented that which we've just enabled.'

Bones nodded. 'That's the truth. But our role is to protect the So'Dal from themselves. To hide them and to keep the Edgelands at bay. Suriin, you must never share this knowledge. I cannot stop you doing it. All I can do is ask you.'

Suriin took in the ring of somber faces that surrounded her.

She laid her hands on Swift's back. 'On the life of Swift, I promise I will share this with no one but my family.' She struggled to her feet, her body weak. 'I need a drink. My throat is sore.'

Boulder offered her a glass from his table. 'I haven't had any. It's just water.'

She took it gratefully. The howler room was so close – she could rest here, but no. She needed to get to her father.

'One last thing.' She reached for the absent pouch at her neck. 'If I'm no longer unwell, how do we explain my return to health?'

'We don't. Once you're well again, you will be expected to rejoin your lessons and your chores. You will not be free to do what is needed. For now, you will have to pretend you are still unwell. You have much to learn, and we need your time. You have a couple of hours. Go outside and see your family. Take joy in things that fuel your power, for we may only have today. As soon as you feel ready, we will get started.'

⌒ ⋏ ☾ ☩ ◉

With Swift exercised and fed, her father notified of her success, and having managed to pick at some soft food, Suriin headed to the library. Now she was able to use her emotions again, she was desperate to learn as much as she could. She was reading a book on the use of dreams as mass communication when the doors burst open, admitting Xedra and her group.

Suriin had barely seen them in the last few tides. With no lessons and her illness, she'd not run across them, except from a distance. Without her crystal, Suriin felt as though the world was brighter, more complex and fascinating. How much was relief and how much reality, she was unsure.

Xedra's contempt was almost a taste in the air, it was so intense. Her companions showed nothing so strong.

Suriin immersed herself in the book to escape their notice. She was free, they were shielded. If she wanted to ... No. She squashed the desire down. Causing pain to anything other than Natke was a waste of her focus, and she knew she was only reacting to Xedra's subconscious attitude. She wondered what would happen if she asked the carpet for a surprise.

Subtly, quietly, she funnelled a tiny amount across the library. Her reach was greatly increased, and her touch no longer needed.

The carpet moved ever so slightly at the edge, enough to slightly catch Xedra's toe as she crossed it.

She stumbled. Suriin returned her eyes to her book, trying to look engrossed. The fussing over Xedra by her friends was sickening, and Suriin wondered what hold she had on them. Did they really believe that her money would ease their lives outside the Black Palace? Watcher, imagine if Xedra could do whatever she wanted, if her reach was like Suriin's own. Her entire crater would be entranced, worshipping her.

Suriin sighed. The Howlers were right. This was too much power. She'd already been tempted to use it, and it had only been a few hours.

She stroked Swift and returned the book to its shelf before slipping quietly out of the library, cloaked in a thin layer of distraction and trust. No one gave them a second glance. It was time to return to the Howlers.

⌒ ⋏ ◖ ✥ ◉

They passed through yet another invisible wall in the depths of the Black Palace. Suriin reached for it and tried to distinguish how it had been made. She found a complex web of emotions that were anchored in something small and white.

She reached down to touch it, and Boulder coughed gently.

'Don't touch it. It serves us well, thank you.'

Suriin withdrew her hand quickly. 'Sorry, it's just ... I can feel things now. I must have been able to before I bonded, I suppose, but now I can detect so much more.'

Boulder pointed at the hound padding alongside her. 'It's not you – it's you unbonded plus Swift. You can access each other's senses more closely.'

They walked for a few more minutes until they reached a branch in the passage. Suriin was far deeper under the mountain than she'd ever been. Boulder turned right, and a breeze caressed her face. There must be an exit ahead.

Natural light passed through what Swift told her was another illusion. Boulder continued through it, as though it didn't exist, leading her onto a shrubby mountainside filled with unfamiliar plants.

'We're on the Surface?' she squeaked.

Boulder laughed. 'Yes, this area is reasonably safe. This is the way the awldrin left the mountain. It's a route into the Black Palace that she knows exists.'

'So we need one of these traps here as an early warning system.' Suriin pulled out the book they carried with them and flicked through it until she found the instructions.

Boulder retrieved his whistle from inside his robe. 'Ready?' he asked.

'Let's try this.'

Boulder began to play. Suriin hummed along, and as she copied his tune, she focused her attention on the doorway ahead. She let him play it a few times before she laid a field of vigilance across the doorway. The book talked about emotional notes that would trigger an alert, and they'd decided that aggression, anger, and sorrow might be the best triggers. All emotions that they associated with Natke. Given her ability for deception, Suriin also added a small amount of distraction. Anyone passing through this entrance with intent to harm should set it off.

With one trap down and several more to go before they could focus on battle magic, they jogged away from the exit and back to an earlier howler entrance. Suriin laid another trap just before the false wall as they returned to the Howler's accommodations.

Bones' list of places to secure were all around the Palace. There were too many people around to be able to set a trigger in the garden itself, so their next challenge was to set one across the top of the steam lift.

CHAPTER 36

DARIN

The garant is the one exhibition of magic that the
*   So'Dal use.*
The fact that no one else has ever been able to
*   persuade a garant to fly*
is put down to generations of expert trainers.
Animalis of Lieus

The Collective unstrapped himself and slid down the Garant's side. He pulled his hood back and strode directly up to Darin.

'What in Lieus are you doing here? I've had people looking for you all over Eye and Pelton. I thought I was going to have to tell your family you'd been killed or eaten. I don't know whether to shout at you or hug you.'

Darin wiped blood from his face as Star wagged a greeting. 'Neither? Thank you for your help. There were four. Chase and Sandy took down at least one other at the rear of the group.'

'Are you all okay?' Chase called as Sandy ran toward them,

with Fleck and Heline close behind. The three hounds reunited with much licking.

'Your hounds are armoured?' Hal rubbed at his head. Chase followed Sandy into the circle of light cast by Hal's glow lamp.

He rushed over as he saw the blood all over Darin, entirely ignoring the garant and Hal.

'Are you alright?'

'Yes. We took the first, then I was struggling a bit with the second, until Hal threw a flash ball at it, then a flame one. I was blinded, though.'

'I did shout to shut your eyes!' Hal muttered.

'Would you close your eyes when something's attacking you?' Chase folded his arms and stared at Hal. He was older, and despite Hal's training as a Collective, it was Chase he'd have wanted to fight the least as they faced off.

'What's going on?' Hal asked again. 'I flew to Dal because I haven't had a message or reply from the Witness or the Soul Anchor there for a tide – no-one has. I fly over, and the town is silent, no light, no movement.'

Darin smiled at Chase. That was good. It meant the rest were doing exactly as they'd agreed and staying hidden.

'The xotryl have been attacking. One even entered the town walls and killed the Soul Anchor,' Chase replied. 'They seem aggravated by magic, so no one has used any more since, even to dream walk.' It wasn't entirely untruthful.

'Why didn't you call for backup?'

'It's Dal. They look after themselves.'

'So why aren't you in Dal now? Why were you there in the first place? And where is the Master of Hounds? Where are you taking all these people? I need to talk to the Witness.'

Darin stepped between them. 'I'll answer those once these people are safe. This is neither the time nor place. The Master of

Hounds is safe. As you have the garant, we'd appreciate it if you could scout the routes down to Clifdon. It would allow the evacuation to proceed more smoothly if we know what we face.'

Hal raised an eyebrow. 'You tell me what to do, apprentice? What has Tralkion been teaching you?'

Chase shook his head. 'He's been double-apprenticed the entire time. And, as far as I am concerned, his actions in the last few days fulfil his requirements for full rank as a Howler. His tattoo will be done once Dal's population is restabilised.'

Darin tried to respond, but the words wouldn't form.

'Howlers don't exist anymore.'

Chase laughed. 'Hold that globe to my cheek and say that.' Darin saw Heline hanging back at the edge of the light with Tian and Krista. All three grinned widely at him.

Hal moved the globe closer to Chase's tattoo. He studied it for a moment, then bowed his head.

'My apologies. I thought your kind long vanished from our ranks.'

'If you didn't, we'd have failed at our task. Now, as Howler Darin said, we need to get these people to safety. Your assistance would be most gratefully received. In fact,' – he turned to Tian, gesturing him forward – 'if you would be kind enough to fly this representative of Dal to Clifdon, he can warn them of our imminent arrival.'

Tian rolled his eyes. 'I know what you're doing.'

Chase shrugged. 'It's true.'

'And you get me there faster.' Tian sighed. 'They probably could do with a warning, though.'

Hal looked at Tian and the straggling group of people clustered around the child-filled wagons, pulled by groups of people. They were filthy, exhausted, and terrified.

'No one would bring an entire town across the Surface

without desperate need,' he said eventually. 'Of course I'll help. I can let Nissa know what's happened here once everyone is safe.'

⌒ ⋉ ⟨ ✧ ◉

They let the folk of Dal and the garant rest for a short time. As the sun crested the horizon, Tian strapped himself onto the garant, and Hal coaxed the huge bird skyward.

'He'll be safe now. Without worrying about him, I feel more able to focus on the job at hand.' Chase grinned widely, his whistle carrying on a light breeze as he returned to his position at the rear of the line.

'Everyone ready?' Darin called. Tired nods greeted him as children were reloaded into the carts. Despite their exhaustion, these were adults poised to pull their offspring to safety. They picked up the harnesses and readied to move.

Krista gave Star a pat on the head as she joined Darin. She checked the straps on her own equipment; her arrows were ready and her bow string taut.

'If we get a good pace going, we might reach the cliffs before tomorrow nightfall. With a garant looking at the routes and protecting us from above, it will take us far less time to get them to Clifdon.

Several times through the night, they heard growls in the vicinity. Darin encouraged Star to howl, and the others joined in. The small pack, so widely spaced, created an eerie sound. Whatever approached had left them alone.

They were taking a rest at midday when they were intruded on by a pack of graaken. People scattered like insects from smoke as the graaken wandered through the line of people. Meals were abandoned in the haste to get away. Darin didn't know what he'd have done had a graaken wandered into Eye before he arrived at the Black Palace, but he was certain he wouldn't have moved as fast as these folk.

They escaped in time, all aside from the parents of one small child. She'd hidden under the cart to play, and when trying to locate her, they got a little too close to the herd.

The resulting stench enveloped the cart, the child, and the parents. Darin didn't envy the person whose task it would be to try to save those food supplies.

He shuddered, and Star whimpered quietly *[Star moving away from the cart]*.

[Star at the front of the line, walking ahead of everyone and the cart] Darin sent back.

'Let's get moving again. Save what you can, and the rest we'll deal with once we get closer,' he called.

Darin and Krista had begun to lead them onward as a garant silhouette appeared in the sky ahead. He hoped Hal carried good news about the cliff paths.

⌒ ⋏ ◖ ⊕ ◉

'The main path is reasonable, but there are a few treacherous sections,' Hal said as they walked, his voice low enough not to carry to those behind. 'I'd be happier if babes-in-arms, toddlers, and the much older did not attempt the descent. I'm not sure they'd make it.'

Darin shrugged. 'We left most of the very old in Dal Town. They preferred to stay.'

Krista nodded. 'If it's not safe, it's not safe. There are three babes and a number of small children. How do you propose we get them down?'

Darin fought the grin that he knew was growing. 'We give

them the ride of their lives. Hal, are you offering to carry them down on the garant?'

'It will take a little preparation, but if I start transporting them now, it's not far to fly. Tian can show them to an area the residents are trying to make safe for you.'

'How bad is Clifdon really? How many houses stand?' Krista asked.

'The houses all stand. It's mainly roofs which have fallen. The main hall will serve as shelter until you can stabilise the other properties.'

Krista grunted. 'I knew we should have pushed Davii to come. We'll need his rope-making skills.'

Davii wouldn't have left if all the all the xotryl of the Edgelands had appeared in the sky, that had been abundantly clear. His fields were in Dal, and without them, he couldn't make a single thread. Darin left Krista to her thoughts, though. They were all tired, and sometimes you had to choose when to let a thought lie undisturbed. This was one of those occasions.

'Who do you want first?' he asked Hal instead.

'Get the smallest walking children to the front of the line, each with one parent, and I'll take them down one at a time. The babes aren't walking, so shouldn't slow your pace.

[Small children on garant from front of line] Darin sent to Star. Then *[Sandy nudging small children].*

Star wagged furiously. A moment later *[Chase and Sandy approaching a group of children and parents]* filled his vision. He fussed Star and sent affection through their bond. Moonhounds were definitely faster and less troublesome than Bones' pebble.

⌒ ⅄ ℭ ✿ ◉

As the first parent and child took to the air behind Hal, Darin breathed a little more easily. They continued to push forward, hopeful of reaching the cliffs before nightfall. He didn't fancy another encounter with the night-roaming Surface creatures at a cliff edge, or being responsible for sending a town of people down a cliff face in darkness.

Not long after Hal departed, the vegetation ahead changed. Mixed in with the thorny brush that the advance group had been clearing, were increasing numbers of spotted leaves and brightly coloured flowers.

'Stop cutting,' he called, as the group started to clear a patch of vegetation.

Star and Darin rushed forward. The wide-leafed plant looked familiar. He stared at it, trying to recall whether it was for good reasons or concerning. As he crouched a little lower to sniff at the leaf carefully, he spotted Gloria's salve growing to his right.

'That one' – he pointed at the wide-leaved plant, its edges almost glowing, despite the daylight – 'will blister you badly. If you do get blistered, you can rub this one on it to ease it, but without proper preparation, it will only reduce the swelling, not heal any damage.' He stood back up, relieved that his instinct had been right.

As they drew closer to the coast, the vegetation became a mix of plants he recognised and things he'd never seen. Not recognising them might mean they had no known effects. He tried to see a way past the large swathe of ringrout by clambering up the side of the pathway. To the East was thick rakbane – not a viable choice for walking through, and far too much trouble to clear. The western side of the path appeared safer, but this would be as far as the carts could go. He couldn't see anywhere they would be able to get them up, let alone the risk of trying to drag them across an unknown surface beyond the path.

'We're going to have to leave the carts. Split the food between us. We only have an afternoon left to travel.' He didn't mention the cliffs all the adults knew were between them and safety. The garant might have time to collect some of what they didn't manage to carry once the children were down safely.

⌒ ⋔ ☾ ✿ ◉

Hal found them next in the middle of the grassy swathe. The garant glided in to land with more ease than it had in the pathway.

'We can't push through that.' Darin gestured to the vegetation filling the path.

Hal glanced over and nodded. 'It's a hard choice, but I suspect I'd have made the same one. Is the back of the group out now?'

[Sandy in the path?] Darin asked Star.

[Sandy seeing people climbing out of the path ahead. Fleck out of the path] filled his vision. The images flashing past one at a time, followed by *[Star eating a big slab of meat]*, accompanied by hunger.

'The middle of the group is out. The back is nearly out.' Given how far they'd walked, the back of the group must be starting to drop behind. Carrying extra food would only slow their pace. He sighed.

Krista reached out and squeezed his shoulder. 'We're doing the right thing. They can catch up and rest as we start to send people down the cliff.'

'Hal, how far before we can get back to the path?' Darin asked.

'Let me look.' He leapt aboard the garant, clipping his safety line on as he took off, and they sprung into the air, flying along the path until Hal was hardly visible on the garant, then turned around.

He circled above, not too far from where they were for a while, then returned. Hal encouraged the next parent and child onto the garant and tied them in place.

'The area I circled is the first point it will be clear to return to. Where I turned around is the cliff-edge. You'll be there soon.'

'Can you fly back over it, so we can get a direction to return in?' Krista asked.

'Of course.' Hal climbed back into his seat. 'Hold tight,' he called to the man and child behind him as they took off.

⌒ ⋔ ◖ ⟁ ◉

They reached the cliff with no further incidents, well before the sun dropped below the edge of the land. Darin tried to look calm and relaxed as he approached the edge. He'd not let himself think about the descent until they got there. It was steep and very high. He knew he'd given his fear away when Krista appeared at his shoulder. 'Would you like me to go first? I'll find the best route down, and you can send them after me until Heline arrives. You'll need to brave the descent at some point.'

Darin quirked a half-smile, hiding his trembling hand behind his back. 'You can see it that clearly, huh? How do I persuade the children that it's safe if I look this scared?'

'You just do. I know you can. I'll see you at the bottom.' She turned to the gathering group of people. 'Those still waiting for the garant, please move to the area behind Darin and Staramine so there is room for take-off without disturbing those of you climbing. Everyone else, form a line. Follow me carefully, and do not rush your descent.'

Darin gestured the last few garant passengers to the area Krista had indicated and set about organising them. They took advantage of the rest to feed the babes. One looked down at the path and laughed.

'That's an easy route! I can walk that. There's no need to waste a flight on me.' She tied her sling tighter and joined the queue of Dal folk waiting to walk down.

⌐ ⋏ 𝄢 ✣ ◉

Darin could hear Krista's voice encouraging exhausted people. He peered over the edge, his legs quaking as he studied the drop. No rope to hold onto, no cage beneath his feet, no rail. He'd have to trust his own unfaithful legs to carry him down the cliff.

Hal collected the next child. Each flight shorter and faster now, as rather than fly them into Clifdon, he took them down the cliff to wait on the beach. Krista was almost at the bottom by the time Darin braved another check. A winding line of people followed her down.

A shadow passed over him, and his heart rate spiked. If anything attacked now, they were all so vulnerable.

He looked up as the garant and Hal flew in to land.

'Two more to go,' Darin said. 'One child is back nearer Chase.'

Heline and Fleck appeared from the end of the pathway, waving. 'We did it!' she called. 'My first howler mission is almost done.'

The line of people behind her belied the statement, but he could more than understand her excitement.

'When do we go down?' she asked.

'When you're ready.'

'I'll wait until Chase and Sandy get here too,' she said, then wandered off to chat to the last nursing mother as they boarded the garant. The down draft from the wingbeats caught him unaware, and Darin scrambled further back from the edge as they glided down to the beach.

The sun had dropped to kiss the sea; they wouldn't have long before the descent became too dark to see. He turned to check on the people still coming out of the pathway, then scrambled onto a stone for a better view. Chase waved at him from the back, and a small knot of tension uncurled from his gut. They should all make it in time.

⌒ ⍀ ⟁ ✦ ◦

The silhouette of the garant filled his view as Hal returned for his final passenger.

Hal shouted, then screamed.

The garant wheeled around, directionless for a moment. It flew past with Hal slumped over its neck.

Darin whistled at the garant, trying to imitate the noise he'd heard Hal make. What on Lieus had happened? The garant blinked. It flew in a circle as Hal remained unconscious in his saddle.

He whistled again, and the garant's head slowly turned in his direction, its feathers raised in an aggressive pose.

'Not her. No. No!' Hal pushed himself up, and the garant turned toward Dal. 'I have to go.' Hal shouted down, and without another word, flew into the distance.

'That didn't sound good,' Heline muttered as she stared after him.

'He's bonded to the Anchor,' Darin replied quietly.

'Oh, flames.'

Darin turned back to all the people looking after the garant receding into the distance.

'Looks like he has a xotryl chasing him, he's going so fast,' one muttered.

'We've got most folk down.' Darin smiled at him. 'We'll manage the last few of you.'

⌒ ⋏ ʚ ✿◦

They remained at the top of the cliff until the final Dal folk reached the base, the last mother carefully supported by others as they carried her young child down.

Krista waved up at the Howlers, then turned to follow the last stragglers along the beach.

'So,' Chase said. 'We're headed back to Dal then?'

Darin nodded. 'Possibly all the way back to the Black Palace. Hal would never abandon us without good reason or the answers he wanted. Something has happened.'

'I'll get in touch with Tian to let him know we are headed back, and Bones to find out the news.' Chase laid on the ground, with Sandy's head on his chest.

He remained in that position for a good few minutes before he sat back up. 'Tian and Krista have got people to safe spaces in Clifton.' He stood up and brushed his clothes down. 'We could have used a sleep, but I'd rather not sleep out here. We'll head back. Heline, it's time to meet the rest of the pack.'

'What's happened?' Darin asked.

'I'll tell you what I know as we walk. If we can get back to that thick patch of ringrout, we can clear a small space inside it to rest.'

He turned and headed down the path. Darin received *[a slab of meat]* from Star, filled with longing.

He took his pack off and pulled out some dried meat for

Star. 'It's the best I can do, until we get back to the abandoned carts I'm afraid, boy,' he said and followed Chase down the path back toward Dal.

Star sent him *[Pack of hounds in the Black Palace barking skyward. Xotryl in the sky]*.

Darin picked up his pace. Something bad was going on in Redpike. They needed to get home.

CHAPTER 37

ELISSA

*It is perhaps good that no human will set eyes on
    me again.
I am no longer human. Nor am I dragon, but a
    strange hybrid.
My skin itches as scales begin to form.
Yet I find I have other, stranger skills. I shall
    investigate more.*
Journal of Otso Dragon-bonded

Elissa burned.

Rapture and Sorrow fed her with emotion, and Elissa burned. Every part of her being was consumed with producing fire – with the glowing mound at her feet that stubbornly refused to become a single lump of echoglass.

It glowed – it had started to melt – but she was close to burning out and near to failure. The knot of emotions she fed the fire had diminished.

Elissa felt rather than heard Rapture's call, her keening cry for more.

She had no true idea how long she'd burned; it could have been minutes or hours, days or tides. She was entirely consumed in the process.

At some point, another dragon had appeared, and then another. Elissa was refilled, refuelled with emotions she barely acknowledged before sending them into the echoglass.

Finally, the staramine began to glow, and a voice called, 'It's melting!'

It might have been her own voice, but she was no longer sure. The staramine burned fiercely as it finally melted, red swirls threading through the molten lump at her feet. She reached out to touch it, and a claw hooked under her arm to pull her back. She willed the fire to burn brighter, hotter, to fuse the glass. She filled it with joy, sorrow, amazement, and, to her surprise, vigilance – guarded protection.

She emptied herself.

Her last conscious thoughts were of Laytha and Makin and their sacrifices for her. She was grateful that she could, in some way, finally repay that. Elissa buckled at the knees and felt a nip on her ear, a set of small talons in her shoulder.

Pain. A sensation cutting through the fire.

'You've done enough. You can stop.' Sorrow. Her friend, the dragon.

Elissa let the flame splutter out. Echoglass glowed red-hot in the dragon scale-lined pit on the floor. When had that happened?

She raised her head to see an array of dragons watching her. Rapture and Amazement filled most of the space, while Sorrow and Vigilant sat closer to her.

'You did it,' Sorrow said softly. 'How do you feel?'

'Empty, exhausted. I could sleep for a tide.'

'Then rest. The glass will take time to cool, and we must discuss how to get you and the echoglass to Lieus safely.'

Rapture sent a flow of joy in her direction, and Elissa took it in greedily. Sorrow pulsed with sadness, which increased as Rapture spoke. Elissa realised she was even more aware of each of their emotions than she had been before.

'You have changed a lot. You are incredibly beautiful. I've never seen a white dragon before.' Amazement's eyes were fixed on Elissa's face. Elissa reached for her skin, finding a host of tiny scales across her cheeks. Maybe they would just wipe off once she was away from Mythos, or drop off.

She smiled at them and leant against Sorrow, snuggling in against his side as she had so many times, before allowing herself to fall asleep.

⌐ ⋏ 𝟨 ⸙ ◉

'She's going to have to go. She still looks mostly human, yet she is dragon enough that they may recognise her as something special. Humans are prone to that. Her difference might be enough to get the awldrin to listen to her too. Her power certainly would be.'

'Will she survive? It is no short distance.'

'She has to. You can see it, we all can. Harmony lives on in her. If we all work together, if we give her our strength—'

'That's not necessary. She has changed, or she hasn't. I will try to fly her around Mythos first. If she survives that, we can attempt the journey.'

Elissa cracked open her eyes to watch the debate. Sorrow and Rapture faced each other, whisper-talking. The others had gone. Dreamer appeared in front of her and shouted a greeting in her face. So much for quietly listening in.

'Hi,' she said, waving from where she lay. 'Were you just casually discussing how I might die? Or did I hear that wrongly?'

Sorrow dropped his chin. His wings drooped as well. 'We were. Now we have the echoglass, you will need to split it and fit it. Both of those things need to be done in Lieus, at the gates. You cannot open the Calderan gate from here, can you?'

'It would be nice if I could.'

Sorrow sighed. 'You know that is not possible, little dragon. You and I, we will fly.'

'Rhymes are bad news from you.' Elissa struggled to her feet, feeling less unsteady than she'd expected. 'So ... we need to fly out beyond the clouds.' She held back a gulp. 'And on to Lieus. Me and you. Through the gap between worlds. You think I can survive this?'

Sorrow looked away, leaving Rapture to reply. 'We believe you have to try. Your white scales mark you apart—'

'Yes, I heard that bit. How long will I need to rest before we can try? Is there any way that my magic can help us?'

'We can try a short flight first.' Sorrow replied. 'Your magic is different to ours – different to that of the humans. It may be that we can find something to help you in the Watcher's records if we travel to there.'

'I think I'd like to get some air.' Elissa stumbled toward the exit. Dreamer flew close to her side, his rippling colours matching her own mood. She stubbed her toe on a stone as she staggered into the dusky light. The mountain loomed above her, and the green globe of Lieus hung low in the sky. She ignored it, searching instead for Tebein, trying to decide if it was in night there. If the side facing her was lit, or a shadow.

'Be safe,' she murmured. 'You said I could save you all, Laytha. I'm trying.' Away from Rapture and Sorrow, Elissa felt an emotional freedom. She breathed deeply, studying the planet with a clear mind, able to think for herself.

Her foot was healed. Her face was scaled. She pulled a sleeve up to discover tiny white scale patches on her arms; they appeared more apparent where the thin, silver-white of her scars were. The most dragon parts of her were the most wounded. It made a sort of sense, she decided as she stared skyward. Out there, scales wouldn't keep her safe.

She reached inside herself to see what emotional reserves remained. Very little. Her memories were there, but the tinges of emotion associated with them had faded. She could revisit memories with a lack of any recognition of how she felt. She'd lost part of what had made her strong. Made her who she was.

Rapture and Sorrow's suggestions of all the dragons giving her emotional reserves reminded her of the way the Chosen had united to help her open the gate. It had worked once, but the dragons might not have the same desire to cooperate as the Chosen. How long would it take to get them all together?

One small accident had put her in this position. From the Untouched to the impossible. She shook her head.

'I don't think I will guard the gates as he did. But I'll help make sure that everyone goes where they should and stays away from the rest of Mythos.' Vigilant floated down from somewhere on the mountainside.

'Thank you for helping me.' Elissa had worried that dropping the strand of trust on him would be temporary, but it must have made him think about what dangers he was looking for and what concerns he truly had.

'I've never flown up there either.' He gestured upward. 'Do you mind if I come, too, when you test it? You are going to fly up there before you do the crossing?'

'I don't really understand the issue, bar the distance. It is a very long way, and I cannot risk falling when I get tired.'

'You wouldn't fall – you would float. There is no fall, much as there is no breathing.'

Elissa blinked. 'No breathing?' she repeated.

'Of course. It's why they want you to be as much dragon as they can make you. It gives you the better chance.'

'No breathing, no talking, no falling.'

Vigilant flapped his wings. 'Exactly. Now you've got it.'

'If I don't breathe, I will die. I know that much.' Dreamer reflected her rising panic, colours flashing across his body so fast that it hurt her eyes.

'You power yourself on dragon fire instead. You can run your body on it at a very low flame. At least, that's what Terror told me. He made the whole thing sound horrific, but then, I don't think he could do anything else.'

'Have you ever tried it?'

'No, I've been too busy guarding the hatchery. But I think you need looking after too. I can just feel it. So when Rapture called, I felt it. This is a very defensible mountain. If she didn't already own it, I'd like to live here.'

They sat in the warm rain, surrounded by charvers chasing fire sprites across the dusk line. Droplet-shaped flowers swung in the breeze, and the blue-spotted leaves that climbed around the cave entrance fluttered. It was peaceful. Elissa felt calmness and, as she had begun to do almost without thinking, saved it for later. They rested companionably, with Vigilant flying around the mountain occasionally to ensure they remained safe.

Elissa needed dragon fire – she needed emotional stores ready for trying to fly above the clouds. She recalled the moment when Laytha had first stepped forward to take her into her hut. The gratitude she had felt, the trust that grew between them. She let herself dwell on her fear of the awldrin, calling up the memory of the body in the fields and their pursuit through the marshes.

As she worked through her memories, slowly refilling her store, threading them into the bundle of emotions she carried, Elissa started to feel less absent and more connected to the world around her. She closed her eyes and laid back on a bed of soft plants, trying to imagine herself in her home on Hope. To her surprise, it was easy now. She was immediately there. She reached for the chair, but her hand still passed through it; maybe that would come with time. Not having to fall entirely asleep would allow her more regular contact, especially once Laytha got there. There had to be some benefit to looking like even more of an outsider.

⌒ ⋀ ☾ ✦ ◉

Elissa lost track of how long they waited outside the cave. Eventually, Sorrow walked out carrying the lump of echoglass in his mouth. Her bag hung round one of his spines.

'You should eat before we try our first flight.' He placed the echoglass at her feet and curled his head around to unhook the bag.

Elissa reached for it and retrieved some easy food. She was finishing her last mouthful when Vigilant returned from his latest circuit of the mountain.

'Are we going?' he asked.

'We?' Sorrow stretched out his wings as Vigilant flapped excitedly around.

'I'm coming too. I need to do a first flight, and you need another set of eyes. Unless you can see behind you if she starts to fall? I will guard her.'

Sorrow's eyes spun slowly as he contemplated them both.

'It's a good idea,' Elissa mumbled through a mouthful of something sweet and very chewy. 'Are we taking the echoglass?'

'It would make sense. By the time we reach above the clouds, we will be getting closer to the Hall of the Watcher, so rather than come back, we should take it.'

The complete lump was harder to fit in her bag than its

component parts. Elissa tried a few times to make everything fit. If she ate just one more thing, she could squeeze the lump into her bag.

She searched for something of the right size and pulled out a lump of the sweet, chewy stuff. Suppressing a smile, she snapped it in three and offered part to each dragon.

'Try it.' Sorrow sniffed it and ate his bit slowly. Gentle moans of pleasure wound out of his snout as the sweetness hit. Vigilant poked it, turned it over. Sniffed it, licked it cautiously, and eventually, took a tiny nibble. Once he was happy, he swallowed the rest whole. Elissa re-packed her bag and prepared to climb up Sorrow's flank. Vigilant was behind her before she realised it, helping her up.

It would be quite a challenge to cope with his constant attentions, now he'd turned his focus from the hatchery to her. Still, knowing he was nearby as they took off was reassuring. She wasn't sure he could take her weight, given his size, but he might slow her fall enough for Sorrow to catch her.

Elissa gripped Sorrow's spine tightly as they flew. Up they rose, passing through the clouds. Sorrow's strong wingbeats carried them ever higher. He said little as they flew, instead leaking sadness at an alarming rate. Elissa tried to take it in, rather than let it take hold of her mind. Vigilant flew alongside her, his small wings beating at many times the speed of Sorrow's.

As they passed through the cloud, Elissa found it harder to breathe and gasped for air, desperately trying to take in as much as she could. Vigilant's wing beats slowed, and he started to drop back.

'Little dragons, you need to burn,' Sorrow sang out. 'Gently, gently, you need to burn.'

Elissa imagined a gentle motion with her arm, too afraid to let go, and a small ball of white fire appeared in front of her.

Sorrow also followed a small flame, but smaller and bluer than hers. Elissa tried to shrink her own. Slowly, it reduced to a flicker, and she grew more comfortable – her lungs no longer hurt. Vigilant caught up with them, his own fire a dark, swirling orb.

'We did it!' he said, his voice so faint that it barely carried to her ears.

He was right. She was flying above the moon, in a void of darkness speckled with stars. Lieus was both far in the distance, and in her future. They cruised for a while, far above Mythos. Two dragons and Elissa, each burning.

They descended to the surface, and for the first time, Elissa felt certain that she could re-open the gates. She would fly to Caldera and bring her people to safety.

Chapter 38

Suriin

The crater garden is a joyful place
Filled with hope and potential.
We plant our dreams, our magic, and our
*   healing here.*
The Bond of Three

A strong tug at one of her traps awoke her. Suriin rubbed her eyes as her heart raced. It had worked, but which one was it? She hoped that her attempt to tie Boulder into the trap alert had worked. Just in case, she needed to get to them.

She threw her covers off and grabbed the closest clothes – the blue dress and her blue scarf. There was no time to co-ordinate things.

Swift was restless; they needed to rush.

She felt again for the trap. She slowed her steps and breathed deeply, trying to calm herself. There it was. The first one they'd set at the far side of the mountain.

'I'm not ready,' she muttered. 'I'm not prepared for this.' Swift sent *[Biting a grey shadow]* and urgency.

Suriin ran.

The Howlers were old men. Their whistles were a nice touch, but their age would slow any response.

[Fluffy waking her father. Image of xotryl and awldrin. Yorynn locking all the doors] Suriin sent as they ran. Swift sent acceptance back, and Suriin hoped that the hounds had built enough of a connection to communicate. Would her father understand? She hoped that somehow Fluffy could get a message through.

She rushed through empty passageways into the silent area, her steps swallowed by the strange magic as she ran. Swift loped alongside, alert and sniffing at the air.

They passed the trap-point where the main living areas began.

It was untriggered, and Suriin breathed a small sigh of relief. In the deeper passageways, she'd be more likely to be alone and closer to the Howlers.

The old men spreading through the palace with vibrating pebbles that they talked to. She'd laughed at them, thinking them little more than a toy, but now she sorely wished she knew where they all were.

As her passage joined another, Silard called from behind. 'Not reached the lift area.'

She slowed slightly so he could catch up, and he shouted. 'Run! You have the only way we can track it! Swift's nose.'

Suriin dug deep, filling her lungs with air, all the recent exhaustion gone. She couldn't run the whole way, but she'd go as fast as she could. Eventually, she slowed to a walk, gasping for breath as pain hit her side.

'Heal yourself, girl. Move! We didn't go through all this for you to collapse in a Watcher-flaming passageway.' Silard dragged her to her feet, pulling her after him.

She struggled on, the trials of the last few weeks and days

hindering her every step. 'Give me a moment,' she said, and quietly hummed to herself, building up the tune that she'd first sung in Nameless. She filled herself with love, and Swift nudged at her affectionately.

'Don't let her help.' Silard huffed. 'She needs her own energy.'

Suriin withdrew her hand, and as the song sunk into her body, she was able to pick up the pace again. Silard's pebble buzzed, and she heard Bones' voice.

'Not through the far illusion wall. Not through the armoury.'

Elissa was glad to know the awldrin wasn't carrying new weapons. But what she'd worn in their last encounter was more than she'd previously had, so she may have found her own store of weapons.

They passed the passageway to the armoury and ran on. Swift had started to scent now. She pressed her nose to the floor and ran faster and faster, vanishing from Suriin's sight around a corner before returning to check they still followed. By the time they reached the exit from the mountain, they'd still seen no sign of the awldrin's passing, aside from Swift's frantic pacing and scenting.

'She must have been following it backward,' Silard groaned. 'It's not her fault – she's been unwell a long time. We have the source of the entrance for definite.'

Boulder joined them, breathing heavily, his dark skin sheened with sweat. 'Something doesn't feel right. We've missed somewhere. There's no way Natke just wandered in and vanished.'

'So, let's track her back. You need to ask Swift about the newest track. Get her to follow that.'

[Awldrin walking out, awldrin walking in. Footsteps into the corridor] Suriin tried to work out how to ask Swift.

[Dark prints, heading down the passageway] Swift sent back.

[Follow dark prints]

Swift ran back the way they'd arrived. Suriin and the Howlers followed closely.

⌒ ⚸ ☾ ✠ ●

They reached the turning to the armoury and seed store. Swift took the turning. Suriin swallowed hard. The awldrin's cell was that way; surely there could be no reason for it to head there. Maybe there was something in the seed store that it needed.

'Headed for the armoury passage,' Boulder said into his pebble.

'We did miss something.' Bones' voice was heavy with dread. 'She spent five hundred cycles watching a door open and close. She's gone straight for the Anchor.'

Suriin's stomach sank. 'Where? How?'

'The door by her cell. Bones went up it while you were being rescued. It leads to the Anchor's quarters on the side of the crater.'

'Surely the Anchor knew about the awldrin then?'

Silard shook his head. 'There are reasons why that information was not passed down to her, and we don't have time to discuss them now.'

They were all out of breath as they reached the smashed door of the awldrin's prison.

The drop bolts had been snapped off, and it swung freely. Inside, as Bones predicted, the locked door was broken too, exposing a sloping passageway. Swift confirmed Natke's entrance.

'We're going into a narrow passageway, after a hunting awldrin?' Suriin asked.

Silard shrugged. 'If we don't, it's all over anyway. If we do, maybe we can limit the damage somehow. Save the boy.'

'Jaer!' Suriin ran. The slope felt endless, her muscles screaming that she couldn't keep going. She just sang at them, urging her body onward. If Natke was there, she wouldn't need any positive emotion anyway. One more day – one more – and she'd have had battle spells to use. Suriin paused, leaning against the wall as she snatched a few deep breaths. *Jaer.*

Up and up she ran until she reached a door that wasn't quite closed. There was a tiny crack, just enough for her to nudge it open. A wall hanging obscured her view, but the voices she heard were clear and familiar.

'Open the gate.'

'I can't. You aren't real. I'm dreaming.'

A boy's whimper from her right. Suriin lifted the blanket slightly to try to locate Jaer. He hid behind a couch, shaking and pale. She quickly sent him a small flow of trust and hope; he turned her way, his eyes widening. She gestured him down. He nodded and made himself as small as he could.

'I am more real than you can imagine, Torturer. You are weak. Time has stolen your abilities. The one I caught in my snare has more strength in her arm than you do in your body.' Suriin drew as much fear as she could, as much distress as she could hold, and stepped out from behind the curtain.

'You called?' she said, trying to hide the shaking in her knees. She pushed the ball of terror at the awldrin, shoving it as hard as she could. Natke stumbled. Her lidless eyes reflected the light as she turned.

'How nice of you to join us,' she replied. 'Strength is nothing without technique.'

Silard and Boulder burst from behind Suriin. Silard leapt forward, grabbing an object as he passed and sending it toward Natke. She flicked it away.

'Old humans and an untrained youngling? What has your army come to, Anchor? You are beneath my contempt. I shall crush you all until you open the gate.' She pulled the crystal from Nissa's neck and ran toward an open balcony and the crater beyond. Nissa took a few steps after her. She moved her hands, clearly attempting her own working. Natke stumbled slightly from the impact, and loathing filled the room as it bounced back from her armour.

Suriin gathered herself for an attack, drawing as much power as she could, preparing to launch it at Natke as Silard struck her again.

'You all tire me,' Natke said. 'I should show you real power.' She grabbed Nissa by the throat and held her over the edge of the balcony. 'Where is my sword?'

Nissa's moonhound snapped at her, biting her calf. Natke kicked the hound away.

'If it attacks again, I will kill it,' she clicked. I have xotryl venom on my glove. She flexed her other hand, showing off the sharpened finger tips.

'It's not here,' Nissa choked out. Her hound took a step back but continued to growl, her teeth fully exposed and spittle flying.

'Where is it?'

'If I tell you, will you let her go?' Jaer stood up, exposing his presence, and Natke paused, tilting her head to one side. 'That would be a fair trade. I agree.'

'Don't trust her,' Suriin urged.

'It's hanging in the Star Tower, the big one,' he said, ignoring Suriin.

Natke's sharpened teeth snapped together as she stepped over the balcony rail.

'You promised to let her go,' Jaer shouted. Boulder grabbed hold of him to stop him running after Natke.

Natke leapt from the ledge, with Nissa held under her arm. The hound leapt forward. Nissa kicked and struggled. She formed shapes with her hands.

Natke flinched as Nissa attacked again, but it wasn't enough.

Suriin and the Howlers ran to the balcony. Boulder still restrained Jaer; he struggled and screamed.

Nissa's moonhound howled.

A huge, red xotryl rose from below, carrying the awldrin.

From a far balcony, Suriin heard a familiar voice as a glowing light grew and grew in brightness. The flash startled the xotryl, and for a moment, Natke lost control. Then she turned the creature toward the source of the flash, with Nissa still dangling under her arm.

Suriin threw her rage at Natke and added the vigilance to guard her father. The xotryl changed direction, heading toward the top of the crater.

'You think you are all safe here, but you are less than my weakest runts. My eggs will hatch, and you will all die. We will reclaim this place as our own. If I cannot get home, I will create a new home.' She held Nissa out and dropped her. 'I keep my word. And my word for you is death.'

The xotryl flew up and out.

Jaer dropped to his knees.

A moment later, Nissa's hound let out a howl that shredded Suriin's soul, and Jaer crumpled, his body wracked with sobs.

He screamed and shouted. 'You could have killed her – you could have. There were three of you against one of her. Why did she take my mum? Why?'

All Suriin could do was wrap her arms around him and be present. He shrugged her off. 'Go away. I hate you all. None of you saved her. I want my mum or my dad.' The sting of his hatred and grief enfolded her, momentarily dragging Suriin in as Swift tried to nuzzle Nissa's hound.

Behind, she heard a distant voice through a pebble.

'She's at the tower. Xotryl smashed through a wall. The Collective are gathering.'

They were trained to fight. They could take a single awldrin. Suriin was left helpless, staring at Jaer.

'She has gone. She has the sword,' the disembodied voice of Fall continued.

Boulder ran his hands over his head. 'Silard, take Jaer and Nissa's hound to the howler quarters, so Bones can care for the hound and we can care for Jaer until his father returns. Suriin, I need you to come with me.'

'But it's over. Your secret is out. The Collective can fight her now. There will be deaths, but we will win. You heard her – there are more of them. She's laid eggs!' Suriin's voice was rising. She shook, and her control was lost. There was too much to process. Poor Jaer.

'That's too risky. We will do this ourselves. Come with me.'

'We failed.' Suriin let herself be led from the room, unable to process what she'd seen. Her tears ran freely as she struggled to keep up. They accessed a tiny staircase that spiralled up to the top of the crater.

At the very top, a large chunk of echoglass rested in a dome-shaped room. Boulder pressed a push-stone, and the ceiling spilt open, exposing them to the night sky.

'This is the Black Palace dream-stone, the focus by which the Soul Anchors and So'Dal are able to manipulate the dreams of our people. Tonight, the only thing we can do to buy ourselves more time is to erase all memory of these events. I need you to try to use your magic. At this moment, you are the most powerful Soul Anchor on Caldera. You need to make

Natke a blur, simply a bad dream shared across the whole town.'

'What about those who are awake?'

He shook his head. 'All we can do is try. You caused this mess. This is a small part of the price you will pay to help us fix it.'

Suriin wiped her eyes and pushed the emotions – the horror of Nissa's death – into her reserves. 'How do I do this?' She reached for the dream stone, resting both hands on it. It almost fizzed with power.

'Imagine the story they need to believe and play it as though you dream walk. You will need to replay it all night and into the morning – as you said, some people are awake.' Boulder locked the door.

Suriin frowned. 'You locked us in? I could just use my emotions on you and make you open it.'

'You could. But you won't. This is your mess, and you feel it deeply. It is as much to keep people out as us in.'

'What about Jaer?'

'We will deal with him separately.'

Suriin sat on the chair alongside the pulsing chunk of echoglass and pulled out her notepad.

'What are you doing?' Boulder asked.

'I'm working out the details. If they all have the same dream, it will be too suspicious. I need a variety of scenarios. If you are going to keep us locked in here until we complete this, then I'd appreciate your help.'

Boulder shrugged. 'I'm sorry, Suriin. We need to do what we need to do. But despite that, of course I'll help.'

Suriin sat on the top of Caldera that night, occasionally emerging from her task to eat or drink. One of the Howlers must have brought supplies at some point. She took short breaks to ensure that she sent no pain-tinged messages.

Boulder was as good as his word. He helped her and ensured Swift was comfortable when she joined them later that night.

Suriin buried her fear and hatred deep as she soothed and clouded dreams.

She was far from done with Natke. Once this task was done, she would learn to fight, learn every offensive trick she could. Then she'd teach her mother. The next time they met Natke, they would both be ready.

Acknowledgments

Having got this far, I thank you, dear reader and hope you enjoyed the new characters you've met along the way and the old ones revisited.

Gates of Sorrow has been a difficult beast to wrestle. Early in its writing last year, it was clear that Archie, my beloved dog would not get to be credited with writing this book. Sadly he left us not long after a new moonhound entered the pages.

Swift is a tribute to the love and resilience of older dogs. Writing her was hard – writing all the moonhounds was hard with a dog shaped hole in our family. I hope they continue to bring joy to you all.

So, this book is a tribute to Archie, with his lumps and bumps. A new canine assistant sits by my side now. She arrived once the edits were complete. Young and enthusiastic, speckled and bossy I look forward to her contribution in future.

The dogs are obviously not the only ones who helped bring this book to a final form. Alex Bradshaw, and Rowena Andrews, thank you for pushing through my early drafts.

Julia, Naomi and Olivia, thank you for your feedback, support and course corrections.

And of course those who have cheered me on and inspired me to keep writing more hounds! My editor Diana, whose unfailing love for this series keeps me working at it, and my friends, Anna and Natalie, and my husband who between them have supplied much needed moral support, flowers, tea, coffee and country walks.

It is always the readers who draw me on, to try and give more moonhounds and more of the So'Dal. So finally, thank you to Jens Helvig Dahl who made a donation to the Save the Children fundraiser to officially adopt Fluffy the Moonhound, and name Eira, Suriin's mother, I name you an honorary Howler.

ALSO BY J E HANNAFORD

The Aulirean Gates

Gates of Hope - Aulirean Gates 1

Black Hind's Wake

The Skin, Black Hind's Wake 1

The Pact, Black Hind's Wake 2

Black Hind Short story, SirenCall

sign up at www.jehannaford.com

Anthologies

So Alone. An Aulirean Gates short story in Through Shadows.

Dark Whale, Skybreaker Anthology

The Last Dance. A Black Hind prequel in Shadows on the Water.
Published by Flametree Press.